Tiger

Laurann Dohner

ELLORA'S CAVE
ROMANTICA®
ELLORASCAVE.COM

An Ellora's Cave Publication

www.ellorascave.com

Tiger

ISBN 9781419968433
ALL RIGHTS RESERVED.
Tiger Copyright © 2012 Laurann Dohner
Edited by Pamela Campbell.
Cover Design by Syneca.
Cover Photography by Fotolia.com.

Electronic book publication April 2012
Trade paperback publication 2013

Prologue

℘

Zandy knew she was in a world of shit. She was still unsure how going out for a few drinks to drown her sorrows had landed her in such a mess, but it had. A glass crashed into the wall near her, beer splashed her skin, and she huddled in her seat to make a smaller target. A body landed just feet away. The man grunted from hitting the floor hard and struggled to get back on his feet. She stood quickly and the wood chair scraped the floor as she turned.

The fight had moved her way. Drunken idiots were doing their best to beat the living crap out of each other and she was trapped on the far side of the bar. Her gaze frantically searched for an exit—a door or even a window to flee through. Three solid walls surrounded her and the only way out would be to struggle through the tight press of combating bar patrons.

"Oh hell," she muttered.

One of the tables close to her toppled when a man stumbled back against it after taking a fist to the face. The table missed crushing her feet by inches and she spun back around, stepped up on the seat she'd vacated and climbed on top of the corner table. There wasn't anywhere else to go. Two more bodies hit the floor too close for comfort. One more dived on top of the fallen pair and they rolled dangerously close to her perch. Blows were exchanged and one even pulled the hair of his opponent.

Her view of the room was much better from the higher vantage point on the tabletop but it assured her she was still trapped. Two small groups of men fighting over the football game on television had turned into a brawl that encompassed the entire length of the room, wall to wall. At least forty men were involved. The few women who'd been inside the bar were rushing out the doors and Zandy envied them. No way could she safely navigate through the fight to follow them outside.

Her back pressed tightly to the wall, her breath came out in pants and she prayed the cops would arrive to break it up before the worst of the fighting reached her. The brawling men on the floor hit the underside of her table, it shook and a whimper escaped her parted lips. She glanced to the next table, ready to jump for it, but a burly man suddenly crashed into it. It collapsed under his weight and she winced as he landed on top of the broken thing.

Regret filled her. She should have stayed home. She'd just wanted to forget her misery by spending her evening sulking over the bitch-slap life had given her. Leaving Los Angeles to move to Northern California had seemed like a dream come true when she'd been offered a better-paying job. She'd relocated, sunk every penny of her savings into buying her first house and had thought everything would work out.

Within three weeks she knew what a clusterfuck of a mistake she'd made after starting her new life. Her boss turned out to be a sadistic slave driver and a chauvinist pig. The jerk knew how much she depended on keeping her job and wasn't above taking full advantage. He'd spent the last week making her miserable. He'd upset her to the point that she'd ended up in Mickey's Bar and Grill. Another mistake.

Two men grappled, wrestling while on their feet. They slammed into the wall near her and tripped over the man still trying to untangle his drunken body from the destroyed table. Both of them fell on top of him. Zandy frantically stared across the room again, praying everyone would just stop fighting.

The doors of the bar were thrown open and she watched several unusually tall men come inside. They all wore matching black uniforms and riot gear. Their black helmets, vests over their chests, and shield-covered faces were ones she was happy to see. Joy rushed through her that help had arrived and they'd get control of the room fast.

She wasn't the only one to notice their arrival. Bodies surged her way—panicked drunks possibly afraid of being arrested—and Zandy screamed as someone fell against her table. It tipped, wood snapped under the man's weight, and her hands flailed to grab something—anything—but she ended up slamming hard into the floor, on her ass.

Pain shot up her spine and stunned her, but she recovered quickly when someone nearly stepped on her fingers. Zandy struggled to get to her hands and knees. She frantically crawled for another table to hide under it since being on top of one hadn't been good but she didn't make it.

Something big and fleshy landed on her back, shoved her flat against the floor, and knocked the air right out of her lungs. The man on top of her didn't get·up. He was impossibly heavy and more weight ground her against the unforgiving hard surface when another body landed on top of him. Their weight shifted enough for her to barely gasp in air.

Someone's heel backed into her hip, a man cursed loudly and weight crashed down over her legs when he tripped backward. Zandy groaned from the pain of having at least three men sprawled on top of her. It rapidly turned even more hellish as more men tripped over the fallen ones.

The horror of her situation filled her thoughts when she tried to move. They had her pinned. She couldn't even drag air into her lungs from the massive amount of weight holding her down and she was about to die on a disgusting bar floor under a dog pile of drunken idiots. She managed to tuck her face against one of her upraised arms in an attempt to protect it when someone elbowed or punched the back of her head.

The bodies shifted as they began to fight each other. She drew in a painful breath, her entire body feeling pulverized, and managed to choke out another terrified scream.

Why don't they realize they are killing me? Don't they know I'm under them? Oh god! More bodies landed over her until her hips and rib cage felt as if they were about to snap from the pressure of their combined weight. It taught her a new definition of pure agony. It hurt so much she couldn't have drawn breath even if she'd been able to inhale.

A fist hit her arm, material tore and something dug painfully into her ass cheek. One of her shoes slid off when bodies rolled a little over it. Rough denim scraped the underside of her foot and most of the weight over her felt as if it centered on her lungs. She couldn't breathe.

Pure panic gripped her when no amount of struggling moved anyone on top of her. She clawed at the wood floor, not caring how dirty it was anymore and she twisted her face. Her eyes opened. She spotted the leg of a table inches from her outstretched arm and managed to curl her fingers around the wood.

Zandy tried to pull her body but her strength waned. Spots appeared in front of her eyes. Her face felt really hot and knew she was suffocating. She blinked, focused on just her hand and her arm shook from straining muscles. Wood scraped the floor. The table moved a tiny bit, instead of her. More spots flashed and she knew in that moment that she was about to die.

Fuck. Her head slumped until her cheek rested on the cold floor. Her lungs burned but no air entered her open mouth. A memory of her mother flashed through her mind — her twenty-first birthday when she'd received the lecture about the dangers of going to bars and how nice, God-fearing girls avoided them. Her mother was all about avoiding sin.

Zandy fought the blackness that threatened to take her, unwilling to let go of life. She could just imagine the police informing her parents of how she'd died, pictured how disappointed they'd be in her once again. They'd turn her death into a lesson about drinking for everyone in the family. They might even go as far as sharing with the entire church how she'd died on a bar floor.

An animalistic roar rose above the sounds of the brawl. Zandy had heard stories of people near death hearing singing angels but nobody had ever whispered about scary noises. In that moment she knew she was going to hell. She admitted she'd probably earned a little eternal damnation for some of the things she'd done in her thirty-one years of life but it still sucked.

Life slipped away from her and she had no choice but to accept her fate as everything just faded to black.

Tiger fumed. The NSO had offered the local sheriff any support that he may need but no one had expected the older human to take them quite so literally. Reservation had received an emergency call from Sheriff Greg Cooper asking them for immediate assistance to break up a bar fight. He and his deputies couldn't handle the disturbance alone.

He glanced with annoyance at the Species males he'd quickly assembled. "Don't hurt the stupid, drunken humans. Just break it up and clear out the building."

None of his Species males wanted to be there. They would have preferred to still be on guard duty. Dealing with humans never boded well. Species were feared or looked down on by full humans. Their altered human and animal hybrid genetics made them different, stronger, and most people couldn't accept them. Being asked to police residents of the nearby town spelled disaster to Tiger's way of thinking but he just followed orders. Justice had reached out to their neighbors, offered help to promote goodwill and they were stuck breaking up a brawl.

The two humans nearest him saw Tiger when he gripped their shoulders to pull them apart. One glance his way and they fled out the door, more afraid of him than whatever anger had made them punch each other in the first place. He moved to the next fighting group, shouldered his way between them and tore off his face shield to make sure they could see his features.

"Stop," he snarled, not hesitant to use fear as a way to empty the bar.

A female scream sounded from the back of the room and Tiger's head jerked in that direction. The female sounded terrified. His gaze fixed on a redheaded female cowering on top of a table in the far corner but she suddenly fell to the floor and out of sight.

Tiger glanced at his men who were working to herd the humans outside but it wasn't fast enough to reach the woman quickly. He kept looking toward where she had disappeared. He was taller than the humans and had a better view but he didn't see her head reappear.

What is a small human female doing in the middle of a fight? He had no answer but figured she had no common sense. Human females were fragile and nonaggressive. Tiger's instincts screamed that she was in danger. He decided to wade in to get her and shoved his way in that direction.

"Get out," he snarled at the humans, grabbing them without care and pushing them apart. The small female still wasn't visible but he saw males dropping in that area. He watched another face disappear in the sea of heads and had a horrible feeling that the woman was somewhere in that tangled mass of falling bodies.

A drunk human spun and threw a fist at Tiger's face but his reflexes were better. He jerked his head to the side. The fist missed him by an inch and his large palm closed over the hand before it could draw back to take another swing. His temper boiled over and he applied a little too much strength. The male he gripped screamed as bones broke and Tiger roared at the drunk before releasing him.

The drunk yanked his injured hand to his chest, began to sob as if he were a female and stumbled toward the bar exit. Tiger moved on, his gaze searching for a small redheaded female as he tossed bodies out of his way.

His enhanced hearing picked up a soft feminine whimper seconds later over the cursing, the sound of flesh hitting flesh, the heavy breathing of the people around him and of furniture being broken. He zoned in on that area, plowed into the bodies and tossed them behind him. The female was in serious trouble and he didn't give a damn if he damaged a few humans in the process of finding her.

Tiger halted where he'd last seen the redheaded female and found a group of males sprawled on the floor. They were throwing punches with elbows and fists. One man kept tossing his head back into the stomach of a man under him who pulled his hair. Tiger quickly scanned the pile and spotted a dainty arm sticking out from under it all. It was a thin, pale one and distinctly female. Her hand was palm down next to the leg of a table, light-pink polish on her fingernails. She didn't move.

Rage tore through Tiger. The drunken idiots were on top of the female, crushing her under their bigger bodies and only that small amount of her could be seen. He couldn't spot any of her body except for her lower arm, her wrist and her hand. Another roar tore from his throat. He bent, roughly grabbed the first body he reached and threw the male away from the pile. The male screamed as he flew through the air and crashed into the wall. Tiger didn't give a damn. He grabbed another male, pitched him in another direction and freed one of the woman's legs.

He finally freed her and dropped to his knees next to the very still female. Her head was turned his way but her long red hair spilled over her features, hiding them. He roared again, demanding help from his males when he realized her chest wasn't rising and falling. Slash suddenly appeared on his knees across from him with the female between them. More males came to his aid, keeping other humans away and cleared the area.

Tiger's hands shook as he quickly but gently assessed the woman. She had footprint marks on her ass, back and thighs where males had stepped on her body. A snarl ripped from his throat. He wished he had killed the ones who had done this to her. He took great care when he turned her over in case of broken bones.

He gently eased her onto her back, guessing she only weighed about a hundred thirty pounds and stood about five-foot-four in height. She wore jeans and an elbow-length pink shirt. The sleeve was torn from elbow to shoulder, proof that she'd not only been trampled but hit. Her bones were small and he quickly pressed his head sideways over the mound of her soft breasts. He heard no heartbeat and made an anguished sound.

"Shit," Slash hissed. "They killed the small female."

Tiger rose and gripped her rib cage, checking it for fractures, but didn't feel any. She was warm as he touched her skin. He calculated how long it had been since he'd heard her whimper and guessed it was under a minute. It wasn't too late. He checked her ribs again, knew if they were crushed it would be hopeless, but again didn't find any broken bones.

"What the hell are you doing?" Sheriff Cooper gasped. "Are you feeling that woman's boobs?"

"No," Tiger snarled. He tore at his vest, ripped it off, and gently lifted the female's head enough to use it to pillow her from the floor.

"She's not breathing," Slash informed the older man. "Those drunks crushed her."

"Son of a bitch!" Sheriff Cooper sighed. "Just son of a bitch."

Tiger ignored the males to concentrate on the female while he tipped her head back and laid her flat on the floor. His heart hammered but he'd been trained to respond to emergencies by Dr. Trisha. Justice had insisted all the officers know basic lifesaving skills and Tiger had agreed. He'd never been happier for those classes than he was at that moment.

His hand shook slightly as he shoved the red hair out of the woman's face. She was pretty with her delicate human features, full, pouty lips, and slender nose. Her cheek that had been against the floor was slightly red but the rest of her skin was entirely too pale. She still wasn't breathing.

He sat up and located the correct area then placed his hands between her breasts. He hoped their generous size cushioned his palms enough to prevent bones from breaking. He did thirty chest compressions.

"What the hell are you doing now?" The sheriff inched closer.

"CPR," Tiger growled.

He tore off his shirt, balled it up, and shoved it behind the back of her neck to keep her head angled. He checked to make sure her airway was clear, pinched her nose carefully, opened her jaw to part her soft-looking lips and pressed his mouth over hers. His gaze diverted to her chest. He stared at creamy cleavage peeking from the top of her shirt and forced air into her lungs. Her chest moved as he breathed for her.

Tiger sucked in air, covered her lips again and blew air inside her. His gaze locked on her cleavage, saw her chest expand. He started a new cycle of chest compressions and she jerked a little under him. He pulled back and watched her facial muscles twitch. He lowered his head to rest his ear over her breasts and heard her heartbeat. She inhaled on her own, a gasp more than a breath, and he relaxed as he straightened.

"She's breathing again and has her heartbeat back." He stared up at the sheriff. "They must have pressed all the air from her lungs until her heart stopped but I got to her in time."

"I'll call an ambulance." The older human grabbed his radio. "Thank you so much."

Tiger studied the female carefully. Her color improved as she breathed and he hated the sight of her on that floor. He had been trained to protect a downed, injured person and wait for assistance once he he'd done whatever he could but something inside him abhorred her lying where humans had injured her.

He bent forward and gently eased his arms under her. She was as light as he'd guessed as he lifted her against his chest and used the strength in his legs to stand. His gaze met Slash's.

"Grab my stuff. I'm going to take her outside for fresh air while we wait for the ambulance."

Slash nodded, grabbing Tiger's destroyed shirt and discarded vest. Tiger shifted his precious burden and turned, assessing the rest of the bar. His males had cleared the humans. The fighting had ceased and his officers attended to the injured. A few of them were the ones he'd thrown to reach the female but he didn't feel guilty.

He strode out of the bar and walked around the building, desperate to get away from the humans who'd harmed the female. They were drunk, stupid, and he didn't want to risk her being in danger again. He carried her to one of the Jeeps they'd arrived in. He used his elbow to test the heat of the hood before he gently laid her across it sideways and kept his arm in place to cushion her head while he studied her face.

Her coloring was much improved, nearly normal but still pale. He surmised it might be her natural coloring with her red hair. The long strands were curly, long and beautiful. It fell probably halfway down her back and was soft. The woman stirred a little, moved one of her legs and her lips parted slightly as a sigh left her.

Tiger prayed she wouldn't wake until the ambulance arrived. She'd see his altered features, realize he was Species and perhaps start screaming. The parking lot lights were bright and she'd see him clear enough to know he wasn't one of her males.

He really hated it when human females saw him and pierced his eardrums with their shrieking. Sometimes they did that and it drove him nuts. He watched her face, hoping she wouldn't wake but he could tell she was going to.

She moved again, shifting her head in the crook of his arm. Tiger looked down at her as she blew out a breath, scenting a pleasant fruity smell. Her eyes opened. Tiger waited for her to notice his features and start screaming.

Her eyes were dark green and beautiful. She stared at the sky, blinked, and finally focused on him. Confusion was an easy emotion to read. She blinked again and studied his features. She took a breath and her gaze traveled over his bare shoulders, arms, and chest. He winced inwardly. He had forgotten that he'd torn off his shirt and knew she'd probably believe she was being sexually assaulted at seeing his upper body displayed.

She didn't scream but instead did the last thing he expected when she looked back up at him. A smile curved her lips and he could have sworn he saw amusement flash in those beautiful eyes.

Zandy had opened her eyes to a sea of stars in a dark sky. Her mind felt foggy, as if she'd just come out of a deep sleep, but she wasn't in her bed. She blinked and shifted her gaze a little only to stare into the most striking pair of catlike blue eyes she'd ever seen. Their color, shape and the really long eyelashes framing them mesmerized her.

The shade of blue was unique and she realized gold encircled the outer rims of the oval irises. She could have stared into them forever but curiosity made her study his regal bone structure, also strange with thicker, raised cheekbones, yet very appealing. He was the most masculine man she'd ever seen—handsome, striking and fascinating all at the same time.

His golden skin tone flattered the mane of thick hair framing his face. Streaked colors of light-to-sandy blond mixed with red were woven through locks that fell over a pair of really broad shoulders. Her gaze stopped just above dusky-colored, flat nipples.

15

She savored the sight of his hairless, wide, perfect chest. Lots of tan skin, well-defined muscles and impressive-sized biceps snagged her attention. Her gaze dipped lower to his flat belly, his tight six-pack abs clearly displayed. Her heart speeded up to thump wildly against her ribs. He was magnificent—a god.

Not a god, a small voice of consciousness stated. *He's got to be an angel.* She frowned, trying to think past her confusion. *Does hell have angels? Wasn't Lucifer a fallen angel?* She was foggy on her bible studies from her childhood but she was pretty certain that's what he was. That meant the gorgeous creature before her had to be a fallen angel too.

"I'm ready to go with you," she whispered.

He blinked and his eyebrows rose slightly. "Go with me where?"

He had a deep, raspy voice and it gave her the good kind of chills. She'd heard the devil could tempt anyone to sin and if he sent fallen angels who looked like this one after the newly dead, she was totally agreeable to do anything he wanted.

She smiled. "You can take me straight to hell if you're there too."

A smile softened his features and made him even more handsome. "You have been drinking too much."

She had known her life would bite her in the ass one day. She should have listened to her mother but it was too late now. Zandy tried to sit up. She wanted to get a better look at him. The pillow under her head turned out to be one of his arms as he gently pulled her up. His other hand curved around her waist, steadied her as she turned to face him and her gaze locked on his abs again. *Pure perfection.*

"I know. I've done a lot of things that I knew I shouldn't. That's how I got here." She licked her lips and noticed how his gaze lowered to her mouth. He was so gorgeous, the best-looking man-creature she'd ever seen, not that she'd ever really seen one before. That was beside the point. She scooted closer to him and smiled.

Oh, to hell with it. I'm already going to hell so why not really earn it? She feared he'd just escort her there and leave. She mentally ticked off the list of bad things she'd done. Premarital sex. She'd stolen pens from her last job. There was that time she'd kicked one of her exes in the balls when she'd found him cheating on her. It had been wrong but, man, had it felt good to watch him hit the floor groaning. He'd broken her heart and hadn't even apologized so she'd made sure he suffered a little too. That brought her to the divorces and she stopped listing her sins.

"You're the most beautiful thing I've ever seen," she admitted to him softly. "I may as well do what I want to most right now since I'm going to hell anyway, right?"

His gaze narrowed slightly. "What do you —"

She made up her mind and cut him off. "Fuck it. I want you."

Zandy reached up and gripped his warm shoulders. She spread her thighs while pulling him closer, forcing his hips to hit the edge of what she sat on. She wrapped her legs around the back of his and pressed her body flush against his tall frame.

He gasped in a breath and looked stunned. She grinned. She was about to show him sin. She locked one hand around the back of his neck while her other one slid down his firm chest wall to enjoy the feel of his warm, smooth skin. Her fingers spread open over his stomach, felt his muscles bunch under her palm and only stopped when she hit the waistband of his pants, which blocked her from further exploration.

"What are you doing?" He growled the words.

That's so damn sexy. "Kiss me."

He blinked but didn't move.

Her grip on the back of his neck tightened, found the hair there and fisted it. She pulled his mouth down to hers and kissed him instead. Firm, full lips pressed against hers. She licked the seam of them and he groaned as he opened up to her. Zandy took advantage, not sure how much time they had before he had to lead her wherever it was she was going. Her tongue entered his mouth. The sharp points of his teeth raked her but it didn't hurt.

He had fangs too. Fangs, cat eyes and growly voice. It turned her on even more and she loved the taste of him when he kissed her back. It seemed that angels carried a cherry flavor in their mouths and it was her favorite. His hands moved on her body, wrapped around her and cupped her ass to haul her tightly against him. Zandy knew heaven instantly when the hard ridge of his erection rubbed against her clit through their clothes.

She tightened her hold on him when he lifted her firmly against his body. She moved against him, grinding on his cock, and it felt so good. Her breasts ached. She wanted him more than she'd ever wanted anything and she suddenly knew hell too. He couldn't fuck her with their clothes on.

Her hand was trapped between them but she found a snap, tore at it and then another to get his pants open. She twisted her hand, encountered bare, hot skin and wiggled her fingers until she found his cock. Her angel didn't wear underwear. Her fingers found him tucked up and to her left as she wrapped her fingers around the thick girth of his shaft.

He purred against her mouth, growled and the kiss became nearly brutal. She didn't give a damn if he cut her with his fangs because his kisses were just making her burn to have him. She tried to position his cock to free him of those damn pants but he was incredibly hard. Their bodies were pressed too tightly together and it was hung up inside them.

Hell! Maybe that is the point, she decided, feeling frustrated. She wanted them both naked, with him buried deep inside her but all she could do was stroke whatever part of him she could reach.

She tore her mouth from his to break the kiss, both of them were panting and she stared into his gorgeous eyes. "Fuck me," she pleaded. "You're huge and I want you inside me so bad I hurt. Get these clothes off us."

He growled, his eyes narrowed and he suddenly had her pinned flat on the hard surface of whatever she sat on. One of his hands left her ass, gripped her shirt and jerked it up. A rough, hot palm slid up her side to her rib cage and he shifted his broad chest, crushing her breasts under him after cupping one of them. He squeezed, snarled against her tongue and his hips pressed tightly between the vee of her spread thighs. His other hand grabbed her wrist as he shifted again and tore her hand out of his pants to force her to release his cock. Then he adjusted his stance until the hard length of it rubbed against her clit.

Zandy moaned. Clothes-fucking wasn't her idea of perfect but she'd take anything he gave her. He rolled his hips, thrust against her again and she gripped his shoulder with the hand that had held his cock. He fisted the side of her jeans. Material tore as he tugged and her level of arousal jolted higher. He was going to tear her clothes off and take her.

YES!

"Um, excuse me?" It was a male voice—loud and close. "The ambulance is coming and someone is going to notice you and the human female. You could say she was having difficulty breathing but I doubt they will believe that is CPR."

Her angel tore his mouth away from hers and swung his head to stare at something behind him. "Damn," he snarled. "Thanks, Slash. I lost all control."

"I assumed." The other man cleared his throat.

Confusion filled Zandy as she was yanked back up to a sitting position beside the angel and he released her. He stared at her with his stunning eyes as he backed away and his hands lowered to close his pants.

Zandy turned her head to stare at another creature standing a few feet away. He wore all black and had catlike eyes too. He wasn't looking at her but instead grinned at her fallen angel.

"Sorry," the creature in black said softly. "If I didn't interrupt you would have taken her where you stood and the ambulance would have arrived to see that. You both would have probably been embarrassed to have witnesses see sex between you on the hood of the Jeep."

Something was written in white lettering on the man's black shirt. Zandy squinted, read three letters and knew she'd seen them from somewhere before. Memory returned to her in a flash. NSO was short for New Species Organization.

Her gaze jerked back to her beautiful fallen angel. He was breathing hard and his eyes were locked on hers as she examined his features. She could actually feel the color drain from her face.

"I'm not dead, am I?"

The man she'd been kissing shook his head. "You thought you were?"

She felt her body cooling fast from the burning desire to leap on the man and take him to the ground, tear off his pants to continue what they'd started. "Oh shit. You're not a…" She couldn't say fallen angel to him, he'd think she was nuts. Hell, she was. *No,* she corrected, *I'm drunk.*

"I'm a what?" His tone deepened and anger seemed to flash in his eyes.

"You're one of those New Species from Reservation, aren't you?"

"Yes."

Zandy closed her eyes and hugged her chest. It dawned that she'd just molested a New Species. They were humans who'd been altered with animal DNA. Some crazy pharmaceutical company had made them part animal and done illegal testing on them. *Son of a bitch.* Her eyes flew open.

She darted a glance at her surroundings and recognized the bar parking lot. The sheriff some of his deputies were visible in the distance near the front of the building under the outside lights. There were some drunks arguing with them. She hadn't died on the bar floor as she'd believed but suddenly wished she had. She closed her eyes again. She couldn't find the courage to glance at the man she'd mistaken for an angel. She waited silently for the ambulance instead.

Chapter One

෨

Zandy tried to mute her anger but it was nearly impossible to do. She had a mortgage to pay. Her life savings had gone for the down payment to get her house and she needed to eat. Having electricity and gas would be nice too. Even if she sold her new house, the market was down and she'd lose the equity.

The thought of returning to Southern California and having to live with her parents at her age was enough to make her desperate. They'd berate her over making another blunder, tell her how disappointed they were in her and rub every mistake she'd ever made in her face. She'd do anything to avoid that, including taking any job, even if she risked running into someone linked to one of the most embarrassing evenings of her life.

She glanced up at the reception area where she waited and knew she'd hit that all-time low. It was the last place she wanted to be but they were hiring. It was a big place. The chances of her running into *him* had to be slim to none and she just had to believe that if she wanted to keep the courage it had taken to come to Reservation.

Hatred for Jordan Parks made her ears warm. The asshole had fired her after she'd repeatedly refused to sleep with the toad. He'd made her life unbearable for weeks, probably hoping she'd quit but she was more stubborn than that. It was a small town, job opportunities were scarce and the next town with jobs was a twenty-minute drive away. Her car was old. It wouldn't endure six months of the mountain driving and the buses only ran once a day. She was in a hell of a mess because the prick had fired her.

She swallowed her anger and forced a smile as a door opened. *A happy perspective employee gets hired more than a grumpy one*, she reminded herself. The receptionist was tall, her features were pretty and she smiled back.

"He is ready to interview you."

Zandy rose to her feet and felt short even in four-inch heels compared to the woman she passed. One glance at the lithe, athletic body also made her feel woefully out of shape. She entered the office, kept her smile in place and hoped she landed the job. It was the only one listed in the paper unless she wanted to work part-time scooping up road kill for animal control. She doubted they'd hire her and it didn't pay enough for her to survive on.

She paused a few feet inside the office to study the man seated behind the desk. He had light-brown hair with blond streaks running through it. Blue eyes stared at her and he waved her to a seat. She spotted the wedding band on his tan hand, noted his wide shoulders and the way his suit bunched over his biceps. He was as fit as his receptionist and she hoped they wouldn't hold it against her that she wasn't.

"Have a seat, Miss Gordon. I'm Slade North."

She passed him her resume as she sat in the big chair and tried to relax but it was impossible to do. She needed the job desperately. The part-time job wouldn't pay her bills but this one would. It was actually listed for more than she'd made at her last job.

He placed the paper flat on his desk, didn't read it, but instead watched her. "I already have a copy of your work history. You had to fax it in along with the other information we asked for to do a background check." He paused. "You have the job."

Shock slapped her. "But you haven't spoken to me."

"I already know everything about you that we need. You have the skills required for the job, you don't have an arrest record and you're not associated with anyone who has caused us problems. Your parents were interviewed and you weren't raised racist." He shrugged. "It's that simple."

"Terrific." She grinned, relieved it was that easy. "That's wonderful. I really need this job, Mr. North. You won't regret giving me a chance."

"Call me Slade. We spoke to your coworkers from your last job." He frowned. "You didn't put it down that your last employer harassed you but you should have. We wouldn't have held that against you. That was unforgivable of your boss to sexually harass you but it won't happen here. I don't want to share sex with you. I am happily married and I'd rather die than touch anyone but my Trisha. No offense to you but that's the truth."

Zandy's mouth dropped open and she gawked at him.

He frowned. "Was I too blunt? I thought that might be a concern of yours after your last job. Your coworkers told us what your last boss attempted and he fired you because you refused to share sex with him. I didn't want you to worry."

It took her a second to recover. "You're blunt. I'll give you that but thank you. I'm relieved to hear it and yes, after my last experience, I guess it is a concern."

"You have nothing to fear here. My people—our males— will leave you alone. Just tell them to stop, that you have no interest in them if any approach you. We appreciate honesty and bluntness. There is no confusion that way. There are also a lot of words and sayings your people use that we are still learning. Sometimes it causes language barriers or misunderstandings. Just speak your mind clearly and we will listen. You can talk to me immediately if any problems arise and I will handle it. We want you to be happy working for us."

"Thank you."

"Could you start working now?"

He surprised her again. "Sure." She hadn't planned on more than the job interview but she wasn't going to say no. It was just after eight in the morning. She didn't have anything better to do other than go home and watch game shows and she didn't mind avoiding that. "That would be great."

He nodded. "Creek, my receptionist, will call for one of our males to escort you to building C. You will be told your duties when you get there." Slade paused. "Because of security you are not allowed to leave the building during work hours until your lunch. One of our males will meet you at the gate every day when you arrive and escort you from there and then back to the gate at the end of your day. At lunch a male will escort you to our cafeteria. I apologize but we can't have you roaming around free. We have many enemies and it has to be this way for security purposes."

"I understand. I could just pack a sandwich so I won't need an escort at lunch."

He smiled. "Lunches are free, Miss Gordon. We serve excellent food and you should take advantage of it."

"Thank you."

He stood and held out his hand. Zandy stood to put her much smaller one in his so they could shake on it. He had a firm hold, released her quickly and nodded.

"Enjoy your work."

"Thank you." She gripped her purse and left his office.

Creek smiled and waved her to have a seat. "An officer was called to take you to building C. You will like working here."

Zandy liked the New Species woman and smiled. "Thank you. I'm sure I will. Everyone I've met so far has been wonderful."

A snort sounded from Creek. "Except for the fact that you have to be searched every time you enter our gates."

"They had a woman pat me down but it wasn't so bad. They were really nice about it."

"We try. We feel bad for having to touch everyone but it's necessary. Just weeks ago a man came in for a job interview and they found a gun stashed inside his underwear. He was from a hate group and wanted to shoot Slade dead."

Zandy was shocked. "That's terrible."

"Some humans hate us." Creek shrugged. "They blame us for what we are though we were never given a choice. Now we just want to live in peace and it offends some of your kind. We fear hiring humans — no offense to you — but many of us don't have the skills to do all the jobs required. I learned how to use computers and type to become a receptionist. A human did this job before me but she sold some documents to the reporters for money. Eventually we'll be able to do most of the jobs as more of us learn skills though the humans we trust will keep their jobs."

"That's just shitty that she did that."

Creek nodded. "Yes. Slade trusted her. She was a grandma type. Is that the right way to say it? I saw Christmas movies and she looked like Mrs. Santa Claus. It was sad when she betrayed our trust and it really hurt Slade's feelings. He liked her and it left him very depressed."

"I don't blame him. There's nothing worse than someone you trust screwing you over. Especially for money."

A look of interest sparked in the woman's eyes. "You have been betrayed for money?"

"I've been betrayed but I never had any money to steal and there were no tabloids to sell stuff to that would hurt me. I just imagine it would be worse if that's why someone did it."

Creek nodded. "Do you have children? I like them."

Zandy shook her head. "No. I've been married twice but neither one of them turned out to be daddy material. Or loyal." She shrugged. "Now I've given up on the whole having-kids plan. I'm past thirty and enjoy not having a man in my life."

"You have had two mates?" Creek's eyes widened. "Did they die?"

"I divorced them. The first one was a cheating jerk who nailed anything that said yes. The second one, well, he was a bum."

"He lived on the streets?"

Zandy laughed. "He probably is now that I'm not around to support him. He liked to sit on his ass all day doing nothing and couldn't find a job to save his life. He was lazy and I got fed up with it. I divorced him and he moved in with a woman two apartment buildings over. While I was working and supporting him, he was sleeping with her. I'm a horrible judge of character when it comes to men, I know that now, and have called it quits on finding another one."

"I don't blame you." Creek reached over and squeezed her hand in support. "Our men are not bums. I heard some of your males are not very strong but our males keep in good shape. You won't find any weak ones here. Our males would die before they expected a female to tend to them as if they were helpless. They don't have that bad trait."

"Are you married? Do you have children?"

Creek shook her head. "I just share sex with different males. I don't plan on mating with one. Our females are unable to conceive children so there is no reason to settle down with just one male. They are a bit controlling. We dealt with that all of our lives and don't wish to be told what to do."

A smile curved Zandy's lips and she liked the woman a lot. "That sounds wise. You don't need a man to complete your life. At least that's what I tell myself every time some cute guy hits on me. No way, no how. I'm better off remaining single."

The office door opened and a tall man dressed in black walked in. Zandy felt the color leave her face as she stared at his features. She'd met him before. She couldn't remember his name but she remembered him all the same. It had been a few weeks ago but she'd never forget his face.

Creek smiled. "This is Slash. Slash, this is Zandy Gordon. She is going to be working in building C. You are her escort for today."

Shit, Zandy's mind screamed. *Maybe he won't remember me.* She stood as the man's gaze landed on her. His blue eyes narrowed and he cocked his head while he studied her intently. A smile suddenly curved his mouth and she almost flinched, knowing he recognized her for sure. She could see amusement in his gaze.

"You're the small female from the bar who was smashed by the drunken males," he confirmed. "How are you, small female?"

"Zandy Gordon," Creek corrected. "You've met her before?"

Slash flat-out grinned. "Briefly. It is nice to see you have fully recovered." He held out his hand.

She had no choice but to shake the man's large hand. His skin was hot as he gripped her hand firmly and gave it a squeeze. He released her but stayed close. She had to tilt her head back to look up at him.

"Call me Zandy. You are very tall."

Creek laughed. "Yes. Our males are all tall but so are most of our females. I am six-foot-one. What are you, Slash? Six-foot-three?"

He nodded, still smiling at Zandy. "Come with me. I will escort you to work."

The urge to quit her new job and flee gripped her. At least he wasn't the one she'd molested. *It could be worse.* That thought barely comforted her. She turned to Creek.

"Thank you. It was nice meeting and talking to you."

Creek grinned. "I would like it if we could become friends. We could eat lunch together. I could easily find you in the cafeteria. Would you like that?"

Zandy smiled. "I'd love that. I'll see you at lunch."

She followed Slash out of the building. He didn't turn around once to make sure she followed him until they were outside and he paused by a black Jeep. He sat in the driver's seat and she climbed into the passenger side, glancing at him warily as he met her gaze.

"You are working here now."

"Yes."

He chuckled and started the Jeep. "You made quite an impression on Tiger."

"Who?" She knew though. Now she had a name for the mystery man she'd molested. She'd never forget those stunning blue-and-gold cat eyes.

"Tiger is the male who breathed life into you."

Her heart nearly stopped. "Breathed life into me?" *It was a hell of a great kiss but that is overstating it a bit.*

"You were not breathing when he threw drunks off your body, which was crushed against the floor. He had to put his mouth over yours and force air back into your lungs to get you to breathe again."

Shock tore through her. "I wasn't breathing?"

"No. Tiger helped your heart pump and he forced air into your lungs. He carried you outside to wait for the ambulance once he breathed life back into you." He chuckled. "I assume he believed you needed more assistance, considering he put his mouth on you again."

Her cheeks flamed. "Could we drop this subject? Please? That wasn't my best night and I keep trying to forget all the details."

"We can drop it. Don't worry. Tiger told me to never mention what happened between the two of you to anyone. I kept my word. We didn't write what happened outside in our report to the sheriff or to the NSO."

A report? Oh hell! Just the thought made her feel even more embarrassed. Slash had just said they hadn't written what she'd done, which meant no one knew she'd molested...Tiger. *Yeah, that name fits.* She pushed that line of thought back. She'd referred to him as her fallen angel and she hated how many nights the memories of what they'd done together had kept her awake.

Slash had said she'd left an impression on Tiger but he'd left a *huge* one on her too. She mentally kicked herself. Every time she thought that word she remembered her hand digging into the man's pants and gripping his cock. *It had to be the alcohol. It just had to be. He really couldn't have been that good-looking and built.*

She smiled as a joke filtered through her thoughts. *How do you turn a man into a perfect ten? Drink a six-pack of beer.* She'd been having mixed drinks, which were stronger. Tiger couldn't really have looked as good as she remembered. He probably wasn't even that great of a kisser. It had to have been the booze.

Slash parked in front of a building with a big C on the front of it above the doors. She glanced at other buildings, saw more letters, and mused aloud, "How come the buildings aren't numbered?"

He held her gaze, looking grim. "We were once known by numbers instead of names inside the testing facilities and seeing them reminds us of bad times. We chose to use letters instead."

"I'm sorry." She regretted asking and sympathy welled up.

"You didn't know. There is no harm in asking questions and we welcome them. We ask many ourselves when we don't understand something. I know you didn't mean to offend me and I hope we never ask any questions that offend you. It wouldn't be our intention." He climbed out of the driver's seat. "I will return to escort you to lunch. You need an officer at your side while you are on NSO property. We apologize but it is necessary. There are cameras inside all of our buildings and even outside. We had to implement this security measure and it is for your safety as well as ours. You working here will make you a target to our enemies. It provides you with a safe work environment."

She slid out of the seat since the Jeep didn't have doors. "I knew that about the cameras. It's in the information packet I had to read before I applied for the job and I know I need to be patted down every day."

He paused next to her. "I'll introduce you to the male you will work with."

Slash opened the door for her and Zandy stepped inside a large, open office space full of file cabinets and two large desks. A man sat behind a computer, glanced their way and grinned as he stood. He approached them.

"Hello. I'm Richard Vega. You must be Zandy Gordon." He flashed a grin at Slash. "How are you doing today, Slash?"

"I am good, Richard. Here she is." He frowned and his gaze narrowed. "Remember what you were told. You don't want to share sex with this one."

Zandy's mouth fell open. She jerked her head to stare wide-eyed at Slash but he just spun on his heel and left. Her new coworker laughed.

"That came out wrong. They just crack me up."

The man returned to his seat, grinned, and she gaped at him.

"I was told why you left your last job. He meant to say that I am not to sexually harass you. They kind of talk in a way that can come across badly at times." Richard chuckled. "Like that. I'm sorry but it was funny. You should have seen your face. I swear I'm not a lunatic. Will you have a seat? That will be your desk right there."

She relaxed and took a seat. The chair was comfortable and she just dropped her purse on the floor, still watching her new coworker. Richard Vega was in his late thirties, Hispanic, with lightly graying black hair and laughing, light-brown eyes.

"New Species, well," he chuckled, "they take some getting used to. They are really good folks. I just hope you have a great sense of humor because you'll need it."

"That did come out wrong." She smiled.

He laughed again. "The last man left because he moved to Arizona to help his daughter with his grandkids. I didn't sexually harass him if you're wondering."

Zandy laughed. "That's always good to know. Is there anyone here who doesn't know why I left my last job?"

"Probably not. They are looking out for you, believe it or not. They wanted to make sure it never happens to you again. As an employee, they will be protective of you. Toss out the rule book for standard work policy if you had one. You're in a whole new world."

"I'm starting to see that."

His smile faded. "My wife got sick last month with a bad case of the flu and had to be hospitalized. We have two small children. Not only did the NSO send flowers to my wife but they invited my children to come to work with me since I insisted on working. They sent two of their women to play with my kids all day to keep them amused. They are amazing and then to top it off, when I took my wife home, they had food delivered to us for a week. They said it was just to help out my family. Those are the kind of people you'll be working for and I wanted you to know that."

"Thank you for telling me. They sound great."

He suddenly smiled again. "Yes. So when they slip with their words just know it was unintentional. Laugh a lot. I do."

"I understand."

"Are you ready to learn what you do? I hope you have a good sense of humor because you'll need it with this job. Otherwise you might get pretty pissed off."

"Why?" She didn't like the sound of that.

"We're the incoming-mail department. All the hate mail, the fan mail, all of it, comes right to us. It's our job to read it, separate it and respond to it. And keep in mind we are supposed to reply nicely no matter what." He stood and pointed. "See those file cabinets?"

She studied the few dozen file cabinets. "Yes."

"That's where all the hate mail goes, the death threats, and the really scary shit."

Zandy gave him a horrified look. "There's so many of them."

"You should see the second floor. That's storage. These cabinets are just from the past five months."

Shock tore through her. "All those are full of hate mail?"

"And death threats. Yeah. Keep your sense of humor if you have one. You are going to need it. If something comes in that is really specific or just gives you the willies, bring it to my attention immediately. Those we hand over to the FBI."

Her gaze drifted around the large room at all the cabinets and it made her chest hurt to see the kind of hate that people were capable of.

"The sad part is that these people are just amazing, hell, better than the people I've known all of my life. They have to deal with all this hatred every single day. The good part about the job though is we do get a lot of fan mail too. Those are fun and nice. Hand it over if you find something really great. I like to give those to the NSO so they think some of us are decent people."

She glanced at two mailbags by the door. "Is that today's mail?"

He chuckled. "It sure is. You tackle the one on the left and I'll tackle the one on the right. And don't worry. All the mail is screened against poisons and bombs."

Her heart rate accelerated for a second. She had never considered that and swallowed hard. "That's always good to know."

Richard laughed. "Welcome to working for the NSO. Did I mention they feed you for free and they serve a great buffet at lunch?"

"That helps. Is it just us here all day?"

"Just you and me."

She hesitated. "Do you mind if I take off my shoes? I wore high heels to my interview but I wasn't expecting to work all day in them. These are the ones that pinch my feet but they look great."

He laughed as he suddenly lifted his foot to show her his socks. She kicked her shoes under her desk.

"You don't have to dress up so much either. They like us to look casually nice. No sweats or stained shirts but you don't have to go all out."

"Thanks." She moved around the desk to the bag on the left.

Richard walked over and gripped the top of the bag on the right. "It's easier if you just drag these to the side of your desk."

She gripped her bag. It was the size of a large duffel bag. She pulled it by the cords to her desk. It was heavy.

"We'll really get through all this in a day?"

"Yeah."

* * * * *

Tiger sighed, ran his fingers through his hair and frowned at the two males. "Enough. You're giving me a headache."

The two males glared at each other. Their clothing was torn and they appeared ready to fight again. Tiger stepped between them and finally twisted his head to arch a questioning eyebrow at the female.

"Kit? Do you want to explain why you invited two males to your room to share sex with you at the same time? You had to know they'd challenge each other."

She bit her lip and put her hands on her hips, a defiant expression on her face. "Would you believe me if I said it was a simple mistake?"

Anger surged and Tiger growled. "Don't lie. It's unacceptable."

She had enough honor to lower her gaze and give him a submissive stance to show remorse. "I was bored. I thought they could fight and the winner could warm my bed for a few hours. It was exciting until you arrived to break them apart." She shot Tiger a pouty look. "You ruined my fun."

A growl rumbled from both males and their anger turned toward the female instead of each other. Tiger was tempted to leave her to her fate. Two pissed-off males who'd been purposely pitted against each other and wanted a little revenge would serve her right. He knew they wouldn't harm her, both males were friends who had good control usually, unless it was directed at another male. He made a quick decision.

"I'm out of here." He spun, storming down the hallway.

"Wait!" The panic in Kit's voice was clear. "Make them leave with you."

Tiger halted and slowly faced her. "You wanted them to fight, you wanted excitement and you have it now. You created this problem so solve it on your own." He glanced at the males. "Will you harm her?"

Both shook their heads. Tiger nodded. "Good enough. I have things to do besides this. Work it out!"

That's why he avoided females. They caused him headaches and were always doing the unexpected. He left the hotel and headed for his Jeep. The memory of one certain female filled his head and he growled. The human. Just thinking of her made his cock twitch so he pushed the images back. Females were bad news but human ones were to be avoided at all costs. Especially pretty redheads with haunting green eyes.

Chapter Two

 හ

Richard sat down hard in his seat. "We don't have to respond to the hate mail. Sometimes if I really get pissed I'll send them one back." He grinned. "Just be polite. That's what I was told. No one said I couldn't be polite and sarcastic."

Zandy laughed.

Richard turned his computer screen in her direction. "Read this letter and let me know when you're done. I'll show you my response."

She walked to his desk, leaned over and began to skim the letter. Her temper flared as she finished it. Some man was calling New Species a bunch of rabid animals who should all be neutered and put to sleep. Her gaze met Richard's and he clicked to the page he was working on.

Zandy began to laugh almost immediately. He'd written an extremely polite letter to tell the jerk that they felt the same way about him and they shared his loving sentiments about men like him. It was all polite unless you actually read the original letter he'd sent. Richard winked.

"I felt compelled to respond to this one."

"That's a riot. I hope when he gets it that it chaps his ass."

"Me too."

The mailbag was filled to capacity and she opened it, grabbed the one on top and used a letter opener to unseal it. Her coworker told her to scan each one into the computer— they saved them digitally as well as filing them—and type any responses she felt were needed. The outgoing department would print and send any letters she typed. It was grim work.

Most of the incoming mail angered her but she did find a few good ones that kids had sent in.

The time flew by. Zandy sat Indian style, her skirt tucked between her thighs, typing out a response to a sweet little girl in Iowa who had written to say that she loved the New Species and thought they were really cool when the door opened. Zandy looked up as Slash walked inside.

"Lunchtime," Richard announced.

Zandy yanked her skirt down and put on her shoes. She grabbed her purse.

"You won't need that. Your money is no good here. Just drop your purse in your desk. It's safe. Theft is never a problem."

Zandy nodded to Richard and followed the men out of the building. Slash studied her when she sat in the front seat of the Jeep.

"How do you like your job?"

"I am happy to have one."

He nodded. "Good." His gaze fixed on the rearview mirror. "How was your day, Richard? Did you lose your temper yet?"

Richard laughed. "Not so far today. Zandy kept me in a good mood through the worst of the mail."

Slash started the engine. "Good. I am glad it is not my job to read that shit. I would be mad all the time."

They were driven a few blocks over to a large building. It wasn't marked but she was pretty sure it used to be a hotel. There were a lot of Jeeps and golf carts parked along the street and in parking spaces. Nervousness struck her.

"It looks crowded."

"We all eat lunch at the same time." Richard climbed out of the back. "They do a huge buffet but the lines move fast. We have an hour to eat."

When Richard said the word "huge" Zandy instantly thought of her fallen angel. She gritted her teeth, knowing she had to stop doing that. He had a name. *Tiger.* She glanced around a big lobby just inside the building as she, Richard, and Slash walked through double doors.

She remembered high school suddenly when they reached the cafeteria. It was all coming back to her as she eyed the gymnasium-sized room. Tables were lined up in rows with trash cans placed strategically. She felt totally out of place. There were four lines and a long steel counter on the opposite side of the room. A lot of the long tables were already filled.

Zandy glanced around at the people as she followed Slash and Richard to one of the lines. The line really did move quickly. There were just a handful of fully human employees and they had to be outnumbered thirty to one. It left her feeling uneasy.

There had to be over two hundred New Species at lunch. The women were tall and athletic looking but the men were bigger. She watched one man walk by her and the amount of food on his tray amazed her. His plate was platter-sized and it was piled about six inches high with meat.

"Don't stare," Richard ordered softly.

She turned her head. "I was looking at the amount of food."

He chuckled. "I guess I should warn you that most of them eat their meat raw inside. Don't be shocked. When we hit the buffet head, move to the left, not the right. The left has fully cooked meats. The right is the raw side. It looks cooked until you bite into it. I made that mistake my first day here and while it was amusing for everyone around me, not so much for me."

"Thanks." She meant that. She'd hate to end up with raw meat as her selection for lunch.

Slash headed right and Zandy followed Richard to the left. Not all of the New Species chose raw meat for their meals since a few remained ahead of them in line. Her coworker handed her a regular-sized plate and grabbed his own. She followed him down the long buffet, amazed at the amount and selection of food. She ended up with meatloaf and gravy, mashed potatoes, corn, a few chicken strips, some fries, and a slice of chocolate cake. She grabbed a soda and silverware last.

They sat by the back wall near the entry doors at an empty table. Richard smiled.

"Did I tell you they really serve a buffet or what?"

She unwrapped her paper napkin, spread it over her lap and nodded. She cut up her meatloaf and took a bite. It stunned her when the flavor filled her mouth and she moaned slightly.

"Just like Mom made, huh? They have a catering service and they are damn good."

"This meatloaf is amazing. The gravy is mushroom and it's so good."

He nodded. "You can always go back for seconds. And thirds. No one is going to look at you weird if you do that. We eat a hell of a lot less than they do."

Zandy saw someone walking toward the table and recognized a familiar face. "Hi, Creek. Are you eating with us?"

"Yes." Creek took a seat next to. Zandy and flashed a smile at Richard. "Hello, male human."

He laughed. "Hello, Creek. I'm Richard."

Creek turned in her seat. "How was your first day so far, Zandy?"

"Great. I love my job." Zandy glanced at her new friend's plate, saw a few steaks with a big salad and then noticed what looked like an iced coffee.

"I didn't see those. I love iced coffee."

Creek pointed. "They are over there in the corner to the right. They have a chocolate flavor, one with mint, and a nutty one. We love caffeine."

"Who doesn't?" Zandy grinned.

She glanced around the room. Everything seemed fine. Some of the New Species were glancing her way but she figured they had to be as curious about her as she was about them. Motion from the door drew her attention as two tall men entered the cafeteria.

It was *him*, her fallen angel. He wore his black uniform, minus the bulletproof vest, and walked side by side with a man equally as large. They were talking softly but she ignored his friend. Her focus locked on Tiger. She couldn't believe she was seeing him again but knew without a doubt she wasn't mistaken.

His hair appeared a striped honey color in the daylight—highlights of red, shades of blond and soft brown combined. It hung freely around his shoulders and she vividly remembered how soft and satiny it felt to the touch. He passed her table and she got a view of the back of him.

Her angel's pants were molded to a nice, beefy ass. He had a trim waist and his upper body was as large and muscular as she remembered. The fact that she'd been drinking had nothing to do with how sexually appealing he'd been since she had to swallow hard not to gasp. He was gorgeous—all man. Even the way he moved showed a grace and sensuality that had her taking notice.

He glanced over his shoulder, almost seemed to sense her intense scrutiny and scanned the area until he came to her. Their gazes met for a few heartbeats before he faced forward, took a few more steps and his entire body appeared to turn to stone. He came to an abrupt halt.

Zandy's heart raced and she forgot to breathe as he whipped his head around again, this time finding her immediately. She studied his breathtaking eyes. They were exactly as she remembered—catlike, an amazing blue, but she couldn't make out the gold color in them from that far away. His face was just as rugged, masculine and fascinating too. His lips parted, forcing her to remember vividly how he'd tasted of cherry when they kissed and how hungry those generous lips could feel on hers.

His friend took a few more steps before he realized he'd lost his companion, turned and said something. Tiger actually jerked, as if startled. Zandy bit her lip and dropped her gaze to her plate. He recognized her. *Shit.* The sound of Richard and Creek talking assured her they hadn't noticed her lack of attention.

She waited a few seconds before glancing up again. He still stood there staring at her. She forced a smile she didn't feel, not sure what else to do. *What if he walks over here? What do I say? Please don't*, she silently chanted. *Please just walk away.* He turned away almost as if he'd heard her and continued toward the buffet. Zandy let out the breath she'd been holding.

It's her. Tiger moved on autopilot to collect his lunch, his mind reeling from seeing the human he'd saved at that bar. It had been a few weeks but he was certain it was the same female. She was eating in the cafeteria, sharing a table with Creek and Richard Vega, and he didn't know why.

His hands trembled enough to feel relief when he sat at his regular spot and placed the tray down. The last thing he needed was to drop his lunch. The memory of the small female not only affected his ability to think and his coordination but his dick stirred too.

"Are you okay, Tiger?"

Tiger stared at Snow, speechless.

The white-haired Species male sitting across from him frowned. "You look angry."

"I'm fine." He wasn't but he refused to admit it.

Snow nodded. "I noticed you saw the female human when you came in. She is hot, isn't she? I spotted her the second we walked in."

Hot? That word doesn't cover it. She'd made his blood boil all right. Tiger wanted to groan but managed to shrug, pretending indifference. "She is attractive."

"Do you think she's into our males?" Interest sparked in his pale-blue eyes. "I wouldn't mind experiencing shared sex with a human if it were her. She looks a little small though and would probably be frightened of us."

Tiger remembered her pulling his hair at the base of his neck to jerk his face down to meet her lips after she'd demanded he kiss her. His dick grew harder at the memory of having her wrapped around his body, pressed tightly to him. She was aggressive for a human female. Her lips had been soft, she'd smelled so good and her moans had driven him insane to be inside her body.

No, she wasn't a human afraid of Species males. She'd known what she wanted. *She went after me and initiated sex.* He wasn't going to admit that to Snow though or anyone else. He'd left out those details on the reports to avoid being teased about making out with a human on the hood of one of the NSO Jeeps, as if he had no control. He had totally lost it with that female. It wasn't exactly his proudest moment.

"Should we sit with her and see how she reacts to me?"

"No." Tiger avoided snarling or lashing out to deck the other male for even thinking about trying to gain the female's sexual interest. The thought of watching her touch Snow put him in a foul mood.

"That's right." Snow's humor died. "You aren't fond of human females. You like ours better."

Tiger just nodded. He didn't want to dwell on the fact that if she decided to share sex with a Species male, he wanted to be the one she chose. They'd started something together they hadn't been able to finish. His dick ached, trapped inside his too-tight pants now that there was a lot less free space inside them. He barely refrained from snarling.

Slash took a seat next to Snow, stared directly into Tiger's eyes and grinned wickedly. "Guess what my duty is today?"

He knows she's here, Tiger guessed, grimly glaring back at his amused friend. He hoped his silent warning came through and held his breath, waiting to see if Slash would say something he shouldn't.

"There's a new human female who works in building C. I get to escort her between doing security rounds. She's sitting at the last table by the door to the left."

"I saw her." Snow chuckled. "Was she fearful of you? I was wondering if she's into our men. She is hot."

"She is hot," Slash agreed. "She didn't seem fearful. Her name is Zandy Gordon and I looked at her file. She is unmarried, single, thirty-one years old, and lives about eight miles from the east gate of Reservation." He never looked away from Tiger, clearly sending his own message.

Tiger's blindly grabbed the top steak off the pile, lifted it to his mouth and viciously bit down. The taste of blood filling his mouth helped ease some of his anger and kept him from staring across the room as if he were obsessed with the female.

Slash refused to stop taunting him. "I get to escort her back to building C and at the end of the day I'm taking her to the east gate. That is where we moved her car since it will be easier for her to drive home from there."

Tiger felt his temper flare. Slash was baiting him by telling him where he could find the female later. Zandy was an odd name for a human but she wasn't exactly typical in any way. He lost the battle and his gaze searched her out.

Her long red hair was in a ponytail and she was laughing at something one of her two companions had said. She didn't wear much makeup, hadn't the night he'd met her either, but she was very attractive without it. He heard her laugher over the din of voices and clenched his teeth. His dick throbbed against his thigh where it was trapped and the urge to go after her gripped him strongly.

He knew he'd regret it if he rose to his feet, stormed across the room and grabbed her. He wanted her back under him, but this time he wouldn't stop and he didn't give a damn who saw him share sex with her. It would warn all the males to stay away from her too. *They will know she's mine.* That thought shocked him enough to leash his desire and even caused a jolt of fear to strike. *What the hell is wrong with me?*

"Tiger?"

He jerked his gaze away from Zandy to stare at Snow. "What?"

Snow laughed. "I was talking to you but you were thinking something so deep you didn't hear me. What is on your mind?"

"I was thinking about something else." Tiger didn't go into detail.

Slash laughed. "I bet you were thinking about your next shift on the night duty and how you hope the human sheriff doesn't call us out on any more emergencies."

Tiger growled a warning at Slash but he just grinned in response.

Snow frowned. "I don't understand."

"The human sheriff is always calling us for stupid things," Slash explained. "We dread it. That is why Tiger just growled. It is annoying."

Tiger planned to kick Slash's ass the first time they were alone. The man definitely baited him by bringing up how he'd met Zandy. He tore another piece of meat off the steak and focused solely on his food. He didn't dare look her way again.

He forced himself to listen and respond to the conversation at the table. Zandy wasn't mentioned again but he couldn't get her out of his thoughts.

* * * * *

"The east gate? But my car..." Zandy said.

"Was moved. At the gate you had to hand over your car keys. This is why. We secure your cars to prevent the protesters from tampering with them. The protesters have been known to spray-paint bad words on visiting cars."

"Oh."

"You live closer to the east gate. It is saving you miles to work if you use it. In the morning return to it. Your escort will be waiting there."

"Will that be you?"

He shrugged. "I do not assign duties."

She nodded. "Oh."

"Tiger does."

Shit.

"Tiger is head of security."

Double shit. She'd molested the damn head of security of the NSO at Reservation. *Just bitchin'.* She hated herself. She really did. She sat in the Jeep quietly mulling that information and how uncomfortable Tiger could make her life if he held a grudge. They drove to the gate and Slash parked the Jeep close to the guard shack.

She spotted four NSO officers patrolling. Two were inside the guard shack and two more were on top of the thirty-foot walls that enclosed the entire perimeter of Reservation. They carried guns.

"I don't see protesters."

"No. You won't here. We recently bought the land adjoining this section. We haven't extended the walls yet but plan to. It's private property so when they arrive we have them arrested for trespassing. Just show up at this gate in the morning. Your car is parked over there." He pointed.

She saw a small parking area and her car. "Thanks."

Slash nodded. "I'll get your keys. Stay here."

Zandy climbed out of the Jeep, grabbed her purse and waited. She watched Slash laugh and talk with the two officers inside the guard shack before he accepted her keys from one of them. He returned to her and handed them over.

"In the morning they will let you in. Park your car where it is and leave the keys in the ignition. They need your keys in case it has to be moved at some point. It's a security measure. They will search your car and go over every inch of it as well so no one messes with your car by planting a bomb."

Zandy just stared at him, too stunned to speak.

Slash smiled. "Have a nice night." He climbed into the Jeep and backed it up. He waved and then was gone.

Bomb? Shit. No wonder the pay is so good. I'm getting hazard pay. She walked toward her car and noticed the two men on the wall watched her closely. She climbed in and tossed her purse on the passenger seat. She started the car and backed up. The gate was opened when she drove toward it slowly. One of the officers nodded at her and she left Reservation.

She drove about a mile through the twisting, forest-surrounded road before she spotted the black NSO Jeep parked across both lanes. She hit her brakes, frowning, wondering where the driver was and why they'd blocked the road. Her gaze darted around the woods but didn't she see anyone. She turned off the car, waited, and hoped the driver would return soon since trees prevented her from driving around the abandoned vehicle. Long minutes passed and she decided to call out to see if the driver would hear her.

The sound of a man yelling reached her ears the second she opened the car door and stood up. She turned in the direction of the obscene curses and bit her lip as he came closer.

"I swear I'm just lost, goddamn it."

"Right," a male voice snarled. "Sure you were."

"You let me go right now, you son of a bitch. How dare you put your freaky damn paws on me? Fuck you."

"You're trespassing and you're going to be arrested for it."

"Drop dead, asshole. Let me go."

Zandy saw movement about fifteen feet to her left. She was tempted to climb back inside her car and turn it around. The gate wasn't far and she was afraid of whatever kind of scene she'd come across. The man cursing seemed pretty belligerent. A rough-looking man in his twenties stepped out of the thick tree line. His face was red from anger but his hands were behind his back. Someone taller moved behind him, forcing him forward, and recognition hit as she saw that second face.

She froze. Tiger didn't see her right away, too intent on controlling the man he shoved forward. The angry man tried to make a break for it but Tiger moved, grabbed him by the shoulder of his jeans jacket and hauled him back.

"Don't make me chase you," Tiger growled. "You won't make it far with your hands handcuffed behind your back."

"Fuck you, freak. Let me go. You got no damn right to touch or handcuff me. I'm going to sue your damn pussy ass."

Tiger growled viciously. "Keep it up, redneck. I can file more charges against you. You're trespassing on NSO property with a rifle. That doesn't bode well for you at all."

Tiger lifted his head and met Zandy's eyes. He blinked at her but didn't seem shocked to see her standing there. He pushed the man toward the Jeep. Zandy was ignored while Tiger hauled the man up and dumped him into the backseat. The man cursed loud and long, making threats of a lawsuit. Tiger yanked out another pair of handcuffs and secured the man to a metal bar with them.

"You goddamn pussy!" the man yelled. "Let me go. You got no damn right to do this to me."

"Shut up," Tiger growled. "And since you're going to jail, I wouldn't be yelling pussy too much. I hear your kind like to bend your males over in there. If anyone else is as stupid as you are then they might take it as you offering to be one."

Zandy smiled, couldn't help it, and knew it was wrong to find that funny. Tiger finally turned and met her eyes. She saw his nostrils flare as he approached her slowly. Her heart rate increased. They were going to talk and she had no idea what to say to him.

"Where the hell are you going? You can't leave me here, freak. I have rights."

Tiger ignored the man in the Jeep. Zandy didn't move as Tiger closed the distance between them until he paused just feet away. They just stared at each other.

"Hey, pussy. Let me go right now, damn it!" The man fought his cuffs.

"Hi," Zandy breathed, deciding to speak first. She was nervous enough to feel the need to say something, anything. "How have you been?"

His beautiful eyes narrowed slightly. "I have been well. Have you been avoiding brawls?"

She blushed at the reminder of her unwise decision to get toasted in a bar. "Yes."

"You are too small to get involved with men fighting."

"I wasn't exactly involved. I was sitting at a table in the far corner when it broke out. It happened so fast that I found myself trapped and they started coming my way. I had nowhere to go but up on top of the table. I would have been fine there if someone hadn't hit it and sent me to the floor." She studied him closely, still certain he had to be the sexiest man she'd ever seen. "Thank you for saving my life."

He tilted his head a little, studying her closely. "Was that why you kissed me? To thank me?"

She knew her cheeks reddened more, embarrassed that he wanted an explanation for her behavior. "No."

"Then why did you? I am curious."

"Do you really want to know the truth?" She stalled, trying to think of a reason that wouldn't sound foolish, but couldn't come up with anything. The man made her brain malfunction.

"I wouldn't ask if I didn't want to know that."

"I..." She sighed, deciding to just be honest. "I was drunk and I thought I was dying. I woke up and was sure I had. You'll think it's stupid and I doubt you really want to hear where my head was."

"I do."

"I thought I died and there you were."

He frowned. "I don't understand."

She wished a hole would open up under her but one didn't. "I thought you were some kind of guide who'd come to take me to hell."

His mouth tensed. "I see. You believed I was a devil." He looked pissed.

"No!" She shook her head, hating the way he looked at her in that moment. She wanted to fix it. "I thought you were an angel." She omitted the fallen part.

His mouth relaxed and his eyes softened a little. "You always wished to kiss an angel?"

"No." Her face had to be flaming by now. "I thought, since I was going to hell anyway, that I might as well do what I really wanted to. That was kiss you." *And more.* She left that part out too.

"Why did you want to kiss me?"

Does this guy ever stop asking questions? She wanted to avoid sounding even more irrational. She shifted her weight, her high heels making her feet hurt. She looked up into his face. *Oh hell. In for a penny and all that.* "I thought you were attractive and I just really wanted to kiss you."

"Thought? Past tense. Now that you aren't drunk, I'm not attractive?"

She frowned. "You are attractive. Don't put words in my mouth."

"So you still find me attractive?"

"You know you are."

He eyed her for long seconds. "Do you still want to kiss me?"

She blinked a few times and decided she did, but she didn't want to admit that. Drunk, she was pretty forward but that wasn't the case when she was sober. She swallowed instead of answering his question and forced her gaze from his to glance at the Jeep.

"Your prisoner over there is falling out." Her gaze swung back to him.

"I don't give a damn. He might shut up if he falls and hits his head."

She smiled, liking him, and agreed it wouldn't be a bad thing if the loud, crude man in restraints stopped muttering curses.

Tiger suddenly stepped forward, invading her personal space. She gasped when two large hands gripped her hips gently to prevent her from backing away from him. Their gazes met and held. His eyes were just as amazing as she remembered, actually more gorgeous in sunlight since the golden rims of his blue irises nearly glowed, enhancing the blue parts. The catlike eyes, combined with his thick eyelashes, were remarkable.

Zandy took a shaky breath, inhaling his masculine, woodsy scent. She didn't resist when he gently tugged her closer until she had to tilt her head back to keep their gazes locked and her body pressed against his. Her hands automatically rose to flatten on his broad chest. The material of his black shirt was soft but the man under it felt very solid.

"I am curious," he rasped. "If touching you is as good as I remember. I'm going to kiss you."

Chapter Three

∞

Zandy knew she should say no and tug out of Tiger's hold. She should... *Oh hell. I'm only going to live once.* The urge to kiss him was strong. She wasn't going to deny it so she slid her hands higher, to his shoulders. They were the broadest ones ever. She pressed tighter against him and parted her lips in invitation.

His eyes widened with surprise and he leaned in a little. A soft growl rumbled from his throat and Zandy's belly clenched. He made the sexiest sounds. Her alcohol-hazed memories hadn't been wrong about that and she closed her eyes in anticipation of his kiss.

The man softly purred when his mouth brushed hers. Zandy took a shaky breath against his lips and lifted on tiptoe to get closer. Their mouths met again and this time he didn't just give her a featherlight tease. His tongue slid past her parted lips and fully possessed her with the kind of passion that would have made her melt to the ground if she wasn't clinging to his shoulders. His arms tightened around her.

Her being drunk hadn't affected her senses after all because the man could kiss like nobody's business. His tongue teased, savaged, and absolutely left her without the ability to think. Another growl came from him. Her nipples responded to the vibrations it caused with her chest pressed so tightly against him and she wanted to be even closer. Her hands wrapped around his neck and she barely noticed when her feet left the ground as he lifted her higher up his body to deepen the kiss.

She kicked off her shoes, wanting them out of the way and needing to feel more of him. Almost instinctively her legs wrapped around his hips. Her back hit the side of her car and he wiggled closer until the hard ridge of his cock pressed against her underwear. She adjusted her hold on him with her legs, clamping her knees over his sides and locking her ankles together until her heels dug into his firm ass, urging him closer.

Tiger's hips ground against her pussy, making her aware of the rough material of his pants against her bare thighs...and that her skirt had ridden up. She didn't care. Instead she kissed him frantically and arched her back, rubbing her breasts and clit against him where they were touching. She moaned, wanting him so bad it hurt. Her body was on fire.

Tiger's hold shifted from her waist to caress down to her ass. His bare hands cupped naked skin where her thong panties didn't cover and he squeezed her firmly. He moved, slowly rocking his cock against her. Pleasure tore through her from how hard he was, how sensitive her clit was to just the slightest movement he made. She ached to come.

It was insane how she reacted to him. No man had ever turned her on more. His mouth was pure sin. His body did things to her. He made her feel wild and needy and she wanted him to take her. She moaned louder, kissing him deeper as her fingernails clawed at him where she could touch his back. She wanted him now, against the car, in the middle of the road and she didn't even care that they were in the open.

Tiger tore his mouth away from hers, breathing hard, and she opened her eyes. "Don't stop."

Pure passion made his eyes the sexiest things she'd ever seen. He flashed some seriously hot fangs at her and the sudden desire to bare her neck for him struck. She could totally go for him biting her. Even the thought of him nipping her with those babies made her hotter. *I'm a sick person but I don't care. He's so damn hot.*

"I—"

Zandy was afraid he was going to refuse. There was a lot at stake considering she'd never wanted anyone as much as she did him. Thoughts left her as she lifted up to place her lips over his to kiss him. He snarled, pressing her tighter against the side of her car.

Her hand fisted in his hair, holding him in place as she rolled her hips. She moaned at the feel of his trapped cock against her pussy and bucked against him to show him how much she wanted him.

"HEY! HELLO? What the fuck? Hey, pussy? Could you stop nailing the chick on the car and let me go!"

Tiger tore his mouth from Zandy's and they stared at each other, both of them suffering. He growled again and took some deep breaths as he watched her.

"I have to deal with that asshole."

His voice was so rough, deep and sexy that she still didn't want to let him go but she'd forgotten about his prisoner. *Damn!* If she had any shame she'd feel embarrassed but she'd passed that point when Tiger had kissed her. All she wanted was him and nothing else seemed to matter. *Maybe I'm going through some kind of early menopausal thing that causes me to be super horny and lose my damn mind.* That made her feel a little better but she didn't believe it for a second. Tiger just made her reckless because there was something about him that pushed her "on" buttons.

Tiger's hold on her eased and she knew she had to release him, even though she didn't want to. She unhooked her ankles and let her legs slide down his body. Her fingers had to let go of his hair and she missed holding on to him instantly as he backed away once she stood barefoot on the pavement. She actually felt cold and at a loss when they separated.

"Let me drive him to the gate and turn him over to the officers." He didn't look away from her. "Wait here for me. Will you do that? It won't take more than five minutes."

She didn't miss seeing the worry that filled his gaze or the regret. An instant *yes* wanted to pass her lips but now that they weren't locked together making out she could think. A smart woman would flee, she knew that, but she'd never met a man like Tiger before. He was worth some risk and doing something totally insane.

"He had a gun or I'd allow him to go with a stern warning. I have to turn him in. He could have been here to shoot at my people and that means he poses a future threat." Tiger inched closer but avoided touching her. "I will be gone five minutes at most. Will you wait here? Please?"

Zandy nodded in agreement and he looked relieved. His gaze finally turned away from hers to study the Jeep as he stepped back. He cleared his throat before he glanced at her again. His voice came out more normal sounding and she missed the gruff intensity.

"I'll hurry. Don't leave, Zandy."

He knows my name. She nodded, a little impressed that he'd taken the time to find out something about her. "I'll be here."

He walked to his Jeep. She leaned against her car to prevent her shaky knees from giving way. They felt as if they just might collapse under her. The man had kissed her senseless and made her body turn to jelly.

Tiger grabbed the man who had tried to climb out of the backseat. The idiot hung a little upside down where his handcuffs had kept him partially inside. Tiger shoved him upright. A growl came from the New Species as he shook his head and jumped into the driver's seat.

"You can't do this!" the man yelled. "Let me go, you talking freak show! I'm an American citizen. This is my country and you don't belong here. I demand a lawyer."

The Jeep reversed. Tiger twisted the wheel and glanced at Zandy as he punched the gas, taking off fast to return to

Reservation. She watched him go, hugged her chest and silently wondered if she was making a mistake.

Common sense dictated that she should climb in her car, leave before he returned and put some space between them. They were going to have sex if she stayed. She wasn't naïve enough to think otherwise and it would probably be just one more thing to add to the long list of mistakes she kept making.

Zandy didn't budge. She took a few deep breaths and stared at the woods around her, appreciating the beauty of what she saw but she couldn't ignore the way her breasts felt achy. Her panties were soaked to the point she'd need to change them when she got home and it had spread to dampen her thighs. Desire still had her heart beating faster than normal.

It would be unwise to risk her new job by sleeping with the head of security at the NSO. The bills, mortgage payment and her eating depended on avoiding getting fired. *Is he really worth risking all that?* Her eyes closed and all she could see was those eyes of his. They seemed to stare right into her soul when he looked at her and she shivered from the memory of his hands gripping her ass. Tiger was dangerous, unlike any other man she'd ever known and she'd never wanted anything more than him.

Get in your car, damn it. Run! The last thing you need is to get involved with another man and this can't go anywhere. You've sworn off men, remember? Two divorces, thirty-one years old and you're always attracted to toxic men.

She didn't budge, just remained there with her eyes closed and silently listed all the reasons she needed to leave. She finally opened them and leaned down to collect her discarded shoes. She tossed them into the passenger side of her car and turned her head to watch the way he'd gone. Wise or not, she wasn't leaving. He was coming back and she'd be there waiting when he did.

On an up note she'd read that New Species were sterile and didn't carry sexually transmitted diseases. He couldn't knock her up or give her anything bad if they did end up having sex.

* * * * *

Tiger hauled the human out of the Jeep, shoved him at two of the officers and then handed over the rifle he'd confiscated from the jerk. "I caught him with this and took him to my Jeep to call it in but then he ran. I had to chase him down. He's stupid so be wary."

The male who accepted responsibility for the prisoner nodded grimly. "Yes, Tiger."

"There may be more of them. Shut down the area, seal the gates and don't allow anyone to leave or enter this way. I am going hunting."

"We'll gather reinforcements to assist you."

"No." Tiger shook his head. "I'm going alone. Make sure all the wall patrols are warned. Be sure they are wearing their protective gear in case of snipers. I'm turning off my radio. I plan to be totally silent while I search the woods."

"I don't think that's a good idea," the second officer growled. "We are stronger in numbers."

"We're also louder. I'm in charge and I just gave you an order. Seal it down. No one in or out and don't be alarmed if you can't contact me. I'll be out there." He spun to stomp back to the Jeep and leaped inside.

His dick was still hard, his body burning to finish what he'd started with Zandy. He really hoped she hadn't been lying. The thought of her being gone when he returned made him want to snarl.

Another part of him hoped she wouldn't be waiting. Touching her made him lose all control. He'd nearly taken her in front of a human witness and he didn't even give a damn. He just wanted her.

Her taste and the feel of her in his arms made him feel foreign, crazy things. He should return home to take a cold shower and find a Species female. They didn't want commitment and were usually easy to understand despite Kit's recent odd behavior. Zandy… Tiger had no idea what she wanted from him besides sex.

No way was he taking a mate. He shook his head as he started the engine and threw it in drive, ignoring the worry on the other males' faces as they watched him leave. He hated the tiny bit of guilt he felt over lying. The fact that he was willing to tell falsehoods to be with the attractive human rang alarm bells in his brain.

Not that it stopped him from driving as fast as he could to return to where she hopefully waited. He took the turns a little too fast, broke the speed laws they had set for safety and only slowed when he came to the last curve of the road, to avoid hitting her car if it was still parked there.

The sight of her made him want to roar in victory. She was his. He was going to strip her bare and do all the things he wanted. Raw hunger gripped him. He wanted Zandy Gordon and he was going to have her.

He grinned, ecstatic all of a sudden as all doubt vanished. He'd worry about what it meant to want her, what *she* meant to him, later. Right now he just wanted to get her alone, away from the road, and put his hands back on her.

There was a wide strip of grass that he used to park the Jeep. He tore the keys from the ignition and pocketed them as he jumped out. He strode right to her and held out his hand.

"Give me your keys."

She blinked, obviously not expecting him to say that, but eased away from the car anyway. "They are in the ignition."

"I'm going to move your car off the road and park it behind my vehicle."

She nodded and inched away from her car as he moved impatiently. The urge to just bend, toss her over his shoulder and carry her deeper into the woods was strong. He doubted she'd appreciate his carnal thoughts of how he'd like to take her on the ground. He tried to cool his heated blood while he opened the door and attempted to wiggle his big body inside her car.

The female had short legs and the steering wheel squeezed him until he got hold of the lever to shove the seat all the way back. The car smelled of her, laundry soap and something he couldn't identify. He drove it off the road, parked it behind his Jeep and reached over to shove her purse under the seat, out of sight. The road was mostly secure but anyone could wander by if they were looking for trouble.

The element of danger wasn't missed by Tiger. He'd already found one human with a gun stalking the woods near Reservation walls. The man could have friends. That gave him pause as he removed the keys from the ignition, pocketed them and locked her car door.

One look at Zandy's steady green gaze and he decided she was worth some risk. He'd be aware of their surroundings and hoped he could remember to stay alert while he touched her. The smart thing would be to have her follow him back to the gates and take her to his house but the officers would talk. Tiger with a human female would cause a stir, considering his outspoken beliefs that Species males were foolish to hook up with them.

Zandy chewed on her bottom lip, an uncertain expression making her appear fragile. He quickly closed the distance between them to scoop her up in his arms. She gasped but gripped his shoulders.

"I can walk."

He resisted grinning, amused. She was light in his arms, felt good so close to him, and he wanted her there. "You're not wearing shoes. I have you." He forced his gaze from hers, turned toward his Jeep, and quickly headed that way.

"Where are we going?" Zandy relaxed in Tiger's arms.

"I'm taking you away from the road. I don't want any interruptions in case others are trespassing." He paused by the side of the Jeep. "Do you see the blanket folded on the back bench? Could you please grab it?"

She had to let go of him with one arm. He bent her over a little and she grabbed it and dropped it on her lap. Her arm wound around his neck again.

"You really should let me walk. It's just grass."

"I don't want you to hurt your feet and where we are going there might be rocks and small twigs. Trust me. I have you."

Yes, you do, she admitted silently. The man was strong. He held her in his arms as if she didn't weigh anything as he maneuvered through the trees quickly. It dawned on her that he was mostly a stranger. She was allowing him to take her deep into the woods and it probably wasn't the brightest idea she'd ever had. He could be a serial killer but she doubted it. Something about him just made her trust him. Her intuition had been wrong before about people but Tiger wasn't exactly a regular guy.

"There is a pretty stream ahead," he rasped. "We will go there."

That sounds romantic. She smiled, liking that. "Okay."

She studied his face. He really was gorgeous in a masculine, exotic kind of way. His hair did resemble a mane. The thick strands waved down his shoulders and the multicolored streaks were a truly striking sight. Her hand turned and she ran her fingers through some of it, enjoying the silky texture. His gaze flicked to hers for a second before he concentrated on where he stepped.

"We're almost there."

He had walked really fast but wasn't out of breath and it made her realize how strong he must be. That probably should have made her a little leery of him but she didn't feel any twinges of fear whatsoever. She was all for having sex with him. The chemistry between them was off-the-charts hot and his size actually made him more arresting.

The woods opened into a small oasis of flowers, a narrow stream and plush grass. Tiger stopped walking, sniffing the air as Zandy gazed around in wonder.

"It's so pretty."

He turned to stare deeply into her eyes. "This is my new favorite spot. We recently acquired the land and I come here to bathe sometimes when I'm patrolling the area. Not many of the officers know about it and only a few of us hunt this section for intruders. We'll have privacy."

He placed Zandy on her feet. Thick, soft grass cushioned her toes. The blanket nearly slipped to the ground but Tiger grabbed it. He straightened, stepped around her and bent to spread it over an area of moss by the water's edge in the shade.

His body twisted her way as he straightened and reached for his shirt to remove it. He exposed his impressively sculpted abs to her view. "Do you need help undressing? I'd like for us to remove all our clothes."

Her heart pounded as she made a final decision—she *really* wanted to have sex with him. It wasn't much of a choice. The memory of him had haunted her since the night they'd kissed in that parking lot, the attraction between them too strong to deny. She wanted him. It had been nearly a year since she'd sworn off men after her divorce and the idea of being touched by him tempted her too much.

Her fingers shook slightly as she unbuttoned her shirt, spread it apart and kept her gaze locked on Tiger. His eyes were stunning, so exotic she didn't want to look away, but the view he exposed when he peeled off his shirt was too tempting to miss. Tan, golden skin, that broad chest, dusky flat nipples and thick bands of muscle was enough to convince her she'd made the right choice. He was perfection.

The zipper at the back of her skirt sounded unusually loud as it came down. The material just dropped to her ankles and she stepped away from it. He softly growled at her as his gaze strayed down her body and she hoped that meant he liked what he saw. She was grateful to be wearing matching underwear. Her hands still trembled as she unfastened her bra, shrugged it off, and reached for her hips to ease her blue thong down her legs.

He stalked closer to her, his pants still on, until only inches separated them. She felt totally exposed, standing there completely naked when he wasn't.

"You didn't take off your pants."

A grin curved his sexy mouth. "I will soon but I don't want to frighten you."

Her eyebrows arched. "Why would that scare me?"

Hesitation made her worry until he spoke. "I really want you and I'm very hard. I'm also different from your males."

That stunned her and she glanced down. The outline of his cock was clear. It was big but appeared the same shape as a normal penis would be. Her gaze lifted and for the first time she really worried about being alone with him, yet she was prepared to deal with any physical differences they might have to overcome.

Tiger seemed to read her mind. "I'm shaped and function the same way but we're just bigger than your males. I don't want you to be intimidated or risk you changing your mind."

"We'll just take it slow." Her hands reached for his waist. "I think I'll risk a little fear."

His hands stopped her from opening his pants as he tugged her along with him. He backed up to the side of where the blanket waited and lowered to his knees, still holding her hands.

Zandy dropped to her knees on the grass then moved onto the blanket. Tiger released her and touched her body instead. She gasped when he suddenly had her pinned down flat with him half over her until their mouths were nearly touching.

"I want you more than I've ever wanted any female." His voice came out gruff and sounded a little raw. "I am trying to slow down but it's so difficult."

Her hands cupped his face. "I want you too. This is insane, isn't it?"

He nodded. "A little, but there is a strong pull between us."

Animal magnetism. She refused to say that aloud in case he took offense. She could have said raw lust but staring into his exotic catlike eyes, the first one fit more. Whatever the draw, it was incredibly strong.

"I've never wanted anyone as much as I do you either," she admitted. "Crazy or not."

A soft purr came from him and it surprised her but, at the same time, turned her on a little more. He certainly wasn't like anyone she'd ever known. It was a good thing.

"I'll try to slow down."

"You don't have to." She decided to be blunt. "I ache for you."

His mouth came down on hers to end any further conversation between them and his aggressive kiss notched her passion higher. Her fingers frantically explored every inch of his chest she could reach. He was hot, figuratively and literally. One of his legs lifted and she spread hers to make room for him as he slid it between them.

Her back arched to press more firmly against him. He snarled and pulled his mouth away as they both panted. His palms flattened on the blanket next to her and he lifted up to sit. He tore at his boots and socks and just tossed them aside. He rose quickly to his feet and grabbed the front of his pants. His gaze held hers.

"Don't fear me. I won't hurt you."

Zandy wiggled enough to rise, bracing her bent elbows behind her. "Show me."

Desire narrowed his eyes and her gaze lowered to watch intently as he released the snap and the zipper. He allowed the pants to slide down once they were open, revealing black boxer briefs. She held back a gasp when she got clearer look at how much he wanted her. He bent, blocked her view of his cock and removed the pants completely. He straightened once more and his thumbs hooked the waist of his underwear.

"We'll take it slow."

"Just take them off."

His chest expanded as he sucked in a deep breath. "Please don't change your mind. It would kill me."

A grin twisted her lips. "I can handle it."

The material lowered torturously slowly, as if he wanted to draw it out as long as possible. She appreciated the feeling of anticipation until the cotton lowered enough for his rigid cock to spring free. Her lips parted and she had to remember to breathe. Tiger was bigger than any man she'd ever seen. The shaft was thick and long and the tip of his cock curved a little upward with a fuller mushroom tip.

"Oh wow."

He froze and stared at her. "What does that mean? Are you afraid?"

"Nope. Just go slow."

The look of relief on his face was near comical to Zandy but she felt a little bad, wondering if he had reason to be so worried. Had some woman seen that bad boy and run from him? She wasn't timid though. There weren't too many challenges that she'd back down from, especially if they looked like something out of her hottest fantasy.

He kicked away the briefs and dropped to his knees. One hand clutched her ankle and lifted, spread her thighs wider and his gaze fixed on her exposed pussy. He made a sexy sound — between a soft growl and a near purr.

"You have hair."

She licked her lips. "Do you prefer it all gone? It's just a little strip."

He let go of her ankle and bent over until his face was right above her spread thighs. "I like it a lot." He inhaled and groaned. "So good."

She'd never had a man do that before but it seemed to turn him on more. One of his hands gripped her inner thigh and calloused fingertips made her shiver in the best way as he caressed her.

"I want to taste you but I want inside you just as bad." His gaze lifted. "You're so wet and ready for me."

Zandy collapsed onto her back and lifted her arms to reach for him. "As good as that sounds, I want you right now."

He crawled over her and lowered his big body until she could feel his hot, thick cock against her inner thigh. They were belly to belly and his mouth sought hers. He kissed her as if it were the end of the world. It was so feverish and frantic it drove her a little out of her mind. She lifted her legs to wrap them around his waist. Her hips wiggled, trying to urge him on and she moaned when he adjusted his body a little higher until the incredibly rigid length of his cock pressed against the seam of her pussy.

He rocked his hips to rub the length of his cock against her clit. It was easy to do since she was soaked with her need for him. It felt so good she had to tear her mouth from his or risk biting him. Her hands gripped his shoulders and her nails dug into his skin.

"Please," she pleaded.

His head burrowed against her neck and he placed hot, wet kisses on her throat, which she bared for him. The feel of the sharp points of his fangs registered and it turned her on more. He could have bitten into her at that point and she wouldn't have cared. He hadn't even entered her and she was ready to come.

He spread his thighs, forcing hers wider apart and rolled his hips in a way that made his cock press tighter against the bundle of nerves.

"Fuck me," she demanded.

He stopped kissing her neck and growled. "Easy."

"Fuck that. Take me."

Her body burned and she was so close to climaxing. Her fallen angel was just too sexy and the man knew how to take her to heaven. Her body screamed for release.

He lifted up enough that she turned her head to stare into his eyes. The blue of them pulled her in and she barely registered when he reached between them and put space between their hips until the broad head of his cock pressed against the entrance of her pussy.

"Yes," she urged.

He pressed against her and his eyes closed. Her body resisted taking him at first but she rolled her hips slowly until the thick crown of his cock eased through. Tiger's lips parted, a look of near pain tensed his features and he growled as he slowly entered her. She was so wet it helped ease him inside and the pleasure of being filled and stretched was exquisite to Zandy.

"Oh god," she moaned.

Tiger's eyes opened. "Tell me if I hurt you. You're so tight."

She rolled her hips again and wrapped her legs tighter around his waist as she adjusted them until her heels pressed into his firm ass. She used them to pull tighter against him and his cock sank deeper.

"You feel so good."

His arms pinned her under him where he braced his weight with his elbows and his fingers curved under her shoulders to grip her. He withdrew a little and slid back in, making her take more of him. She couldn't look away from his eyes staring into hers. They were the most beautiful thing in the world and nothing had ever felt better than having him slowly fuck her.

"Faster," she urged once her body adjusted to him after he'd fully worked his entire shaft inside her pussy. "Please?"

He lowered his head and tried to kiss her but she turned her head to the side to bare her throat instead. "I'm afraid I'll bite you. It is too good. I'm going to come."

His mouth found the line of her throat and he kissed her there as he began to move faster, his strong body pinning her down. The feel of his muscles rippling almost sent her into climax. His cock hit a spot inside her that made her cry out and her nails dug in deeper. Sharp teeth clamped down on her skin and his hips bucked rapidly, fucking her hard and fast.

Zandy threw back her head and cried out as pleasure tore through her. The climax was brutal as it spread through her body. Her vaginal muscles clamped down hard on his driving cock and her body seized from the intensity of it.

Tiger released her from his teeth. The roar that came out of his mouth nearly deafened her. Heat shot inside her as he came. She could feel every jet of his semen filling her as his hips slowed to sharp, short jerks and he kept his cock buried deep inside her. Another climax hit, shocking her, and she lifted her head to muffle the scream she couldn't hold back against his chest. She was afraid he'd mistake it for pain. Her mouth opened on his smooth skin.

Tiger's head fell forward and his weight pushed her back flat. She was shocked that she'd bitten him. She had been afraid she would. He panted against her skin when he finally stopped fucking her. Zandy eased her grip and loosened the hold of her legs, which were still wrapped around his hips, as her body began to recover and relax. A sense of deep satisfaction filled her and she smiled. She didn't even care that Tiger roared like a lion when he came. It sounded scary but it was a real turn-on.

Chapter Four

🔊

The sounds of the woods penetrated finally to Zandy. The stream bubbled and the wind not only sent a gentle breeze along their heated skin but made the trees rustle above them. Her eyes opened and she stared through the branches full of leaves at the pretty blue sky with clouds.

Tiger hadn't moved off her and seemed content to keep their bodies joined while he kept her pinned under him. She could breathe fine but his weight was heavy enough to keep her exactly where he wanted her. There was zero motivation on her part to move though.

She discovered, in the aftermath of the best sex she'd ever had, that Tiger's cock still felt incredibly hard and big inside her. She'd be worried he hadn't come if she hadn't felt him do it and heard his roar of completion. Her ears still rang a little from that roar of his.

Lips brushed her skin. "Did I hurt you?"

A smile curved her lips. "Nope. Wow. That was amazing."

His body tensed for a split second before he relaxed again. "It was."

Her hands moved, roaming down the broad expanse of his back, and loved the feel of his smooth, firm skin. It was something she could get used to and never tire of. Her hands trailed down to the curve of his ass before making their way upward to finger his silky hair.

"That feels good."

"For both of us," she agreed. "I really like touching you."

"You can do that as much as you like, anywhere on me." He laughed and shifted so he could look down at her. She had to release him to focus and peer into his eyes. They were so stunning. She felt as though she could stare into them forever. His hands released her shoulders and one of them brushed her hair off the side of her face. His touch was tender.

"You are so beautiful right now. Your lips are swollen from my kisses and your eyes are such a pretty shade of green. They remind me of a beautiful meadow when I look into them."

She grinned. "You're the beautiful one. Trust me. You're the most beautiful man I've ever seen. You're like a living sculpture of the perfect man."

He grinned. "You mean an angel?"

She laughed. "You will never let me live that one down, will you?"

He shook his head, smiling. "No. I'm flattered. I've been called a lot of names but never one so nice."

She just smiled at him.

"Did I hurt you at all? Tell me if I have. You're small and I was rough."

She shook her head. "No. Did I hurt you? Your back maybe? Your chest? I bit you a little. I don't see any blood though." She glanced at the red spot and winced. She could see teeth marks. "I'm sorry."

He grinned. "It felt good. I was just afraid I may have been too rough with you. You make me lose my control."

"Thanks. I might have cut up your back with my nails."

He shrugged. "It was worth it if you did. You completely drained me."

She reached up and brushed his hair back. "I drained you?"

He smiled. "You made me shoot so much of myself inside you that I don't think there's anything left. I almost passed out it felt so strong but I was afraid I'd crush you." He paused. "I roared." His surprise was clear.

"Don't tell me I'm the first one who ever made you do that," she teased.

He didn't smile back and instead seemed disturbed a little when he frowned. "I have never lost so much of myself inside a female before or felt that strongly that I couldn't hold back my instincts."

A little pride swelled inside her and she had to admit it felt good to know she'd affected him as much as he had her. They both had experienced some firsts. Then grim reality set in next. They'd had wild, passionate sex in the woods together but they didn't really know each other. They probably had nothing else in common and they weren't in a relationship.

Men were different than women. She had two failed marriages in her wake to prove that fact. Saying vows with a man had meant everything to her but both husbands had broken them as easily as they had her heart. Sex and love were separate for men and she needed to remember that.

He just wanted sex. Put on the big-girl panties. You wanted this too but don't read anything into it. The mental pep talk helped her keep things in perspective. It saddened and depressed her but she'd have great memories.

"I guess we should get dressed and go back to our cars before someone drives by and wonders where we are."

His gaze narrowed and his voice noticeably deepened. "You want to leave already?"

"I, um, well, someone will see our cars and wonder where we are. They might even come looking for us." The idea of being caught naked in the woods unsettled her. She never had trysts with strangers—he was her first. She liked to keep her sex life private. "I'd have to post bail," she joked.

"I closed the road. No one will know."

She stared up at him. "You did?"

70

He smiled. "I turned over the asshole to officers at the gate and told them I wanted the road closed. I told them I would hunt the woods alone and see if anyone else was out here. No one will disturb us. I'm in charge and they have to follow my orders."

She laughed. "That's pretty cool. I guess it's good to be in charge, huh?"

"Very cool." He shifted and eased his cock out of her body. "Come on."

Zandy released him and he rose to his feet. He was so muscular and perfect that she couldn't resist staring at his body a little. The fact that he still had a major hard-on wasn't lost on her either. He reached out to her.

"Take my hands."

She put her hands in his and he helped her to her feet. He stepped backward, still holding her hands. He led her to the creek and into it. It was a warm, sunny afternoon but the water was a bit chilly. He kept hold of her until he stood waist-deep and she was up to the tips of her breasts. They instantly responded by tightening and she knew Tiger noticed when he grinned.

"Come over here. There are some rocks."

They moved downstream about five feet and he suddenly sat on something hidden beneath the surface that made the water level with his nipples. He maneuvered her to sit on the mossy-feeling stone next to him. She relaxed and enjoyed the movement of the water around them.

"This feels good since we got a little sweaty."

"I love to come here whenever I can. I enjoy cooling off before I stretch out naked on the rocks over there to dry in the sun."

It sounded so sensuous to Zandy that she followed the direction of his gaze to the smooth, flat boulders. She could almost imagine his naked body as he stretched out on his back with his arms up to use his hands to cushion the back of his head. Her attention returned to him and his body. The water made his nipples taut, hard tips of dusky temptation. She got the urge to taste.

Oh hell, why not? She knew this would be the one and only time she found herself sitting in a creek with a super-sexy guy. Her tongue darted out to lick her lips before she turned into him and lowered her face. He gasped as her mouth latched on to him and he arched his back to give her easier access. One of her hands slid across his flat belly under the water while her other hand gripped his shoulder to keep her balance.

His fingers slipped into her hair to encourage her. She shifted even closer to him, released his nipple and kissed her way to the other one. Loud purrs made his entire chest vibrate. Her hand lifted from his belly to his chest, to feel them better. She was amazed and aroused at the same time by his reaction.

The hold on her hair tightened until he fisted it and tugged her away from sucking and teasing his nipple. She met his gaze for a split second before he lowered his head and his mouth took possession of hers. Firm, desire-hungry lips forced hers apart and his tongue explored and stroked, as if he wanted no doubt left in her mind that he wanted her again. She tried to lift her leg to climb on his lap but he suddenly broke the kiss to stare at her.

"Hands and knees, right here, but turn around," he snarled, his voice harsh.

His stern tone didn't scare her. She understood why he sounded half out of control since she wanted him more than her next breath. Letting go of him wasn't easy since her hands loved the feel of him but she managed to do it. The rock they shared was similar to a ledge and she rose to her knees on it. The embankment directly behind them was a sharp incline covered with grass and clover.

"Grab something," he growled.

Big hands gripped her hips and pushed her forward enough that her hands shot out to claw at the soft greenery when he bent her over and stood behind her. A knee bumped her thighs, she spread them apart, and suddenly Tiger curled his body over her back. One of his hands opened on the grass inches from her left one and he braced.

His cock nudged against her pussy and he was entering her. He wrapped his free arm around her waist and anchored her firmly in front of him. Zandy moaned from the way he drove into her with one slow but forceful thrust of his hips. He made her take all of him without any hesitation. The feel of him inside her was wonderful and the new position felt even more amazing than him facing her had.

His hold on her waist adjusted until his hand cupped her pussy from the front and located her clit. He pressed a finger against it. Tiger growled and withdrew almost totally from her body before he slammed into her hard and deep. Zandy cried out from the pleasure of it and he wrapped around her tighter as her fingers dug into the earth.

Tiger pounded against her mercilessly as he rubbed her clit. Ecstasy swamped her. She couldn't think. Nothing existed but his driving cock, hitting wonderful nerves that were drawing her dangerously close to climaxing. It felt so good it nearly hurt as he pounded against her ass harder, hammering her rapidly, and his purrs were loud enough that her body seemed to vibrate with his.

"I could mount you until I die," Tiger snarled.

"Yes," she cried out as he thrust into her even faster and harder.

A snarl came from his throat. It brought the sex up another notch instead of frightening her. She felt his teeth clamp down on her shoulder and the sharp points of his fangs actually seemed to bite into her that time. It didn't matter. The jolt of pain only took her closer to climax.

"God, that feels good," she panted. "I'm so close."

He snarled again and his teeth bit down harder on her shoulder as he continued to pound into her from behind while his finger strummed her clit. Zandy felt her body tense and she screamed his name as she came so hard she nearly blacked out.

His teeth released her as pleasure tore through her entire body from her center outward. He roared as he came too with blasts of his release deep inside her body. She could feel him coming, the warm spread of his semen filling her as his hips slowed.

Zandy panted, trying to catch her breath. The only thing keeping her from slumping sideways and sliding into the creek was Tiger's hold. Her body totally felt boneless and limp as she basked in the afterglow of that bout of sex. It didn't matter that her head had lowered and that her cheek rested against the ground. A smile curved her mouth when she realized she wouldn't have cared if they were lying in mud.

The feel of Tiger withdrawing his cock slowly from her pussy made her groan. She felt connected to him and her vaginal walls clamped down almost as if they were protesting the loss too, possibly trying to hold on to him a little longer. He backed away enough to take his weight off her back while his hold on her waist eased. Cold water chilled her overheated clit when his finger left it.

He sat down and pulled her onto his lap sideways. Their gazes met and she smiled.

"Did I say 'wow' before? I was wrong. Wow!"

He nuzzled her head aside with his face and she thought he wanted to kiss her neck. He lowered his head instead and his hot tongue licked at her shoulder. It was a slightly strange sensation but she liked it. She felt a little sleepy and really loved being cradled on his lap. His tongue kept flicking at her shoulder, over and over, and curiosity prompted her to speak.

"I'm not complaining, but why are you licking me?"

His tongue stopped. "I bit you hard enough to break the skin this time. I'm cleaning your wound. It will be sore later and hurt." He didn't lift his head to look at her while he spoke. "I'm so sorry."

"Don't worry about it." It was odd that he'd bitten her but it didn't hurt so it couldn't be more than a scratch. She wasn't alarmed over it. "Sex injuries happen sometimes and that was totally worth one. I don't even feel it." She laughed.

He didn't. "It's going to hurt later when you warm from the cold water and the endorphins from sexual gratification subsides." His voice deepened to a gruff tone. "It may scar. Damn. I didn't mean to do it." His tongue lapped at her again.

She thought it was really cute how he'd put that. She'd never met a man who said "endorphins" but wisely didn't laugh. She was afraid of hurting his feelings if he mistook her reason for finding humor in it. He was sweet and his concern touched her. It even made her fall a little in love with him.

Don't do that, she sternly ordered. *It's just sex. Don't forget that*. Her humor vanished. "I'm okay."

His tongue stopped again. "I took you too rough. Are you sore or feeling no pain at all yet?"

She pushed her head against his and he lifted his until their gazes met. The look of regret in his eyes almost broke her heart. So much for their perfect one-time tryst in the woods. Her head turned and she twisted her shoulder enough to see where he'd bitten her. There were two small puncture wounds on the top of her shoulder and she couldn't see if there were more on the back side. A small amount of blood came from them but the skin wasn't torn. It didn't look too terrible and her gaze returned to his.

"Don't feel bad, okay? Honestly. I'm tougher than I look and that was pretty awesome. The sex and even the bite felt really good. I'm fine." She smiled. "You didn't break me."

He pulled her tighter against his chest and she found her cheek resting against the curve of his throat as he held her. She stared at the woods around them and figured he might be doing the same.

"It's really beautiful here."

"It is. Do you know what makes this place perfect?"

"What?"

"We're here together."

Damn. I could totally fall in love with him. He sounded so sincere that she turned her head enough to see his face. He glanced down and honesty shone in those beautiful eyes of his. *Correction,* she amended, *I am falling in love. Not good. Love at first sight or in our case, after having sex, is a mistake. He's still a man, despite being so different. He'll break my heart.*

He shifted his body, forcing her away from his chest. He glanced around and sighed. "The water is cold and I don't want to risk getting you ill. Your body temperature doesn't run as hot as mine, nor do you have my endurance. I need to warm you."

Tiger fought panic and confusion as he followed Zandy out of the water. He hovered close to her to make certain she didn't fall and every protective instinct inside him demanded nothing less. His gaze lowered to her ass as she climbed up the embankment. She was rounded and soft, very different from a Species female. Her skin was so pale he could see the traces of blue veins on some parts of her body. It fascinated him.

He bent and grabbed the blanket, shook it, and turned to open it for her. "Here. I'll help you dry." *What is wrong with me?* He wasn't sure but the desire to tend her was strong. A Species female would have hit him by now and never allowed him to coddle her in any way. Zandy stepped closer and he wrapped the blanket around her body firmly while drying the water from her skin. She didn't even stare at him as if he'd lost his mind.

He was pretty certain he had. The urge to just bend, toss her over his shoulder and carry her to his Jeep was strong. She was little and couldn't put up much of a fight if he took her to his home. Images of tying her to his bed and using his mouth and hands to convince her to stay there made him step behind her to hide the fact that his dick had just hardened.

Sex had never felt as good as it did with Zandy. She was amazing and giving. He bit back a purr, remembering how tight and hot she felt wrapped around his cock. Soft and wonderful. Her small body fit perfectly against him and made him feel completely male. His hands lingered on parts of her body while he continued to help her dry. He didn't want to release her. The fact that she was submissive to him without him having to display aggression during sex left him reeling.

No, she's not anything like a Species. This is how it starts, he realized. Those poor males who ended up with human mates had to have felt what he did. Protective. Possessive. Maybe even blown away by intense feelings while sharing sex. That sobered him enough to back away from her and get dressed. *This is probably the definition of broadsided.* He had been broadsided by a small female with green eyes.

His hands shook as he pulled on his underwear and pants. His interested dick protested being contained but he ignored it. He had bigger problems at that moment. He needed to figure out how to handle the situation and the emotions he'd never experienced before.

Instincts were a bitch. He was more than aware of their constant existence, a side effect of being altered with those feline genes. He glanced back in time to see her bare body as she neatly folded the blanket and bent over to display her ass while reaching for her clothing.

He closed his eyes and took calming breaths. The baser side of him wanted to just take her. Keep her. The human side of him knew it would be wrong to do that. The part of him that remained in the middle prevailed. He used logic and common sense. He didn't know much about her. He didn't need or want a mate. His duties took up a lot of his time and he'd be sidelined if he took a mate. Justice made sure all males were given safer jobs if they had families.

Sometimes he lived at Reservation while at others he resided at Homeland. He also worked closely with the human task force. He enjoyed being around the human males and leaving the NSO occasionally. All that would change if he became too attached to a female and she actually agreed to be his mate. Slade managed to divide his time but his mate was a doctor whose job demanded she work in both locations.

The whisper of a zipper made him open his eyes to watch Zandy finish dressing. She was human and wouldn't fit in his lifestyle. He'd already bitten her and mounted her too roughly. He'd make a bad mate even if he were willing to consider the idea. It would also put her in danger but that worried him little. She'd never leave NSO if she were his and he'd make certain she was safe.

Humans date. That option didn't alarm him. That way he could have her without committing for life. If she was willing. He hoped the sharing of sex had been so intense due to the sexual frustration he'd experienced after the first night he'd met her. He'd wanted her but never thought she'd be in his arms again.

Tiger knew he was clinging to that concept a little too hard but he could live with that because it didn't unsettle him. Dating a human couldn't hurt and perhaps it was the pent-up desire he'd had for her that had made their coupling so incredible.

The female turned and smiled. His dick jerked, wanted her, and so did he. He knew he should force a smile in return to assure her everything was fine. He didn't. Words blurted out of his mouth before he could stop them.

"Why don't you go home with me tonight? I have a private house on Reservation. You could share my bed."

He wanted to roar when her smile faded and she glanced at the ground instead of agreeing instantly. Rejection stung him as sharply as if she'd slapped him. Every muscle in his body tensed.

"I don't think that's a good idea." Her gaze rose and met his.

Anger and pain burned through his chest. He'd been torturing himself with thoughts about a mate but she didn't even want him beyond the time they'd spent together. The idea that she hadn't enjoyed his body as much as he had hers made him feel even worse. He knew he'd been too rough despite her protests and now he had proof. Shame wasn't an emotion he suffered often but it struck then.

"I mean, it wouldn't be the best idea, right?"

"Why not?" He worried about her answer but needed to hear it.

"Well, for one thing, we have to pass the guards at the gate. I work for the NSO now and I'm pretty sure it's probably against the rules to date other employees. Secondly, I'm new and it would just look bad if it got around that I spent the night with you on the first day of my job. Third, I don't have an extra set of clothes. It screams bad impression when you wear the same clothes two days in a row."

Excuses. She didn't want to hurt his feelings. He respected her for that and appreciated it. His pride was stung though, despite her kindness. It was another reminder she wasn't Species. One of their females would have just told him he'd been too controlling and hadn't placed her sexual gratification above his own.

"I understand." He finished buttoning his shirt, knowing he'd messed up. She didn't even want to date him. "I'm carrying you back to your car." He would make sure she wasn't harmed by walking barefoot. "That isn't up for debate."

She nodded. "Thank you. Are you sure I'm not too heavy?"

"I could carry you in my arms all day," he answered honestly. "Hold the blanket and I'll pick you up."

Zandy gripped the blanket as he approached her and didn't protest as he scooped her up into his arms. Her scent tormented him. She smelled strongly of her distinctive scent but it was mixed with sex now and his own scent. Any Species male who came within sniffing distance of her would know they'd shared sex. That idea didn't alarm him. It would warn other males not to approach her for sharing sex, if they were smart.

Her arm wrapped around his neck and she peered deeply into his eyes. "Thank you, Tiger."

He wanted to kiss her but refrained. She'd made a choice and he had to respect it. He wasn't an animal despite his urges to ignore her refusal to share his bed. He was a male. He wouldn't force her to go home with him even if he wished she would — it wouldn't be fair. She wasn't strong enough to keep him in line the way a Species female could when a male became too dominating, though he'd never hurt her.

"Thank you for today," he said honestly.

Chapter Five

ଛ

Zandy liked that Tiger made her feel petite and womanly in his arms. He carried her as easily as he'd said he could and wasn't even out of breath when they reached their vehicles. No one seemed to have disturbed them. He didn't halt until he gently placed her on the hood of his Jeep. He tossed the folded blanket off her lap and over the windshield to land inside the vehicle.

He smiled. "We are back at the beginning. Here I stand and you are sitting in the same spot as when we first kissed."

A smile tugged at her lips. She was more than a little amused and touched by his romantic streak. It also impressed her. "I like this time better."

"Why?"

"No one interrupted us."

His striking blue eyes stared deeply into hers. "Meet me here again tomorrow after work. I'll bring food and we'll have a picnic."

It was a bad idea but she refused to say no outright. She was falling for the guy big-time and it would end badly. It was a weakness of hers to get involved with men too fast. He seemed too good to be true and she knew how that worked out. Badly, and divorce lawyers cost a lot of money. *Not to mention the dreaded phone call to my family to tell them I screwed up again.* She nodded anyway. She just couldn't resist Tiger but she didn't need to worry that he would ask her to marry him. He didn't seem the settle-down type of man.

"Okay. Do you want me to bring anything?"

"Just you."

"I can do that."

He cleared his throat. "Good. I might be a few minutes late after your shift ends but wait for me. I will come."

"Okay. Are you going to close the road down again to make sure no one goes searching for us when they spot our cars?"

"I'll think of something." Amusement flashed in his gaze and he stepped closer.

She nodded. "I better get going. Lunch was a long time ago and I worked up quite an appetite."

He chuckled. "I still think you should go home with me."

"Don't tempt me."

"I don't want to make you sore either. I definitely would if I took you home."

"I just told you not to tempt me."

He threw back his head and laughed. His hand came up as he caressed her cheek. "Thank you for waiting for me today. I was afraid I would return to find you gone. It would have greatly disappointed me."

"Me too. That's why I stayed and waited."

"You are very unique and wonderful, Zandy."

"So are you."

He moved suddenly and his mouth brushed hers. She kissed him back. The purr that rumbled from him made her instantly hot and horny as memories flooded her mind of what he could do to her body. He shifted his hips and moved between her thighs until the hard length of his trapped cock rubbed against the seam of her underwear as she spread her thighs wide to make room for him. Zandy wrapped her arms around his neck, clinging to him. She wanted him again and it felt as if he wanted her too.

His hands cupped her breasts and squeezed. She moaned against his tongue to encourage him. One of his hands lowered down her stomach and fisted her skirt to tug it up her hips.

She shifted her ass, helping him bunch the material around her waist to get it out of the way. His hand slid between her thighs to hook a finger in the band of her panties and she felt them jerked out from under her ass. He easily tore them off.

Excitement gripped her. It wasn't just the danger of them being caught—no one had ever torn her clothes off her body before. It was a fantasy he'd just made a reality. Her nails dug into his shirt and she wished she could touch his skin.

Tiger tore his mouth away from hers to break the kiss and she opened her eyes. There was something wild-looking about his eyes in that moment when passion flared through them. Eyes were the window into someone's soul—she believed that—and his were promising hot sex.

His hand left her thigh and gently pressed between her breasts. He pushed her flat on her back over the hood of his Jeep. The trees had shaded it and the feel of cool metal against her bare ass was a little naughty. She really liked it. She liked him.

His hands gripped her hips and tugged her closer to him until she should have worried about slipping over the edge. It didn't concern her since she'd wrapped her legs around his waist when they'd kissed. He slid his palms upward, shoved her shirt up until it bunched over her breasts and his gaze lowered.

"Beautiful," he rasped. "But this is in my way."

She gasped when he gripped the center of her bra and tugged. It didn't stand a chance against his strength as it broke apart and freed her breasts.

Zandy panted a little as he leaned forward, cupped her breasts again with his bare hands and his mouth opened over her nipple. He sucked it into his mouth and she felt his teeth clamp down on the skin around the taut tip. He didn't hurt her but he had a good grip. She felt a second of fear, knowing if he bit down it would hurt. Instead his tongue started to slide across her nipple and he sucked on her harder.

She gasped. It felt as if her breast and her clit were connected. Her fingers slid into his hair to keep it out of the way, while making sure he didn't stop. She breathed his name, "Tiger…"

He growled as he slowly released her breast when he lifted his head. Their gazes met. He reached up and his fingers encircled her wrists to tug her hands free from his hair. She let go and was stunned when he used his hold on her to lift her arms above her head until they rested against the hood of the Jeep.

"Keep them there."

She nodded. He broke eye contact with her to peruse the length of her body spread out in front of him and growled again. His hands gripped her knees and he nudged them, indicating that he wanted her to release him. She freed his hips and he lifted her legs straight up against his chest and spread them enough to brace them at his shoulders.

He reached down and she heard his zipper as he opened his pants. His gaze held hers. "I wanted to do this the first time you were here," he rasped.

She expected him to just enter her but Tiger wasn't so easily predictable. His finger traced the seam of her pussy. She knew he'd find her wet and ready to take him but then he decided to play with her clit. She moaned as he rubbed small circles around the bud.

"Tiger…" she moaned.

"I'm right here."

Yes, he is, she agreed, reveling in the raw enjoyment of the pleasure he gave. She really wanted to touch him but he wanted her to keep them above her head. It was almost torture and her legs tensed, unable to take much more.

"Please?"

One of his arms locked across her legs to pin them against his chest and his gaze lowered between them to stare at her pussy. He adjusted his hips until his cock pressed against her.

84

The feel of him entering her body broke her focus on his face and she threw her head back. He lifted her enough that her ass hovered over the hood and he began to fuck her in long, firm strokes.

She moaned and could only feel the drive of his cock and him continuing to play with her clit. The overwhelming urge to come burned her from the inside out.

"Faster," she urged.

He growled. "No. I'm in control."

Her wrists twisted and she clawed at the metal under her palms. Tiger suddenly thrust into her a little deeper and rocked his hips at a faster pace. He massaged her clit to match. The sounds that came from him were a mixture of a purr and a moan.

"Come for me," he ordered in a harsh voice. "Now. I can't hold back."

He pressed a little harder against her clit and Zandy screamed out his name as she did just that. Her vaginal muscles convulsed from the force of her climax and Tiger threw back his head. A roar came from him that drowned out everything. His hips ground against her as he jerked with each jet of semen he shot into her.

Zandy panted as she tried to recover and kept her eyes closed as Tiger eased her ass back down onto the hood of the Jeep. His hand slid away from her clit and he gripped her thighs, spread them and bent over her. His body settled over hers and he kept them connected by refusing to withdraw his cock from her body.

"Look at me."

She stared deeply into his eyes, just inches from her own. His hot breath fanned her lips and she loved the smile he gave her. Her hands moved to cup his face. He turned his head a little to press tighter against her palm.

"Hi."

He chuckled. "Hi."

"That was amazing."

His lips brushed across hers but he didn't deepen the kiss. "You're very sexy, Zandy. I can't get enough of you. I was more careful this time not to be rough."

"I like it both ways."

He braced his arms on the hood next to her, caging her in his hold. She liked the feel of having his body over hers but wished her bare breasts and stomach were against his skin instead of the shirt he still wore.

"What did you like best?" he asked.

"I can't decide. How about a rematch tomorrow so we can both decide?"

"Maybe I'll come up with more to judge. It might take days to really figure this one out."

Days with Tiger sounded heavenly. She laughed. "It sounds good but I'm not sure I'll be able to walk if we have sex this much every day."

His gaze became serious. "I can carry you. You won't need to walk. It will give me an excuse to keep you flat on your back."

Damn. He's charming and so handsome. Her fingers caressed his warm skin and explored his strong bone structure. His cheekbones were slightly prominent and so was his jawline. It gave him a very masculine appearance, which she appreciated. He waited for a response so she gave him one.

"That's true."

He pushed her hair away from her neck and he pulled her torn bra out from under her shirt to remove it. He tossed it over the glass windshield into the Jeep. Zandy watched him study her shoulder.

"What are you looking at?"

"Your bite. It's not bleeding anymore."

"It's fine. It was well worth the sex injury." She grinned. "How is your back?"

He didn't grin back. "You are the first woman who's marked me. Has a man ever bitten you before and marked you?"

"I can't say I've ever been bitten before."

Gentle fingertips probed the wound. "You will need to hide this. Someone will think I've mated you if they see this."

"Mated?"

"It's like marriage to my kind but we don't divorce. You would be thought of as mine and I would be thought of as yours."

Shock reverberated through her. "All over a bite?"

He smiled finally. "Species tend to bite sometimes during the sharing of sex but we never break the skin. There are only two ways this usually happens. I had to bite you to assert my control if we fought for dominance during sex or because I wanted to mark you to show other males you belonged to me." He blinked. "I am sorry. I lost control and I wanted to completely own you in that moment. I wanted all of you."

His words sank in and she realized she didn't hate that idea. *Oh no. Don't go there. He is asking you to hide the mark, which means he didn't intend to do it. Remember that.* "Well, I think you successfully owned me there for a while."

"It goes both ways. There is nothing but you when you are in my arms." His eyes narrowed and all traces of humor fled. "You're dangerous, Zandy."

"Me?" It was her turn to laugh as her gaze took in those massive arms next to her and the broad chest that blocked out the world above her. "You're the one who's really big and strong. I'm not dangerous in the least."

He suddenly gripped her face and moved closer, until they were nearly nose to nose. "You are very dangerous to me. I'm not the type to take a mate, Zandy. I never want to be tied down that way. I enjoy my freedom after the lifetime I have spent without it. A mated male lives for his female. I've seen it firsthand. The males want to kill any other males who go near their females. They can't sleep without their females in their arms. They go insane at the thought of losing their mates. We scent imprint our mates. It's…" He stopped talking.

"It's what?" She was curious. "I've never heard anything about this."

"We get pretty much addicted to her scent after we claim a female. We need them to smell like us and we need their scents on us. The mated males can't stand having the scent of other female on them once they imprint their mate's scent. If a male has imprinted a female he can't share sex with another one. If his female were to ever share sex with a male I think the mate would go completely insane and kill anything in his path blocking him from the male who touched his mate. He would definitely tear apart a male who touched her. It's…" He paused. "Scary as hell and something I never want anything to do with. If I were ever interested in taking a mate, you would be her, Zandy. That's what makes you dangerous because you make me consider it."

She was really shocked. "I've been married and divorced twice, Tiger. I'm not cut out for marriage obviously since I seem to suck at it. I got really hurt by them. I swore I'd never put my heart out there to be stomped on again. The idea of allowing someone to become my entire world scares me." She wanted to be honest. "I am so drawn to you that it's not funny and you're amazing. I just don't want to get hurt."

"We're quite a pair, aren't we?"

She nodded, unable to disagree. They were both strongly attracted to each other but neither of them wanted to become too involved for their own reasons. She respected that about him and instinctively knew he understood about her reservations too.

"I want you to meet me here tomorrow. I don't know how long this can last but I know I want to see you again," Tiger said.

"I'll be here after work."

"I'll bring a picnic."

"I should be going. I really am hungry."

He grinned. "So am I. It will be dark soon and we missed dinner."

They silently stared at each other until Tiger finally lowered his face enough to brush his lips lightly over hers. He eased out of her body to separate them and helped her sit up. Strong hands gripped her hips to lift her down to the ground.

He let go with a reluctant expression. Zandy fixed her clothes, minus her bra and underwear. She forced a smile she didn't feel. It was time to go but she hated leaving him. It just felt wrong to walk away and that assured her she really needed to get in her car.

"Bye. See you tomorrow, Tiger."

"I'm looking forward to it." Sincerity shone in his eyes as he righted his clothing and dug her keys from his pocket.

She took them and had to force herself to turn away from him. The urge to spin back around, throw herself into his arms and ask him to take her home with him was there. *Damn.* She climbed in her car and refused to look at him again. It was too tempting to ask him to spend the night with her.

She glanced in the rearview mirror as she drove away. Tiger stood where she'd left him, watching her. A sigh of regret passed her lips.

It dawned on her halfway home that she hadn't retrieved her torn underclothes. She'd left them with Tiger. A groan escaped her lips and she hoped he remembered to toss them away.

She stopped at the only fast-food joint in town with a drive-thru, not feeling up to cooking. It was a relief when she let herself into her house, collapsed on the couch with her dinner and reflected on what had happened. *No. I don't regret it,* she decided. She just hated the strong desire she felt to know where Tiger was and what he was doing. *Is he obsessing over me too?* "Damn."

Zandy knew she'd made the right decision to go home. She couldn't let herself get too attached to Tiger. She didn't want her heart broken and the last thing she needed was to fall in love with a man who clearly didn't want a relationship any more than she did. They had that in common.

* * * * *

Tiger stood still long after Zandy's car disappeared from his sight. The urge to leap into the Jeep and chase her was strong. He battled his instincts and finally won. He turned and noticed her discarded, torn panties. He reached down, fisted them and shoved them inside his pocket.

The sight of her bra on the passenger seat when he got in the Jeep made him sigh. He'd totally destroyed her undergarments but didn't regret it. He picked up the soft material and put it in another pocket. Moments passed as he sat there trying to figure out how his life had gotten so complicated by an attractive little redheaded human.

He knew he needed to return to Reservation but the officers would know in a heartbeat that he hadn't been hunting if they got a whiff of him. He reached down and dug out the emergency bag from under the seat where he kept a spare set of clothes. He carried it back to the stream, glanced at the flattened area where he'd spread out the blanket and memories assailed him.

His hands were jerky as he stripped everything off, removed the fresh clothing from the bag and shoved his used ones inside. He sealed it and walked into the chilled water to wash off her scent.

He used handfuls of moss to scrub his skin. He dunked his head under the water and stayed there for as long as he could hold his breath before he broke the surface again. That would take care of any lingering traces of her scent.

Tiger climbed out of the stream. He stood there in the fading sunlight as the strengthening evening breezes dried most of his skin. He shook his head to help dry his hair faster. It would be wet but no one would question it.

The trip back to his Jeep was fast and he replaced the bag under the seat. He'd have to wash his clothes when he arrived home to remove her scent from them. He started the Jeep and returned to Reservation.

"You didn't find any more idiots?"

Tiger shook his head at the officer. "It was all clear. Just remember to warn the next shift that more of them may be out there."

"Will do. Good evening, Tiger."

"You too, Smiley."

He waved and drove to his home. He liked the cabin he had been assigned at Reservation a little better than his house at Homeland. It was more secluded. He didn't have any immediate neighbors and it was far enough from the Wild Zone that he wouldn't have to fear any of the males harassing Zandy.

A growl tore from him over that reason. Zandy had refused to come home with him so it wasn't a concern that any of those males would pick up her scent. No one would come investigate why a human was near unless one was actually there. He parked the Jeep, removed the bag, stalked inside his house and went directly to the laundry room.

The scent of sex and Zandy hit him when he opened the bag. His eyes closed as he inhaled and his dick instantly hardened. He wanted her again. Now. A growl rumbled from his throat and his eyes jerked open. He slammed the clothes on the dryer top while he dumped soap into the washer then he threw the shirt in the machine. He paused when he gripped his pants.

He needed to toss away her destroyed underthings but he decided to wash them first to erase her scent from them. He doubted anyone would go through his trash but he knew how humans were. NSO sent their trash to the out world and reporters had been known to go through everything looking for a story. It's why they shredded or burned all paperwork instead of throwing it away. With his luck someone would find her things and believe a female had been sexually attacked.

He withdrew her panties from the pocket and dropped them in the washer. Her bra he lingered over. The cups were soft and silky. They had held Zandy's breasts and his hands itched to do the same at that moment. He lifted it to his nose and inhaled her scent.

His cock throbbed and painfully ached to be released from his suddenly too-tight pants. A snarl tore from him as he dropped his soiled pants into the washer and slammed the lid closed. He turned it on, still clutching her bra and headed for his kitchen. Shame hit him full force as he grabbed a Ziploc bag out of one of the drawers and stomped through his house to the bedroom.

He sat down hard. *What am I doing? It's not normal or sane to want to keep her scent. I've lost my mind.* He stared at the plastic bag and her bra, something he wanted to put in his nightstand drawer. The bag would keep her scent longer, make it last.

He inhaled deeply. Her scent drove him more than a little crazy. It scared the hell out of him as he worried that he might have become addicted to her. She wasn't his mate, he didn't want one and he'd never heard of a male locking onto a female's scent that fast.

"Fuck!"

He released the bag and reached for the waistband of his pants, almost tore the things to free his cock, and he sighed in relief as the pain of it being confined abated. He glared down at his stiff dick and snarled. It made him more than angry that it was in that condition over a female he shouldn't want in the first place.

Chapter Six

ဢ

Creek nodded. "It is true. I swear!"

Zandy laughed, watching her friend and coworker talk at the lunch table, more than a bit amused.

"There's a bar in the hotel and you guys all love to dance there? I didn't know about it." Richard shook his head. "I was never invited."

"You work here and are always welcome. Just inform Security you want to go and bring your mate. They will escort you there." Creek smiled and glanced at Zandy. "What are you doing tonight? I would love to take you."

"I have plans." *With Tiger,* she added silently.

A glint of amusement shone in the New Species woman's eyes. "Are you meeting with a male?"

"Maybe." Zandy glanced away but purposely didn't search the large room to see if Tiger was there. She was afraid her two companions would notice.

"You are meeting a male. Is he going to be husband number three?"

Richard choked on his drink. "Three? I take it you're divorced from the last one?"

"There's not going to be number three." Her fork stabbed into her cut steak and met Richard's curious stare. "I was married and divorced twice. I learned my lesson. I'm a loser magnet."

"I've been married to the same woman since we graduated from high school. We're going on twenty-two years now." He shot her a sympathetic look. "Happy marriages can exist. We're proof of that."

"I thought you said your kids were pretty young."

"They are. She is a lawyer and we put off having children for her career. She finally made partner and the pressure was off. We had our first one six years ago and the second one two years ago. We're thinking about having one more."

Zandy stared at him. "Wow. Sex with the same person for twenty-two years? How is that?"

He laughed. "Really great. You should rethink the whole marriage thing. I hear the third time is a charm."

"No way, no how." Zandy laughed. "I'd probably get hit with the third-time loser scenario if I ever decided to roll those dice again. My taste in men sucks and I'm aware of it."

"You just need to find a different kind of man." Richard winked.

Tiger is definitely a different kind of man. Personality wise and physically. She'd tossed and turned all night, regretting saying no to going home with him. Creek reached over and touched Zandy's arm to draw her away from her thoughts of the man who was responsible for her exhausted state.

"Our males look at you and one of them could make you happy. They are hard workers and we do not cheat when we mate. I could introduce you to some of the best of them if you go to the bar with me and go dancing. I've shared sex with many of them and could tell you which ones were the best."

It stunned her that her new friend wanted to hook her up with men she'd slept with. "No thanks."

Creek nodded. "You are a small female while our males are large." Creek hesitated. "Their sex part is bigger than a human's. They might hurt someone as small as you if one tried to mount you."

Richard choked on his food and laughed when he could. He grinned at Zandy. "See what I mean? I'm always laughing."

"Did I say something wrong?" Creek glanced between them. "It is true. Our males are large all over. They would have to be careful if they shared sex with you, Zandy. I would avoid the canine species for sure. They swell at the base of their dicks at the end of sex. There isn't much to you and I would be afraid it would be quite painful."

Richard laughed, shooting soda out of his mouth and sputtered as he hit his chest. "I love this job. Yeah, Zandy. You might want to avoid that. Any other advice for her, Creek?"

Creek hesitated. "I would give you the advice that feline species have hot semen. It doesn't burn but it is noticeable. The primate species would probably be the best for you. They don't swell or have hot semen. They love to cuddle and touch a lot. I shared sex with one recently and he enjoyed rubbing my hair on his body while he ran his hands all over me. It was nice." She nodded. "I could introduce you to our primate males. They look more similar to humans with the softer bone structure and eye shaping."

"No thank you." Zandy was slightly blushing. She shot Richard a dirty look when he didn't try to hide his glee at the embarrassing topic. He didn't look regretful in the least so she turned her attention on Creek. "I'm meeting someone tonight after work. He's a nice guy."

"My kind would be better but you *are* small. It is probably best that you stick with a smaller human with a smaller male part."

"Hey," Richard said, and chuckled. "I resent that. I'm not tiny or anything."

Creek lowered her gaze to his lap. "Drop your pants and show me."

What she had asked him to do sank in and all humor fled. It was his turn to blush a little. "I…"

Creek laughed, nudging Zandy with her elbow. "I got him. I was kidding, human male. I do not want to see your male part. I watched porn videos and have seen plenty of them. I appreciate the sight of our naked males much better. They have less body hair. How is that for odd? We are altered with animal genetics yet we have less body hair than full humans."

"I'm not hairy either." Richard grinned. "I'd be willing to show you my back. It's all smooth skin."

Creek laughed. "No thank you. You are mated and I don't want your mate to feel the need to attack me for seeing you undressed in any way."

"It's just my back."

Creek smiled. "That would be enough for a mate to go after someone. Species don't appreciate anyone looking at anything on their mates."

Zandy finished her lunch while her friends continued to tease each other. Her gaze wandered around the cafeteria, unable to resist any longer, and located Tiger sitting at a table by the buffet area. He happened to look up while she watched him and their gazes met. She couldn't look away but he finally did. He glanced at the man to his left, said something, but focused back on her immediately. She smiled and lowered her eyes that time.

Creek suddenly sniffed loudly and turned to frown at Zandy. A smile curved the woman's mouth and she winked.

"What?"

The smile widened. "You are interested in one of the males here."

"No," she lied.

"Scents don't lie. You are aroused. It is very faint but there. I wouldn't have picked it up but we are sitting close together."

"She's aroused, huh? Damn. Love this job." Richard chortled.

Zandy shot him a dirty look. "Knock it off, Richard." She addressed her friend next. "Can we never discuss that again? Please?"

"Oh." Creek nodded. "You are shy about sex. I understand but one of them has caught your attention. I will introduce you to whichever one holds your interest if you want to share sex with him." She smiled. "Just don't go near him if you aren't ready to do that because he will know you are aroused. I would actually avoid going within five feet of any of the males while you are in this state. They will scent it and ask you to share sex with them."

Richard laughed so hard he nearly fell out of his chair. "Oh man."

Zandy sighed, glaring at him. "I'm glad you're so amused by this."

Creek studied Richard. "You are amused by her shyness? Are you shy, Richard? You should shower before you come to work if you share sex with your mate. You did that with her this morning and she is in heat."

Richard stopped laughing and paled. "She's in what?"

"Heat. She is able to get pregnant right now. I think you call it ovulating?"

It was Zandy's turn to laugh. "You did the wife this morning, huh? Didn't you say you were thinking about another baby? Maybe you got one."

"You can smell that?" He gawked at Creek.

"Yes. I suggest you stay five feet from my kind as well until you shower." She winked at Zandy. "He isn't laughing anymore."

"Nope, he's not. He kind of looks embarrassed. Thank you from the bottom of my heart."

"My pleasure."

Richard stood. "Time is up. We need to meet our escort."

Zandy waved to her friend as she stood, took care of her tray, and followed her coworker outside. Snow was a very tall blond Species male with sky-blue eyes and shoulder-length hair. He kept glancing at her as they walked to the Jeep and continued to keep looking at her as he drove them back to her building.

It bugged her enough that she finally said something when they reached the door. He had insisted upon following her all the way to the entrance. "What?"

A grin twisted his lips. "Do you find me attractive?"

Richard began to laugh. Zandy clenched her teeth, a bit annoyed with her coworker. It wasn't funny. She was more than a little embarrassed.

"You're very attractive but you aren't the reason if you're smelling me."

"Too bad." His gaze traveled down the length of her body. "You really smell good and I would share sex with you." He stared into her shocked gaze. "It would be very enjoyable for both of us."

Laughter sounded behind her as Richard opened the door to their office. Zandy just wished he'd trip and land on his face as heat blossomed in her cheeks. The whole smell thing with New Species wasn't humorous in the least.

"I'm flattered but no thank you."

Disappointment showed clearly on Snow's features. "I'm your escort today and will take you to your car when your shift ends. Think about it."

She fled inside and was glad to close the door. Richard flopped into his seat, gave her a wink and chuckled. "See why I love my job? Never a dull moment."

"Shut up, Mr. Sex In The Morning. Don't you have death threats to read?"

He turned to his computer screen. "At least I had sex. It seems you just want to have it. You should take that tall blond guy up on it. He's good-looking."

"You nail him then." She sat at her desk and turned her chair to avoid facing Richard.

"I'm happily married," he teased. "Plus, I'm not his type. He didn't ask me." He laughed again. "Of course, according to Creek, her males are bigger than humans. Isn't that tempting?"

"Throwing my coffee mug at you is starting to sound good."

"Okay. I'll behave." He laughed once more. "Don't you love this job?"

She did enjoy the job but she'd have to be more aware of things. *Is there anything a New Species can't smell? Damn. This is a learning experience.* It meant that every time she was turned-on, Tiger would know by smell. It gave him an advantage over her if they continued to see each other. She would only be able to guess what he wanted from her. Their next date was only hours away and she felt nervous.

It's not a date, she reminded herself. *It's sex and a picnic dinner. Maybe not even sex. Yeah, right. It's totally sex. You know it and so does he. Then what?* She didn't have an answer. Part of her was tempted to cancel. It just smacked of foolishness to get involved further with him when they both admitted it couldn't go anywhere.

She glanced at the clock on the bottom corner of the computer screen and decided she'd meet him one last time after work. *That's it though. Just to say goodbye before I get in over my head.*

* * * * *

Worry nagged Tiger as he glanced down the road again. He'd been hung up with the shift change when a male who had transferred from Homeland had questions. Zandy hadn't been waiting when he'd arrived fifteen minutes late. Had she given up? Left already? He stared at the clock on the dashboard of the Jeep and decided he'd wait another ten minutes. The idea of returning to the gate and spending the evening sulking over their broken date really irritated him.

The sound of an engine perked him up since Zandy was the only person who should be traveling on the road. A grin spread across his face as he climbed out to greet her. She parked right behind him on the shoulder, in the grass. He opened her car door before she could unfasten her belt, eager to get his hands on her.

A small gasp escaped her lips when she stood and he lifted her into his arms until they were face level. He inhaled her scent, softly groaned, and his cock reared instantly to life when blood rushed there. He just wanted her naked.

She laughed. "Did you miss me?"

The feel of her arms wrapping around his shoulders made him grin. "You have no idea." The scent of her arousal teased his sense of smell and a soft growl escaped in response. "You missed me too. I wasn't the only one looking forward to our time together."

Pink tinged her cheekbones. "You can smell that, right? That I want you?"

He nodded, backing away from the open car door with her in his arms. He closed it with his knee. "You'd smell my desire if you could. I've wanted you all day."

She adjusted her hold on him and gripped his butt with one hand, squeezing the firm cheek through his pants. "You have the nicest ass." Her keys jingled from where she had them hooked on her thumb by the ring.

"Put your keys inside my back pocket." He turned with her in his arms, striding toward the woods. "Wrap your legs around me."

"I'm wearing shoes. You can put me down."

"No." The need to keep her close was too strong. His fascination and near obsession with Zandy worried him but he'd deal with that later. His hand slid lower, cupped her ass when they hit the line of trees, and he jerked on her skirt. He wanted to feel her skin. "You're no burden to me."

The hold he had on her impeded what he wanted to do and he halted. Zandy's green gaze met his and he could tell she was curious about why he'd stopped. "Let go of me for a second."

She didn't question his order, just followed it and the feeling of possessiveness for her intensified. No female had ever done anything he asked without argument first unless it was obvious what he wanted. She either trusted him or was just naturally submissive. Both concepts turned him on even more.

He adjusted her body in his arms and chuckled when she gasped as he lifted her, ducked his head to the side, and bent her over his shoulder. Her ass was right next to his cheek when he straightened and started walking again.

"I'm upside down." She sounded surprised.

One arm wrapped behind her knees to keep her in place while his other hand slid up the back of one of her soft thighs, delved under her skirt and didn't stop exploring until the underwear covering her pussy halted him. He hooked the satiny fabric with his finger, shoved it out of the way and another growl rumbled from him when his fingertip dipped inside her moist pussy. She was ready to take him.

Zandy moaned and her body tensed when he slowly fucked her with his finger, pushing into the tight confines as far as he could go. He withdrew almost all the way before driving into her again. Her hands clamped down on his ass, his dick hardened even more, and he realized how much his cock envied his index finger.

"Tiger," she panted.

"We're almost there."

The desire to lower her to the grass was nearly overpowering. The human made him insanely horny and impatient. He adjusted his hand enough to press his thumb over her clit and rubbed while he banged her faster with his finger. The scent of her arousal grew stronger as her pussy grew wetter, sleeker and hotter. He had to bite back a snarl, the animal side of him demanding he put her down and fuck her immediately.

Her hands kneaded his ass through his pants, her soft cries of pleasure tortured him and he came to the sad conclusion that he wasn't strong-willed enough to make it to the clearing. His dick throbbed and each step was agony. He pulled his hand away from the vee of her thighs, grabbed her hips and dragged her down his body until her arms wrapped around his neck.

Her eyes were narrowed with desire and he could see how much she wanted him. "Hold on to me and wrap your thighs around me."

She did as he ordered and he managed to tear open the front of his pants. He hadn't worn underwear so some of the pain eased as his stiff shaft, which had been bent at an awkward angle, was freed. One arm grabbed her around her waist to lift her a little higher. His fingers hooked the center of her underwear, tore them, and he fisted the base of his cock. He never looked away from her beautiful eyes as he adjusted the direction of his shaft until the crown slid through the seam of her pussy and he drove up into her with one fluid thrust.

Pleasure made him quake as she cried out his name again and the tight walls of her pussy squeezed his dick, which was buried deeply. No pain showed on her face from his quick entry and he spread his thighs to brace. His arms shifted under her spread thighs and he cupped her ass to slam her up and down on his cock. Moans of ecstasy and the need to come urged him to fuck her faster.

Zandy's head tipped back and her fingernails dug into his skin through his shirt. He wanted to kiss that mouth that panted his name but he was afraid he'd bite her. The desire to mark her was there. He didn't care if it was by bite or his seed filling her but he wanted something to show that she belonged to him.

That urge grew stronger as her climax hit and her vaginal muscles clamped down around his shaft almost painfully. He had to slow his thrusts as her body shook and he threw back his own head. A roar tore from his mouth as his hips jerked at every blast of his semen filling the woman he held.

Tiger's knees gave way and he collapsed onto them to land on the grass. His strength and agility kept them both from falling over as he adjusted his hold on her to keep them upright. Zandy's face fell forward and she nuzzled his neck as her arms hugged him tightly around his neck. They were both breathing hard from their shared pleasure. They were still connected, his dick buried deep inside her and he didn't want to separate them.

He shivered when she licked her lips and his throat in the process. He turned his head slightly to give her better access. Just the thought of her sinking her teeth into his skin and biting him made his cock twitch. Desire gripped him again, although it was more manageable after the sex they'd just shared.

"Bite," he demanded.

"You didn't bite me."

Her soft words startled him and he jerked out of his haze of after-sex bliss. "What?"

"You just whispered the word bite. You didn't get me with your teeth."

He knew that. But he had wanted her to bite him bad enough to say something he hadn't realized he'd uttered. She wouldn't leave a mark the way a Species could but it still tempted him to ask her. She could bruise him if she bit hard enough. Her marking him again with her teeth filled him with a mixture of emotions. Fear, confusion, desire, and longing.

The sound of her stomach grumbling roused him from his musings and reminded him they hadn't eaten. A feeling of shame filled him next. He'd gone to the trouble to set up a nice outing for her but his passion had overridden his intentions.

He'd taken her while standing in the middle of the woods. Her needs should have come first.

His hold on her eased and he forced his hips to move. The feel of withdrawing from her body wasn't a satisfying one—he liked being joined with her.

"Stand up," he urged.

She didn't appear any happier than he was when she unlocked her thighs from around him and her feet lowered to the ground. He rose to his full height and released her in the process. He closed his pants.

"We didn't make it to the creek. Are you ready for dinner, Zandy?"

Her face tilted up and she peered at him. A slight smile curved her lips. "I am hungry."

Tiger didn't ask permission but instead just leaned forward and scooped her into his arms. He spun, heading for his original destination. Her arms wrapped around his neck without complaint and she rested her cheek against his shirt.

She felt right in his arms and no amount of denial could change that. He didn't act rational when it came to the human he held. She wasn't typical in any manner, in his defense. He inhaled and muffled a purr. He could sniff her all day and night without tiring of her scent.

The sound of the creek led him to the spot he'd left an hour earlier. He admitted he might have gone a little overboard with his preparations but he didn't regret it. He'd soon find out if she appreciated the effort. Human females were a mystery to him and he had no idea if she'd find it romantic or disturbing.

I'm losing it, he admitted silently. *I have it bad for her.* A mental image of him falling off a cliff flashed through his mind. *Fuck. Maybe it's just a temporary fascination. I'm not mate material. I enjoy my freedom too much.*

Chapter Seven

ຮາ

Zandy admitted Tiger had a way of making her feel small and sexy in the cradle of his arms, as if he were the strongest man in the world and she the most feminine woman. It made her even more attracted to him.

"I went to a lot of trouble. Look," his husky voice urged when he stopped walking.

Her head turned and a soft gasp escaped her parted lips. Tears filled her eyes next as she stared at the scene before her, deeply touched. An air mattress had been placed in the shade under a tree next to the moving water. Thick, comfortable-looking bedding had been neatly spread across it to make a romantic bed for them to share. Next to it a blanket had been spread out with a large picnic basket. A bucket of ice with either champagne or wine was placed next to the food. He'd even brought real plates, silverware and glasses. A pile of towels cushioned a camping lantern.

"What do you think?"

She turned her head to stare into his gorgeous eyes. There was no missing the worried look lurking there, as if he questioned if she would love the romantic gesture.

"I can't believe you did all this for me."

A frown curved his mouth. "I made you cry? I see tears. You don't like it?"

"I love it. This is the best surprise ever, Tiger. No one has ever done something for me like this before." She blinked back more tears. "Thank you."

His features smoothed out. "You are worth all the time I spent setting this up." He carried her to the edge of the picnic spread and put her on her feet.

Zandy sat and carefully arranged her skirt while removing her shoes. Tiger sank down next to her and his hand cupped her cheek. The tip of his thumb brushed her mouth.

She regretted it when he released her and focused on the basket instead. The smell of fried chicken teased her nose when he opened it and began to remove food. He'd also brought mashed potatoes, gravy and corn on the cob. A box of donuts had her hiding a smile. He grabbed the bottle from the ice bucket, popped the top, and she glimpsed the label. He'd brought a fruity wine and carefully filled both glasses before setting it back in the ice. She accepted the glass he offered her.

"Here is to us being together tonight."

She touched her glass lightly to his. "This is fantastic, Tiger. Thank you so much."

Broad shoulders shrugged and she could have sworn she saw a hint of red color his cheeks as his gaze darted away from hers to the food. "I hope you like to eat fried chicken. I know this is a favorite picnic food for humans."

"I love it." She sipped the wine and put her glass down. "You really outdid yourself and I appreciate it. This is perfect."

"It was nothing." He looked at her again. "I wanted to encourage you to spend more time with me."

"You succeeded."

He chuckled and relaxed. "Eat. I want to get you out of your clothes afterward."

Amusement made her smile. He was blunt and she liked that about him. "I like that plan."

The clearing was beautiful and Zandy appreciated the scenery as they ate. There was a small waterfall upstream. Birds sang in the treetops above them, the weather was warm and they had a few hours before the sun would set. Any doubts she'd had about meeting Tiger faded.

The amount of food he put away stunned her a little but her gaze took in his sheer size. She deduced it probably took a lot of calories to maintain all those muscles. He opened the donuts last and offered her one. She accepted and noticed he avoided the chocolate ones. She shook her head when he offered to fill her glass a second time.

"I have to drive home later. One glass is it for me."

He hesitated. "You could sleep here with me. It is safe. I wouldn't allow anything to happen to you and I checked the weather. It will be a nice night."

The idea of sleeping with Tiger was too much of a temptation to resist. "Okay. I'll just have to leave early to have time to go home to shower and change my clothes. It seems your people have a supersensitive sense of smell. I know now that they can pick up just about everything a person does if they get close enough."

"Yes. I planned to warn you about that."

"I already learned that lesson today."

"What happened? Did someone inform you of what shampoo you use? It smells nice."

"That would have been way less embarrassing than what happened."

Tiger frowned and stared at her. "Someone embarrassed you? Who?"

It seemed amusing now. "At lunch I was staring at you and kind of remembered yesterday. I guess I got a little turned-on. I didn't realize New Species could pick that up." She grinned. "You are hot."

He didn't smile back. "What happened? What was said?"

"Nothing really. Creek pointed it out to me in front of Richard and offered to introduce me to whatever guy I liked. Richard thought it was pretty funny. Then my escort noticed and asked me if I thought he was attractive. It was a learning experience, let me tell you. It was embarrassing at the time but I'm over it."

Tiger softly growled and didn't look amused in the least. "Did your escort ask you to share sex? Did he touch you?"

That took her by surprise. Was he jealous? "No."

"Good." He relaxed. "Who was it? I don't remember who was assigned to you today."

"Snow. He's nice."

"He is attracted to female humans. I will make sure he isn't assigned to you again."

She managed to keep her mouth from dropping open. Anger glinted in his eyes as he watched her and she swallowed a protest. Tiger *was* jealous. "He's fine. He didn't hit on me or anything. He just assumed I might be attracted to him and that he was the source of what he smelled. I set him straight."

"Did you tell him it was me who aroused you?"

"No."

A muscle in his jaw flexed as he seemed to grind his teeth together. "You need to tell any males who approach you that it is me who arouses you. You smell incredible when you're in that state and many of them might ask to share sex with you."

Zandy was a little amused and curious. "I do, huh? What do I smell like?"

He leaned closer suddenly and inhaled deeply. "It is hard to explain but it makes me hard for you. I crave burying my tongue in your pussy to taste you before I mount you."

His answer stunned her just a bit. She was not used to men being so blunt. He stood before she could come up with a response to that and offered her his hand. She took it and allowed him to pull her to her feet.

"Strip out of your clothing. We'll wash up."

Her gaze darted to the water nervously. "It's going to be a little cold."

He grinned. "I'll warm you up and I have plans."

"I love your plan so far," she admitted, as they both removed their clothing.

Tiger held her hand and led her into the water. She gasped a little at the chilly water but it wasn't too bad. He waded in deeper as she trailed behind him until he sat on a rock beneath the moving water near the opposite embankment. Firm hands turned her to face away from him and he tugged her down on his lap. He adjusted her legs to the outside of his, spread both their knees apart with his, and one hand slid to cover her pussy.

Her back pressed tight against his warm chest as his fingers played with her clit. A soft growl heightened the pleasure she experienced at his touch. The water was chilly but his body wasn't.

"You're so wet," he rasped, brushing a kiss on her shoulder. One of his arms hooked around her waist and lifted her.

A gasp escaped her as he lowered her straight onto his hard cock. The sensation of being filled by him was amazing. He continued to stroke her clit as his hips bucked upward, fucking her slowly. Zandy gripped his biceps just for something to cling to. He moved her easily up and down on his lap with his arm. All she could do was lean back, enjoying him.

"I love what I feel inside you when I do this, Zandy. You grip and squeeze me the more excited you become and you're so hot and wet. We're in water and you're the one soaking me."

The water was level with her nipples and every time he lifted her, they hit the air and tightened painfully. Her entire body tensed as she prepared to come but he seemed to know that. He stopped rubbing her clit to just tap the bundle of nerves. It was torment.

"Please, Tiger!"

His arm tightened around her waist and he pounded his hips up, using the rock behind him to support his back as he braced his feet on the creek bed. His fingertip pressed down on her clit and he fucked her faster. Raw ecstasy gripped her. She moaned louder and bucked her hips, just trying to keep some sense of control, but Tiger wouldn't have it. He fucked her even faster, harder, and frantically strummed her clit.

Zandy threw her head back against his shoulder and cried his name when the climax struck. Her vaginal muscles quivered from the force of how hard she came. Tiger's body seized, every muscle seemed to turn rock hard where she was against him or gripping his arms, and he threw back his head. The animalistic roar that filled the woods was extremely loud.

Hot jets of his semen filled her as his body jerked under hers. The roar cut off and his hand left her clit to wrap around her breasts until he hugged her tightly to his chest with both arms.

"Zandy," he rasped.

"Tiger," she panted, out of breath.

His mouth nuzzled her throat and his hot tongue licked her skin. It made her shiver in a good way, only amplifying the after-sex glow. The water felt good now on their overheated bodies as they both relaxed.

"Do you think someone will come from Reservation to investigate? We were kind of loud."

Tiger shook his head. "We're far enough away from the wall where the officers patrol for them not to have heard us."

"Good." The idea of officers swarming the area looking for the source of the noises made her inwardly cringe. His assurance put her at ease.

"I could stay inside you forever."

"I wouldn't complain." She smiled.

"We need to get out of the water soon. You're more fragile to the elements than I am." His hands explored her skin. "I don't want you to catch a cold from the cool water."

His arm around her waist tightened as he lifted her high enough to break the connection as his cock withdrew from her pussy slowly. She felt the loss instantly but didn't complain. His hand slid down her body and he slipped a finger inside her, fucking her slowly with it. She was surprised but it felt too good to protest.

"I thought you wanted us to get out of the water. Keep that up and I'm going to want you again."

"I'm cleaning you."

She moaned. "You're doing more than that."

A chuckle tickled her ear as he nuzzled her again. "We'll finish this once I get you dry." His finger withdrew and he cupped her between her thighs, rubbing lightly. She just leaned against him, enjoying his touch until he stopped and his thighs closed.

"Walk toward the towels." He released her waist and gripped her hips with both hands, urging her to stand.

Zandy's legs were shaky as she walked through the moving water to the other side and climbed up the grassy embankment. Tiger remained close behind her in case she lost her balance. She found it cute and gentlemanly. No man had ever been so attentive to her. He didn't even allow her to dry herself. He grabbed a towel before she could, flipped it open and wrapped it around her. His big hands carefully rubbed it over her skin.

She stared into his eyes as he bent enough to reach her lower body and realized that she wouldn't ever stop being fascinated by their exotic shape and color. A smile tugged at the corners of his mouth when he was done. The towel was torn away and she gasped when he gave her a push. She fell backward and landed on the air mattress. An extremely soft bedspread cushioned her body as well. Her fingers brushed against it.

"Is this sheepskin?"

Tiger used another towel to quickly dry off as his gaze raked over every inch of her body sprawled before him. "Yes. I brought it from my own bed. You haven't been to my home so I thought I'd bring part of it to you."

He was a romantic or at least seemed so. It made her like him even more. *Hell*, she admitted silently, *I am falling in love with him.*

He dropped the towel and stepped closer. "I want to take you on it. It is the only thing that will do your soft skin justice." He dropped to his knees, gripped her ankles and bent her legs up and apart to expose her pussy to his view. He stared at it and licked his lips. "Hold your legs just like that, tight to your chest."

Zandy gripped her knees and Tiger growled, the only warning she received before he let go of her ankles to grip her inner thighs. His face lowered and his hot mouth fastened over her pussy. His tongue teased her already swollen clit and she moaned. He burrowed in, lashed at her clit in rapid flicks of his tongue and zoomed right in on that tiny spot that drove her insane as raw rapture struck.

It was too much, felt too good after her recent climax. She tried to close her legs. Tiger refused to allow it as his hold on her thighs tightened when her heels dug into his shoulder blades. He held her down tighter to the bed.

"Tiger, you're killing me," she whimpered.

He began to purr loudly and vibrations added to the sensations. Zandy's back arched and her fingers clawed at the bedding. Pants and moans mixed until she feared passing out. Another climax brutally tore through her body. She shook from the force of it and screamed when he released her clit to drive his tongue inside her pussy.

She was certain he was attempting to actually kill her. Wave after wave of pleasure rolled through her body as she jerked and twitched under him until he finally withdrew and released her thighs. Her body went lax as he rose to his knees and used her hips to drag her ass to the edge of the air mattress.

"I can't," she rasped, struggling to sit up. "Give me a minute."

His tight expression showed his displeasure. "I want you now. I need you."

She managed to roll to her side and pat the bed next to her. "Lie here."

He moved, the mattress dipped with his added weight and she rolled into his side as he sprawled out on his back. The sight of his hard cock pointing up drew her attention as she still fought to regain the ability to think. Her hand curved around the thick shaft and he responded with a groan.

Her tongue darted out to wet her lips as she scooted down the bed while she continued to stroke him with her fingers and regained some control over her heavy breathing. He groaned when she took the head of his cock into her mouth.

His hand tangled in her hair but it didn't hurt. He was careful not to pull it or force her head down to take more of him. The sweet taste of pre-cum made her moan. She usually wasn't overly fond of going down on men but of course he couldn't even be typical in that way either. He tasted good, which encouraged her to keep going.

"Stop before I come," he groaned. "I'll warn you."

She had no idea why he'd want to do that as she opened her mouth wider, exploring him with her tongue as she took him deeper, tightened her lips around him and sucked. Tiger was a mouthful and she had to be careful with her teeth. The loud sounds of him purring became music to her ears and she loved hearing how he responded to her. Not only was his shaft rock hard but his taste just grew better as she worked him. He vibrated where they touched too, his entire body seeming to be affected by it.

He tugged frantically and she lifted off him to peer at his face.

"Stop. I'm about to come. Use your hand. I'm so close."

"Why? I don't want to stop."

"You feel me when I come inside you, don't you?"

"Yes."

"I would choke you if I came in your mouth. I shoot hard and hot."

"I think I could handle it." She tried to capture his cock with her mouth again but he twisted his hips before she could, forcing her gaze back to his.

"Our females can't handle it. That's why they don't do this to our males. I shoot about six feet."

A mental image surfaced and she grinned. "How do you know how far it goes?"

He sat up a little. "I'm male. How do you think?"

A laugh escaped her. "You measured the distance, didn't you?"

"I hurt, Zandy."

Her hand squeezed his shaft and she stroked him. Her gaze dropped to his dick as he slid flat on the mattress again and she watched him come. He hadn't been mistaken about how far his semen could shoot. It didn't even land on the bed. Watching his stomach became more interesting as his muscles tensed, revealing a sexy pattern.

His hand grabbed hers and tore it off his cock. She realized he hadn't roared that time. Groaned and panted but no loud, animalistic roar. It surprised her a little since most men enjoyed head more than intercourse. She started to ask him what he preferred but decided to discover that answer on her own. It would be fun.

She lowered her mouth to the crown of his cock when his body relaxed and he stopped coming. The flat of her tongue traced the ridge of his still-stiff cock and the sweet taste of him drew a moan from her. His taste reminded her of warmed honey with a hint of maple syrup. He could become her breakfast of choice.

"Zandy!" He snarled her name and fisted her hair, tearing her away as he rolled her onto her back. His weight came down on her to pin her beneath him.

Tears filled her eyes from the stinging pain of having her hair pulled. She stared at him as he relaxed his hold, his intense gaze locked on hers. Her ears still rang from the harsh, brutal sound of her name.

A jolt of fear shot through her that she must have done something really wrong and he looked enraged as their gazes held. Had she hurt him? He was on top of her and she couldn't even breathe. His weight was crushing her into the air mattress and she couldn't move with his legs and arms holding her down. He took a deep breath before lifting off enough for her to get air into her lungs.

"I smell fear. I'm sorry I scared you. I didn't mean to."

"You snarled at me. Did I hurt you?"

His hand near her face stroked her cheek. "No, Zandy. I didn't mean to yell. It was just that you were killing me."

Her fear eased. "In a literal sense?"

"No. It felt so good that it was too much to take."

She could relate. "Oversensitive?"

"To put it mildly." He cupped her face. "I'm so sorry I frightened you." He inhaled. "I made you really afraid, Zandy."

She wound her arms around his shoulders. "I know that. You just kind of scared me there for a second."

"I'm so sorry," he rasped.

"It's okay."

He purred and shifted on her, stretching his body lower down hers. He buried his face in her neck and nuzzled his mouth there. "I'd never hurt you. Never. I don't ever want to smell fear on you again."

"I'm fine. I know you wouldn't hurt me. It startled me more," she lied. He was really upset that he'd frightened her. "I'm okay."

His head lifted until he could peer into her eyes again. "You are so much more than fine." He reached between them and gripped her thigh to adjust it enough for his hips to fit between legs. "I can't get enough of you."

Zandy moaned as Tiger's rigid shaft entered her pussy. "How can you still be hard?"

He brushed his mouth over hers. "I'm not human, Zandy. It's the animal in me. I can fuck you until I drop from exhaustion. I just need a minute to recover."

She moaned, moving against him, matching his thrusts. He moved slowly, setting a pace that drove her to pleasure. He shifted on her and put his hand between them.

"I can't last long with you, Zandy. You make me come over and over again." His finger found her clit and stroked. "Come for me now."

She thrashed and moaned. The pressure against the bundle of nerves grew as he rubbed her harder and faster. His hips kept perfect time with his finger. She cried out his name and climaxed. Tiger snarled her name as he found his release.

* * * * *

Tiger rolled to his side and drew Zandy against him as they recovered from another round of sex. The sky began to darken above them as the sun lowered in the sky behind the treetops. He didn't have to watch her drive away any time soon. She was his until morning.

The smell of sex and their mingled scents seemed right to him. His hand caressed her hip as her hot breath fanned his chest where she faced him. Her eyes were closed and her face relaxed in near sleep.

He'd frightened her. The smell of it was gone but the memory remained. It only reminded him of how different they were. A Species female would have just snarled back at him, known not to fear him. Zandy was human.

He closed his eyes to take deep breaths. The bird sounds faded as a cool breeze picked up. It felt good against his heated skin but the female against him burrowed closer. Another reminder that she wasn't Species.

"Let's get under the covers. I'll keep you warm."

Her lips brushed near his nipple. "I know you will."

They both shifted enough to get under the thick comforter he'd taken from his bed. The sheets were his as well, ones he'd stripped from his bed after lunch. His scent was strong on them and it was almost as if he were in his own bed. The air mattress was just a lot softer. He settled on his back to allow her to cuddle into his side and use his arm as her pillow. He carefully tucked the blankets to make sure she wasn't chilled.

Her hand stroked his chest sluggishly and she yawned. It couldn't be much past seven but she was tired. He'd worn her out after her day of work. It made him feel a little guilty. She hadn't complained but Species had a high sex drive. He should have taken it easier on her.

"A penny for your thoughts."

He glanced down and found her peering up at him with a curious look. Her green eyes were beautiful to him. "Sleep. I'm right here."

"It's too early."

"You've had a long day."

A smile softened her lips. "It ended really well."

He couldn't help but smile back. "It has. I could take a nap," he lied. He wasn't tired but she was exhausted.

"Okay." A yawn broke. "We'll do that but wake me when you do."

"I will."

She closed her eyes as he stroked her lower back. She was small compared to Species females and they rarely allowed a male to pet them after sharing sex. They also didn't cuddle against his side or use his biceps for a pillow. He enjoyed the feel of her so close.

Her breathing changed quickly to that of a deep sleep but he continued to touch her. She'd wanted to know what he was thinking but it wasn't anything he wanted to share. Zandy Gordon didn't fit into his life but she fit perfectly into his arms. He was at a loss over what to do.

A mate would leave him vulnerable in a way he never wanted to be. Mercile had taught him young to never value anything he couldn't live without. They'd used any weakness they discovered against him and others of his kind to try to control them. He was a survivor but a mate would expose him to untold pain if he were to lose her.

It's just sex, he tried to convince himself. He wasn't buying that thin excuse though. A small female with red hair and green eyes had broken through his barriers of self-protection when nothing else ever had.

He'd allowed himself friends. He'd even learned to depend on other Species. It had been a risk but he'd known deep down he could survive their loss if something ever happened to them. It would cause him a lot of pain but he'd go on. The thought of something happening to Zandy made him grow icy cold inside. His hand paused on her lower back to just feel her breathing.

He could only protect her if she were with him twenty-four hours a day, seven days a week. He'd have to take her to his house, barricade the doors and windows and allow no one close to her. That wasn't any kind of life for her to have. It would be a prison similar to the one he'd grown up inside. Mercile wouldn't be her captor—he would be. She'd grow to hate him and he wouldn't blame her. He knew he'd have to let her go soon before he became too attached. His chest hurt from the thought.

Chapter Eight

ဢၵ

Zandy fought a yawn but lost as Richard watched from his desk. He grinned.

"Didn't you get enough sleep?"

"Nope."

"I take it your date went well last night?"

Zandy just grinned.

"I'm glad to hear it. Did you get any sleep at all?"

Memory surfaced of the times Tiger had woken her during the night to make love to her — at least four times. "Not much. At dawn I had to drive myself home to shower and get ready for work."

"You spent the night with him? That good, huh?"

She winked and focused on the letter on her computer screen.

"Does he have a name?"

"Yes." She refused to glance at him. No way was she telling him Tiger's name.

"I'm not going to leave you alone until you tell me who it is."

That made her turn her head and stare at him. He looked serious. "Fine. His name is Angel." She grinned at the private joke. Tiger would probably laugh too if she told him about calling him that.

"One of my kind." Richard wiggled his eyebrows. "We're sexy, aren't we?"

"One of your kind?"

"Angel is a common Hispanic name. Latin lovers and all that."

"You're off base there. It's his nickname."

"He must not be too angelic if he kept you up all night."

"He took me to heaven quite a few times."

Richard laughed. "I'm glad that you met someone. So, is this going to be marriage number three?"

"Bite your tongue, man." She hesitated, thinking it wouldn't be so bad sleeping with Tiger every night and waking up his arms every morning. He wasn't looking for anything long-term though. "No. Neither one of us wants something too serious. I've been married and divorced twice. He's not looking for a wife. We're just having some fun together so don't expect a wedding invitation."

"Do you know that saying about never saying never? Just remember that. You might fall for the man and I've heard the third time is the charm."

"Or three strikes and you're out."

"Bah humbug. You're too young to be so pessimistic."

She shrugged. "He's not up for it even if I were willing to take another shot at a relationship. He seems to enjoy his freedom too much."

Richard smirked. "That's what all men say until they meet the right woman. I thought about becoming a priest before I met my wife in high school. She changed my mind when I realized I couldn't live without her. I have no regrets."

"That's really romantic."

He shrugged. "I do need some help. Will you leave Reservation with me at lunch? Her birthday is coming up and I need a woman's opinion. I want to buy her something nice but I have terrible taste in jewelry."

Zandy nodded. "Sure. What does she like?"

"Not butterflies." He chuckled. "I bought her a broach last year, thinking it was pretty but she wasn't so thrilled."

"I bet. I'll go with you."

He smiled. "Thanks. I don't know too many women. My wife's best friend was supposed to go with me but she's sick. I have to buy it today to make sure I have time to have it inscribed. I also figure we're going to be swamped here for the next week."

"Why?"

"That press release last night is going to draw in some hate mail."

She wasn't sure what he was talking about since she'd spent the night in the woods with Tiger but didn't want to reveal that part. Her coworker would ask too many questions but of course the NSO had a lot of press conferences. They were already pretty busy but she figured they could handle an increase in mail. The system they had implemented for incoming mail was pretty effective and smooth.

Thoughts of Tiger made the time pass quickly as she wondered how long they'd last and how their relationship would end. He wanted to see her again but hadn't given her a time. She hated that he'd kissed her goodbye at her car and promised to call her. Her teeth dented her lip, worrying it might have been a brush-off line for goodbye.

"Zandy?"

She turned her head to peer at Richard. "Yeah?"

"It's lunchtime." He stood. "Snow just pulled up to escort us. Don't forget your purse today. I doubt they'll ask for it since you're with me but you don't use the front gate, do you? I'm not sure they all know you. You should take your identification."

It stunned her that time had passed so quickly as she put on her shoes and followed him to the front door. Snow opened it before they reached it. A few minutes later he dropped them off at the parking lot near the front entrance of Reservation.

"You drive a white minivan?"

He chuckled as they climbed inside. "My wife has a matching blue one. We thought it was cute."

"It is." She put on her seat belt.

Richard drove them to the gates and whistled. "Wow. Look at that."

Zandy was shocked at what she saw. "Is it always this bad around lunch? I never leave this way." They slowly drove past at least a hundred protesters after they exited through the gate. They were glared at as some of them shouted.

"I guess they aren't happy Justice North took a mate."

Zandy jerked her head to stare at him. "He did? If the locals had such a problem with them why did they buy land here for Reservation?"

"How did you miss that news conference last night? It was on every channel. He married the daughter of some popular senator and all of them announced it together. Daddy was thrilled, she's kind of hot, and Justice swears they are really happy. They sure looked it." Richard paused. "These aren't the town residents. Everyone who lives around here loves the New Species. All these assholes drive here to cause problems. The local motels won't rent rooms to them so maybe that's why they are so bitchy. They have to drive over an hour to stand out here being idiots and then at the end of the day drive another hour back."

Zandy laughed. "The local motels won't rent to them?"

Richard shook his head. "Nope. They put out big signs. Haven't you seen them? They state 'no anti-New Species persons' allowed right there with the 'no shoes, no shirt, no service' signs. It's kind of funny."

"That is. I've never visited any of the motels. I bought my house online and did all the paperwork by fax. I just moved here after the house closed. I'm glad Justice North is happy. I like him. I'm glad he found someone but I thought he'd take a New Species mate."

"You and everyone else." Richard accelerated once they reached the highway that would lead them into town. "The fact that she's human is going to stir up every asshole out there who has a problem with the NSO. We're going to get slammed with hate mail but just remember to respond nicely." He turned his head and winked. "Insult them back with polite sentences."

"Dear sir, your thoughts are much appreciated by our entire mail department because we laugh daily over your views and hope you have the kind of day you've wished on us too."

Richard chuckled. "Too bad we can't just tell them to fuck off."

* * * * *

Tiger snarled as he hung up the phone and glared at the males around him. "Lock it down and triple security. I want the males from the Wild Zone patrolling the long stretches of walls where we're spread thin. Have them break into two groups, twelve-hour shifts and they can tear apart any trespassers if they somehow make it over the walls."

Flame cocked his head. "Seriously?"

"No. It would be nice though, wouldn't it? Tell them to terrify but hold anyone they find until we can send someone to collect the morons."

The other male grinned. "I know I could think of a few humans on the other side of the gate I wouldn't mind beating on."

Harley nodded next to Flame. "The loudmouth with the blow horn would be at the top of my list to get an attitude adjustment."

Tiger's sense of humor returned as he grinned. "The male in the red beer shirt?"

"That's the one," Harley confirmed. "Just two minutes with him and I'd send him home with that horn in a bad place that would make walking difficult for him."

Moon shifted his stance. "I'd go after the male in the fatigues. He isn't really military but someone should put him through my version of boot camp." He lifted his foot to show off his military-issue boot.

Tiger's bad mood dissipated. "Try to keep your sense of humor. I know it is difficult but we'll get through today."

"What about tomorrow?" Harley smirked. "I don't think this is going to blow over fast. I think those losers out there just realized we can give their women a lot better than they can." He softly growled. "I could show them with that brunette beauty in the blue suit."

Moon growled too. "Hot. She could do an in-depth report on me anytime."

A deep chuckle escaped Tiger. "Don't flirt with the reporters."

The phone rang again and Tiger dismissed the males. He reached for it and was glad it was Justice who called. "How is Jessie holding up?"

Justice hesitated. "She's angry. We expected a backlash but it's been worse than we feared. Brass said you've had a lot of protester issues since late last night."

"It wasn't actually bad until a few hours ago. I wish you'd given me warning before you announced this. I wasn't even aware of what had happened until this morning when I came on shift."

"I tried to call you but you didn't pick up. I was told you wanted time off and didn't want to be disturbed." Justice paused. "Are you well? Brass said you'd called to say you were spending the night in the Wild Zone."

Tiger hated to lie. "I just needed to commune with nature." An image flashed of Zandy under him while he'd fucked her. His dick stirred at the memory of her parted lips and sexy green eyes staring into his. He'd gotten in touch with his animal side all right. A lot. Guilt struck next. "That's a lie," he admitted. "I refuse to speak of it but I was with a female."

The silence on the other line lasted long seconds. "Okay. I don't understand the reason for secrecy but I'll respect it. You know you can discuss anything with me."

He was tempted and hesitated. "Maybe later. I want to work this out on my own."

"Understood. Our females can be complicated. Do you need more males there? We're spread thin here but you have more territory to protect."

"I've just sent my team to recruit the help of the males from the Wild Zone. They won't be real stable but they love to hunt. I don't think they'll kill anyone if they find a human. Harley and Moon will assign them in teams to even out the calmer ones with the more feral. It's now standard procedure here in case of emergency. I'd qualify this as one. How are you holding up?"

"I'm furious. I knew it would cause problems when we released a statement about me taking a human mate but we hoped for the best with her father at our side."

"Why did you do this now?"

Justice hesitated. "Jessie's brother was shot. He'll live but she flew to be at his side. The press saw some of our males on her security team. They contacted us to ask why. We had him transferred to Homeland to recover. It's safer for her to be with her brother here than at a hospital. Jake agreed and our doctors are caring for him. The reporters weren't going to let it go."

"You had no choice."

"That's how we felt." Justice sighed. "I apologize for the difficulty but she's worth it."

"I know you love your mate."

"Love is an understatement. She's my life. Her brother however is a thorn in my side. I hadn't met him until they flew him in. He's difficult."

"Anti-Species?"

"No. Just an asshole. Think of a younger version of Tim Oberto without the leash since he works for us. Jake quit the military to work for a private security firm. He's already demanding to see our entire security protocols to fix them. He's a very protective older brother. I admire his love for my mate but the male is annoying."

"Humans come with family," Tiger teased. "He is yours now."

"Bite your tongue. I know I'd enjoy punching him in that loud mouth of his."

"Resist. Your mate wouldn't approve."

"Jessie wants to punch him too. She threatened to shoot him in his other leg so the scar on his thigh will have a matching one if he doesn't back down. They have this strange sibling relationship where they argue a lot and make dire threats against each other."

"My day doesn't seem quite as stressful now," Tiger teased. "Enjoy getting to know Jessie's brother."

"Take care."

Tiger hung up and entered the main room of Security. The cameras were filled with scenes of protesters. "Are they behaving?"

"No one is throwing anything since we hosed down the first twenty feet in front of the gate," Zest answered with a grin. "They didn't enjoy getting icy water baths."

"Good." He brushed his fingers through his hair. "How about the town? Has the sheriff returned our call?"

"He isn't reporting any trouble. Most of the protesters are avoiding it and instead hanging out here."

"That's a relief. I don't want the town to grow to hate us."

At least something was going right. Tiger knew it was going to be a long day. He'd had hopes of calling Zandy to arrange a meeting with her after work but she'd be sleeping by the time his shift ended.

* * * * *

"That was fun." Zandy shot a glance at Richard. "Thanks for buying me lunch in town."

"My pleasure. You have great taste. I think my wife is going to love that locket with the rose design. It's beautiful."

"Just remember to take those pictures in tomorrow when you pick it up after they inscribe it for you. One of you and one of your kids. Every woman would love that. It was actually fun to shop for someone else."

"Hey, I'm glad you think so. At Christmas, may I borrow you for a few hours? I really need help then." Richard grinned. "Not only do I have to buy for my wife but my mother too."

"Ah," she teased. "You don't want me as a friend. You want me as a shopping assistant."

"Damn straight!"

The van had to slow when a large crowd blocked the road ahead of them in front of the Reservation gates. Richard tooted his horn to get some of them to move out of the way. Three off-road, full-sized pickup trucks were in line ahead of them to be searched.

Richard sighed. "We might be a little late."

"It's not our fault. The NSO officers can see us up there on the wall." Zandy peered up at the well-armed security officers patrolling the catwalk along the top of the thick barrier. "I don't remember there being so many of them up there the day I came for my interview."

"That's because there usually aren't." Richard paused. "Are you feeling as nervous as I am? Notice the way some of these jerks are eyeing us." He hit the locks on the door but they were already down. "I don't like this."

Her gaze darted around to find a lot of strangers glaring at them. "I don't like this either. Maybe you should back up and drive to the other gate that I use."

"That's miles away and we'd really be late. We're safe. No one would be stupid enough to try anything with all those guns up along that wall. We're technically on NSO land here on this side of the gate. It's posted everywhere and those officers can open fire if need be."

She studied the faces around them. "Do they know that? Those aren't our finest and brightest holding those racist signs. They are total dipshits."

Richard chuckled. "It will be fine. Look, there are a few deputies from town trying to do crowd control. I've worked here for a while and I've seen worse."

Some idiot wearing jeans and a T-shirt climbed up into the back of a pickup truck in line at the front to yell obscenities at the NSO officers. A news crew shoved forward with their cameras to capture the tension.

Richard softly cursed beside her. "They are such assholes."

"Maybe he'll fall out of the back of the truck and break his neck. We can always hope."

Richard gave her a wink when she glanced his way. She smiled and returned her attention to the jackass making a fool of himself. The NSO officers ignored him but the camera crews were eating it up while filming the action.

"I'll bet you five bucks that makes the six o'clock news. It only hurts their cause so I hope they do run it. What a prick. I know two-year-olds with better language skills." Richard's fingers tapped the steering wheel. "We're really going to be late."

"It's not our fau—" Shock cut her off when a tarp was thrown from the back of the truck bed in front of them. It landed on the slanted hood of Richard's minivan and two men stood up from where they'd been hiding under it. Both of them were gripping long weapons.

Zandy froze in horror as the men opened fire. The sounds of gun blasts were deafening and the brake lights on the truck holding the two men suddenly went off. It was such a small detail to notice but it drew her attention. Reverse lights came on a second before the vehicle ahead of them slammed into the front of the minivan. Zandy's belt dug painfully into her shoulder with the rough impact and Richard yelled. It wasn't a word, just a sound of terror and confusion.

The NSO officers responded by firing canisters that exploded on the pavement around them. Thick white smoke began to fill the air to block the sight of the gates ahead. Something hit the window next to Zandy, jerking her attention there. A man with a bandana over his nose and mouth hit the window again with the hammer he wielded. The glass next to her face spider-webbed as it started to crush in.

The protesters attacked the minivan by the dozens, their bodies pressing against it and rocking it wildly. Zandy cried out as her fingers frantically clutched at the belt release. It popped open right when the man hit the window again and broken chunks of glass hit her lap as a hand gripped her arm. Richard jerked her roughly and shoved her between the open space between the seats.

Someone bellowed for calm from a loudspeaker but the words were lost between the screams from the protesters, the shouting and more gun blasts. Zandy hit the floor hard between the captain chairs in the center of the van. Someone grabbed at her foot and tore her shoe off. She kicked away and her legs slid off the center divider until she was curled in a tight ball.

"We need help," Richard yelled.

She couldn't see him from where she lay but she saw his uplifted arm that had to be holding his cell phone. He might have called 9-1-1 or the gate, she wasn't sure. The side door next to her slid open suddenly and she twisted her head.

"Fucking animal-loving bitch," some man yelled.

"It's her," some other man shouted. "It's Justice North's wife."

Rough hands reached inside to grab at her. Zandy screamed when the thick smoke poured inside, blinding her. Her fingers clawed for any purchase as they dragged her out of the van. They had her legs though and were strong. She slammed hard into the pavement and had a coughing fit when she tried to scream again.

The hands released her legs when she fell and a man grunted. Someone fell next to her and she realized people were running by them. She crawled forward and bumped her head on part of the van. She couldn't see anything but she had found it. Heavy footfalls came closer, people screamed and coughed and she rolled under the van.

It was a tight fit but she hoped it would save her from being trampled as everyone fled. The smoke grew thicker until she couldn't breathe at all. Zandy fisted the front of her shirt and tucked her head, covering her nose and mouth. It only helped a little.

"Zandy!" Richard screamed her name before he broke into a fit of coughs. He sounded close and out of the van.

She took a deep breath and freed her mouth. "I'm under the van!"

Hands gripped her and dragged her out from her hiding spot. She started to struggle but a vicious growl stopped her.

"I'm NSO," the male informed her.

Her body went lax and she was amazed when he just scooped her up from the ground. She was held tightly against a padded chest—his protective gear—and he quickly rushed her through the thickest part of the smoke.

She had to blink back tears and stared up at the face shield of the officer carrying her when it cleared enough for her to see again. The gates came into view and he jogged through the open space they'd made to get her inside.

"Breathe against my shirt and don't inhale more of the smoke," he demanded roughly. "Just hang on."

The sound of someone else coughing made her twist her head a little and she spotted Richard being helped by another officer. Her coworker clutched a mask over his face that his escort had obviously provided as he was led inside the gate too. She fought back more tears of gratitude that they'd both survived.

Chapter Nine

❧

The officer assessing Zandy had removed his helmet after carrying her inside the guard shack. He grimly frowned as their gazes met. He released her arms as he stepped back. She was pretty sure he'd visibly searched about every inch of her before he was satisfied.

She tried not to stare at his face. His features weren't as harsh looking as some of the males she'd met. His black hair was tied back in a ponytail and he was really cute. His eyes were more rounded in shape. She realized that he wasn't canine or feline. He was one of the primate-mixed New Species that she'd heard about from Richard. There weren't a lot of them. He only stood about six feet tall but his muscular frame left no doubt he was in great shape, despite being shorter than other New Species males she'd come in contact with.

"You have some scratches, bruises, and you're bleeding."

"I'm fine. Thank you for coming out there to get me. I'm Zandy. You are?"

His eyes narrowed. "I'm Smiley. You work for NSO. You are one of ours." He glanced down and suddenly he grabbed her shirt with both hands.

She lowered her chin to watch him pull both ends of her torn shirt together. Her bra had been showing...and a lot of cleavage. That was the least of her worries and she refused to be embarrassed. Those assholes who had dragged her out of the van had destroyed her clothing in the process. He crouched down a little to stare into her eyes again, looking concerned.

"Did you hit your head? Are you in any pain? Your knee is bleeding badly. We are taking you to Medical immediately as soon as a Jeep arrives. I'll personally escort you there."

She avoided glancing down at her right leg. The sight of blood wasn't her favorite and knowing it was hers only made it worse. It hurt a lot but she didn't want to be a crybaby about it. "My head is fine."

Richard suddenly stepped next to the officer and she was happy to see him. He looked a little worse for wear but unhurt.

"Are you all right, Zandy? I tried to get to you but I couldn't get my door open. They pulled you out of the back faster than I could say shit."

"I'm a little dinged up but they dropped me once they got me outside."

"Thank god." Richard sounded and looked pretty shaken. "I thought they'd run off with you. I can't believe they actually attacked the gates." He studied her face. "Your cheek is bleeding. Did one of them hit you?"

"I think I bumped it on the side of your van. I couldn't see anything but I found it with my face." She refused to reach up to touch the throbbing spot, afraid it would be worse than it felt. She didn't want to know. "It all happened so fast. All I could think to do was get under your van to hide and keep from being trampled."

He reached out to touch her but the New Species officer blocked his hand and scooped her into his arms. "I'm taking you to Medical now."

Zandy gave Richard a stunned look over Smiley's shoulder before she was carried outside. Snow waited behind the wheel of the Jeep that had arrived and she was carefully placed in the passenger seat. The officer climbed into the backseat.

"Go."

The Jeep took off quickly. Snow glanced at her as he drove. "Are you harmed, Zandy? We apologize for you being attacked."

"It's not your fault there are assholes in the world. I'm just a little banged up but I'll be fine."

Snow glanced from her to the road, then back. "They shot one of our males but he didn't suffer any lasting effects. The vest stopped the bullet from piercing his skin. We got both males who opened fire on the NSO."

"Good." The memory of seeing that tarp hit Richard's hood and those men standing up suddenly, holding those weapons, made her shiver. She had little doubt it wasn't something she'd ever forget and it would probably be the source of many nightmares. She didn't say it but knew if they'd fired at her and Richard, they'd have been easy targets strapped in their seats. "I'm glad you have them in custody."

"They believed she was Jessie North," Smiley added.

She hadn't remembered those men yelling at her until that second. "Who is Jessie North?"

"Justice took her as a mate." Snow concentrated on driving as he parked in front of a building with glass windows. "She's human but looks nothing similar to you except you both have red hair. Didn't you watch the news last night?"

"I missed that."

"They say our kind are hard to tell apart." Snow snorted. "It seems your kind can't tell each other apart either. You don't look anything like Jessie except for your small size and the long red hair. Her hair is much longer though and it is very red."

Smiley jumped out of the back and scooped her into his arms before Snow could even turn off the engine. "Thank you. I have it from here."

Zandy put her arms around his broad shoulders while he carried her inside the building once the automatic doors opened. A Dr. Harris waited inside for them with a New Species female at his side. The man was in his mid-thirties and introduced her to Midnight. The tall blue-eyed female smiled grimly.

"Bring her this way, Smiley."

He carefully placed her on an exam table in one of the back rooms and hovered there until Dr. Harris walked in. "Thanks for bringing her. We've got it from here."

The officer hesitated. "I need to stay with her."

"We're making her strip," Midnight informed him. "I see your interest but approach her later."

"It was an order to protect her."

"Wait outside." Midnight smiled. "Human females are shy about their bodies."

He spun around and Zandy watched him leave. Midnight closed the door. "Males." The woman shook her head. "Did he drool on you?"

"No."

Dr. Harris laughed. "That was Smiley and he has a thing for humans." He turned his back. "I won't peek."

Midnight pulled out a cloth gown and offered it. "You need to strip down to your panties if you wear any."

It hurt to stand on her injured knee and the tall Species female kneeled down to help her remove her only shoe. The other one was lost. She had forgotten that since she'd been carried everywhere since her rescue. Midnight took her clothes and she put on the gown, leaving it open in the back.

"She's decent, handsome."

The doctor turned his head to grin at Midnight. "Thanks, gorgeous."

Zandy was surprised at their exchange. The doctor had put on gloves and he pulled a stool closer to sit. He examined her bloodied knee when she took a seat on the exam table.

"He's mine," Midnight announced, pointing to the doctor. "The young one. Not his father. There are two Drs. Harris. Don't get ideas about him."

"I wouldn't," she managed to get out, stunned that the tall muscular nurse was dating the doctor. He wasn't a bad-looking man and was fit but it was obvious his girlfriend could kick his ass.

The doctor chuckled. "Yeah. I'm hers." He prodded Zandy's injured knee. "You won't need stitches but it needs to be cleaned. It's going to hurt."

Midnight got him what he needed and Zandy clenched her teeth while he worked on her knee until it was bandaged. He examined her chest where her shirt had been torn, found a scratch above her breast, and even prodded the bruise on her hip where she'd landed on the pavement after being dragged from the van.

"Any dizziness? Double vision? Nausea?" He blinded her with a penlight he flashed in both her eyes while studying the cut on her head. "What happened here?"

"No, no, and no." She winced when he started to clean it. "It isn't bad, is it? I was crawling and hit the side of a van."

"It's not bad," he admitted. "This is going to sting."

Shit.

* * * * *

Tiger was furious. "They attacked the gates?"

Timber nodded grimly. "They shot Torrent. He is pissed but fine. They tagged his vest hard enough to leave some bruising."

Tiger's gaze wandered around Security, watching his males hard at work, keeping an eye on everything with the cameras. "Has Justice and Homeland been informed?"

"Immediately. We had to warn them about potential attacks on Jessie. One of our human employees was attacked. The idiot humans thought she was Justice's mate."

"Why would they think one of our human employees was Jessie?"

"She has long red hair. She had left for lunch with a human male and they were returning when the idiots attacked the gate. Some of them saw her and assumed she was Jessie. They broke the windows of the van she was in and dragged her out. The smoke made them run and they dropped her. She will be fine. I ordered Smiley to stay with her. He escorted her to Medical for treatment. We have the shooters and driver who brought them here in custody. They have been prepared for transport to Homeland."

Tiger growled. "You should have contacted me immediately when this happened."

"You were tending to the Wild Zone incident. It was all handled well. The only real destruction done was to the van the two humans were in. We are taking care of that. Good thing we pay for insurance for this stuff with the money we fine the idiots. The repair bill will be costly. The driver of the truck hiding the gunmen reversed his truck into the front of the van when they attempted to flee and then the windows were smashed in an attempt to get to the human female when the protesters attacked. They also dented the van greatly since they tried to overturn it."

"Son of a bitch," Tiger snarled. "Is the human female well? Is she going to quit? It is hard to find trustworthy humans."

"She is well. I just spoke to Midnight. The human has been treated and has asked to go back to work. We offered her a few days of paid vacation to recover but she refused."

"I will go smooth things over with her. What is her name?"

Timber hesitated, thinking. "It was an odd name. Zane? Zany?"

Tiger's heart almost stopped beating. "Zandy?"

Timber nodded. "That is the name. Small human female, green eyes and long red hair."

"Fuck!" Tiger snarled. "I'm going to Medical."

Timber gaped at him. "You know this female?"

Tiger spun and sprinted out to his Jeep, not bothering to answer. Zandy had been attacked. The details sank in as he drove quickly to reach her. He wanted to know why she'd left Reservation for lunch and what human male she'd been with. He decided it had better have been with Richard Vega. The male loved his mate and that would mean it hadn't been a date. Just the idea of another male touching her made him want to roar with rage. She'd been hurt and he hadn't been there to protect her.

He took ragged breaths, trying to control his rage. A mixture of jealousy and fear gripped him hard enough to make his chest hurt. They hadn't agreed on any dating terms. Had Zandy gone on a date? He shook his head. That didn't matter at the moment.

She'd been attacked by humans and he was tempted to call Timber to put a hold on the prisoners. He'd love to spend five minutes with each of the males until he made certain they were injured as well. The thought of what could have happened to her left him with a deep need to reach her side as quickly as possible. He punched the gas to an unsafe speed and took a turn too fast. Species stared at him as he passed but he didn't give a damn.

* * * * *

Zandy put on the new set of clothes. Midnight had brought her a gray T-shirt with NSO lettered on the front pocket and matching sweatpants. Her torn clothing had been thrown away. Her knee throbbed. Dr. Harris told her to go home and keep off it for a few days but Zandy had refused. The last thing she wanted was to go home to her empty house. She'd rather be around people after her close call with nearly being kidnapped.

Dr. Harris wasn't happy with her decision. He held out a plastic bag. "I put a few shake ice packs in here too. Do you know how to use them?"

She smiled. "Um, I shake them?"

He grudgingly smiled back. "Yes."

"Thank you."

"Your purse was retrieved from the vehicle you were in." Midnight handed it to her. "We are glad that you weren't really harmed. Are you sure you don't want a few days to recover? There is no shame in that. You are human and not used to this kind of stress."

"Honey," the doctor said softly, "we're not invalids just because we aren't as tough as you. She wants to go back to work. I'd do the same."

She smiled at him. "You are very brave. For a human."

"I'm glad you think so." He turned to Zandy and asked, "Do you want crutches? That knee is going to hurt worse in the morning. You're already limping."

"I'm good. I won't lie and say it doesn't ache but I banged up my knees worse when I was a kid. I was a bit of a tomboy and liked skateboarding."

"I saw the faded scars and wondered."

"We lived on a hill."

"Got it." He grinned. "I hope you wore a helmet."

"I plead the Fifth."

"Don't forget to take the pills I gave you for the pain and the ones I prescribed to help reduce any swelling. They are inside the bag. Use condoms for a month if you're on birth control. They will mess with it since it's also an antibiotic. I'd rather be safe than sorry to help you prevent any infection. I cleaned the cut well but you were in contact with the pavement. I have no idea what kind of germs you were exposed to. Stay off that knee as much as possible. I know you have an office job and work behind a desk. Have someone else fetch anything you need. Elevate it if possible."

"Thank you. I'll take the pills as soon as I get to my office."

Midnight offered to escort her out but Zandy refused. Smiley was pacing outside in clear view of the front windows. She limped out there and he turned, his expression grim.

"Allow me to carry you."

She shook her head. "No, I'm okay."

"I called for transportation. You shouldn't be standing from the amount of blood I saw on your pants. I strongly suggest you go home." He paused. "You've had a trauma. Your family should care for you."

"I live alone. The idea of staring at my walls isn't real appealing. I'd rather be around someone right now."

"I understand." His expression softened and his pretty brown eyes fixed on her. "I could request to end my shift and take you to my home. I'm not offering to share sex but someone should care for you. I have a large television and I'm safe."

She highly doubted his version of safe and hers lined up. Midnight and the doctor thought the New Species was attracted to her. The only man she wanted fawning over her had blue eyes and purred during the heat of passion. Her mouth opened to tell him no thanks but the sound of a car careening around a corner drew her attention first.

The Jeep was speeding at them and she recognized the driver instantly. Tiger's streaked hair was easy to spot and so was his enraged expression as tires locked up on the pavement when he hit the brakes. The vehicle came to a screeching halt by the curb. He was out of it the second the engine cut off.

"This is Tiger," Smiley stated, as if she didn't know who stormed around the front of the vehicle to reach them. "Hello, Tiger. I take it you heard what happened. She is well. How did it go with Vengeance?"

"Give us a moment alone," Tiger snarled, his gaze locked on Zandy. "I need to speak to her. Take a walk."

Smiley gawked but backed away. He spun on his heel and went to the end of the building. He'd seemed pretty shocked at Tiger's abrupt dismissal and she could relate, stunned a little herself. Tiger waited until the other man had moved away before he stepped closer. He ran his gaze down her body before meeting her eyes again. His hand lifted and he gently gripped her jaw, forcing her head to tilt a little to get a better look at the cut on her face.

"Why did you leave Reservation and who were you with? Are you all right? Who did this to you?"

She wasn't sure which question to answer first. "I'm okay. Richard and I went shopping for his wife on our lunch break and the protesters attacked while we were in line to get back inside the gates."

A deep growl rumbled from his throat. "Where are your clothes?"

"They threw them away. The shirt was history and the pants were bloody."

He sniffed and another growl came from him, the second one deeper and almost scary. Rage narrowed his eyes and she hoped it wasn't directed at her. His touch remained gentle where he held her jaw.

"I still smell blood."

"I'm okay. I got a few scratches. My—"

"Where?"

She paused. "My knee got the worst of it. I have a scratch on my chest and you can see my face. I didn't get a good look at the men who tried to grab me but they thought I was someone else."

His other hand gripped her hip. "I heard the attackers thought you were Jessie. I can't believe they thought you were her. Your hair is much lighter and shorter than hers. Humans are stupid. You shouldn't have used the front gates. Didn't you realize it would be dangerous?"

She let that one slide since he was obviously upset and didn't she really want to be lumped into the same category as the protesters at that moment by reminding him she was human. His words made her feel a little defensive though.

"I guess we missed the news conference last night when Justice North announced he'd gotten married to the woman they mistook me for. I had no idea it wasn't safe to leave the front gates. I take it that you know her?"

He nodded. "I know her very well and you two look nothing alike." He took a deep breath. "I am agitated. I'm sorry. I should have called your office the moment I found out Justice had to tell the press about his mate and warned you it would antagonize the protesters."

Zandy studied him and a hint of jealousy struck. How well did Tiger know the other redhead? It was going to bug her if she didn't ask. "Did you ever date this Jessie?"

His mouth tensed. "No. She is Justice's mate. I've never mounted her. Why would you ask that?"

She hated the fact that she was glad he'd never slept with the woman she'd been mistaken for. The idea of being a replacement version of a woman he'd lost to another man had set her on edge. "Curiosity, since some people think we look so much alike. Never mind. It's been a stressful day."

He caressed her cheek before dropping his hand. "I don't want you leaving Reservation. It's not safe. The protesters are out in full force and some have even shown up at the gate you use. That's a long stretch of road I don't want you traveling and someone could follow you home. They already attacked you once, thinking you were Justice's mate. I insist you stay here for a few days until things calm."

Disappointment hit her that he wasn't inviting her to stay at his place. Smiley had offered to take her home and he didn't even know her. It was a painful reminder that Tiger didn't want anything long-term between them. It was what they'd agreed on and she'd made her bed. Sleeping in it suddenly seemed really lonely and painful.

"Okay."

"There is space open in human housing. It's similar to your apartment buildings. I'll assign officers to guard you. Some of the protesters have tried to breach our walls and I want to make sure you're safe. I will try to check on you but I'm not sure how late my shift will end. It's going to be a long day and worse night. We've learned that they tend to think just because the sun goes down that it will be easier to sneak onto NSO lands."

"I don't have any clothes. I'll need to take at least one trip home to get my stuff."

"No. I'll order you clothes from our store." He glanced down her. "I apologize but we don't get too many small females staying here. You'll probably have to wear more sweats and T-shirts."

"There's a dress code for work."

"Don't worry about that. I'll make certain no one says anything. You are safer here at Reservation until this blows over. We'll extend the same courtesy to all NSO human employees."

That killed her assumption that he'd done something special for her by asking her to stay where he knew she'd be safe. It drove home another reminder that they didn't have a relationship. It stung.

"Fine. You do that. I need to get to work. I guess I'll see you later."

She turned away from him and he had no choice but to release her hip. The limp was noticeable as she headed toward Smiley. He saw her coming and came at her quickly.

"Zandy?" Tiger hissed.

She paused and turned her head to meet his gaze. "Yes?"

"Is something wrong? Are you angry with me?"

She swung back around and limped so close to him that she had to tilt her chin up to stare into his handsome face. He looked past her and held up his hand to halt the officer. His hand dropped to his side.

She was in pain and had been assaulted, her patience already at the limit. They didn't have a real relationship but she wanted to be honest. It was probably the last time they'd talk anyway. She might as well give him a piece of her mind.

"I'm having a shit day if you haven't noticed. I'm sure you are too since I know you're the head of security here. I guess when I saw you speeding around that corner I assumed you'd heard what happened and it shook you up enough to want to see me." She paused. "Hell, this is why I don't get involved with men. I suck at it and we don't have a relationship, right? Thank you for caring and checking on me. I know you need to get back to work. We're fine." She turned away again.

Tiger's hand clamped down on her arm to prevent her from getting away from him. He stepped around her until he blocked her path. "Are we in a relationship?"

Her gaze dropped to his NSO work shirt. "I don't know. Are we?" She gazed back up at him.

"I wanted to invite you to stay at my house but you'd already told me no. I didn't want to be rejected a second time. I also have to work long hours and my home is too far from the office to sleep there while this crisis is happening. You'd be out there alone. I wanted to keep you close."

"It wasn't a rejection. I just said no because we barely knew each other then."

His exotic eyes narrowed. "We know each other extremely well now."

Sexually. "I don't know where we're heading and it's scary. I missed you today and hoped you'd invite me to meet you later." *I'm falling in love with you.*

"I missed you too." He hesitated. "I will come visit you tonight and we'll talk."

"Okay." She wasn't sure if that was bad or good.

"It might be late."

"I understand."

His cell phone buzzed and he reached for it, never looking away from her eyes. "Yes?" He paused. "Understood. I'm on my way." He hung up. "I have to go. Some of the humans outside the gates are acting up again." He lifted a hand and waved Smiley forward. "Try to take a nap before I arrive." His voice lowered even more. "I plan to do a lot more than just talk to you." A soft purr came from him before he backed away.

Zandy's body instantly responded to the sexy noise. The idea of seeing him later and possibly spending another night sleeping together had her nipples growing taut and her belly quivering. Him licking his lips only reminded her of what he could do with that tongue and her clit throbbed.

He faced Smiley. "I'm reassigning you to Zandy today. Take her to work and I want you to stay close to her building until after her shift is over. She'll be staying at building H, apartment HJ until this mess ends. It's too dangerous for her to leave Reservation. I'll have officers meet you there later. Wait for them if they are running late. She isn't to be left unguarded."

"Understood."

Tiger glanced at her one more time before he strode back to his Jeep. Another one turned the corner, probably the transportation Smiley had called. She resisted waving at Tiger as he drove away. The officer next to her sniffed loudly and she jerked her head to stare at his face.

He frowned. "Forget about that one, Zandy."

"What?"

"You are aroused and Tiger isn't a male you wish to pursue. He isn't the type to take a mate. He avoids sharing sex with human females."

Her cheeks warmed as she blushed. *Oh hell.* "Is there anything you guys can't smell?"

He hesitated. "I'm not opposed to taking a mate and open to a possible lasting bond with a female. You're injured and having a stressful day but keep me in mind if you wish to share sex. Just think about it."

A new officer watched them from the waiting Jeep while Zandy limped toward the passenger seat. She wasn't going to touch that one with a ten-foot pole. Not the man or the offer. She wasn't even sure how to respond.

Chapter Ten

ᔓ

A noise woke Zandy and she glanced at the clock on the nightstand. It was just after eleven. Tiger had finally arrived. She was on her stomach under the covers but had left the light on in the living room of the one-bedroom apartment. Her hair was still damp from the shower she'd taken. She used her arm to lift up and turn in bed. The covers slid down a little as her gaze swept the dark room until she found his darker shape near the dresser.

"I was wondering if you'd ever show. Thanks for the clothes and all the stuff you had deliv—"

The shadow lunged at her, hit the bed hard enough to knock her flat, and a gloved hand clamped around her throat. Shock tore through her as fingers squeezed painfully tight until she couldn't breathe. Her mouth opened to scream as the body on the bed with her scooted even closer when she tried to struggle under the covers.

It wasn't Tiger. She couldn't see the man's face. The hand felt big and he was heavy as he tried to pin her body down. Panic and sheer terror made her claw at her throat—he was strangling her. She found his skin just above the leather gloves and dug her fingernails in. Her lungs burned from lack of oxygen and she focused on hurting her attacker.

He cried out and the hold on her throat loosened for a split second. It was just enough time for her to suck in much-needed air. She screamed. The sound came out as more of a shriek. The man let go to roll away. He fell off the edge of the bed as Zandy screamed again, blindly turning the other way to put space between them.

A dark shape lifted from the floor and rushed toward the corner of the room. He hit the glass window hard enough to break through when he slammed into it. Cool air filled the room while she continued to pant. Wood splintered from the other side of the apartment and two New Species rushed inside her room from the living room. One flipped on the light, both of them sniffed the air and the blond rushed toward the destroyed window.

"Stay with her. It was a human male," he snarled before he leaped out the opening to chase her attacker.

The remaining officer held up his hands in an almost calming way to show he posed no danger to her. "Are you all right?"

She nodded and tried to speak but coughed instead. Her throat hurt. It took some work to swallow before she tried again. "I woke up and someone was in the room."

He stalked slowly around the bed and bent down. One hand gripped the sheet and lifted it to her upper chest. "You're naked." He sniffed. "He didn't sexually assault you."

She clutched at the sheet that the officer had handed to her, still gripping her throat with the other. He'd seen her bare breasts. Her hair falling over her shoulders hadn't totally hidden them but at that moment she was too confused and frightened to be embarrassed.

"Did you see his face?" He backed off as soon as she held the sheet up without his assistance. "Do you know who it was?"

She'd thought it was Tiger but couldn't state that without admitting they were sleeping together to explain why he'd be in her bedroom. "No. It was too dark."

He crouched and gently moved her hand from her throat. A soft growl came from him as he studied her neck. "He hurt you."

"He tried to strangle me. He was wearing gloves. I felt them when I tried to make him let go."

The officer took her hand and sniffed her fingertips. "You made him bleed. Wipe them on the bedding. We will want his blood scent."

Shock prevented her from responding so the officer used part of the bedding to clean her fingertips. Blood stained the material and she realized she must have really nailed her attacker. He released her hand and rose to his feet.

"I will guard the door. Go into the bathroom and wash your hands. Human males can carry diseases. Use soap."

"I'm naked," she reminded him.

He paused to glance at her. "I won't look. Hurry, more officers are on the way." He strode to the dresser and removed some of the clothes Tiger had ordered for her. He returned to her side and offered them. "Just come out when you are dressed."

He spun, moved to the bedroom door and turned his back to her. She glanced at the broken window, the curtains swaying in the breeze, before tossing back the sheet to streak to the bathroom. Once the door was closed she realized how badly she was shaking.

Someone had attacked her in her bed. When she looked in the mirror she saw red marks on her throat where she'd been squeezed. She tilted her head to get a better look. She'd probably have bruises. Her hand rose to touch the sore spots but the sight of blood on her fingers stopped her. She lowered her gaze to the sink to turn on the water. Her hands trembled badly as she soaped them and scrubbed under her fingernails.

The T-shirt and sweatpants were too large but she didn't have a choice. She opened the door when she'd put them on. Two officers were in her room. The one who'd tended her was stripping the comforter off her bed. He folded it to keep the blood stains on top.

"Here," he passed it to the other officer. "Take this to Security immediately." He turned to face Zandy. "Are you well? We're tracking the male who attacked you. Did he say anything to you?"

"No. He was by the dresser when I woke and he just attacked me. He grabbed my throat and I couldn't breathe."

"He wanted to keep her silent," the second officer stated. "He had to have known we were posted outside."

A third officer walked into her room. "We found his point of entry. He broke through the kitchen window in the back. Smashing this window to escape cost him severe injuries, judging by the amount of blood we found outside. It shouldn't take us long to track him. He won't be able to get away." He grimly regarded Zandy. "Are you well, female?"

"I'm okay. Shaken, but I'll live."

"He harmed her throat," the first officer informed the one who seemed to be in charge. "We should escort her to Medical."

"It's just red. I can breathe fine now and it's just a little sore. I'm sure I don't need a doctor."

"Are you sure?" All three of them studied her.

"Yes. I just want a drink." She inched past them and entered the living room. Her purse was on the floor and all the contents had been dumped out over the coffee table.

She picked up her wallet and opened it. Her cash was still there and she showed it to the officers who'd followed her. "He wasn't a thief. I don't know what he was looking for though."

"Don't worry. We'll find out when we catch him."

She dropped her wallet on the table and entered the kitchen. It was small and her gaze immediately focused on the window. It was closed but she could see where the lock had been broken along the bottom.

* * * * *

Tiger was furious as he glared at Vengeance. The male snarled at him, in a foul mood. He was really testing Tiger's patience. He had spent the past few hours trying to calm the male but admitted to being ready to call in someone to tranquilize him and put him down for the night.

"You attacked a female human while working for the task force and that's how you ended up here. I know you want to do something but you blew it. I'm not arguing with you anymore, Ven. I have things to do tonight and I'd like to get some sleep. More important things are happening than you throwing a fit because you aren't happy here."

"I should be doing something."

"I understand but you tried to force mate a female." Tiger's cell phone rang and he reached for it. "Tiger here."

"The human female, Zandy Gordon, was attacked at her apartment at human housing."

Tiger snarled from rage and shock that someone had harmed Zandy again. "How? Who did it? Is she well? Where were the officers I assigned to guard her?"

Timber sounded angry too. "They were near the curb, in front of the building. You said to keep them outside. A human male broke in through a back window. He tried to strangle her in bed but she managed to scream. The human attacker is injured and bleeding. We're tracking him now and he's heading toward the Wild Zone. He's going to be one sorry bastard if he makes it there. The unstable ones will kill him if they find him before our officers do."

"Is Zandy all right?"

"She's fine. She refused medical treatment and officers are with her now."

"I'm in the Wild Zone with Vengeance. I'll see if I can head him off."

"He's bleeding a lot."

"She did that much damage to him?" That surprised him since Zandy wasn't a big female but a little pride swelled inside his chest too.

"No. He jumped through a window after she screamed. It must have cut him badly."

"Good. I'll call you if I find him or you call me if he's found." He ended the conversation.

"What happened?"

Tiger studied Vengeance and fought down his rage. He wanted to punish the human for touching Zandy. "I have a job for you. You're an excellent tracker, aren't you? A human male has somehow trespassed onto Reservation and attacked a female human employee. He's heading this way and I want your help finding him. Just don't kill him. I want to know what he is doing here."

Vengeance nodded. "I could use a good hunt."

Tiger nodded. "Me too. Just remember to keep him alive and he needs to be able to talk. I want a piece of this one myself."

Tiger and Vengeance got in the Jeep. Tiger would find the male and remove the hand that had tried to kill his Zandy. He forced himself to take deep breaths to try to calm down. If he hadn't gotten tied up at work, he would have been with her and he wouldn't have allowed anyone to cause her harm.

He drove to meet the tracking team. A comforter had been taken from Zandy's bed and offered to all the males to sniff. He spotted the blood stains on the spread and rage gripped him. He didn't calm until he realized it had come from the male. The stench of the human male mixed with Zandy's fear set him on edge. He leaped back in the Jeep and glanced at Vengeance.

"Do you have his scent locked?"

Vengeance nodded. "Who is the female? She smells good. She's showered recently."

"Forget the human female," Tiger growled. "Let's find the male."

Vengeance stood from his seat and sniffed the air. "It's faint but I got him." He pointed. "The wind is blowing from that direction."

Tiger punched the gas and watched the Species. Canines had a stronger sense of smell than felines. It was the one thing he hated about his heritage. Right now he wanted to be the one to sniff out the human and locate him. His fingers gripped the steering wheel painfully due to his rage. Soon enough he'd have his hands on the male. He'd be one sorry son of a bitch for going after Zandy.

* * * * *

Zandy stared across the coffee table at Smiley as he watched her. She sat on the couch while he'd taken up residence in the chair. "You got to babysit me, huh?"

He shrugged. He'd shown up ten minutes before in a pair of sweats and a loose T-shirt. His hair was wet, hanging loose and he wasn't even wearing shoes. "Snow was called to Homeland since they needed extra help. You are familiar with me and Timber asked me to sit with you. He wanted someone here that you've spent some time with."

"You were off duty."

He shrugged again. "I don't mind. I'd eaten and showered. I was bored anyway. How is your throat?"

"It's better. I put some ice on it." She shifted her position. "You don't really need to sit with me."

"The human is still at large and we'll feel better if someone is with you."

"You're not even wearing shoes."

He grinned. "A lot of us hate to wear them but we're required to on shift. I'm off."

The silence was a little uncomfortable. Zandy wasn't sure what else to say. Smiley sniffed and smiled.

"What?"

"Your scent is changing."

"What does that mean?"

He hesitated. "You will be ovulating soon."

"What?" She gaped at his out-of-left-field statement.

"You are about to go into heat, Zandy."

Her mouth opened but no words came out.

"Our females try to hide the scent from our males. It's arousing."

"Ovulating? You can smell that? Really?"

"Yes."

"Bitchin'," she muttered sarcastically. "How the hell does Richard find this amusing?"

"I don't understand. Richard warned you already that your heat was coming?"

"Never mind. So, did you enjoy the weather today?" She decided to change the subject quickly.

"It was a nice day. Thank you for asking." His gaze narrowed as he watched her. "Your cheeks are pinker. Is this an uncomfortable conversation for you? Going into heat is perfectly natural."

He wasn't going to let it drop. "Women don't go into heat. And yes, this isn't a topic I want to discuss."

"Females do experience heat. There is nothing to be embarrassed about. My nose doesn't lie and you are going into heat. You should speak to one of our females about how to hide it from our males before you fully hit that stage. It's very faint now but every male will scent it when it grows stronger. They will offer to share sex."

"Why?" She was stunned and curious.

"Nothing smells better or tastes better than a female in heat." His gaze roamed her body. "May I ask you questions that might make your cheeks pinken more? It is attractive."

"Um, I guess. What do you want to know?"

"Our females strongly desire to share sex while they are in heat. Don't humans react that way?"

"No. We don't even know when we're ovulating."

He frowned. "Really?"

"Obviously. You're telling me something I didn't know. I had no clue."

"Don't you feel an increase in your sex drive?"

She had since she'd met Tiger but he was hot. "No," she lied.

He leaned back in the chair and his fingers tapped the arms. "Shared sex between us would be good, Zandy. I can be gentle. Are you sure you aren't interested? Have you had time to think about it?"

Her eyes widened. "Thanks, but no."

"You want Tiger." His fingers stopped tapping. "He will never be open to taking a mate. You're a single female. Don't you want a mate?"

She was starting to feel uncomfortable. "Look, Smiley. You're an attractive man but I'm not interested in you. I'm flattered but it's a firm no."

"You were aroused by Tiger. You are also human. Our females don't enjoy bonding with males but I've been told yours do. He rarely shares sex with the same female more than twice a year. I haven't heard about him ever touching a human one. You have needs he is never going to meet."

"Just because I'm attracted to someone doesn't mean I want to have sex with just anyone."

He smiled. "I will never understand human females."

"It's not just you. All men don't understand us."

"I have something in common with your males then after all."

"I guess so." She stood. "You can go home. I don't need a babysitter and it's late. I'm going to try to get some sleep."

He didn't budge. "Are you sure you don't want company in your bed? I'm skilled with sex. You've had a trauma and shouldn't be alone. I could distract you."

The guy was persistent. "I'm very sure."

"I'll stay here until the male is caught. That's what I was ordered to do. I won't bother you." His gaze roamed down her body. "I would never go where I wasn't wanted. Have no worry that I'll enter your room. Rest well, Zandy."

"Thank you."

She fled and closed the door between them. She wasn't worried he'd come after her. Her gaze drifted to her bed. New bedding had replaced the old ones. One of the officers had made the bed for her.

Tiger wasn't coming. That was obvious. Disappointment gripped her and she changed out of the heavy sweatpants into a pair of thin shorts. The window had been boarded shut and someone had turned up the heat too much to compensate for how chilled the room had grown after the window was smashed.

A yawn broke from her as she stretched out on top of the comforter. It had been a long, traumatic day. She'd been attacked at the gates and then again on Reservation. The day couldn't end soon enough. Smiley was in the living room and she knew no one would get past him. She was safe.

* * * * *

Tiger jogged to the left of the trees while Vengeance dodged to the right. The human had taken to the forest and they'd had to leave the Jeep behind. The human had made a mistake since his scent was easier to follow with the thick vegetation blocking the wind. Tiger crouched, sniffed the air and knew he was close to finding his target. The scent was strong and the prey was terrified. He'd made it almost two miles but it wouldn't be far enough to escape. The human had slowed from exhaustion and his weakness was sure to get him caught.

Tiger ran, following the scent. He saw something ahead and sprinted quickly for it. His eyesight was good at night. It was a gift of his altered DNA. He was grateful for it tonight.

The human was limping. Tiger smelled Vengeance coming from the other side to trap their prey between them. This was the male who'd touched Zandy. He silently slowed before leaping to land next to his target.

The human gasped and fell back on his ass. Tiger roared. The male screamed in response. The stench of terror intensified — a bittersweet smell. The urge to tear the son of a bitch apart was strong but instead Tiger reached down, fisted the male by his shirt and yanked him to his feet. He was big for a human male.

"Why did you attack the female and trespass into her quarters?"

The smell of urine was strong. The human had wet himself. Vengeance laughed. Tiger waited for the human to respond.

"We thought she was Jessie North," he sobbed.

Tiger growled. "She is not."

"I know. I saw her driver's license."

The man's front pocket started to beep. Tiger tore the material open, grabbed the cell phone and looked at the caller ID. He growled and turned it to face the male he held. "Who is this?"

"One of the guys. He said he's going to meet me over the wall to get me the fuck out of here."

Vengeance growled. "You will not be meeting him. I'm hungry, Tiger. How about you? I say we chow down on this son of a bitch."

The human moaned in horror, almost causing Tiger to smile. Vengeance was good at terrorizing the stupid ones. He believed they'd eat him now. If the male had a brain, he'd know they didn't eat people and, even if they did, they sure as hell wouldn't want something that reeked of body odor and piss.

"What did you want with Jessie North?"

Tiger snarled when the male refused to answer. He knew it was just the thing to do when whimpering sounds came from the human.

"I was ordered to kill her. Okay? I was told to slice her damn throat. She's betraying mankind by sleeping with one of you animals. It's just not right."

"Why did you attack the human female in her bed?"

"She is living with you assholes too. All bitches deserve to die if they let one of you screw them."

In a fit of rage, Tiger threw the son of a bitch. The male's back hit a tree hard. He groaned as he fell to the ground and kept whimpering in pain. Tiger had the urge to kill him but Vengeance's presence prevented him from doing it.

"I am about to lose my temper and we need him alive. Will you haul his ass to the Jeep, Ven? I'm going to make a call. We need to interrogate him and see who he's working with so we can round up the stupid bastards."

Vengeance nodded. "I think I will dunk him a few times in the river first. I don't want to smell him while we take him in."

"Good idea." Tiger lowered his voice. "Make sure you don't drown him but I won't mind if he thinks you might."

Vengeance chuckled and hauled the human male to his feet. "Let's go, piss pants. The river is calling your name."

The human screamed. The sound was high pitched and Tiger cringed. He heard Vengeance snarl in response.

Tiger opened his phone and dialed Security. "We have the human male. Check all the walls. He said someone would meet him for pickup. Locate and grab them. I have his phone." Tiger flipped it open. "He made two calls since the attack, to two different numbers. Get ready to trace them. I want all these bastards caught. They thought the human female was Justice's mate. He was here to kill her. Call Homeland and have them tighten security around Justice and Jessie." He hung up.

Tiger had ordered Zandy to stay at Reservation, thinking she'd be safer behind their walls. Instead she'd been attacked for living on Reservation and being human. He stomped to his Jeep to wait. He glanced up at the sky, wishing he were in bed with Zandy. He wanted to see her to make sure she was really fine. He turned when he heard Vengeance and the frightened, wet human male coming from the woods.

"He's clean." Vengeance chuckled.

"He tried to kill me," the human male sputtered.

Tiger grinned. "Shut up or I will ask him to keep trying until he succeeds."

The drive back to Security was a short one. Tiger sped. He dropped off the human to be interrogated. Usually he'd do it himself but he wanted to see Zandy. He needed to see her. He tossed his keys at Vengeance.

"Take the Jeep home and stop being an asshole. I have better things to do with my time right now than deal with your temper tantrums. Patrol Wild Zone if you want to do something. Bring them in alive if you find humans."

Vengeance nodded. "I will patrol."

"Good."

Tiger took off, jogging toward Zandy's building. He needed the time to calm before he faced her. He didn't want to frighten her and he was still suffering from bloodlust. He felt much calmer when he knocked on her front door. He hated finding it locked to keep him out. Smiley answered the door.

Smiley frowned. "She is sleeping. I assume you wish to ask her questions. It should wait until morning. She's told us everything she knows."

Irritation rose quickly at being told what to do by the other male. "You're relieved. I'll stay here until she wakes."

Smiley hesitated. "She is attracted to you physically. I smell it on her when you are near. I like her a lot, Tiger. I would like to talk her into dating me. I can't tell you who to share sex with but please keep it in mind if you scent arousal on her. I don't want another obstacle in my way if she doesn't enjoy the outcome of you touching her when it wouldn't mean anything to you."

Tiger was instantly enraged. "Leave," he growled.

Smiley knew he'd gone too far. He lowered his gaze before he inched past Tiger's rigid frame. Tiger wanted to slam the door but he closed it quietly, locking it. The male had openly just admitted to wanting Zandy but he wasn't going to have her. He spun on his heel, walked to the bedroom door and eased it open.

The bedroom was dark with only a narrow beam of light coming from her bathroom. Zandy was sprawled on her stomach on the top of the covers. The scents of other males masked a lot of hers. It drove him a little crazy, knowing how close she'd come to dying and that he hadn't been there to protect her. Others had come to her rescue.

The loose shorts showed off her bare legs and one side had slid up to reveal one rounded ass cheek. She wasn't wearing underwear and the baggy shirt rode up to reveal inches of her spine. The thought of Smiley seeing so much of her made him want to track the male and punch him in the face.

A soft growl refused to be denied but she didn't stir. He reached down and unfastened his pants. His cock flared to life. The desire to touch her and have her under him made him quickly strip. He breathed in the mixed scents in the room and wanted her immersed in his. He knew he was being irrational, she wasn't his, but he couldn't help it.

His dick hurt from wanting her so much as he put his knee on the bed and crawled up until he crouched over her. Another growl ripped from his throat when he picked up a faint scent coming from her. His heart raced. Zandy was going into heat. Whatever control he had left slipped away.

Chapter Eleven

ॐ

A deep, scary growl roused Zandy from a dead sleep and she jerked when she was flipped over. Her mouth opened to scream but one word stopped her terror.

"Zandy."

Tiger was on his hands and knees next to her. His hair was down and he was naked. The room was dark but not pitch black. She'd left the bathroom light on and the door cracked so just enough light enabled her to see him. He shifted, gripped her thighs and parted them.

His hands gripped the waist of her shorts next and the material ripped. It shocked her that he'd so easily destroyed them. A quick tug to get them out from under her and he tossed them to the floor. Her eyes widened as she watched him lower his face until his hot breath was on her lower stomach. One hand fisted her shirt, shoving it up until he'd bared her breasts. His hot mouth kissed her ribs.

"Tiger? What are— Oh!"

He nipped her with his teeth. It didn't hurt but a jolt shot through her from his sharp canines. His hand released her shirt to cup her between her legs. His fingers teased the seam of her pussy before one of them pressed down on her clit.

Her hands rose to grip his shoulders as his hot mouth trailed kisses over her bare breast until he sucked the nipple inside his mouth. He wasn't gentle as he suckled her. Passion hit hard and fast.

"Yes," she moaned as she spread her thighs wider to encourage him to keep touching her.

His finger slid from her clit to the opening of her pussy. He entered her with the thick digit slowly and finger-fucked her. Her hips moved, unable to stay still. Her fingernails dug into his shoulders and he tore his mouth away from her.

"You're wet for me already." His voice came out gruff and super sexy. His finger slowly withdrew from her body.

"Don't stop."

"Muffle your sounds, Zandy."

She wasn't sure what he meant by that because she hadn't thought she was being loud. She didn't get a chance to ask though as he gripped her hips, rolled her over and jerked her ass up in the air until she was on her knees. Suddenly he was behind her and his cock entered her slowly.

She moaned and clawed the bedding. His hold on her hips kept her in place and he adjusted his legs to the outside of hers, pinning her there as he drove his cock deep. He eased his hold on one hip, bent forward and one of his hands flattened next to one of hers to brace his body as he curled over her back. His mouth ended up next to her ear.

"I'm going to fuck you. I need you now. Grab the pillow and use it. There are officers outside."

The "muffle" comment suddenly made sense as she struggled to find the pillow somewhere above her head. She dragged it closer and Tiger almost withdrew from her body before his hips slammed hard against her ass. She dug her face into the pillow and cried out in pleasure at the feel of his thick shaft stretching her vaginal walls. He moved fast, fucked her hard enough that it nearly drove her flat, but his arm slid from her hip to encircle her waist as if he knew she was about to collapse.

All she could do was feel as he took her in a near frenzy. It felt so good it nearly hurt. His balls slapped against her clit and his ragged breathing matched her own. He adjusted his hips, took her at a new angle, and the crown of his cock hit a spot that made her moan louder.

The arm around her middle tightened and he growled. He kept fucking her until she lost it. The climax struck and she bit into the pillow to keep from crying out. Her body jerked under his and suddenly Tiger's mouth locked on her shoulder. Pain made her cry out as he bit down. Pleasure and agony mixed until she nearly passed out. His teeth released her as he ground his hips against her ass and, jerking violently, he came hard. She could feel his semen shooting deep inside her.

The only thing keeping her up was Tiger's strength. He stopped coming and just collapsed to his side, taking her with him. They were still joined and he held her tightly around her waist to make sure they stayed that way.

Her shoulder ached where he'd bitten her. He was breathing as heavily as she as both of them recovered. He lifted his head and put his lips next to her ear.

"Another male isn't to touch you, Zandy. Swear that to me. I'm the only one you share sex with."

His words stunned her.

He growled softly and his mouth nipped her shoulder. "Swear."

It didn't hurt but her oversensitive body jerked from the soft bite. "I swear."

His tongue licked the area he'd bitten. It was an odd sensation as he lapped at her skin. His cock inside her twitched and he slowly started to move, fucking her again. She moaned and turned her head against the bed. Her fingers found his arm around her waist and she clung to him.

He rolled onto his back and took her with him until she was sprawled on her back over him. His free hand cupped her mound and played with her clit while his hips drove his cock into her pussy. Zandy threw her arm over her face and used her wrist to muffle some of her moans.

She wasn't sure what had gotten into Tiger or why he'd made her swear he'd be the only man she was with but she didn't care at that moment. He felt so good inside her and massaging her clit that it was all that mattered. She wasn't sure what felt better. The way he'd taken her fast and furiously on her knees or the slow, languid way he fucked her now.

Sweat made her body slide on his by the time he'd made her come a second time and found his own release. They relaxed and panted. Zandy turned her head to rest her cheek against Tiger's chest, where she remained. Her fingers on his arm caressed him and her hand over her mouth dropped back over one of his shoulders.

"Drained," he rasped. "You take it all from me. I feel almost turned inside out."

She lifted her head to peer at him. His head was tipped back and she couldn't see his face. Disappointment struck over not being able to see his eyes. He seemed to read her mind as he lifted his head enough for their gazes to meet.

"What do I take from you?"

He blinked. "You make my seed come out so hard it nearly hurts."

"Oh." Her shoulder throbbed. "Are you all right?"

A smile played at his lips. "It's a good kind of ache right now."

His head fell back and his hand flattened on her lower belly, caressing her. "I bit you again."

"I felt it."

His body tensed under hers and she was too sluggish to protest when he rolled them onto their sides. His tongue licked at her shoulder again. His cock twitched against her vaginal walls where they were still connected and he slowly withdrew from her. His tongue kept lapping at her.

"Am I bleeding?"

He paused. "Yes."

She wasn't sure how to react. She knew he'd bitten her hard and he'd broken the skin. It wasn't the first time and she remembered what he'd told her. She'd have to hide the injury or someone would think he'd mated her. The other bite was healing quickly since it was just a few light scratches. The one he'd just done felt much worse, had hurt more, and she wondered how bad it was.

"I didn't mean to do it." He lowered his head to rest it against hers. "Did I hurt you?"

"A little but it isn't bad now."

"I got you far worse this time. It will leave a scar."

She hesitated. "Why did you bite me again?"

"I lost control."

"It's okay." It was done and she wasn't going to bitch about it.

"It isn't. Damn." He nuzzled her with his cheek against the side of her face. "Sometimes it's hard to be me."

"Why?"

He took a few slow, steady breaths before answering. "I'm a male but I'm more. I have instincts that sometimes rule my thoughts. I wanted to mark you. Smiley warned me away from you when I arrived here and stated his intentions to try to talk you into sharing sex with him. The idea of him touching you sent me into a rage."

"I'm not interested in anyone but you. Is that why you had me swear off other men?"

"Yes. I think I'd attack any male who touched you. I am trying to be honest. I don't want a mate but I feel things for you, Zandy. It confuses me and drives me a little insane. I'm not someone who should take a mate."

She could relate to that. The memories of two broken marriages haunted her. She'd tried to make her relationships work but they hadn't. The thought of opening herself up to another serious commitment was frightening. Tiger and she came from two different worlds, or so it seemed. His past was completely foreign to her and hers would be to him. Opposites attracted but long-term it probably wouldn't work.

The silence between them stretched. Zandy finally pulled herself away from her grim musings. "May I ask you something?"

"Anything."

"Smiley said something that worried me."

"Did he threaten you?" His voice turned scary.

"No. He said my scent is changing and that he thinks I'm going to ovulate. He said I should hide it from New Species men. Can you smell anything?"

"Yes. He's right."

"That's so weird. Will men really be attracted to me because of that?"

"Yes."

"I'm trying not to freak out that your sense of smell is that good. It makes me wonder about all the other little things you can pick up with your nose. I hope my deodorant is working well enough." She rubbed his arm as she babbled, knowing she was doing it but couldn't stop. "Good thing we don't have to worry about pregnancy. I hope it's not an offensive smell like body odor. Please tell me I don't stink." She inwardly winced at the thought.

He said nothing.

"Did you fall asleep on me?"

"No. I'm awake and you smell wonderful. It's an attractive scent. I wish I could stay the night but I can't. I have to leave soon."

"Oh." Disappointment hit. "I like sleeping with you."

"I like that too."

He lifted his head and she turned to peer into his eyes. "Do you have to leave right now?"

"Soon. I have to use your shower first. Otherwise the officers outside will smell you all over me the second I walk out the door."

Pain hit and her gaze darted away from his. "I guess that would be a bad thing if anyone found out we were sleeping together."

He gripped her jaw and she met his eyes again. He was frowning. "I am not ashamed of us or what we do. Is that what you think?"

"I'm not sure. You confuse me. You told me to tell other men it's you who turns me on if they smell that on me but now you're going to shower to hide that you were with me. That's a contradiction."

"I think we should figure out what is happening between us before we allow others to know we are seeing each other."

"You are the head of security and I work for the NSO. I guess that could make things complicated. You're not officially my boss, are you?"

"I don't believe so. That would be Slade. He's in charge of hiring human employees."

She took a deep breath. "I've had enough relationships fail to really want to avoid the pitying looks and personal questions if we stop seeing each other."

The image of Richard and Creek interrogating her over what was going on between her and Tiger was enough to be in full agreement that they should hide their relationship a little longer. Then there was her family.

She inwardly groaned. One more lecture from her mother about dating men who weren't right for her was the last thing she wanted to hear. The fact that Tiger was New Species was going to be a huge drawback in her family's opinion. It wasn't as if she could take him home to meet the family on holidays either. She was pretty certain they weren't allowed to leave the NSO compounds to take vacations.

"So, we're exclusive."

He stared at her. "What does that mean?"

"I swore I wouldn't see anyone else and I expect the same promise from you."

He smiled. "You're the only female I want."

Her eyebrow lifted. "You're a man."

"What does that mean?"

She hesitated. "We're exclusive, right?"

His expression turned serious. "I'm not human, Zandy."

"Is that man code for you expect me to be loyal to you but you won't make the same commitment?" Anger stirred. "That's bullshit."

"I won't be sharing sex with any other females. You have my word on that."

Zandy studied his eyes and saw honesty there. "Okay. Good. I'm not a doormat."

"You're sexy and beautiful." A chuckle escaped him. "I take it that's a human saying that means you won't allow me to step on your feelings?"

"Good guess."

"Hurting you is the last thing I want."

"Yeah. Me too. It sucks."

"Males have hurt you before."

"Married and divorced twice, remember?"

His hand massaged her lower belly. "They were idiots. They should have known how to treat you to make sure they never lost you."

She had nothing to say to that, unsure how to respond. Tiger could have her easily if he said he wanted something more serious between them. It scared her to leave herself open to possible heartbreak but she couldn't deny her strong feelings for him, which were deepening every moment they spent together.

"I need to get a little sleep. I have to be back at work in a few hours. We're still dealing with a lot of threats. The protesters have thinned but they will return first thing in the morning. They always do."

He lowered his mouth and brushed a tender kiss on her lips. Her arms wrapped around his neck and her fingers played with his hair. She loved to fist the soft strands. A low growl emitted from him as he deepened the kiss. He slowly pulled away, to her regret.

"Don't tempt me to stay, little one. I couldn't say no to you right now and I need to."

Temptation was a bitch, she decided, as she released him. She really wanted to seduce him into staying with her but he looked tired. He hadn't gotten to take a nap the way she had before he'd woken her. "Go shower. When will I see you again?"

"Tomorrow evening. I'll come back."

"Okay."

He cupped her cheek and stared deeply into her eyes. "I'll be thinking about you."

"Ditto."

He chuckled as he released her and rolled away. She watched him strut naked into her bathroom, appreciating his firm, gorgeous ass. The room darkened when he closed the door between them, blocking out the light. She turned onto her stomach and closed her eyes.

* * * * *

Tiger eased out of the bathroom and stood watching Zandy sleep. Her slow breathing assured him of that. He couldn't resist sitting on the edge of her bed for a little while. Her face was turned his way and he reached out to brush a strand of her hair away from her cheek.

It would be so easy to scoop her up, blankets and all, and just take her to his house. Of course he wasn't going there tonight. He'd bunk at Security on a cot. His gaze turned to the clock to learn it was well after midnight. He wanted to just curl up against her side and sleep, holding her in his arms.

It took every ounce of willpower to stand and get dressed. He left her bedroom quietly and exited the apartment. Two officers sat in a Jeep at the curb and both males stared at him. He made sure her door was locked before he avoided them by jogging off toward Security. He waved to the other officer he'd assigned to guard the back of the building after the breach. The exercise was always welcome when he had a lot on his mind.

He might not want a mate but the idea of losing Zandy to another male set him on edge. He was possessive of her and he'd marked her. The taste of her blood was something he'd never forget. Or her scent. He ran faster until he stressed his body to the point of exhaustion.

You can run but you can't escape the truth. You are obsessed with Zandy Gordon.

Leaving her bed had been beyond difficult. She was about to ovulate. The smell was undeniable. He'd have to make a decision quickly about what to do about that. She assumed he couldn't get her pregnant. He changed directions until he ended up at Medical. Someone was always on duty.

The elder Dr. Harris was dozing at a desk in the reception area when Tiger entered the building. The male jerked awake at the sound of the automatic doors and peered at him with confusion for a few seconds.

"What happened?"

"Relax. I am not injured."

The doctor located his glasses on the desk and put them on. "What time is it?"

"Late. I'm sorry to disturb you but I have questions."

"Okay." Harris waved to another chair. "Do you want to take a seat?"

"Sure." Tiger collapsed into one. "What I say is private."

"Of course."

"I'm sharing sex with a human."

The doctor appeared surprised. "I thought you avoided them. It's not exactly a secret how you feel about your friends mating those women."

"She is starting to ovulate. The scent is still faint but it's about to happen. Can she get pregnant right now?"

"How faint? Are you sure that's what you're smelling and not some soap she uses?"

Tiger lifted a finger to tap his nose. "It doesn't lie."

"Right. Okay. I will assume you just noticed the change in her scent. You're safe if that's the case but I would use condoms from now on. You know you can't risk getting her pregnant unless you're willing to mate her. I can get you some condoms if you don't have any. Your supply store closes early and you'd be surprised how many of your men have recently asked for them. We started keeping some on hand."

"She's never asked me to use one so I assumed she is either taking something or has heard we're unable to conceive children."

"She's not on anything if she's ovulating strong enough for you to smell it and you'd definitely know if she were using a method that involved something with spermicide."

Tiger's eyebrows arched.

The doctor chuckled. "It's someone else's private story but I'll just say you can smell and taste it. Not a good experience from what I was told."

"It doesn't sound good. Thank you for talking to me." He rose to leave.

"Tiger?"

He paused by the door and turned to stare at the doctor. "What?"

"Do you want to talk about this?"

His eyebrow arched.

"The woman. You. The fact that she's human."

"I'm not looking for a mate."

"So it's just a casual affair?"

"Nothing about her is casual."

Surprise widened the doctor's eyes. "You're feeling things for her then?"

"Yes."

"That's a good thing."

"I'm not so sure." Tiger sighed. "I don't want to grow dependent on anyone."

Sympathy showed in the older male's face. "I understand but could I give you a little advice?"

Tiger nodded.

"I fell in love with a woman once but I put my career first. I was in med school and I let her slip through my fingers. That was forty-eight years ago. To this day I regret it. I married someone else but it wasn't the same. That relationship didn't last more than a few years. I got a wonderful son out of the deal but his mother and I never really loved each other. Don't let this one get away if you love her."

"Why didn't you go after this female if you still have strong feelings for her?"

The doctor sighed. "She married my best friend after I dumped her. He could appreciate what I couldn't. They are happy but it's a knife to my heart every time I see them together. Get your priorities straight, son. I know you have issues after the life you've been handed but it's better to face your fears than live with regret. Trust an old man on this one."

"Son?"

The doctor smiled. "I think of all of you as my kids. It happens when you reach my age. You have a life now. Live it. Make every moment count."

"Thank you." Tiger left knowing he had to make a decision. He either needed to break it off with Zandy for good or fully commit to her.

Chapter Twelve

ൈ

Richard shook his head. "I can't believe you were attacked at Reservation. It's so safe here. Did they figure out how the douche bag got in?"

Zandy shrugged. "I'm not sure how the guy breached the walls but they caught him." She'd heard that from her security detail when they'd escorted her to work. She'd completely forgotten to ask Tiger about it the night before. "They are having a lot of problems with the protesters."

"And the reporters." Richard made a face. "You should have seen all the news vans lined up along the front gates this morning. It's insane. Someone reported that Justice North and his wife might be here so they are everywhere, hoping for a sighting."

"I didn't know he was here."

"He isn't," Smiley announced as he entered their office. "We had a helicopter fly in from Homeland and they incorrectly assumed it could be Justice and his mate." He glanced at them both. "Are you ready to be escorted to lunch?"

Zandy rose from her desk and put on her shoes. "I'm starving."

Smiley sniffed loudly at her as she approached and it caused her to frown.

"Stop doing that."

"The scent is growing stronger. Perhaps you shouldn't go to lunch. I can take Richard and bring your meal back."

"What scent?" Richard glanced between their escort and her.

"Zandy is beginning to ovulate."

"Uh-oh." Richard backed away and used his fingers to make a cross. "It's that time of the month, huh? You should have warned me. I would have brought chocolates to toss your way when you hit the worst of the PMS stage. It does my wife wonders."

"Ovulation. Not menstruation," Smiley scoffed. "How is it that I know more about females than you do when you have a mate?"

A blush heated Richard's cheeks. "Oh." He suddenly grinned. "That's good news. The other monthly visitor scares me."

She shook her head. "Nice. Can we drop this subject? I'm starving and I want to go to lunch."

Smiley opened the door before she reached it. He inhaled deeply and softly growled. "You do smell good."

"Stop saying that."

"Do I see a hint of romance between the two of you?"

"Shut up, Richard. No." She gave Smiley a pointed look. "Behave."

"I am trying," Smiley said to Richard, grinning. "So far she keeps turning me down."

"Smiley is a nice guy," Richard vouched. "You should date him."

"I'm seeing someone, remember? I'm also starving so let it drop. My personal life isn't a topic I want to discuss."

They drove to the cafeteria but Smiley paused by the door. "Your scent really is growing stronger. Tomorrow you need to do something about it or I'll have to bring you lunch at the office for a few days. The males will begin to notice and pick it up. I suggest you don't get too close to them."

Richard chuckled. "No offense but I'm glad I can't smell you."

"You're missing out." Smiley's gaze traveled slowly down Zandy's body in a clearly sensual way. "She smells good enough to eat."

Heat warmed her cheeks. "Slade North told me to be blunt so here goes, Smiley. You're a good-looking man but I'm never going to be interested in you. It's starting to get on my nerves."

He gave a sharp nod of his head. "I understand. I will not state my desire for you again."

She smiled at him. "It's nothing personal. You're a great guy. Very hunky. Please don't be offended."

"I understand. You are aroused by another."

"Let's not go there," she said quickly. "It's…well, that's private. Being aroused by someone shouldn't be discussed or shared. It's a human thing. We can't tell that about each other and it's a good thing."

Smiley's gaze slid to Richard. "I understand."

Richard gasped. "I arouse you? Really? Wow, I'm flattered."

Zandy snorted. "It's not you so don't even go there. I want this dropped now. Enough." She glanced at Smiley. "And you need to stop sniffing at me and making comments about my body."

He sighed. "Fine. I won't bring up the subject again but you're banned from coming here after today for a few days. Your scent will draw the attention of males."

"Okay. I'll take your word on that. Can we eat now?"

He nodded and waved his arm for her to precede him. "Just try to keep at least five feet of space between you and males today."

"I'll try my best."

It quickly became apparent that there was a problem when they joined the line for the buffet. New Species turned in line to stare at her. She caught interested stares from more of them at nearby tables. One of the males walked right up to her with a serious expression.

"I'm Ascend. Would you like to eat lunch with me?"

She gawked a little at the big, handsome male officer wearing an NSO uniform before her brain began to function again. "No thank you."

He spun away to return to his table. Smiley stepped closer to her until they were almost touching. "It's stronger than I thought. I'm primate and my sense of smell isn't as good as the canines or the felines. I'm going to stay with you today while you eat until we leave. It will dissuade most of them from approaching you again."

Zandy was stunned by the amount of male attention she drew. She couldn't glance anywhere in her vicinity without meeting men's intense stares. Her cheeks warmed, knowing the reason for their sudden fascination with her. She didn't complain about Smiley being nearly glued to her side.

"Shit," Richard whispered. "Is it just me or are we being stared at?"

"She is drawing attention," Smiley sighed.

A chair scraped loudly on the floor and Zandy turned her head to see the source of the noise. Tiger stood up across the room and came at them quickly. The tense expression on his face made him appear angry. He stormed right up to them and glared at her escort.

"Back off from her. You're too close. I assigned you to escort her, not rub against her body."

Smiley took a big step back. "She is beginning her ovulation cycle. The canine and feline males are picking it up stronger than I did. I thought I'd stick very close to her to dissuade other males from approaching to ask her to share sex with them."

Richard chuckled and Zandy shot him a murderous glare for being amused. It wasn't funny to her. It was embarrassing, bordering on humiliating to have her body functions discussed so openly.

Tiger's gaze held hers when he stepped closer. His beautiful eyes narrowed as he sniffed. "You should go to your apartment now. I'll have lunch sent to you. Take a few days off until your cycle passes."

"It's fine. I'm going to have lunch and go back to work."

Tiger bent a little until he was almost nose to nose with her. "You should go back to your apartment. Any male who comes in close contact with you will notice your scent. It's only going to grow stronger until the entire room can smell you."

"Richard can't and he's the only one I work with. Can we drop this? I'm here and I'm starving. I missed breakfast. I'll eat lunch in the office for a few days, starting tomorrow."

He straightened to his full height and his anger showed in his glare. "Fine. Don't listen to me. More males will approach you." He spun on his heel and stomped away.

Zandy watched him go. She wasn't sure why he was so pissed but it upset her that he was. Richard whistled softly under his breath.

"Not good when the head of security gives you an order and you refuse. That's what it amounted to." He glanced at her. "You're brave. He scares the shit out of me."

"He's worried about her security," Smiley intervened. "That wasn't an order or he would have made sure she left. It was more of a suggestion that she leave. It will be fine. I'm eating with you both today and my presence will tell the other males that she already has a male ready to tend her sexual needs."

"Needs?" Richard's face twisted into a grin as he laughed. "Oh boy. I can't wait to tell my wife about this."

"You suck." Zandy sighed. "This isn't amusing." She ignored the stares and the sniffs she heard from the men around her. It was a relief when she carried a tray of food to the table and Creek was already seated there. "Hi."

The tall woman sniffed the air. "You are about to go into heat."

Zandy sat down hard and put her tray in front of her. "I've heard."

"There are ways you can disguise it. You'll need to or the males will grow aggressive in trying to gain your attention and impress you in hopes of you wanting to share sex with them."

"How does she do that?" Richard had a look of pure glee on his face.

Zandy wanted to toss a grape at him and only resisted for a second. It hit his chest and he chuckled.

"Good shot."

"It's not funny."

Creek leaned in to speak softly. "You need to get perfume and spray it on a panty liner. You have to buy it in town though. Do you know what one of those is?"

Her humiliation was complete as Richard chuckled again.

"Yes."

"Use baby wipes to clean that area hourly and change your panty liners at the same time. It will hide the scent of you being in heat from the males. It's what our females do who wish to continue working during that time. Otherwise males would follow them around and pick fights."

"Fights?"

Creek nodded. "Our males get really aroused and aggressive if you're in heat and they smell it. We've had males fight amongst themselves to show who would be the strongest to try to win our interest in letting him mount us. When you are in heat they will actually follow you around. It makes them very aroused."

Smiley nodded his agreement. "Very aroused."

"Wow. See what kind of interesting things you can learn?" Richard winked.

She sighed, staring back at him. "Can you bring me some perfume? I'm not supposed to leave Reservation after being mistaken for Justice North's mate and I can't shop for it here."

"Sure. Not a problem. My wife has a ton of the stuff. I can bring it to you in the morning."

"Thanks."

A big male paused by their table and drew their attention. His dark eyes locked on Zandy for long seconds before he took a seat at the next table. Clearly, he sat there so he could watch her while he ate. More men came to sit at the same table. All of them watched her. It made her super self-conscious as she tried to eat her lunch.

"Maybe you should leave now," Creek whispered. "The scent is growing stronger. I believe you're about to hit your full-heat cycle. The tables near us are usually empty but they are quickly filling."

"Holy shit," Richard muttered. "You're like a porn star or something by the looks of it." He flashed her a grin. "Look at all those adoring fans you've got."

"Sometimes I wonder why your wife allows you to live."

He laughed. "She thinks I'm cute."

Zandy lost her appetite as even more men sat at the tables and she knew they were staring at her. She stood. "I think I should leave."

Smiley rose to his feet. "Good idea."

Creek and Richard followed them out of the cafeteria and through the hotel to the front door. Zandy almost collided with a tall, bald New Species guy who was rushing inside as she tried to leave. His big bulk missed her by inches. He snarled. A mean look showed on his face and cold blue eyes met hers for a second. He stepped around her and she kept going until a hand gripped her arm to jerk her to a halt. Her head twisted to see it was the same bald guy who had her.

"You're in heat." His voice came out super gruff. He pulled hard on her arm until it caused her to slam into his body. One arm kept hold of her while the other wrapped around her waist. He sniffed and yanked her off her feet.

"Let me go!" Fear gripped Zandy instantly when the man stormed back outside. He carried her easily. She didn't know where he was taking her but knew it didn't bode well for her. "Put me down!"

He sniffed at her and kept walking. "No mate and I smell no male. Mine!"

"Vengeance!" Smiley snarled. "Release that female."

The big New Species who held her spun fast enough to make Zandy dizzy. "No!" The bald Species snarled louder than Smiley had, showed some sharp teeth and spun back around to carry her away from the building. "Get your own. This one is mine."

Something hit the man in the back and he stumbled. Another snarl came from him and he dropped Zandy gently to her feet, let go of her and turned to face Smiley. "She's mine!"

"She isn't." Smiley tried to reach her but the bald Species shoved him.

"Get your own. I found her and I'm keeping her."

Creek pulled Zandy back until her body was between her and the bald man. Richard came to stand near them, watching the confrontation go down. Smiley was in great shape, tall, but the bald New Species was thicker chested and had beefier arms.

"She's human," Smiley tried to explain. "She's not Species. She's not really in heat. It's just ovulation to her. She doesn't need a male, Vengeance."

"You lie and want her yourself." Vengeance snarled. "Mine."

"Shit." Smiley cursed. "You can't take her."

Zandy was horrified as her escort was grabbed and tossed about six feet in the air to land on the grass. Creek growled and shook her head at the man who stomped closer.

"No, Vengeance. She's not for you."

"Move, female."

Creek snarled and tried to push him back. It happened fast as Vengeance spun Creek and carefully put her on her ass behind him. Richard lunged to put his body between Zandy and the advancing New Species but he didn't stand a chance. Vengeance just shot his palm out flat and hit her coworker in the chest. It knocked Richard about four feet back until he landed hard on his ass.

"Mine. I won't harm you. Don't fear me." The bald man advanced at Zandy.

Someone landed between them. Tiger leaped between them and crouched just inches in front of her. She was shocked at how he'd gotten there. She'd never seen anything like it and the snarl he let loose in warning was terrifying.

"Don't, Vengeance."

"Mine!" The bald Species snarled back and flashed his sharp teeth.

Tiger's voice came out harsh. "Don't do it, Vengeance. We'll fight to the death. You aren't taking her."

Tiger reached back and gently pushed Zandy, nudging her belly. She backed up, her heart pounding, wondering if they were really going to fight.

"She's not mated and smells of no other male."

"Damn it, Vengeance. Go. Now. I will kill you if you leave me no choice."

"Mine," the bald Species snarled as he tried to get around Tiger to reach Zandy. Tiger tackled him. Both of them landed hard on the ground and the fight was brutal as fists were exchanged.

"Stop it!" Zandy frantically looked for help. More officers rushed out of the hotel and a few of them approached but stayed back from the two men on the ground. Creek stood and rushed to Zandy's side.

"See? They fight for you to show you who is more dominant. Which one do you hope will win? That is so sexy, isn't it?"

Zandy's mouth fell open in stunned disbelief. "Damn it, stop them! I don't want them to fight and it's horrible."

Creek snapped her head around to stare at a few of the other New Species. "Stop them, officers. You heard her. She isn't impressed."

The sight of Tiger and Vengeance fighting was vicious. They punched hard, rolled on the ground trying to pin each other and the sounds they made were animalistic. One of the officers tried to break it up but Tiger kicked out at him, making him jump out of the way.

Jeeps rushed to the scene and locked up their brakes as more uniformed officers arrived. Zandy hoped they'd break up the fight but they just stood there watching. She bit her lip and frantically grabbed Creek.

"Stop them. Please?"

The Species female sighed. "Okay. This is normal though. Males fight and you should be impressed by it." She lifted her hand and signaled to the new arrivals. She made a fist with her hand before opening her fingers and bringing them down flat in the air.

One of the males grimly nodded. A few second later he and his partner lunged at Vengeance when Tiger threw him off his body. They grabbed his arms behind his back and a third officer planted his big body between him and Tiger.

"Enough, Tiger."

Tiger rose to his feet and snarled but he didn't attack. He was breathing hard and had a cut on his cheek. His shirt was torn from the fight and the officer he faced looked foreboding as they watched each other.

"We have him. We'll return him to the Wild Zone."

"Thanks, Flame."

The redhead sniffed the air, his gaze drifted to Zandy and he sighed before addressing Tiger again. "You should talk to her. She's obviously new."

"I've got her."

Flame jerked his head in understanding and spun. "Let's take Vengeance home."

The two officers holding Vengeance had handcuffed his hands behind his back and lifted him into the back of the Jeep. Vengeance snarled and a shiver ran down Zandy's spine as a pair of cold blue eyes fixed on her. The redheaded officer drove away with their staring prisoner. She bit her lip and released Creek to rush to Tiger's side. He was holding his face where it was cut.

"Let me see how bad it is."

He turned on her and snarled, pure rage in his expression. "I told you to you go to your apartment." His other hand shot out and gripped her arm. "I'll take you there myself. This is what happens when you don't listen to me."

She was shocked at his rage and the way he practically dragged her to a Jeep. He didn't hurt her but he was abrupt as he steered her into the passenger seat, stomped around the front of the Jeep and climbed into the driver's seat.

The engine started and he snarled at Smiley who approached.

"You're done escorting Zandy. Take Richard back to work. You didn't protect her."

Smiley looked shocked and his mouth opened to defend himself from the verbal attack but Tiger punched the gas. The Jeep shot forward and Zandy grabbed hold of the seat and the bar in front of her since the things didn't have doors.

Tiger refused to even glance her way as he drove quickly back to her building. One hand stayed on the wheel while the other kept hold of his bleeding cheek. Hot tears filled Zandy's eyes. He'd gotten hurt protecting her and he obviously blamed her. She couldn't have guessed some crazy, bald New Species would attack her.

He finally spoke. "I told you to leave the cafeteria but you refused. You don't know us or what we are capable of. You aren't in your world." He growled the words and each one of them hurt her feelings. "You aren't to leave here until you're out of heat. I won't be fighting other males again to keep them from showing you just how unlike human males we are."

He stopped the Jeep in front of the apartment building and Zandy didn't wait for him to turn off the engine. She jumped out and quickly walked toward her door. Two New Species were standing on the sidewalk and they parted to allow her to pass. She didn't glance at either of them as she hurried toward her door.

"Zandy? Where are you going? We're not done talking," Tiger snarled.

She kept going and blinked furiously to hold back her tears. The front door wasn't locked—no need for it since officers were stationed outside the building at all times. The door closed firmly behind her and she spun, twisting the locks. Seconds later Tiger tried to open the door.

"Zandy? Open up."

The tears fell. She had been terrified when Vengeance had come after her. Tiger blamed her but it wasn't her fault some of them were freaky about ovulating women.

"Fuck you, Tiger. Go teach your men some control. It's not my fault what happened."

The door shook when he tried to jerk it open. "Zandy? Open this door."

"Did you hear me? Fuck off." She wiped at her tears. "How dare you yell at me for being a victim? Screw yourself." She turned her back on the door and rushed into the bedroom.

He punched the door and she winced from the sound. He didn't kick it down though, something she was pretty sure he could have done. It hurt that he'd blamed her. He was wrong

185

for that and she wasn't going to take that bullshit from anyone. Even him.

* * * * *

Tiger was furious as he listened and heard the sound of water inside the apartment. Zandy had turned on her shower to avoid hearing him knocking. He lowered his hand and turned to face the two males watching him. He glared.

One of them hesitated. "Is everything all right, Tiger? We smell that you have been in a fight with Vengeance and you are very angry with the little female."

Tiger gritted his teeth. "She started her heat cycle and wouldn't leave the damn cafeteria. I had to fight off Vengeance so he didn't tear her clothes off and force himself on her. I'm pissed."

"I smelled her fear," Torrent admitted softly. "It was strong and she had tears in her eyes."

Tiger suddenly felt like shit. He'd been so angry he hadn't noticed her fear or her tears. He'd been oblivious in his rage. If he hadn't been there Zandy could have gotten hurt. He was ready to kill Vengeance. The damn male was out of control.

"We'll make sure she's safe," Tree promised. "We're trained well about human females. They don't understand how some of our wilder males will react to something they don't give a second thought about. I'm sure she didn't mean to start trouble."

Tiger nodded. "I'm going to go have a chat with Vengeance."

Tiger spun away and went to his Jeep. He wanted to kick some ass and he knew a male who would be damn sorry for attacking Zandy. He grew angrier every mile he drove until he reached his target's home. He turned off the engine and climbed out.

"Vengeance!" Tiger tore at his shirt, kicking his shoes off as he neared the house. The door was unlocked and he barreled inside. The male he sought sat in a chair facing him. "Get up. Go outside. We're going to fight."

Ven slowly rose to his feet. "I expected you."

"I'm sure you did." Tiger backed out of the house. "You touched Zandy."

The canine lumbered outside, limping from their earlier fight. Tiger rolled his shoulders as he stopped some distance from the house. He expected Vengeance to come at him but the male just hung his head while he kept his arms loose at his sides.

"Fight me."

Vengeance's chin lifted and he grimly met Tiger's glare. "I won't hit back. I know what I did was wrong. Punish me." He put his hands behind his back and locked them there.

"Why did you do it if you knew it was wrong?" Tiger's temper nearly boiled over but he managed not to lunge forward to attack.

"You never had a mate." Tears welled up in the other male's eyes. "I miss her so deeply."

Tiger's fists unclenched. It was hard to feel rage in the face of such raw pain.

"I am empty inside. I don't sleep well. I force myself to eat and live. Some days I wish I'd died with her. I fought for so many years to survive. You know how strong our will to live is. I lost that when she was killed."

Hot tears slid down Vengeance's face and the shock of seeing a Species male cry left Tiger speechless.

"She had feelings for me. She would play with my hair and comb it with her fingers." He reached up to touch his bald head. "It's why I refuse to allow it to grow back. It reminds me of her. Some nights I howl from my grief. I run until my legs give way and I wait for winter to come. Maybe I will fall in the snow from exhaustion and the cold will keep me from waking. Do you think there really is a heaven? Do you think she's waiting there for me? Will she be angry that I didn't die right after she did? Sometimes I dream that she is mad at me for surviving when she didn't."

Emotion made Tiger's chest hurt as he breathed. "Ven…"

The male lowered his gaze to the ground. "Our females aren't interested in taking a mate. They resist any form of attachment now that they have been freed. Mercile gave me a female to see if mated couples could produce children but I grew to have deep feelings for her. It makes it worse when I've shared sex with a few of our females. They don't touch me the way my mate did or allow me to hold them while I sleep. The human females seem so fragile that they should have a mate. I'd take such good care of one." He wiped at his tears and met Tiger's gaze. "I don't mean to frighten them. I just want a mate again so bad. I think Species females would fight to the death to avoid being with one male now that they have choices but a human one accepts it. I keep thinking if I could just claim one that I'd have the time to show her how I'd never hurt her and that I would do anything for her. She would be here to get to know me."

"Damn it, Ven, you're breaking my heart. I came here to bust your head. You can't keep going after human females."

"I know. I see them though and something inside me just reacts before I can think it through. I'm so lonely and I would be an excellent mate." His shoulders straightened. "I have no one."

Tiger stalked closer and touched his arm. "You can't just carry one off. It would be cool if it was that easy but it's not."

"I'm skilled at sharing sex and I have learned how to cook. I'm an excellent fighter. I would keep her warm in my arms and die to protect her."

"I'm sure you would."

"I've been learning more about their culture with the television. I know if I am ever to have another mate she is going to have to be a human. That's how much I want one. They used to be the enemy but it doesn't matter. I can't stand being alone anymore. Mercile made me dependent on my mate and she had feelings for me. I just want that again."

"Learn that they need more from a male than just being stolen and claimed. That's why you scare them. It's barbaric to toss her over your shoulder and run off."

"They believe I would hurt their bodies by forcing shared sex. I would make her want me first."

"You can't make them do anything."

Vengeance's eyes narrowed. "I am very skilled with sex. My mate taught me well."

A smile curved Tiger's mouth. "Seducing a female and making her love you aren't always the same."

"They should be."

"Life isn't that simple."

"I'm lost in this world."

"We all are but we have each other. Stop charging after human females, Ven. You said you're learning about their culture? Learn that. I'd suggest coming at them gently and talking to them. Allow them to get to know you first before you try to convince them to go home with you."

"She isn't with a male. I thought she might want one."

"Yes. She is." Tiger's voice deepened. "She's mine."

"Your scent isn't on her."

"My mark is."

"How did you lure her into being yours?"

Tiger released him. "It's a long story and I've made mistakes."

"So have I."

"Let's go inside and talk."

Vengeance turned. "You are lucky, Tiger. Mate her and know happiness."

Tiger wanted to curse. He'd really screwed up with Zandy. She'd locked him out of her apartment and refused to speak to him. He didn't know how to make it right.

Chapter Thirteen

ಐ

Zandy bit her lip and stared at the locked door, wishing there was a peephole. "Who is it?"

"It's Creek," a familiar female voice stated. "I brought you dinner."

Zandy quickly unlocked the door and opened it wide. The New Species female smiled, holding a bag in one hand and a bottle of wine in the other. She stepped inside the apartment and swept her gaze around the room.

"I thought you could use a drink after today. I know human females enjoy wine. Are you all right? Richard is fine but a little shaken up. I hope you are in the mood to eat a steak. I know you like to have that for lunch sometimes."

"That sounds wonderful." She took the bag and the wine. "Have a seat. I'll get us some glasses."

"I brought my dinner too. Do you mind if I eat with you?"

It explained how heavy and big the bag was. "I'd love that." She put it on the coffee table and rushed to the kitchen to get silverware and glasses. She hunted up a bottle opener.

They sat side by side on the couch and Creek sniffed the air. Zandy turned her head to stare at her friend.

"You are in heat. It's not just a faint smell now. It's hit you full force."

"That's so weird. I hope I don't stink." She hated the thought. "Women can't tell when they ovulate."

"Species can. We get very aroused for sex and want it often. You don't suffer that condition?"

"Nope."

"You are lucky. I am sorry Vengeance went after you. He lives in the Wild Zone and hasn't learned manners. Some of our more uncivilized males live there and they tend to allow their animal sides to rule. I'm sure he wouldn't have harmed you but you would have had one horny male on your hands."

"He would have forced me?"

Creek hesitated and then smiled. "He would have convinced you that you wanted sex. Our males would never take us unless our bodies were prepared for them. They can be very persuasive when they really want a female."

Zandy shook her head. "He wouldn't have convinced me."

"I would disagree." Creek took a sip of wine and looked surprised. "It is fruity but not bad."

"You never had wine before?"

"No. We don't drink alcohol but I like it." She set the glass down. "Vengeance would have stripped you bare and buried his face against your sex. They can convince you to want them." A wide grin spread across her face. "They are good at that. You being in heat would have assured he wanted to do that to you. They go crazy over the taste of a female in heat."

Her mouth was hanging open and Zandy had to force it closed. "Okay."

Creek chuckled. "You should see your eyes. Does this shock you? Don't your males love to lick your sex and taste you?"

"Um, most of them prefer women to go down on them."

Creek's amusement instantly died as she gawked. "Why?"

"What do you mean, why? They like getting head."

"What is that?"

Zandy blinked. "Oral sex. Men love getting oral sex from women."

"Our males don't ask." Her chest puffed out a little. "They want to convince us to share sex with them. There's no reason for us to tempt them that way to share sex with us. We are few and they are many. They have to work harder at sex to impress us since we have a large selection of males to choose from."

"Wow." Zandy sipped her wine. "So you never go down on the guys?"

"No."

Zandy decided to change the subject. "I feel horrible about that fight today. I should have just left when Tiger told me to."

"It's not your fault you didn't understand how tempting you were to males or that they would come after you aggressively. You're human."

"Tiger was hurt. His cheek was bleeding."

She laughed. "Don't worry about him. Males fight often and we heal fast. Besides, the females will hear what he did and want to reward him. He was a hero."

"Reward him?" Zandy didn't like the sound of that one bit.

"Tiger is one of our best fighters. That's why he heads security here. The males respect and fear him at the same time. The females will hear what he did for you and offer to share sex with him. Some female will be more than happy to tend to it."

Pain sliced through Zandy at the thought of some Species woman going after Tiger. He was mad at her and they were probably over. Would he sleep with someone else? She lifted her wineglass and downed the contents.

She listened to Creek talk about missing Homeland and how she'd been assigned with fifteen other women to live and work at Reservation. She drank a few more glasses of wine and managed to finish her dinner. Creek finally seemed to notice how quiet Zandy had grown.

"Are you tired?"

"Yes."

"I'll leave then. You aren't supposed to go to work but you can. Tiger will get over his anger. You work with a human and they have no sense of smell. Richard also has a mate and I've never smelled arousal on him when it comes to you. I'm sure you'll be safe with him."

Zandy stood up too fast after so many glasses of wine and stumbled. Creek gripped her arm to steady her and laughed.

"I think you drank too much, my little friend."

"Probably. It's been a long, bad day."

"You should call that male you are involved with and talk to him. It might make you feel better. You haven't been able to see him since you've been asked to stay here for your safety."

"We had a fight and I think we're over. Thank you for dinner and the wine."

"I'll walk you to your room. You're wobbling on your feet."

"Thanks." Zandy couldn't deny she was a bit drunk.

Creek led her into the bedroom and pulled back the blankets. The other woman sniffed the air and got an odd look on her face as she stared at Zandy.

"What?"

"Have you changed your mind about wanting to share sex with one of our males?"

"Nope. I was seeing someone and it just ended badly. Didn't I just tell you that I think we're over? We got into a fight."

"That's right." Creek helped her remove some of her clothes and climb into bed. "Were you seeing that male for long?"

"Long enough that it really hurts that we're over," Zandy admitted. "I knew it couldn't last." Tears filled her eyes and she blinked them back as she stared at her friend. "I envy you that whole refusing-to-get-serious-with-a-man thing. It sucks when you care about them and they don't feel the same way."

Creek tucked her in. "I understand. Did you allow him to sleep with you?"

"Yeah."

"He held you while you slept?"

"It was really nice," Zandy admitted. "Falling in love sucks."

"I'm sure it does." Creek moved away and paused at the door. "Sleep well, Zandy. I will see you in a few days after you're out of heat and allowed to return to the cafeteria."

Zandy closed her eyes when Creek turned off the bedroom light. She heard the other woman cleaning up the other room and felt a little guilty. Hot tears spilled out though when she thought about Tiger. Was he with another woman? He hadn't called her to apologize and he hadn't shown up again at her door, trying to talk to her.

The living room light went out and Creek closed the exterior door as she left. Zandy rolled onto her stomach and tried to push thoughts of Tiger away. She should have known better than to fall for him.

* * * * *

Tiger paced his bedroom, his thoughts on Zandy. He wanted to go to her but wasn't sure she'd talk to him. He paused to stare at the phone. Would she answer if he called? He'd really lost his temper when Vengeance had gone after her. He'd hurt her feelings but wasn't sure how to fix it. Humans were so different from Species females. One of them would have just hit him if he'd angered them but humans were known for holding grudges.

He sat on the edge of his bed and opened the nightstand drawer. He withdrew the Ziploc bag he kept there and opened it. Zandy's scent still lingered on her bra as he breathed her in. It only made him miss her more. The desire to go to her grew stronger so he sealed the bag again and put it away. Tormenting himself wasn't going to help matters.

His doorbell rang and he quickly strode to his front door. He shouldn't have come home but he'd needed some time away from everyone. He grabbed his cell phone out to check it, saw he hadn't missed any calls and jerked open the door, wondering who had come to visit him. It surprised him to find Creek standing there.

"Hello, Tiger." She peered at him. "May I come in?"

He opened the door wider and moved to allow her to pass him. "Is something wrong? I spoke to Vengeance if that's what you're here about. He's sorry for what he did today."

She turned to face him as he closed the door. "I had dinner with Zandy and we shared wine." Creek grinned. "She can't hold her alcohol. She was swaying on her feet and talked funny after a few glasses. It was very cute."

"Is she all right after today?" He inwardly winced, wondering if Zandy was more upset with him or with the male who'd tried to take off with her. He hadn't beaten on Vengeance after their talk. He'd felt bad for him and had no longer wanted to beat on him. "Is that why you're here? He won't go near her again."

All trace of humor left Creek's expression and she stared at him for long seconds. "Vengeance was out of control today but you stopped him from seducing her. I wanted to say thank you. Zandy is my friend. She doesn't understand about our males or what going into heat does to them."

"It was nothing. He was out of line."

She took a step closer to him. "I could share sex with you if you are interested. You were a hero by fighting him."

Tiger took a step back. "No thank you. I appreciate the offer."

She stalked closer and he backed away. Creek's gaze narrowed and he wondered why she was being so aggressive. It wasn't common for a male to turn down a female's offer to share sex. His back hit the closed door and he softly growled at her. "I said no."

Creek paused inches from him and stared into his eyes until he felt uncomfortable. "I could call another female to come here if it's me you're not interested in."

"I would find one on my own if I wanted a female. You should go."

Her expression softened as she retreated a few steps. She turned, took a seat on his couch and crossed her arms over her chest as her gaze met his again. "I tucked Zandy into her bed. She was unstable on her feet. Imagine my surprise when I smelled you and sex on her blankets. I know the real reason you are turning away my offer of sex. You don't want me because she's the female you do want."

Tiger frowned and remained against the door. "She's your friend and you were testing me to see how I felt about her by offering to share sex with me, weren't you?"

"Yes."

Anger stirred. "What do you want?"

"I like her a lot. She is my friend. She's hurting because you aren't seeing her anymore." Her voice deepened into a growl. "I saw pain in her eyes that you've caused. She isn't Species and sex isn't casual to them. She has feelings for you, Tiger. I wanted to tell you this. You'd be stupid not to see what a good female she is and try to coax her into a mating."

Tiger's anger burned hotter. "I plan to see her again. We just had an argument. I didn't say it was casual. We are both confused about what is happening between us."

"You don't want a mate and she doesn't want a third husband."

He pushed away from the door. "That's true."

"That's bullshit." Creek shook her head slowly. "You appear unhappy and I know she is. You refused to share sex with another female. She has refused to share sex with other males who have offered. That's already a commitment. We are

Species, Tiger. I know you spend a lot of time with human males from the task force but don't forget what you are. We don't lie or hide from our nature."

He took a seat in the chair. "I don't know what I want anymore."

Creek smiled sadly. "You know. Listen to your instincts. What do they say?"

"I want Zandy. I'd like nothing better than to go snatch her from her bed and bring her to mine."

"You enjoy sleeping with her in your arms?"

"Yes." Admitting it was a relief. "I want her there every night."

"Males can be so stubborn." Creek stood and reached into her back pocket. "Here."

He stared at the key she held. "What is it?"

"The spare key to Zandy's front door. I snagged it from the wall where it hung. I'll distract the officers while you sneak in. Humans are strange about sharing sex and allowing everyone to know about it. Go to her and fix her pain. She thinks you don't want her anymore."

Tiger rose to his feet and took the key. He stared deeply into Creek's eyes. "Thank you."

"She's my friend. Stop fighting your instincts and remember she isn't Species. They seem to enjoy being dominated by a male. It makes me curious about human males since obviously they are a lot softer. Females always want what they don't have."

"Will you come in the morning to give me time to sneak out? I want to stay the night with Zandy."

"Piece of cake. I'm off shift tomorrow and will bring the officers breakfast. They will flirt with me." She smiled. "One of them won't turn me down if I offer to share sex."

He reached out and clasped her shoulder. "Thank you."

"I care about Zandy and you are my friend too." Her smile faded. "Don't hurt her or I'll hurt you."

Causing Zandy pain was the last thing he wanted. "I owe you one."

"I'll remember that."

"Let me grab a change of clothing. Thank you."

"Just allow those male instincts of yours to rule and you should be fine. Humans seem to think it's cute when males get possessive." She chuckled. "Their males don't taste them often either. They expect the females to tempt them into sex. No wonder so many of them appreciate our males. I never fully understood why they'd so easily take mates until she shared that information with me."

He hoped Zandy would easily accept him as a mate. He'd just have to go slow and talk her into it.

* * * * *

The bed moved and it woke Zandy. She gasped and rolled over, expecting to be attacked again by some stranger. Instead she stared at Tiger. He'd turned on the living room light and had left her bedroom door open so she could clearly see him sitting on the edge of her bed.

"I'm sorry we had bad words." He hesitated. "I was angry because Vengeance could have put his hands on you. It wasn't your fault and I shouldn't have yelled at you. Just the thought of him touching you put me in a rage."

It took a stunned moment for her mind to process his words. "What are you doing here?" Her gaze dropped to his bare chest and legs then back up. He had one leg tucked to hide his sex but his bare hip made it clear he wasn't wearing anything. "You're naked."

"I was hoping you'd allow me to sleep with you. I want to stay the night."

He wasn't with someone else. It was almost sad how relieved she felt after Creek had told her that other women would offer to have sex with him. He'd chosen to come to her instead. She threw back the covers and opened her arms to him.

His gaze lingered on her clothes. "Will you take them off?"

She sat up, grabbed the T-shirt and tore it over her head. Tiger softly growled to encourage her as she dropped flat on her back, lifted her hips and grabbed the waistband of the sweats to wiggle out of them. He helped by pulling at the ankles, tugging them down her legs. In seconds she was bare and Tiger shifted positions until he stretched out on his side against her. One hand cupped her face as he peered deeply into her eyes.

"Do you have any idea how insane you make me? All the things I want to do to you?"

"No. Tell me."

He dipped his head and nuzzled her cheek with his while he inhaled deeply. "You're in heat. You smell so good I could eat you alive."

Her belly clenched in response and she turned on her side to face him while her hands opened on his chest to flatten there. His hot skin felt satiny and she loved to touch him.

"More biting, huh?" She knew that wasn't what he meant and smiled when he met her gaze.

His tongue wet his lips and his gaze lowered down her body to her lap. "Open up for me. You know what I want."

She rolled to her back and spread her thighs, lifting her legs at the same time. Tiger moved fast and slid down the bed. Zandy's heart raced as she watched him crouch over her and his hands gripped her inner thighs. He softly purred and lowered his face.

"I could stay here for hours."

"You'd kill me."

His gaze jerked up. "Don't say that."

"It was a joke. I just meant I'm not sure I could take hours of that."

His features hardened and his voice came out deeper. "I'm trying to keep in control for you. I don't want to frighten you."

"You being right there isn't scary unless you bite. I really like it when you go down on me."

He caressed her thighs with his hands. "I want to do more than that."

"What do you want, Tiger?"

He closed his eyes.

"Tiger?"

He opened them to stare at her and she saw something in his gaze that made her hold her breath. There was a raw hunger showing but she didn't understand what caused it.

"I want it all with you but I'm afraid I'd frighten you if I let go of my control. You're in heat and it calls to me in ways that would shock you."

"I'm feeling really brave," she admitted. "Really turned-on."

"I'm not totally human."

"I know."

He blinked. "Do you really understand that?"

She nodded sharply. "You purr, Tiger. You growl. You've got those amazingly beautiful eyes that I love to stare into. You've got the sharp teeth. Trust me, I get it. I'm still here naked with you. I'm not afraid. You won't hurt me. I trust you so stop holding back."

"There are officers outside. Remember that." It was the only warning she got.

Tiger dipped his head and his mouth fastened over her clit. Zandy closed her eyes when his hot tongue began to tease her by rubbing strongly against the bundle of nerves. He nuzzled his mouth in tight against her, his hands shoving her thighs wider apart to make room for him.

Pleasure gripped her—fast and furious. Her back arched to press her pussy tighter against his hungry mouth. One arm lifted and she threw it over her open mouth to muffle the sound as she moaned. Tiger showed no mercy as he manipulated her clit, found that tiny spot that drove her insane and she climaxed hard.

He tore his mouth away and the bed moved. Zandy opened her eyes just as his hold on her shifted from her inner thighs to her ankles. She looked down as he slid off the end of the bed and yanked her down it. His intense stare held hers until he flipped her over, grabbed her hips and her knees softly hit the carpet. He bent her over the side of the bed and his legs spread on the outside of hers.

The head of his cock brushed the seam of her pussy as he reached between them to adjust it, found right where he wanted to be and slowly entered her. She moaned and clawed the bedding at the wonderful sensation of his thick shaft stretching her apart to take him.

"I can't stop," he growled. "I need you."

His body wrapped around hers to pin her tightly against the bed. His hands grabbed hers where they clung to the bed and his mouth brushed hot, wet kisses on the side of her throat. He drove into her deeply and fucked her hard, fast.

Zandy moaned loudly and pressed her mouth against the bed. She couldn't move at all the way he had her pinned. She could just take him and feel every thrust of his cock. Her vaginal muscles were still twitching from her climax. It didn't take long for him to bring her to a second one. She cried out, muffling the sound against the bedding as she felt him come.

His body shook over hers as hot jets of semen filled her deep inside. He growled, stopped kissing her while he panted and groaned. His hips bucked with each jerk of his release. She expected him to slowly withdraw after he seemed to recover but instead he began to move again, fucking her a little slower.

"I could take you for hours," he rasped. "I'm going to. I can't stop. You're so hot and wet for me. So tight. You're mine, Zandy."

She moaned. He might kill her but what a way to go. "I—" She stopped, shocked by what she'd almost said.

Tiger paused. "You what? Do you want me to stop? Are you sore?"

"Keep going," she urged. She'd almost told him she loved him. "Don't stop."

His teeth lightly raked her throat. "I won't." He began to move again, fucking her deeply and steadily.

Pleasure rolled through her. He brought her to climax again and found his own. She didn't protest as Tiger lifted her afterward. He put her back on the bed and curled up behind her. Light kisses brushed her shoulder and cheek as he held her tightly.

"I'm going to wake you during the night. You're exhausted though. Try to get some rest."

"That was incredible."

He softly purred. "It was and it will be again. Rest, Zandy." Amusement sounded in his voice. "I think I wore you out."

She grinned and closed her eyes. "You totally make me understand why men pass out after sex."

* * * * *

Tiger knew when Zandy fell asleep. His dick was still hard and he ached to take her again. Because she was in heat, he'd stay in his aroused condition as long as the tempting scent of her filled his nose.

She was in full heat and he hadn't used condoms. She didn't know he could get her pregnant. Guilt ate at him for not warning her of what could happen but he didn't regret it. He'd need to tell her the truth though. Their relationship had reached the stage where he knew it was time to share the classified information with her. He wanted her for his mate and she'd need to be informed of the truth to make that decision.

What if she said no? Pain tightened his chest. She could tell him she didn't want another male in her life. She'd had two of them who had harmed her heart and betrayed her. They'd been human but she might not understand how different he was from them.

* * * * *

Tiger's buzzing cell phone woke him before dawn. He hated to turn away from Zandy but he had to answer it. He grabbed it from his pocket and walked into the living room, closing the door to prevent his voice from waking her.

"Tiger here."

"This is Brass. We've had a full-out assault at Homeland. Two of our males are injured, two humans are dead and we're facing a riot from the protesters. We need help immediately. The human task force is here and we have human police helping but Justice wants you here too. You have a way with our males, of keeping them calm."

"What happened?" Tiger instantly was alarmed.

"Two of those damn crazy humans drove right up to the gates and came out screaming about how we are animals. The car just blew up. We suspect a car bomb they set off. The humans died instantly. Two of our males were blown right off the walls from the force of the blast. They are in bad shape but they'll survive. Our males are furious. The protesters are lying, saying we blew up the car. It's turned into a nightmare. The human law enforcement and our task force are trying to handle the situation but our males are fit to be tied. They are tired of being attacked and Justice thinks your good nature and humor are desperately needed. How fast can you be here?"

"I'm on my way." He hung up and dialed Security. "Get the helicopter ready. I need to get to Homeland now."

"Understood."

He hung up and stared at the closed bedroom door. He didn't want to leave Zandy but he had no choice. He'd only be gone a few hours.

Chapter Fourteen

ھى

Zandy woke alone but Tiger had left a note on the pillow. She read it and smiled. He planned to take her to his house for dinner later. That had to be a good sign that he planned to keep seeing her. She showered, dressed, and turned on the television when breakfast was delivered to her door by a grim officer.

She thanked him and took a seat on the couch, opening the bag. The commercial ended and the opening news story left Zandy gawking at the screen. The background sight of the scarred, twisted gates to Homeland held her attention as a chipper, blonde news reporter accounted what had taken place there in the middle of the night. Two suspected members of a hate group were dead while two New Species had been injured.

"Shit." Her appetite was gone.

She flipped the channels, picking up more of the story from different reporters. The two New Species would live. It had been a car bomb and both the men who'd driven the car to the gates had died in the explosion. Her mind went over all the hate mail she'd read but no one had made threats against the NSO with car bombs.

Was Tiger okay? Upset? She wouldn't blame him if he hated humans. She just hoped he didn't lump her in with the ones who'd attacked Homeland. Were the injured New Species friends of his? She stood and turned off the television. He'd call her and she'd ask him about it. She'd be there for him if he needed her. She put on her shoes and walked to the door, wanting to get to work.

* * * * *

Richard looked surprised to see her when she entered the office. "I thought you were taking a few days off."

"No."

He grinned. "I take it you're wearing panty liners?" Amusement lit his dark eyes. "I didn't see your escort sniffing at you or drooling."

"Yeah. I got some of those delivered to me. Did you see the news?"

His humor vanished. "Yeah. They didn't send in any threats to warn us."

"That's what I was going over in my head when I saw the news. I hope we didn't miss something."

"We didn't. The real fanatical ones rarely send warnings. They just attack."

"What have you heard that isn't on the news?"

"I talked to someone at Homeland first thing this morning. The officers are going to recover. They mostly suffered cuts and bruises from the fall. They were lucky to hit a grassy area and not the pavement. Their protective gear also helped avoid more severe injuries. We got lucky this time. Expect a lot of threats to come in. Copycat idiots and crazies tend to do that after one of these events."

"Events?" Zandy sat down hard in her chair. "That sounds like such a tame word for what happened. I keep thinking about how much worse it could have been."

"What else do you want me to call them? It's fucking horrific. I shudder to think what could have happened or how many New Species could have been killed if they'd used more explosives. Did you see the damage to the gates? It twisted part of them."

"I saw."

Richard got up from his desk to crouch in front of her and stare into her eyes. "Are you okay? You really seem shaken by this."

Tears filled her eyes. "No. It could have happened here." She thought about Tiger, Creek and everyone else she had met. "New Species are so great. Why can't those assholes leave them alone?"

Richard took her hand. "I know, honey. It's upsetting. We can't control the idiots of the world but this time it worked out in our favor. None of the New Species died. We help where we can. That's why we read all this shit that comes in. Just concentrate on work and maybe we'll find a real threat today. That's how we find and stop the morons we can. Okay?"

She squeezed his hand. "Thanks for the pep talk."

"No problem." He straightened and released her. "We'll have lunch brought to us. We'll put in as many hours as we can today. Throwing myself into work always helps me."

"Thanks."

He shrugged. "Oh. I brought you perfume." He opened one of his desk drawers and lifted a small bottle. "I was planning on giving it to Creek today to get to you."

She smiled. "Thanks and please thank your wife."

His smile returned. "She loved hearing about women going into heat. She said it was really interesting."

Memories of Tiger in her bed made her lower her gaze. It was flat-out sexy. It was some of the hottest sex she'd ever had. She couldn't wait for a repeat later when Tiger came to get her to take her to his home. She wondered what his house would be like.

They worked through lunch, her mind still on Tiger, and she was startled when her desk phone rang. Richard stared at her as she met his gaze.

"Answer it."

She reached for it. "Hello?"

"Hi, Zandy."

Tiger's voice was music to her ears. "Hi." She turned away from Richard, ignoring his curious stare.

"I had to fly to Homeland this morning after it was attacked. Did you hear about that?"

"I did. I'm so sorry. Is everything okay? Are you okay?"

"Our males will recover and the situation is improving by the hour. I'm stuck here though. I'm not sure I'll be able to return tonight."

Disappointment struck. "I understand. You need to do whatever you can."

"I wanted to make you dinner at my home."

"I wanted that too. We could make plans to do that tomorrow night."

"It sounds good." He hesitated. "I'll call you tonight around nine. We can talk longer then. I have a meeting to attend."

"Do you have my cell phone number?"

He paused. "Give it to me."

She gave him her number and he said, "I'll talk to you tonight. Be careful."

"I will."

He hung up and Zandy returned the phone to the cradle. She knew her coworker watched her.

"Was that Angel?"

"Yes."

"Why does he have to be careful? What does he do for a living?"

"Don't you have work to do?"

"Fine. Don't spill the beans. Leave me pondering about this mystery man. It sounded as if you're planning another date with him. Do you know what that tells me?"

"What?" She twisted her chair to face him.

209

"The third time is the charm." Richard winked. "So much for not getting serious. How many dates will that make?"

"I'm not keeping track," she lied.

"She protests too much." Richard wiggled his eyebrows. "Do you know what that sound is?" He cocked his ear.

She didn't hear anything and eyed him with suspicion. "What?"

"I think I hear distant wedding bells."

"Shut up." She threw a paperclip at him, which he caught.

She turned back to her computer screen and smiled. The idea of getting serious with Tiger didn't fill her with fear anymore.

* * * * *

Tiger was stressed and tired. It had been a long day and the evening wasn't getting any better. He stared at the males who shared the helicopter with him and knew they were all more than ready to return to Reservation.

Thoughts of Zandy filled his head. It would be after ten by the time they landed but he planned to visit her to make up for not being able to call. He wanted to climb into her bed and just hold her. She'd still be in heat. His cock came to life just remembering the previous night.

Motion drew his attention and he met Zest's cool stare. The male tossed a headset his way and he put it on. They'd reach Reservation soon.

"Long day."

"Yes," Tiger agreed. "I'll be glad to get home."

"Would you like to go for a run when we arrive? I doubt I can sleep. The stress was palpable. I thought Justice was going to have a stroke yelling at the local law enforcement for not giving the NSO enough support."

"No. I have plans. The last thing I want to do is something outdoors."

The other male grinned. "Which female is it?"

Tiger pulled off the headset and tossed it back, smiling. Zest caught them and laughed. He hung them back on the wall next to the pilots behind his seat. Tiger closed his eyes and tried to ignore the way the wind battered the helicopter. Flying wasn't something he enjoyed, a firm believer he'd have been born with wings if he were meant to fly.

Something dinged metal in a rapid succession. His eyes flew open as the helicopter suddenly dipped drastically. An alarm bell screamed and he saw flashing red lights coming from the cockpit. Zest threw him a headset and he put it on as the helicopter rose and fell again. It was a violent movement that made all the males glance at each other with dread.

"Mayday," the human pilot yelled in the headset. "This is Reservation Blade One. We're under attack from armed fire coming from the woods and have taken damage."

Shock reverberated through Tiger. He wasn't even sure what that meant. Something else hit the helicopter and the glass spider-webbed on the door across from him. He realized someone had fired some type of weapon and struck them again. The alarm from the front grew louder and the pilot shouted out coordinates and veered so hard to the right that Tiger would have been thrown out of his seat if not for his belt.

"We're going down," the pilot shouted. "They hit a fuel line and we're losing pressure. Mayday, I repeat, mayday. This is Reservation Blade One. We're under fire from the ground and we've suffered multiple hits."

Tiger's gaze met Zest's, saw the other Species' fear, and knew his own expression must mirror it. He glanced at the two other males. Both stared at him for guidance until the power cut out and everything went dark.

"Brace for impact," the pilot yelled at them. "We're going down."

The helicopter tilted dangerously to one side. The feeling made Tiger's stomach protest and the engines that were usually so loud just cut out. No one yelled. It was a sick feeling as they dropped in the eerie silence.

Seconds later they hit something hard, stunning Tiger since he had expected to fall for a while. Glass and metal took the brunt of the impact with the treetops. The helicopter seemed to roll over before it slammed with bone-jarring force into the ground.

Pain gripped Tiger around his middle where the belt held him in place. His leg and arm ached badly. Lights flickered inside the damaged interior and he saw movement from the bench across from him. Something wet blinded him and he tried to wipe his eyes. One arm refused to move and dizziness gripped him.

"I smell gas," a deep voice growled. "Are you alive?"

He knew that voice but his brain couldn't identify it. He hurt and breathing caused stabbing pains in his chest. The stench of blood and gas did seep into his fogged senses. A hand touched his throat.

"Tiger?"

He fought to open his eyes and when he did, he could barely make out Zest's face. The male was bleeding from his nose and had a cut along his forehead. Tiger tried to speak but nothing came out.

"I've got you, Tiger," Zest growled. "The helicopter is leaking gas. We need to get you out of here. I'm sorry. This is going to hurt."

The pressure around his waist suddenly disappeared and hands caught him. He snarled from the pain and nearly blacked out. He knew he was being lifted and another pair of hands gripped him under his arms. His leg bumped something and he cried out. It felt as if that leg had just been torn away from his body.

* * * * *

Tiger woke to the sound of moaning. His eyes opened and flames blinded him. He blinked a few times to try to clear his vision but the fire was too bright. He thought he could make out the outline of the destroyed helicopter on its side somewhere in the high flames.

A big male dragged someone away from the fire and he recognized Zest's back. He brought whoever he pulled closer and Tiger knew that was the person making those horrible sounds.

It was the human pilot. The injured male had some burns on the arm he waved in the air when Zest backed away after releasing him. His friend dropped to his knees, blood staining his side and a howl tore from his open mouth.

* * * * *

Tiger woke again when someone touched his face. He peered into a pair of blue eyes. Zest looked like hell with his bloodied face and his matted dark hair with streaks of blood.

"Hang on, Tiger. We got you out before the helicopter caught fire but the pilot wasn't so lucky. He's got some severe burns." Zest put his hand over Tiger's forehead, holding it tightly. "You have broken bones. We crashed close to Reservation. Help is coming." He turned his head. "Ascend?"

"They are close," the other male answered. A howl came from him and a distant one answered in seconds. "Hear them? They aren't that far."

Zest leaned in. "Did you hear? They will be here soon. Medical will be on alert and ready for you. Don't give up. Fight to breathe, Tiger. Do not die on me."

Tiger closed his eyes, too dizzy and weak to try to focus his failing sight anymore. He wouldn't be climbing into Zandy's bed tonight. He'd probably never see her again. Agony stabbed at him with every breath and his head felt as if

213

it were in pieces. A pair of beautiful green eyes filled his thoughts and the memory of her face was all that kept him fighting to live.

He never should have gotten involved with Zandy Gordon. She'd grieve his loss and he'd exposed her to the kind of hatred that most likely had killed him. The helicopter had been shot down. They'd been approaching Reservation when the attack happened. It couldn't have been unintentional.

He wouldn't be around to protect Zandy anymore. She'd be defenseless against the humans who hated Species and they'd come after her for working for the NSO. It would only make her a bigger target if anyone found out she'd shared sex with him. He wanted to roar in rage at the thought of anyone hurting her.

Regret filled him. He'd been selfish to be with her and should have thought of her safety first. Fury had taken Ellie as a mate and humans had tried to shoot her. Slade and Trisha had nearly been killed by hunters who'd stalked them after striking the vehicle they'd been traveling in. Valiant's Tammy had been kidnapped just for being his mate. Justice couldn't fall in love without it causing a bombing at the gates of Homeland from the idiots who believed Species and humans shouldn't form relationships.

Tiger admitted that was real reason he'd been so reluctant to ever consider taking a human mate. He'd watched all his friends suffer the terror of having the females they fell in love with tormented in some way. Being with a Species had caused them grief. Guilt ate at him, knowing a stronger male would have thought of that before it was too late. He'd been selfish to expose Zandy to danger.

"Tiger?" Zest kept hold of him. "I hear engines. They are so close. Hold on, my friend."

His mouth parted. He wanted Zest to swear to guard Zandy with his life. The male was his friend and would do it. A soft groan came out but no words. He tried to focus harder but he was slipping away. The pain intensified and everything faded into blackness.

* * * * *

Zandy stared at her cell phone. Tiger hadn't called and it had been over an hour since he said he would. She lifted her gaze to the clock with a loud sigh. It was almost ten thirty. She had to work in the morning, needed sleep, and tried not to feel hurt that he must have forgotten about her.

She stood and carried her glass to the kitchen. A string of excuses formed in her mind. He could have been stuck in a meeting or was so exhausted he'd fallen asleep. Whatever the reason, she missed hearing his voice. She longed to talk to him but had no idea how to contact him. She scooped up her cell phone and turned off the lights as she headed to bed.

It was empty and cold without Tiger's big body and his heated skin. She tossed and turned, thinking maybe he'd forgotten her phone number. He could have misplaced the number. Maybe the switchboard had been too busy to connect his call.

"Fuck," she sighed. He hadn't called. It wasn't the end of the world. He had a life and more important things to do than tell her good night. An emergency had happened at Homeland and he should be focused on that.

She tried to drift to sleep. She'd see him at some point tomorrow, hopefully. They'd have dinner at his house. She wanted to tell him how she really felt. He might dump her when she admitted that she was falling in love but at least they wouldn't be pretending their relationship was just sex anymore.

Chapter Fifteen

ᴔ

Zandy had overslept and was running late when she opened the front door to greet her escort. She had missed breakfast. Someone had left a covered dish on her coffee table but she hadn't had time to eat any of it.

Smiley and three other males were grouped together in the courtyard when she stepped outside. Four pairs of grim gazes turned her way. Some of them looked so angry that she winced.

"I'm sorry I'm ten minutes behind. I had a rough night. I hope I haven't made any of you late."

Smiley walked closer. "It's not you. We're upset about what happened last night." He glanced at his watch. "I didn't even notice. I should have driven you to work already. Let's go."

"What happened last night?" She fell into step with him as he led her toward one of the Jeeps parked at the curb.

He stopped and his gaze met hers. "You didn't hear what happened yet?"

"No. I didn't even turn on the TV this morning." Her heart plummeted. "Was there another attack at Homeland? Did one of the injured officers take a turn for the worse?" She really hoped not.

"Last night one of our helicopters was shot down. We're still trying to figure out how they did it but it crashed. It happened right outside NSO walls. They were incoming to land but didn't make it."

"Oh my god. Is everyone who was on board okay?"

He hesitated. "One of the human pilots is touch and go. He has burns and broken bones. Most of our males had injures but Tiger is the worst of them."

Her knees almost gave out beneath her. "What?"

He blinked. "I'm sorry. You know him. Tiger was on board."

She clutched Smiley's arms just to keep from falling. Hot tears quickly filled her eyes. "Is he alive? Where is he?"

The tall Species grabbed her hips to steady her and frowned. "Zandy, you are very pale suddenly. Are you ill?"

"Is Tiger alive?" Her nails dug into him where she had his arms. "How bad is he hurt?" She refused to believe he was dead. Fate couldn't be that cruel. "Where is he, Smiley?"

He studied her eyes and softly snarled. "You shared sex with him, didn't you?"

"Is he alive?" she yelled, frantic to get an answer.

"He's alive but in critical condition. He suffered multiple broken bones and a head injury. We were told the pilot was able to get them to a low altitude before the engines seized. He did some kind of maneuver to halt their momentum. They estimate that the helicopter fell about a hundred feet into the tree branches at the crash site. That cushioned the crash somewhat but it landed on the side where Tiger sat."

Every word he spoke was like a dagger to her heart. Tears slid down her cheeks. She'd been sleeping and Tiger had been fighting for his life. It was beyond horrific. Someone should have told her when it happened. She'd have been at his side.

"His ribs are fractured, as well as one arm and his leg. He suffered cuts and a blow to his head. Our doctors suspect swelling in his brain but they aren't sure how extensive the damage is."

"Take me to him."

Smiley frowned. "He's not here, Zandy. His injuries were severe and our doctors felt he needed a neurosurgeon. We don't have one of those. He was airlifted to a trauma center a few hours from here last night. He is under heavy guard and protected where he is."

"Where? I want to go there." The desire to get to Tiger's side was nearly overpowering. She just had to see him to make sure he was really alive. Inside she was falling apart. "I need to get to him."

"How many times have you shared sex with Tiger? You're really upset by this. *Did* you share sex with him? You didn't answer me."

"What does it matter?" She wanted to shake him. "Where the hell is Tiger?"

Smiley's hold on her hips tightened and he leaned down enough to stare into her eyes. "Answer me."

"Yes! Are you happy now? Where is Tiger? I want to see him."

Smiley released her and grabbed for his cell phone. "How many times? I need to report this immediately."

Her mouth fell open. "What? It's no one's business how many times Tiger and I have slept together. I demand to know where he is, damn it. I want to see him."

Smiley took a deep breath. "He's under heavy guard by both the NSO and the human task team assigned to protect him. I'm going to have to get you clearance, Zandy. You can't just go to his hospital room to see him. They'd never allow you near him without them being ordered to do so. I have to contact Timber, he's in charge of Reservation with Tiger injured, and he'll have to give permission for you to go where Tiger is being treated. He'll want to know the extent of your relationship."

She wiped at her tears. "We've been seeing each other since the first day I started working here. We've spent the night together a few times. We're dating. I was supposed to have dinner with him last night at his house but he was called to Homeland, okay? He said he'd call me last night but he didn't." She sniffed. "He couldn't because he was in that accident. Please, Smiley. I need to see him."

The male's gaze softened. "You have deep feelings for Tiger."

"Yes."

He dialed, watching her. "It's a few hours away. You might want to get a spare set of your clothing while I get this cleared. I'll try to put together an escort for you as quickly as possible. We don't have another helicopter at our disposal."

She spun and fled back inside the apartment. Her hands shook badly as she rushed into her bedroom to grab clothes. All she had to pick from were shorts, sweats and T-shirts provided by the NSO.

Smiley hung up the phone when she walked outside carrying one spare set of clothes. "Timber is calling the task team to clear you to visit Tiger." He paused. "You need to wait until dark when some males can be freed from their current duties to escort you off Reservation and to the hospital where Tiger is being treated."

"No. I want to go to him right now." Impatience burst forth and so did the need to get to Tiger as quickly as possible.

"That's the best we can do."

"Take me to my car. I'll go alone."

A soft, animalistic sound came from Smiley. "No. It isn't safe."

"I don't give a damn. No way am I going to be able to sit here all day waiting for someone to get around to driving me. Tell me what hospital he's at and take me to my car."

"No."

Her anger surged. "You can't stop me. I'm leaving. Tell me where Tiger is, damn it. He's hurt and I want to see him."

"Smiley," one of the males interrupted. "She wishes to go. She's not a prisoner." He cleared his throat and red-hued engrossing eyes fixed on her. "I'll escort you to your car. You'll need identification for the human task team. They'll want to see that if you arrive without escorts to prove your identity." He sniffed. "You don't carry Tiger's scent."

"Stay out of this, Jericho."

The big male had black hair that was pulled back in a long braid. He growled at Smiley while glaring at him. "The female is highly agitated. We both know if Tiger is sharing sex with her that she must mean a lot to him. I know she's in heat and that may be making you irrational but she wishes to leave." He hesitated. "She might be little but I would bet she isn't one you wish to anger. Females have a way of getting even." He stepped closer and held out his arm to her. "I'll escort you to your vehicle. Do you have identification? They will ask for it."

"In my purse," she admitted, grateful as she curled her fingers around his upper arm. His eyes were so strange she couldn't help but stare a little.

He hesitated. "I'm primate like Smiley but those traits are more pronounced with me. There aren't a lot of us." He tugged her forward. "You probably haven't seen eyes similar to mine before. I get stared at often when I come in contact with humans."

"They are really pretty."

He made a snorting sound. "Scary perhaps but not attractive." He helped her into a Jeep.

She glanced at Smiley and saw how unhappy he looked when he frowned deeply. Her escort climbed into the driver's seat and pulled away from the curb as soon as he started the engine.

"Smiley was highly interested in you. He spoke of you often. He also was clear that you turned down his offers. Don't feel bad for him."

"Right now all I feel is terror and worry. Is Tiger going to be all right?"

"He is a strong male in good hands with medical professionals. We heal at an accelerated rate—faster than typical humans do. They designed us this way and it's a good sign that Tiger has survived all these hours. I would bet a week of my cream pies that he will live."

She gawked at the New Species. He smiled, his attention on the road. "I can feel you staring at me. I have a fondness for cream pies and wouldn't give them up easily or bet them away without being certain I am right." He chuckled. "And no, banana isn't my favorite. I enjoy chocolate and coconut more."

She appreciated his attempt at humor and his assurances that Tiger would make it. He gave her the name of the hospital and told her to ask for Trey Roberts when she arrived there. "He is heading the human task team protecting Tiger. He'll ask for identification. Don't forget that."

"I won't."

He drove her to the east gate and parked. "I'm going to have two officers follow you down the stretch of highway to the main road. We don't want to risk you being attacked." He leaped out. "Go to your car. I'll arrange it now."

"Thank you so much."

He cocked his head to stare at her with those strange yet appealing eyes. "I am hoping your presence will help Tiger heal faster." His gaze swept quickly over her body. "He will be motivated to heal at the sight of you." A small smile appeared. "Not to mention that we joke about how the scent of a female in heat could make us do anything they desire. You want him well."

Zandy liked the man. He spun away to talk to the officers at the guard shack. They had two of the heavily armed ones come down from the overhead walls and climb into a Jeep. She followed them for a few miles until they pulled over to the side of the road to wave her past them when they were sure no one hung around the wooded area looking for an easy target.

She gave them a grateful wave and drove toward her house. She needed to print out a map and grab some of her own clothing. The area was still unfamiliar to her and she wished she had a GPS system in her car. Money was always tight though and it was an expense she couldn't spare. Seeing her house after a few days away made her realize she hadn't missed it much.

The two-bedroom home had been in her price range and her budget. She'd bought it for that reason more than loving it. She unlocked the front door, stepped over the mail on the floor that had been pushed through the mail slot, and walked over to her desk. She turned on her laptop while she rushed into her bedroom. In minutes she'd changed into a pair of comfortable jeans, a tank top, and had packed a small overnight bag.

It only took her a minute to pull up driving directions to the hospital where Tiger had been taken and print them out. She grabbed the overnight bag and left her house. She wanted to get to him as soon as she was able. Worry ate at her. Would he really be all right? Jericho had seemed so certain that it helped keep her calm over the next few hours as she drove.

* * * * *

The woman at the front reception area stared at her blankly when she asked to speak to Trey Roberts. "I don't know who that is."

Zandy lowered her voice. "He's in charge of a security detail here. A New Species was brought in last night. His name is Tiger and he might be listed under the last name of North."

The woman's eyes narrowed. "We have no New Species patients."

"You do," Zandy insisted. She reached inside her purse and slapped down her driver's license. "Call his security detail and let them know I'm here. They are expecting me."

The woman reached out and took the identification and studied it before glancing around. Her voice came out low. "No one is to know he's a patient here. The press would be all over it. Have a seat while I call upstairs."

"Thank you."

She sat, nervous and worried. In minutes she watched a tall, beefy man in a gray, cotton, long-sleeve shirt and jeans approach the front desk. The woman she'd spoken to handed over her driver's license to him and pointed. Zandy rose to her feet when his gaze met hers.

"Zandy Gordon." He passed her license back to her. "I'm Trey Roberts. Please follow me."

Excitement and worry gripped her as the elevator doors closed. "How is Tiger?"

He suddenly moved and his hands roamed her body. "Sorry. I have to pat you down."

She didn't resist. "Is Tiger okay? What's his condition? They said he had some broken bones and a head injury."

He spun her around, patting down her back. "I'm just taking you to the NSO team. They will answer your questions. You're clean." He released her and held out his hand. "Give me your purse and your bag. I have to check them out."

She gave them both up easily. The doors opened and they stepped out on the eighth floor. He pointed to two men dressed similar to him and both of the muscled guys stood out in the hospital setting.

"Go to them. I will have to go through your bags here."

She followed the men down a hallway and into a room. Two large New Species were inside. They wore T-shirts and jeans too, and frowned when the door closed behind her as the human guards left her alone with them.

"I'm Bestial," the black-haired giant stated. "This is Jaded. You are Zandy Gordon." He sniffed the air, walked a circle around her to study every inch of her body and glared when he paused in front of her. "You don't smell of Tiger and I doub' your story. He isn't into human females."

The black-haired New Species with bright-green eyes growled softly at the other one. "Be kind, Bestial. It's not impossible. She is attractive. It's possible she's telling the truth."

"I don't believe it." His dark eyes narrowed. "Prove it, female."

"How is she going to do that? Tiger is unconscious. She doesn't carry his scent." Jaded crossed his arms over his chest. "The male Species who called seemed to believe her. He knows this human. We'll need to have faith it's the truth."

"She's not getting near Tiger." Bestial blocked her path.

Frustration and anger rose in Zandy. She reached up and grabbed her shirt, tugged it to the side and turned enough to toss her hair out of the way to reveal the back of her shoulder. The scratches and bite marks from Tiger's teeth couldn't be missed.

"Is that enough to prove to you that I'm telling the truth? Those are from Tiger." She glared at the much-taller New Species in defiance. "You could send someone to the apartment at Reservation where I'm staying and have him sniff my bedding. Tiger has slept there with me. There isn't maid service and I haven't been able to wash my sheets."

Shock widened Bestial's eyes as he stared at the injury to her skin. "You're his mate. Why didn't you say so?"

"We're not mated." She released her shirt and faced him. "He didn't mean to bite me. I never would have shown anyone since he said people would assume that but I'll do anything it takes to see him." She took a step closer. "Is he in that room behind you? Please move if he is. I've come a long way and I'm not leaving until I make sure he's okay." Her hands clenched at her sides, ready to do battle if need be. "You might be bigger but I'm determined."

Bestial's mouth parted but it was Jaded who spoke. "I'd step aside."

The big man backed up and pushed on the door. It led inside a hospital room and the sight of the still form on the bed caught Zandy's full attention. Tears blinded her when she saw how pale Tiger looked lying on the bed. A bandage covered most of his long, streaked hair. A bruise marred one cheek. Her gaze lowered to his bare chest where monitor leads had been attached. His left arm and leg were in casts, his ribs were wrapped and cuts marred his skin.

"Oh god." Her legs nearly buckled but she made it to his side. Her hand trembled as she gently touched his shoulder, a spot free of damage. "How bad is he?" Hot tears streaked down her cheeks. "Is he going to make it?"

"We're giving him special drugs designed to help us heal faster. He hasn't woken yet." Jaded drew next to her. "He had internal injuries, nine fractured bones in all, and some swelling in his brain. He is improving though. His blood pressure stabilized and the bones are repairing."

She nodded.

"As I stated, he was given special drugs we recovered from Mercile records that were salvaged. The fractures weren't severe. Our bones tend to heal fast but with the drugs it is just a matter of days. It helped that they weren't total breaks."

Her fingers caressed Tiger's jawline. "What about the swelling in his brain? Will these drugs help with that?"

"We think so. They gave him a scan two hours ago. The doctors said there was no bleeding and no fluid accumulated. He said the swelling had lessened. They didn't have to operate. The head doctors said it's a waiting game now to see if he has any damage when or if he wakes. They said he has a much better chance than a human would and his condition is remarkable, considering his injury."

She leaned down and her fingers played with some of his long hair that was free of the bandage around his forehead.

225

"I'm here, Tiger. Can you hear me? You need to get better for me. I'm going to stay with you."

"No, you are not."

Zandy twisted her head to glare at Bestial. "I'm not leaving him."

"The drugs he was given have a serious side effect. It's not safe for you to remain in this room. That's why Jaded and I are here. He could become very aggressive if he wakes."

"Tiger won't hurt me." She believed that.

Bestial hesitated. "Our kind have been known to get sexually aggressive as well as unreasonably combative from this drug. He was given high doses because he is so injured. He could hurt you and not mean to. He could wake to the scent of your heat cycle and force sex with you. He wouldn't mean to but your scent might drive him over the edge of sanity."

Zandy eyed the large man. "I'll be ecstatic if he feels well enough to want to have sex with me because it will mean he's getting better. You can't force the willing."

Bestial blinked but then laughed. "Fine."

"Thank you for letting me stay."

He nodded. "I will be sitting over there. One of us has to remain inside this room at all times in case he is aggressive when he wakes. We don't want him killing one of the medical staff. One of our human doctors came with us but she is sleeping right now."

Zandy returned her gaze to Tiger. He could have died, still could. She should have told him how she really felt. It might have made him dump her for fear that she was getting too attached to him but at least he'd know she loved him. Regret twisted at her.

No more fear. She silently made that promise. When he woke—she refused to consider anything less—she'd tell him that she was in love with him. He might not feel the same but she wasn't going to hide behind uncertainties anymore. Their future would be in his hands. He could end their budding relationship or take it to the next level.

She kicked off her shoes and assessed Tiger again, more closely now that the shock had worn off. The scratches were healing, not raw wounds. The bruises on his body appeared days old rather than from the night before. The drugs they were giving him were obviously some kind of miracle treatment for New Species. Gratitude for them struck her hard. It would give the man she loved a better chance at survival.

"He is tough," Jaded stated.

"Yes. I know." More tears threatened to fall. "I'm not giving up on him."

She ignored the two men who watched her every movement as she touched and softly spoke to Tiger. They didn't trust her perhaps or maybe it was just strange to see a human tending to one of their own but she didn't let it stop her from doing what she wanted.

At one point she walked into the bathroom to wet a washcloth and began cleaning the blood off Tiger's skin.

"The nurses will do that," Bestial informed her from his seat in the corner.

She ignored him and kept gently scrubbing Tiger's arms and chest. Zandy wanted something to do to feel as if she were helping him.

Chapter Sixteen

🔊

Zandy was tired when she woke. Jaded had touched her shoulder gently where she'd fallen asleep curled in the chair next to Tiger's bed. Her gaze lifted to the bright green stare of the New Species.

"I'm going to order breakfast for you. You should take a shower before it arrives."

"Thanks." Her gaze shifted to Tiger. Her palm rested on his chest where it rose and fell with each breath he took. The cuts looked almost healed and the bruising far less noticeable. "He looks better."

"The drugs are working. We'll feel better when he wakes and talks to us."

"I'm concerned about that myself," she admitted.

Jaded released her shoulder and backed away. "Bestial is talking to the task team here. Will you be all right for a few minutes alone? They make me fill out request forms for our food at the nurses' station." He rolled his eyes. "It's a silly human rule."

A smile curved her mouth at his expression. He was a handsome man but looked a little too stern. "Yeah. We're all about making silly rules sometimes. I'll be fine."

"He could wake. Yell if he does. We have no idea what kind of mental state he'll be in."

"You've warned me half a dozen times that the drugs could make him violent. I've assured you every time that he won't hurt me."

"Just yell if he wakes."

"Will do."

He left her alone and she stood, stretching her limbs after sleeping in the cramped position. Tiger's color looked better and she bent over him, brushing a kiss on his cheek.

"Wake up for me, sexy. I miss you."

The door opened behind her and she straightened. It was a doctor who stepped inside the room and he frowned when he spotted her. "Hello. I'm Dr. Razner." He drew closer to glance at Tiger, then the machines, before turning his attention on her again. "What agency do you work for?"

"Agency?" She had no idea what he was talking about.

"The nurses said you've been on duty since yesterday. You've bathed the patient and kept vigil at his bedside since you arrived. No one knows what agency you were hired from and I am slightly alarmed by that. Did you get permission to work here? This isn't a private home. Are you a registered nurse? A certified nurse practitioner?"

Her mind was still a little sluggish from lack of sleep. "I'm not a nurse."

"You're a doctor? What's your field?"

"I'm not one of those either. I'm here for Tiger."

The older man shoved his glasses a little higher on his nose and frowned. "What are you to him?"

She hesitated. "I'm his girlfriend."

The doctor's expression slowly changed to one she could easily read. Disapproval wrinkled his face and a coldness seeped into his gaze as he regarded her.

"Shame on you," he accused softly.

"Excuse me?" Shock slapped her at his words.

"Didn't your parents teach you right from wrong? It's abhorrent for humans to have intercourse with animals. That's just sick, young lady. This hospital boasts an excellent mental-health facility. You should go check yourself in immediately to get the treatment you need. You're an attractive young lady who doesn't need to stoop to dating those things."

It took a few seconds for Zandy to recover from the astonishment of his verbal attack and to let his insulting words to sink in. "How dare you speak to me that way." Her hands curl into fists, the urge to slap him strong. "Why don't you go find another doctor to pull your head out of your own ass?"

He sputtered. "What did you say to me?"

"You heard me. How dare you talk to me that way about Tiger. He's a better man than you'll ever be, you prejudiced loser. I deal with letters spewing hate and stupidity from pricks like you all day at work. You went to med school? Let me guess. Was it by any chance the school of doctors without brains? Where did you do your residency? Assholes anonymous?"

His fists clenched. "Get out of here before I call security. You're banned from this patient and the entire hospital."

"Fuck you." She flipped him off. "You're the one out of here. You're not touching Tiger. You're fired. I demand someone else treat him. I wouldn't let you near him with a ten-foot pole." She remembered that the NSO had their own female doctor somewhere on the premises who'd been sleeping when she'd arrived. "I want the NSO doctor right now."

"Security!" the creep yelled.

Jaded and Trey Roberts rushed into the room in seconds, both of them focused on Tiger, probably expecting him to be awake and violent. Zandy moved to block the doctor when he tried to step closer to Tiger's bed.

"Get the hell away from him."

"Get her out of here," the doctor demanded.

"Over your dead body," she threatened.

"What the hell is going on?" Trey Roberts stepped closer, glancing between them.

"He's fired," Zandy ground out. "I don't want him near Tiger ever again."

"This is my hospital. Get her out of here." The doctor glared at Trey. "I want our security staff in here and she's to be removed from the hospital property immediately."

"This piece of shit just lectured me about how sick it is to date an animal and called Tiger a thing." She took a threatening step closer to the doctor, ready to deck him. She was that angry. "Tiger is a wonderful person and you don't deserve to breathe the same air he does."

Jaded growled and the door opened again as Bestial and another task team member rushed inside the room.

"What is going on?" Bestial glanced at Tiger. "He didn't wake?"

Jaded moved slowly, cupped Zandy's hips, and tugged her away from the doctor. She didn't resist but kept glaring at him. The big New Species holding her growled again, deeper. The threatening sound caused her to turn her head to peer up into his face. His sharp teeth were showing as he watched the doctor with about the same amount of anger as she felt.

"Get out, Dr. Razner," Jaded demanded. "You're done here. You will no longer treat our male."

"This is my hospital."

Trey Roberts stepped between the doctor and where Jaded stood holding Zandy in front of him. "Get out, Dr. Razner. You're fired."

"You can't do that."

"Yes, we can," Trey argued. "I have the administrator of this hospital on speed dial." He pulled out his cell phone. "She assured us that Tiger would get the very best care and we would get her total cooperation on everything we need." He stepped into the doctor, bumped him back with his bigger body and glared at the shorter man. "I need you to get the fuck out before I lose my temper. Tiger is my friend, not a thing, and the only animal you need to worry about is me. I'm feeling like going a little savage on your dumb ass right now."

231

The doctor paled and stumbled back. Bestial growled, showed his sharp canines to the terrified doctor and Zandy watched the jerk flee the room. Trey shoved his phone back into his pocket and turned to stare at Jaded.

"That went well, don't you think? Did he piss his pants?"

"No."

"Too bad." Trey's gaze lowered to Zandy. "Are you okay?"

She nodded.

He turned to Bestial. "I'll let you handle Justice on that incident report, who will hopefully tell Tim not to jump my ass. I'm going to have a heart-to-heart chat with the administrator before that asswipe calls her, crying about us being mean to him." He chuckled. "I think we handled that well. No blood was spilled." He walked out of the room.

Bestial sighed, staring at Zandy. "What did I miss?"

"He is anti-Species," Jaded answered for her. "He insulted Tiger's female for being with him."

"Got it. I'll call Homeland to let them know what happened." He spun and left the room.

Jaded's hands released her hips and she faced him. "Thank you."

"You're lucky the humans are honest about their hatred with you. That same doctor was on duty when Tiger was brought in. He helped treat him but never showed his distaste for our kind. He could have harmed Tiger or not done his best to make him well without us realizing it."

"I can't believe he said that shit."

Jaded sighed loudly. "Get used to it, Zandy. You're with one of us and it unfortunately comes with the territory. I'm sure you knew it wouldn't be easy when you decided to be with Tiger."

"I really haven't thought much about it. Our circumstances are a bit odd."

He took a seat. "Talk to me and tell me how you two met."

"I'd rather skip that part."

His gaze narrowed while he watched her.

"It's kind of an embarrassing story I'd rather not share."

"How long have you been seeing him?"

"Not long." She walked over to Tiger and watched him rather than the man intent on getting information out of her.

"You're in heat. I asked one of the human task team members to pick you up some supplies to hide your scent."

That made her look at him and she blushed. "Sorry." She wasn't sure what else to say. It was still weird that they could smell her ovulating.

"It's a pleasant scent." He smiled. "That's the problem and why I asked them to get you a few items. Did Tiger tell you how to hide your scent? I could explain it to you if need be. I'm a council member and used to educating humans about Species habits."

"No. Creek told me how to do that."

"The male I asked to buy your supplies was upset by the request. You're blushing and so did he. I'll never understand why this causes that reaction in humans."

"Well, you asked him to buy me panty liners." She laughed. "My ex-husbands would never have done that for me."

"You have been married?" He frowned.

"Twice. And divorced."

"You don't have a good history of loyalty to men. Tiger is my friend. Do you plan to leave him as well?"

Zandy tried not to take offense since he was New Species. "My first husband cheated on me with another woman. My second husband turned out to be a bum. He didn't live on the streets, before you ask. He wouldn't get a job and he just wanted me to feed him and pay for everything. I got sick of it pretty fast. He also slept with one of our neighbors. I was always loyal to them but it wasn't returned. I just have shitty luck finding the right guy."

His expression softened. "I understand. They betrayed your trust and weren't mate-worthy." His gaze darted to Tiger before meeting hers again. "Tiger is a male who has sworn to never take a mate."

"I know. That about sums up my history with men. I'm always picking the ones who won't be in my life for long."

"I've watched you with him since yesterday. You have deep feelings for Tiger. Is he aware that you love him?"

She wasn't about to deny it. "No. He's been really clear that he's not looking for something lasting and I can respect that. I wasn't looking for a relationship either after being burned twice by love. Now, I wish I'd told him."

"He'll survive. He's a tough male."

"I hope so." Hot tears filled her eyes and she blinked them back. "I'm going to go take that shower. You're staying with him, right? I don't want him left alone."

"We have another room next door where Bestial and I are sleeping. It has a private bathroom. Go use it. Your bags were taken there. They are in the corner."

"Thanks." She checked on Tiger one last time before crossing the room. She had opened the door when Jaded spoke again.

"Zandy?"

She turned toward him. "Yes?"

"Please come here."

Nervousness pitted her stomach. "Why?"

"Curiosity. I won't harm you. I would like to see those bites again please."

She could refuse but Jaded had stood up for her with Dr. Razner. She stopped before him and he stood. His hands were gentle as he lifted her hair out of the way and tugged her shirt to the side to expose the back of her shoulder.

"I can see two distinctive times you were bitten." He paused. "They were done at different times. Did you ask him to do this to you?"

"No."

"You're a small female and we're strong. Did he accidentally take you too rough and cause you to try to get away from him during sex?"

"No."

"For someone who doesn't want a mate, he's extremely possessive of you." He released her shirt and stepped away. "Has he bitten you anywhere else?"

She shook her head.

"We don't usually bite females during sex unless we are in the middle of it and they try to move away. We will grip them with our teeth to hold them in place during highly passionate moments. It's instinct to finish the sex with us after a certain point. The only other time a male has been known to bite a female is possessiveness. The urge to have all of them, including to know the taste of their blood on our tongues. To mark them for that reason is very rare. It's a trait we've discovered in males who want to make the female their mate. Tiger has bitten you twice, one of those times deep enough to scar. It's a lasting mark that will warn off other males who see it. They'll know there's a male willing to kill them if they mount you."

"He said he just lost control. He didn't mean to do it. You're making too much out of this."

"I'm educating you, Zandy. I don't care what he said. Actions speak with Species. Those bites assure me that my friend isn't easily going to allow you to leave his life. Think about this while he recovers. He might not have wanted a mate and you might not have wanted one either but you both are feeling strongly for each other."

She nodded her understanding and hope flared to life that perhaps Tiger was falling in love with her too. "I'm going to take a quick shower."

"Go." Jaded took his seat. "Breakfast will be here soon."

The other room was empty but four cots had been set up in there, all obviously used by Tiger's security detail. Her bags were neatly stored in one of the corners and she walked into a towel-messy bathroom. Clean ones were folded but a pile of used, wet ones were on the floor. She closed and locked the door behind her.

The shower felt great after spending a rough night sleeping in a chair at Tiger's side. Jaded's words were stuck in her mind. The thought that Tiger wanted to mate her didn't make her fearful. It wouldn't be easy telling her family about him but she'd deal with them. They'd be leery of any man she fell for after two divorces.

It would change her life but he would be worth every single one. They'd have to live at the NSO. She loved the people there and wouldn't miss her house. She wasn't attached to it except for the mortgage payment. Tiger was one in a billion and worth taking risks for.

She dried off quickly, dressed and returned her bags to the corner of the room. Bestial had exchanged sitting duty with Jaded when she entered Tiger's room. He was eating and met her gaze.

"You showered."

"I did." She approached Tiger's bed. His coloring had improved and the scratches were healed. It amazed her how much better he looked in a twenty-four-hour period. "The drugs he's on are amazing."

"Mercile did a lot of bad things but they were an excellent pharmaceutical developer. They wanted the ability to heal us quickly after the abuse they made us suffer at their hands. Sick test subjects weren't useful to them."

That sobered her appreciation. She reached out to caress Tiger's cheek. His nose twitched when her fingertips traced his jawline and his mouth tightened. Excitement made her heart race as she leaned in closer to him.

"Tiger? Can you hear me?" She didn't look away but spoke to Bestial. "He moved."

The chair squeaked and the New Species rounded the other side of the bed. "Talk to him," he encouraged. "I'm right here in case he wakes violently. If he does, get back and I'll handle him."

"Tiger? Please open your eyes. It's Zandy. I'm right here. Come back to me. Come on and open those beautiful blues for me."

His hand moved and she grabbed it with her free one, squeezing it gently. His chin lifted a little as his head turned in her direction, seeming to seek her out.

"Wake up for me," she urged. "Tiger?"

His eyelids parted and he stared at her, looking confused. His tongue darted out to lick his lips. "Zandy?"

"Yes!" Joy hit her hard. He was awake and knew who she was. She had to blink back happy tears that he had come out of his coma-like sleep. "I'm right here. You're going to be fine."

His expression changed, hardened. He tore his hand out of hers and a deep, mean snarl came from his parted lips. "Get away from me." He turned his face away as if her touch burned him. "Go! I can't have a mate. Stay away from me. You aren't safe."

Her horrified and hurt gaze lifted to Bestial's. He appeared just as stunned as she was by Tiger's reaction to her. He glanced down.

"Tiger, you're in a hospital. Zandy is fine. You—"

"Get her out of here." Tiger reached up and grabbed his friend by the shirt and snarled again. "Get her away from me. I won't ever see her again. I won't take her for a mate. Never!"

"Tiger," Bestial snarled.

His heart rate was so fast the alarm he was hooked to started beeping in warning. He turned his head and roared. "Humans are the enemy. They attack for no reason and there's no safety. Get away from me!" he roared and tried to get out of bed.

"Stay down!" Bestial threw his body forward to hold his injured friend down. "Get help, Zandy."

She stumbled back, horrified that Tiger blamed her for what had been done to him. He fought Bestial and turned his head to glare at her. Another roar tore from him and pure rage showed on his face. The door behind her burst open as Jaded and two human task team members rushed inside.

"Get Dr. Allison," Bestial shouted. "Tell her we need to sedate him."

"Get her away from me," Tiger snarled. "She's not safe. The enemy is everywhere. I will never take you for a mate. I never should have touched you. Get away from me!"

She spun and rushed for the other door. Seeing her made him fight harder. Her bags were still in the other room and she grabbed them. Her shoes were near Tiger's bed but she wasn't going to go back in his room to retrieve them. Another roar sounded as she stepped out into the main hallway barefoot. Nurses and doctors rushed toward Tiger's room.

She ended up in the elevator alone, crying. Tiger and she were over. He regretted ever touching her. Those words still rang in her ears. It devastated her. So much for hoping he loved her and wanted something serious. He'd demanded his friend throw her out of the room.

She completely broke down in a fit of tears when she reached her car. Tiger would live but he wouldn't be part of her life anymore. It tore her heart apart. She finally pulled herself together, paid for parking and began the long journey to her house. She might need her job at the NSO but she wasn't ready to return to work until she had some time to harden her heart.

* * * * *

Bestial glared at Tiger. "Why did you say all that bullshit to Zandy?"

Tiger snarled. "Mind your own business."

Bestial growled back. "You were very wrong to do that."

The door opened and Dr. Allison Baker rushed in with her medical bag. "What is it? Is he having a violent reaction?"

"He's having a something," Jaded snarled. "Sedate him."

She shoved her bag at one of the human task team members who held it and she withdrew a syringe. Tiger wildly fought at her approach.

"Get that human away from me. They aren't safe."

"Knock it off," Jaded hissed. "Give him the shot. He's strong for someone so injured. Do it before he reopens his wounds."

The doctor jabbed Tiger in the hip and jumped back as he fought the two males holding him down. "It's going to take a minute. I didn't want to risk over-sedating him."

Tiger panted but his thrashing lessoned. "What happened to the others? We were in a helicopter crash."

Bestial answered. "You were hurt the worst. The others lived but one of the pilots suffered severe burns. He's being treated in the burn unit."

"Tell me what two plus two is," Allison demanded. "I need to know if you've suffered any brain damage."

Tiger growled. "Four. Did they catch whoever shot us down?"

"Yes," Jaded said, nodding. "There were six human males trespassing in the woods. We've changed the flight patterns to prevent them from trying to shoot at more of us. The helicopter was a total loss. We're going to be down one for a few weeks. We've ordered another but the company said that is the quickest they can do the modifications we need."

Bestial growled. "Why the hell did you say all that to Zandy?"

Tiger snarled. "Mind your own business."

Jaded gave him a disgusted look. "She sat with you and wouldn't leave your side except to go to the bathroom. She threw a doctor out of this room because he called us animals. She held your hand."

"She bathed you," Bestial added. "She talked to you while you slept until she was almost without a voice. I told her how dangerous you could be because we had to give you the healing drugs but she didn't care. She said she knew you wouldn't hurt her. She was wrong, wasn't she, Tiger?"

Tiger growled. "Zandy doesn't belong with me."

Bestial drew back when Tiger ceased struggling, the sedative taking hold. "I want her if you don't. I see what kind of mate she'd make. I'm not a fool but you seem to be one."

Jaded growled at Tiger. "I'll definitely take her. You hit your head really hard to have no sense left."

Tiger tried to get up but both males moved, pushing him back down. Tiger snarled and tried to fight while they struggled to hold him down.

"You need to stay put!" Jaded roared at him.

Tiger snarled and snapped at Jaded, almost biting into his friend's forearm. Jaded roared again at Tiger, barely escaping his snapping teeth.

"Hold him down," Bestial ordered the other New Species and human task team members. His gaze sought Dr. Allison. "When is the sedative going to knock him out?"

"Any second. His heart rate is high and the adrenaline from his anger is fighting the effects of the drugs."

Bestial relaxed his hold on Tiger when the male turned limp and his eyes closed in sleep. "He is strong for someone so hurt."

Jaded softly growled. "We should have let him get up and hit the damn floor for what he did to Zandy."

Bestial sighed. "He hurt her deeply. I saw the pain he inflicted on her emotionally."

Jaded growled. "Asshole."

Bestial nodded.

Chapter Seventeen

🔊

Zandy parked her car in the driveway and just sat there. It had been a long, horrible twenty-four hours. She'd learned Tiger had been in an accident and now she'd lost him. He was alive. That was all that really mattered. Tears threatened to spill again but she pushed them back. Ice cream was definitely going on her list of what to do next.

She unlocked the door and pushed it open, instantly shocked at the sight that greeted her. Her couch was ripped up and the stuffing from the cushions spread on the carpet. The table next to it lay on the floor in pieces with the lamp smashed. Something red had been smeared on the walls and her nose picked up the smell of paint and something offensive.

"What the…"

Someone had broken in and vandalized her house. She took a few steps backward, afraid whoever had done it might still be there. She spun to rush to a neighbor to call the police but gasped instead, jerking to a halt. A tall man blocked her door where he stood on the porch. He appeared to be in his late twenties. He frowned.

"Hello, Satan's whore."

His words sank in. She heard glass crunch under someone's heel and jerked her head to stare at her living room again. Two more men in their twenties walked out of her kitchen area. They had paint smeared on their hands—at least she hoped that was the source of the red. It looked a lot like blood. Her gaze darted to the wall and she was sure the nasty words scrawled there were done in paint. Her head twisted back around.

"I have fifty bucks in my wallet. Take it." Her hands trembled as she held out her purse in one hand and her car keys in the other. "Take the car too. They are just things to me and not worth my life." She took a shaky breath. "I never saw you or your friends. Take whatever you want but please don't hurt me. I swear to God that I won't even call the cops."

The one she confronted snorted loudly. "What would you know about God? We're not here to steal your possessions. We're here for you."

Fear tensed her entire body. "Why?"

"You work at Reservation and help the demons who walk this earth."

Confusion was her next emotion. "What?"

He stepped forward and closed the door behind him, trapping her inside her destroyed living room with him and his two friends. "We thought you might be Jessie North but our Brother told us your real name and address. That's how we found you. He gave us your information before those demons killed him."

"He can't be dead," one of the men behind her whispered. "Don't say that, Brother Adam."

She darted a glance at the speaker, the youngest of the bunch. He had a severe acne problem and she pegged him to be in his early twenties. Tears filled his eyes as he stared at the man in front of her. She looked at Brother Adam since he seemed to be in charge.

"He never got out of that den of evil. They either killed him or his soul has been compromised. They spread their evil into others. I'm sorry about your cousin, Brother Bruno. He gave his life to hand us this sinner." The jerk in front of her stared down at her. "We'll make his sacrifice count."

Zandy knew she was in deep shit. Her terror level notched higher.

Brother Adam smiled—a cold, scary sight that didn't reach his dark glare, which was directed at her. "She's going to

243

set an example to all God-fearing women to stay away from those demons."

The third man chuckled behind her. "I think she'll look good nailed to a cross and set on fire at the gates of that hellish place. It will be shown worldwide to all the potential sinners and dissuade them from stepping away from the righteous path. We'll call all the media outlets to be there to witness the first strike at evil."

She'd heard enough. The three men were nuts and no amount of reasoning would make them sane. Her gaze darted around the room before she addressed the one in front of her. Hate mail had come in from enough religious fanatics that she could guess these were a few of them.

"Are you with the Woods Church? Your leader has sent in a lot of mail to the NSO. I read it." She darted her gaze around the room, hunting for an escape route. "We could discuss the grievances he has with New Species."

"That hack?" Brother Adam snorted. "He doesn't speak for God. We do."

She lunged toward the kitchen to reach the back door. A scream tore from her throat in hope that one of her neighbors would hear it and call 9-1-1. Her quick movement surprised the men but there weren't just three of them. She slammed into a fourth one when he jumped around the corner into her path.

"Got you!"

She collided with him hard enough to bounce off his body and her ass hit the floor hard. Zandy screamed again and rolled away. Pain shot up her arm when her palm came down on broken glass from the lamp. A hand fisted in her hair and dragged her to her feet. Agony made her gasp.

The one holding her hair used it to control her as she was flung forward and crashed into the wall. Her cheek hurt from the force of hitting the plaster. Hands grabbed her from behind to yank her arms behind her back. The hand in her hair pulled and she screamed again as her attacker rammed her face into the wall.

"Let's get out of here. Someone could have heard her."

"Get the van," Brother Adam demanded. He was the one gripping her hair.

A hand wrapped around her throat and squeezed. Zandy fought but a body leaned in and pinned her painfully between it and the wall. He had her hair in one fist and her neck in the other. She couldn't breathe, her face got really hot and pure panic surged when it dawned that she was suffocating.

She tried to claw at the hand on her throat but more hands grabbed her and pinned her arms to the wall. She kicked and struggled but couldn't get away. Spots appeared before her eyes before blackness swept reality away.

* * * * *

Tiger awoke to stare at a white ceiling with thousands of tiny holes high above where he lay. The smells hit him next. Humans, antiseptic and air-conditioning. He wrinkled his nose at the hospital smell he recognized as he struggled to remember how he'd gotten there.

Memory returned quickly of the terror he'd experienced when the helicopter had been struck by ground fire and gone down. The crash had been painful but he'd obviously survived. He turned his head to stare at the male seated in the corner.

"How are you feeling now?" Bestial growled. "Feel like less of a bastard?"

Tiger was shocked by his friend's words. "It wasn't my fault the helicopter crashed. Did everyone make it?"

Bestial nodded grimly. "One of the human pilots was touch and go but they said he'll live. He is in the burn unit. You were given the Mercile drugs. You suffered broken bones and a head injury. You will be in some pain for another day but you should be fine by tomorrow night at the rate you're healing."

Tiger relaxed. "I need a phone please. I have a call to make."

Bestial growled. "No."

Tiger felt stunned. "No?"

"No. I wouldn't do anything for you at this moment. I wouldn't even be here anymore if Justice hadn't unfortunately ordered Jaded and me to protect you."

Tiger looked confused. "Why are you so angry with me? What is your problem?"

"Don't pretend you don't understand my issue. I meant what I said. I'm going to pursue the female and mate her myself. You're a fool, Tiger. A dumb fool."

"I have no idea what you're talking about. Her who?"

Bestial snorted. "She sat at your bedside and tended to you. She slept curled in a chair at your bedside just to hold your hand while you were unconscious."

"Who? How long was I out?" Tiger felt shock. "How injured am I?"

"Were. I told you the drugs are working. Your bones were broken but they are mending fast. Your arm and leg are fine but they haven't had time to remove the casts yet. Your head suffered a severe enough injury that the doctors suspected you might not wake. They say you are fine now but I disagree. I think you have major brain damage. You lost your common sense."

"What is your problem? Why are you so angry with me?"

"She pushed her chair next to you to keep touching you while you slept. I watched her bathe and tend to you. She almost lost her voice whispering to you to get better and wake for her. She wouldn't go to another room to sleep on a bed. Hell no. Instead she sat there worried about you."

"Who did?"

Bestial frowned. "You know who."

Tiger shook his head, puzzled. "I have no idea what you are talking about."

Bestial softly cursed. "You don't remember Zandy being here?"

Tiger tried to sit up but gasped in pain from his ribs. His gaze darted around the room frantically. "Where is Zandy?" He inhaled but the hospital odors messed with his sense of smell. Her scent didn't linger. He stared at his friend.

The big male slowly stood and approached his bed. "You made her leave. You said harsh words until she cried and fled."

Tiger's eyes widened. "What are you talking about?" Rage hit him hard. "I wouldn't do that. Where is Zandy?"

A snarl came from Bestial as he gripped the bed railings. "You honestly don't remember your verbal attack on her before you demanded she leave?"

"No." Tiger struggled to sit again. "I wouldn't have done that."

"You did." Bestial pushed him flat. "Stop struggling. You need to stay down!"

Tiger glared at his friend. "Where is Zandy? I have no memory of seeing her. She was the last thing I thought about before the crash. She is in danger being with me and I need to protect her from humans harming her."

"She arrived here yesterday morning after hearing about the helicopter crash and demanded to see you. She even showed us your bite marks to prove she was with you because it was difficult to believe you were involved with a human female. You woke and verbally attacked her."

"I wouldn't do that." Tiger had a sinking feeling he had though since Bestial wouldn't lie to him. "What exactly did I say?"

The door opened and Jaded walked in. "He's awake again? Do we need to sedate him again?"

"He claims no memory of waking before or seeing Zandy."

"Shit." Jaded paused by his bed, frowning. "Honestly?"

Tiger stared at his other friend and felt his heart squeeze in his chest. "What did I say to her?"

"You yelled at her that you didn't want a mate and you'd never take one. You ordered her thrown out of your room." Jaded paused. "You said she was your enemy."

Tiger stared wide-eyed at them both. "Tell me this is payback for some of the pranks I've pulled on you both. I didn't really do that."

Bestial's gaze softened. "You did. She cried and took off out of here fast. She was in pain and shock. You hurt her deeply. She didn't deserve that, Tiger. She loves you. She sat here tending to you and not leaving your side. She left Reservation as soon as she heard what happened and drove her own car here. Smiley tried to talk her in to waiting for an escort but was told it would be hours before they could free up males to escort her. She refused to wait and had to get permission to be allowed to see you. She loves you and anyone could see that from the way she looked at you. You were a total ass and she is a good female, Tiger. You are a stupid bastard not to have taken that one to mate."

"I don't remember. I…" He was in shock. "I wouldn't say any of that to her."

"You did." Bestial softly cursed. "You really don't remember?"

"No. I wouldn't do that, damn it. I wouldn't drive Zandy away. That's why I want a phone. I need to call her."

"You did it," Jaded confirmed. "You made her flee in tears and in pain. It must have been the drugs. We didn't know. We just thought you were being an asshole since you've always been so vocal against Species mating humans."

"How long ago did she leave?" Tiger felt his chest squeeze in pain.

"Five hours. She's had time to get back to Reservation." Bestial withdrew his cell phone. "I will get her on the phone for you and tell her it was the drugs talking and not you."

Tiger nodded. "Please."

Bestial dialed and asked to talk to Security after identifying himself. "Direct my call to Zandy Gordon's escort."

He listened. "You are sure?" He paused. "Fine. I want to be called immediately when she gets there." He hung up and grimly gazed at Tiger. "She never arrived back at Reservation."

"How far are we from there?"

"Almost three hours by vehicle."

"She must have gone home." Tiger softly cursed. "Give me your cell. I'll call hers."

Tiger dialed the number he'd memorized but it just rang until it went to voicemail. "Zandy? It's Tiger. I just woke up and don't remember what happened before. I didn't mean anything I said. I was out of my head. Please call me, little one. This is Bestial's number you see on your phone so call it back." He hung up.

Bestial eyed him. "Little one?"

Tiger frowned.

Jaded chuckled. "You have it bad, don't you?"

Tiger hesitated. "She's all I think about, so yes, I have it bad."

Bestial sat back down. "The feeling is mutual. She loves you very much and is completely dedicated to you. It was very obvious. She was terrified you wouldn't make it and she tended to you as if she was your mate. It was very impressive."

Tiger relaxed. "She is very impressive."

Bestial suddenly laughed. "She might not forgive you. She would make a wonderful mate."

"Try to go after her and die," Tiger growled. "She's mine."

"But you haven't mated her," Jaded pointed out, grinning.

"I am confused," Tiger admitted. "I never wanted a mate but I hadn't met her. She has been hurt by males and I've been trying to take things slow."

Jaded shook his head. "It isn't our way. We take what we want."

Bestial snorted. "Tiger spends too much time around the task force listening to those males. The human condition must be rubbing off on him."

"Bite me," Tiger growled.

"You nearly bit Jaded," Bestial informed him. "I think that's enough near-blood draws for the day."

Tiger glanced at both males and saw honesty in their faces. He couldn't remember snapping at one of them with his teeth. "I have to explain to Zandy that I didn't mean the words that were said."

"He has it bad." Jaded leaned against the wall and grinned. "Tiger is going to take a mate."

"Perhaps not. She might prefer me," Bestial boasted with a chuckle.

Tiger forced his body to move despite the pain and struggled until he sat upright. He glared at his friend. "I will get up and beat you if you keep threatening to go after what is mine. She's all I think about when I'm not with her. It's gotten hard to leave her side and her scent nearly drives me insane from wanting to touch and mount her."

He knew he shocked his friends as they gaped at him, all traces of humor gone from both males. He didn't care what they thought. He'd messed up badly by sending Zandy away.

"I love the feel of her in my arms when I am going to sleep and waking with her is wonderful. I think of her when she isn't with me but I want her to be. Zandy is exceptional. She's different. She's —"

"Your mate," Bestial cut him off. "Idiot. Whether you wanted one or not, you have her, Tiger. At least you did. You caused her tears. It was hard for me to watch and I can't imagine how it would harm a mate to hear those words. You inflicted great damage. I don't know if she would wish to stay with you after today."

"Get her home number. Maybe she doesn't have her cell phone with her. She might have forgotten it when she heard of the accident."

Bestial nodded and called the NSO again, asking for Zandy's home number. He memorized it and dialed while watching Tiger. "I will tell her it was the drugs and offer her an escort back here."

Tiger was relieved. "Thank you. I have to tell her I never meant what I said."

Bestial frowned. "Her phone is busy."

Impatience drove Tiger insane after many failed attempts to reach her. "I can't stand this anymore. Help me up. We're going to her home."

"No," Jaded stated. "You're staying put until you're healed."

"I need to get to Zandy."

"Remain calm," Bestial ordered. "I have a plan. Human females talk too much but I know there is a way to have an operator do an emergency interrupt. I would call this urgent." He made a phone call and then finally hung up. He eyed Tiger. "Her phone is off the hook. The operator said so."

Tiger tried to climb out of bed. "I'm going to her. She is upset and I need to clear this up."

Bestial moved fast and pushed him back. "She only lives a few miles from Reservation, correct? I'll send a few of our males to her house and make them hand her the phone to talk to you."

Tiger grinned. "Thank you."

Bestial shrugged. "Remember this if I find myself a human mate and I screw up. I might need a few favors."

Tiger smiled. "My word to you."

* * * * *

Zandy's face hurt when she roused and her mouth felt swollen. Her bottom lip throbbed when she ran her tongue over it and she tasted blood. She tried to sit up but something kept her restrained. She slowly took in her surroundings and realized she was on a bench inside an old motor home.

Handcuffs chained her wrists together in front of her and thick straps at her shoulders, waist, thighs, and ankles secured her flat. She tried to wiggle her arms out from under the straps but they were too tight. She strained to hear anything but didn't pick up any sounds.

The motor home had seen better days with its fading orange-and-brown décor. She tilted her head back to see the kitchen and found the source of the smell that bothered her when she spotted a lot of dirty dishes. Whoever it belonged to was a slob.

Her head turned and she stared at the scattered pamphlets littering the floor. She twisted her head enough to read a few. They were targeted toward spreading hatred for New Species by using religion.

"Fuck," she sighed, dropping her head back on the padded bench. Memory returned and fear grew into terror.

They had mentioned burning her at the stake. She'd read enough hate mail to guess what their basic beliefs were. Some fanatic religious groups had popped up, stating that the human/animal hybrids were really spawn of the devil put on Earth to bring the destruction of mankind. They'd watched too many horror movies in her opinion but unfortunately they weren't prone to listening to a voice of reason. They were firm in their conviction that only evil beings could have fangs and growl.

Think! Calm down. You need to get out of this mess.

A man's voice penetrated her thoughts, growing louder. Her head turned toward the closed door, expecting someone to check on her at the very least. Her only chance would be to trick them into releasing her. Her arms and legs strained against the restraints but they had no give in them.

"Tonight we'll show all those devils that they can't win."

Another man spoke, sounding nervous. "It will make women think twice before associating with evil. Are you sure we shouldn't drug her first? I don't know if I can stomach listening to her scream while she burns."

Zandy's stomach heaved. They really planned to burn her alive. It was beyond horrific. Her terror returned full force as she struggled harder against the strong belts.

"We are righteous in this, Brother. It's our duty to show what must be done when one embraces evil."

"You're right, Brother Adam. I believe that as strongly as I believe in our charter. We must show the sinners how they will be punished to prevent this plague from spreading."

The door to the motor home creaked loudly as it opened. The bright sunshine that poured inside momentarily blinded her and she blinked a few times. She'd been unconscious all night. The first man who stepped inside was the one who'd blocked her exit last night at her front door. He met her frightened stare with a frown.

"You are awake. I will listen to you now if you want to confess your sins before your soul cleansing this evening."

Zandy refrained from calling him some choice, insulting names and from telling him what a stupid, crazy son of a bitch he was. Another man, a new one, who appeared to be in his mid-sixties followed Adam up the few stairs. His wrinkled gaze narrowed on her.

"She doesn't look evil, Brother Adam."

"She allies herself with the devils. Don't forget that. Evil comes in many forms and her innocent looks are just a ruse for the foolish."

The older man nodded grimly. "That is true. She might end up a bride of a demon like the other women who visit their den of evil if we don't intervene."

Adam nodded. "We're saving her soul. She's a mere woman and we all know how weak and foolish they are when they see masculine skin. That is why those NSO demons are all so big. Women take one look at them and it drives them to the sin of feeling lust. They hide their women from us because they know we're stronger and can resist sins of the flesh."

Oh, hell! She couldn't hold back anymore. These guys were flat-out ridiculous. "You know what you could save me from?"

The old man peered at her curiously. "What do you want to be saved from, child? Do you wish to embrace God and take the right path before your soul is cleansed of evil on this night?"

"I want to be saved from you crazy morons. That's the biggest load of horseshit I've ever heard. Men are the ones who think with their dicks. If you're so religious have you ever heard of the Ten Commandments? Thou shall not kill. Does that one ring any bells?"

Adam sputtered. "See? Her soul is already gone. She probably fornicates with the devil himself. It's just as I stated. Those demons flash their muscles and they turn the women into lusting whores. This is why she must be nailed to the cross and her soul cleansed with fire."

Fear was replaced by anger quickly. "If I was doing the devil he'd be here and torch your asses, like having a big weenie roast. Ever consider that? The devil knows all, right? He'd come get me if I belonged to him. Let me go, you stupid bastards."

"See?" Adam nodded at the old man. "Hatred pours from her mouth."

"Hatred? You're talking about nailing me to a cross and setting me on fire. You honestly think I'm hateful because I can call you stupid bastards? Hello? Can you use your brains for once? You might want to ponder that one before you commit murder."

The old man frowned. "We aren't really going to nail you to a cross. We're going to bind you to it. Putting nails through your body would be too cruel."

Zandy's mouth opened in shock. "Are you kidding me? You don't think setting me on fire is cruel? Who the hell are you people and what is wrong with you? Lay off the damn drugs, people. Put down your joints and smoke some common sense."

"That's enough," Adam snapped. "We are saving your soul. We are cleansing you and showing others that working for the devils will bring nothing but death and destruction."

The older man eagerly agreed. "Fire cleanses the soul."

"What do you assholes do in your spare time? Go hunt down teenagers who listen to rock music while wearing black, accuse them of being witches, and dunk them? Give me a break. Ever hear of medication? Get on it."

"We do not need medication!" Adam yelled. "Our mission in life is casting out all evil and doing God's will by fighting the devil and his spawn, created by his minions."

"Minions? For real? How many comic books have you read? They aren't real. Newsflash for you, nut job. The only evil happening is you twisting religion to suit your narrow-minded bigotry against people you don't understand." She glared at him. "I might not be able to get free but I want you to know one thing, Brother Adam. You're a pathetic idiot." Her gaze cut to the older man. "The only things more pathetic than a moron are the ones who follow him."

She might not have long to live but damn it, she would make them miserable while she had breath. Both men looked ready to explode in rage after she'd insulted them. It was slightly satisfying and encouraged her to go on. She'd always wanted to vent after reading hate mail and she suddenly had a chance to unload—if she could hold back her fear.

"I think your real problem is you have no life and this is the only way you can get a woman. You have to kidnap them and tie them down to make them listen to this bullshit. It must be rough knowing you're both such losers and it's a jealousy thing, isn't it? New Species are hot and you both couldn't get laid if you walked into a whorehouse wearing hundred-dollar bills."

* * * * *

Bestial's phone rang and Tiger felt his heart jump in his chest. Zandy would have to forgive him after he explained about the medications and how he didn't even remember what he'd said. He'd tell her how he felt about her and she would hopefully believe him. He wouldn't give up until she did. He could be very convincing when need be and he refused to give up on getting her back into his life.

His friend answered the phone. "This is Bestial."

Tiger watched the male's face pale and his mouth tighten. Anger glinted in Bestial's eyes as a growl burst from his lips. "Tell me what it looked like." He paused. "How many? Could you follow the trail?" He listened. "Are you sure?"

Alarm gripped Tiger, sensing something was seriously wrong. Had the NSO been attacked again? Another helicopter fired upon? He struggled to sit up in bed, his ribs feeling much better since he'd gotten several hours of sleep.

Bestial refused to look at him. "Call in all law enforcement, even the humans. This is priority. We must find those males immediately and I want to be called the second you know anything." He hung up.

"What has happened? Are any of our people hurt? I am so tired of the stupid humans. Why can't they all be reasonable, like the majority of them?"

Bestial rose from his chair by the door and finally held his gaze. The cold, angry look in them only made him more certain something horrible had happened. His friend stalked closer to the bed before he paused within arm's reach.

The male pulled in a deep breath. "We couldn't free any task members to escort our males to Zandy's home until this morning."

Tiger's stomach knotted and his hands clenched into fists at his lap. The rate of his heart raced and he had a sick feeling something bad had happened to the female he had such strong feelings for.

"Is she well?" He knew he couldn't stand it if the answer wasn't positive.

"Her home was vandalized and they smelled four human males." He reached out and gripped Tiger's upper arms to keep him in place. Sympathy softened his gaze as they stared at each other. "They also found her blood. Her car was in the driveway but she wasn't there. They believe she was attacked and stolen."

The information was too horrifying to be real but Tiger knew Bestial wouldn't lie to him on this matter.

"They lost her scent outside by the curb. They spoke to neighbors who saw a van there yesterday evening. Two of them thought they heard a few screams but believed it was someone's television playing too loud. More of her blood was found outside. She was alive and actively bleeding when they took her. There wasn't much, if that's a comfort. I'm sure if they meant to kill her, they would have left her body. We're doing everything we can to try to find her, Tiger."

He lost his mind. It hurt too much to think and a roar tore from his throat as he tried to shoot out of the bed. Strong arms shoved him down and he fought. Zandy was out there, injured and kidnapped by human males. She needed him.

"Stop it," Bestial shouted. "You're still healing."

The doors were shoved open as more of the task team rushed into the room and they tried to hold his body flat. He fought hard, snarling and biting at anything that came near his mouth.

"Let me up! I need to find her."

"Calm!" Jaded roared, drawing Tiger's attention.

He stared at the other feline Species and battled his emotions. "Get me my clothes now. I'm going after my female. Help me or get out of my way!"

"I understand but you're still weakened by injuries."

Tiger flashed his sharp teeth. "They took my female. Would you lie here meekly while others searched in your place? She's mine."

Jaded hesitated.

Bestial eased his hold. "I'd feel the same if it were my mate. Let me get you some of my clothing. Your clothes were damaged. We'll find her, Tiger." He spun away and left the room.

Tiger yanked out the lines to the monitors and in seconds was shoving his legs over the edge of the bed after all the males released him. He tore off the hospital gown.

Misery and fear flooded Tiger as he swayed on his feet waiting for Bestial to return, ignoring all eyes on him except Jaded's. A sharp jab of pain dug into his heart at the thought that his Zandy might be dead. He shoved that concept away instantly. If they'd just wanted to kill her then they would have done so. They would have left her discarded body inside her house. No. They'd taken her for a purpose. Tiger snarled.

"I'll kill them all if they hurt one damn hair on her head."

Bestial walked in carrying the clothes. "We will help you do it."

Jaded reached out to help steady him. "We will find her."

Chapter Eighteen

∞

Zandy fought the urge to cry, refusing to give Brother Adam the satisfaction of seeing her break down. She rarely hated people to the extent of wishing she could choke the living shit out of them but for him she'd make an exception. The idea of wrapping her hands around his throat and watching him turn blue while she squeezed calmed her. She'd had to listen to his rambling hate until she'd given up on insulting him. It only seemed to encourage him more.

A new man entered the motor home to address Brother Adam. This one looked fresh out of high school and needed a haircut. His shirt had holes and his faded jeans were in just as poor shape. His gaze avoided her completely.

"We are ready to test it, Brother. We need to make certain it will work for the real thing. Brother Davey said it should hold her weight but we don't want it to break during the cleansing."

"No, we don't." The jackass stood from the table and shot Zandy a glare. "We want her to burn without any glitches. We don't want to create any bad press that would hurt our cause."

"Yeah, committing murder will really endear you to people," she snorted.

"Shut up!" Brother Adam ran his fingers through his hair, looking enraged. "She never stops." He glared. "I wish we had taken a different one."

"Me too. We finally agree on something."

"You are a vile woman."

"You're a crazy dickhead, hiding behind a warped Bible."

His face turned red and he took a threatening step toward her. The older man stepped between them. "She's tempting you to sin, Brother."

"Send Brothers Bruno and Fred in here and we'll carry her outside."

Zandy couldn't do anything but lie there waiting until the other men arrived to crowd into the tight confines of the motor home's living room. The bench she was strapped to reminded her of a rescue backboard. They hoisted her up and tried to carry her out the door but it was too wide. Pain gripped her where the belts dug into her skin when they turned her sideways.

She screamed from the pain. It seemed to amuse Adam and he laughed. The sunshine blinded her again when it directly hit her face as they straightened her out. A sick feeling made her grateful that they were starving her, otherwise she might have thrown up.

Her eyes adjusted to the bright light and she took note of all the trees around the clearing the group had turned into a temporary home. Other motor homes and campers were parked nearby and the smell of a campfire filled her nose. Women were outside staring at her as the men took her to the back of the motor home where she'd been imprisoned. Their plan sank in when they began to talk again.

"How are we going to get her up there?"

Her gaze lifted to the high roof and desperation struck. She had to escape. "I have to pee!"

Adam shot her a glare. "Piss your pants. I don't care."

"Brother!" a stern voice barked. "Shame on you." The owner of that voice walked forward—a thin-lipped woman in her fifties. "Where is your compassion? Let her use the bathroom."

"It's best if we leave her tied up, Sister Deanie."

The woman glared at her leader. "I raised you better than that."

His voice lowered. "Come on, Mom. Not in front of everyone."

Zandy's eyes widened in astonishment. The older man got involved. "Son, it will turn your followers against you if you abuse that woman. Listen to your parents."

Holy shit. Her gaze darted between the three of them, seeing a resemblance. They were obviously a really screwed-up family.

"Fine." Adam nodded at the men. "Put her down but make sure she can't run away."

The bench was eased to the ground and the two large men unfastened her restraints. She'd been flat for so long that she felt a little dizzy when she sat up. The older woman approached, looking fearful.

"Now, don't you spin your head at me or anything."

Zandy's smart mouth kicked in. "I think you watched way too many horror movies. I'm not possessed."

The woman frowned. "Do you need to go pee-pee?"

Pee-pee? Really? Just bitchin'. I've been kidnapped by idiots who use a two-year-old's vocabulary. "Yes."

They didn't remove the handcuffs which held her wrists locked in front of her. The woman gripped them in the middle and led Zandy over to one of the campers, tugging on the chain as if she were leading a dog.

"Don't try anything evil," Deanie warned. "I'm watching you."

Zandy's gaze swept the interior, looking for a weapon but the place was pretty bare. Dishes had all been put away and the woman refused to release the chain on the restraints. The bathroom was a tiny one.

"Go ahead. You hurry up." Her voice lowered. "Stop giving my son grief, young lady. You're trying to make him look bad in front of his followers. Do you know how hard it was for him to gather so many of them?"

It was a struggle to get her pants undone and use the bathroom with her hands locked together. "No. Not really. I haven't read much about cults."

Deanie gasped. "Shame on you for even saying that. We're—" The woman glanced down and gasped a second time. "Sinner! I see that whore's underwear instead of what should be decent covering for your private area. *Tsk, tsk!* No wonder you were lured to the dark side."

Zandy blinked a few times. "They had really good cookies and they approved of thong underwear. What can I say? I didn't stand a chance."

Her sarcasm was totally lost on her captor as Deanie frowned. "What does that mean? What kind of cookies?"

"Oh geez. You people are seriously screwed up. No wonder your kid is so messed up."

"You're an evil sinner with a potty mouth. Shame on you." She turned around and jerked open a drawer built into the wall. She turned, holding out bright blue shorts. "Remove that whore garment and put this on."

"Are those swimming trunks?"

"Yes."

"No."

"You will. You can't cleanse your soul when you're wearing that bright-red sin tempter. We're trying to save you, not send you to hell."

"I'm already there, lady."

Deanie's face reddened. "Change or I'll have the men come in here to do it for you. These are clean and pure."

The thought of Adam or those other creeps taking her pants off made Zandy decide to comply. The men's swimming trunks were a bit big but it seemed to have soothed the upset woman when she almost smiled.

"Much better."

The irony wasn't lost on her. They were going to burn her to death wearing swimming trunks. *Fire and water. It just keeps getting better and better.* She was led outside and shoved back down on the bench. Zandy tried to struggle but couldn't get away from four men. They tied her down tightly.

"Now how do we get her up there?" It was the young kid with the holey clothes.

Zandy realized they were talking about the top of the motor home. She had no clue why they wanted her put on top of the motor home but she didn't like it. "Oh hell no."

Brother Adam glared at her. "We'll turn her on her side. Two of us will grip the sides and climb the ladder while two will hold the bottom and push. We'll get her up there. She doesn't weigh that much."

"It hurts when you do that," Zandy informed him.

Brother Adam smiled and a gleeful look crossed his features. "I know."

"You bastard," Zandy hissed. "Do you know why I think you're so mean? I bet you have a tiny little dick and have to behave like a huge one, trying to compensate."

The man gritted his teeth and rage turned his face splotchy red. His lips opened but no words came out.

"That's what I thought, tiny dick. Or should I just start calling you prick?"

"You bitch!" he yelled.

"Dickless," she taunted.

"Enough!" Deanie snapped. "She's baiting you, Brother Adam."

"Baiting him?" Zandy snorted. "He's too small. I'd have to toss him back if I caught him."

Brother Adam screamed and lunged for her but two of his followers grabbed him to hold him back. She smiled grimly. He might set her on fire later but he looked ready to have a stroke. She could only hope something killed him before he ended her life.

* * * * *

Tiger was glad to be out of the casts. His leg still ached a little and his ribs hurt but he wasn't really in pain. He'd had to swear to Dr. Allison to take it easy. The normal speed of bones healing for a Species was two weeks. The enhanced drugs had mended him in days.

Slade North pointed to one of the chairs in his office. "Sit down, Tiger. Stop pacing. You need your strength when we find her and your bones aren't completely healed yet. They will hold your weight but don't press your luck. I know Dr. Allison didn't want to release you for another twenty-four hours but you refused to stay in the hospital."

"Zandy is out there somewhere and I need to find her."

Slade grimly nodded. "I know this but the good news is they didn't kill her right off the bat. They took her for a reason and they will hopefully keep her alive until they make whatever they want known to us."

"Mercile employees could have her." Tiger was miserable as he took a seat.

"I doubt it. They wouldn't have vandalized her home. They would have just taken her. This isn't their way."

"They held us captive for most of our lives," Tiger snarled. "They could be hurting her if that's who has stolen her from me."

"It's not them," Bestial agreed. "Slade is right. This has to be one of those hate groups or someone who wishes to ransom her for money if they learned she is an NSO employee."

Richard shifted in his seat. "I've given all the information to the FBI and local law officials about the groups that have been the most vocal about female employees and about women who hook up with New Species. Hopefully they can track them down and find Zandy soon. I'm hoping that's the case or we have no leads if it was the criminals' intent on using her to blackmail the NSO out of money."

Justice North and Tim Oberto were on speakerphone conference call in Slade's office. "They have to know she's not Jessie. We held a news conference here an hour ago to make sure of that. My mate addressed the press and it was on every channel. Whoever has Zandy Gordon would have heard about it or seen it."

"No one has contacted us for a reward?" Tiger sounded hopeful.

"No one who panned out. One male called to say she was being held prisoner by aliens from another planet." Justice sighed. "He is in need of medical care but we are checking out every call that comes in, Tiger."

"I'm never letting her leave Reservation again if I get her back," Tiger growled. "Ever. I don't even want her out of my sight."

"Was there any connection to the males who shot down the helicopter?" Bestial glanced at Slade.

"No," Justice answered instead. "We thought of that already. Those humans just wanted to kill some of us. They have no interest in our females. They came at us like hunters."

Tiger growled. "Zandy wouldn't have left Reservation if it wasn't for them."

Smiley bit his lip. "I'm sorry, Tiger. I should have restrained her and forced her to wait for an escort to and from the hospital."

"My female is strong willed and unstoppable when she's made up her mind to do something she feels passionate about. She wanted to reach my side as quickly as possible. This is my fault. She was safe there until I drove her away."

"It was the drugs," Bestial reminded him. "Stop beating yourself up over this, Tiger. We should have stopped her and made her calm before leaving the hospital if you want to assign blame."

"It doesn't matter who wants to feel the blame," Justice stated. "She was taken and we need to get her back."

"We have teams of your men and mine going around the area asking questions," Tim Oberto said. "Some of these hate groups have been known to camp out in the woods since no motel wants to put them up. They might still be close if they are the ones responsible for this kidnapping. There's a hell of a lot of ground and we don't have enough air support with one helicopter down." He paused. "Thank you for lending us your helicopter from Homeland, Justice. It has helped, having two birds in the air."

"I could hire out local helicopters and pilots if it will help," Justice offered.

"Let's do that," Tim agreed. "The more land we search around here, the better. Just tell them to report any signs of life they find. Our teams will check out anything they spot."

"I'm on it," Justice stated before he broke the connection of the conference call.

Tiger closed his eyes, his thoughts on Zandy. *Where is she? Is she still alive?* The rage inside him built. She needed him but he didn't know where to find her. He hated feeling helpless and he'd experienced that emotion often since he'd grown to care so deeply about the human female.

* * * * *

Pure terror gripped Zandy as they strapped her to their crazy contraption. She fought back a scream for a second but then let it loose. They'd kept her strapped to the bench but had tied that to a large cross that had been flat on top of the motor home roof. They used a winch from the front of the vehicle to raise it upright. The cross was connected to some welded-on hinge system.

She hung a good fifty or so feet from the ground and knew that at any second the ropes attached to the bench or even the belts holding her body could break. She'd plummet to the roof of the motor home or worse, fall farther to the ground. She frantically searched the area, seeking help from her high perch but didn't see anyone in the surrounding woods. Miles of trees seemed to stretch around her and the only signs of life came from the group who had kidnapped her.

"Do you feel closer to God?" Brother Adam grinned at her from below, his hands on his waist, looking smug.

"Fuck you." She really wanted to kill him.

"We're going to pile wood and pour gasoline all over the roof up there with you. A tarp will hide you and cover the smell until it's too late for anyone to help you." He looked totally pleased with his insane plan. "We're going to drive right up to the gates of hell, hoist you up for all to see and show the world what happens when someone submits to sin."

"I've marked the cable line," one of his men called out. "We'll be able to get the cross raised quickly without fear of snapping the line."

"Great." Brother Adam beamed. "How many seconds will it take to get her up there? I need to prepare my speech accordingly."

"We'll test it."

Zandy squeezed her eyes closed as the cross shook violently as it lowered. Her stomach rolled from the sick feeling of fear that the wood would just snap at the base where it had been connected to the top of the roof by the hinge they'd created. The entire thing finally rested on the roof and she breathed a sigh of relief when she lay flat again.

"You count, Brother," someone shouted. "Ready?"

"Oh shit," she muttered, afraid of what would happen next, not wanting to find out.

"Here we go!"

Her eyes flew open as the motor from the winch increased in sound. The entire cross and bench shook and another scream tore from her throat as it rose quickly, flinging her upward until she was suspended once again high in the air. Wood creaked and groaned, she could have sworn that the ropes holding the bench made a sound of protest but it stopped as suddenly as it had started.

"Six seconds," a new voice announced. "Is that enough time?"

"Sure," Adam nodded, no longer looking at her but digging into his pants to remove a pen and a palm-sized notepad. "Any longer and it might give them time to react. I'll get to say my lines before the show begins."

Show? They were talking about killing her as if it were a Broadway production. Hot tears filled her eyes and she blinked them back as some of the people below her started a line to pass kindling and chopped wood to the top of the motor home. They lined the edges first until someone suggested they lower the cross.

The ride down made her clench her teeth to avoid giving them the satisfaction of hearing her scream again. Once flat, she watched them stack wood closer to her sides, covering the entire roof surface with at least two layers. The smell of cut wood usually appealed to her but not under those circumstances.

The five people silently working avoided making eye contact with her. She decided to try though. "Please help me. You know this is wrong. My name is Zandy. I have a family and a life. I'm not evil."

They kept working, refusing to look her way or speak. Frustration rose and she closed her eyes. The warm sun beat down on her but she felt cold inside. None of Brother Adam's followers were going to grow a brain. They had a cult mentality and thought the idiot could do no wrong.

"Should we soak the wood with gasoline now?"

The voice belonged to the teenager with the holey clothes. He had climbed on top of the roof and held a dull red gas can in both hands. The sight of it made Zandy hyperventilate, each breath a fight for her to control.

They were really planning on setting her on fire. It was barbaric, horrific, and worse—idiotic.

"No. Brother Adam thinks those evil spawns might smell it despite having the entire top covered with the tarp. He wants to make a more dramatic approach for the cameras. He envisions it will really reach out to viewers and draw out the suspense if they see the gasoline being poured."

"I get it." The kid nodded vigorously, smiling. "That's a really cool idea. It's going to be epic."

"I'm glad you think so," Zandy commented dryly. "Want to trade places with me if it's so cool? What the hell is wrong with you?"

He glanced at her and met her glare. "You're a whore and sinner tainted by Satan. Don't speak to me."

She took a deep, calming breath. "You're so young. Don't you understand that you're throwing your life away over this? None of you are going to get away with killing me, especially if it's in front of a bunch of reporters with cameras. You'll grow old in prison. Is Brother Adam worth that? Don't you want to meet someone and have a family one day? Don't you have dreams you want to fulfill? It's not too late. Just untie me and we'll both get out of here. I won't tell anyone I saw you. You can walk away from this mess."

He walked closer and shook the gas can to make certain she could hear it slosh and took the time to slowly secure it somewhere by her feet. He winked when he straightened without it. "This is my dream and we are going to be heroes. We're saving souls."

"You're going to go to prison for murder. That's how this is going to end unless you let me go and we both escape."

"Shut up. I refuse to listen to you."

She glanced at the other two people with him, both avoided her gaze, and she tried to talk some sense into them. "Did you hear me? You will all go to prison. It doesn't have to be this way. Just untie me. Please?"

"I said shut up," the kid muttered. "We're not listening. Brother Adam knows what he's talking about and we are on a mission."

Zandy said nothing as the kid left, climbing down the ladder at the side of the motor home and out of her sight. The two other people followed him, leaving her alone. The wind blew and she stared at the blue sky above. There wasn't a hint of rain, something that would have been really great to wet all the kindling piled around her. It just wasn't her day.

She concentrated on thoughts of Tiger. He was going to survive his injuries but they were over. It was probably best. It hurt that he'd ordered her to leave his hospital room as though everything they'd shared had meant nothing. It broke her heart but at least her death wouldn't devastate him. That was the last thing she wanted.

Tears spilled down the sides of her face and she couldn't even wipe them away. She loved Tiger. She'd fallen for him hard and wondered if he'd feel guilty when he found out what became of her. Time passed as she tried to come to terms with what would happen to her soon.

She struggled but couldn't break free. The sound of someone climbing the ladder drew her attention and she twisted her head to watch Brother Adam join her. He had to step carefully over the wood but made it to her side without falling. Two more men climbed up on the roof, both geared up with hammers and boards.

"What are you going to do now?"

Adam refused to answer her. "Do it."

Zandy opened her mouth to ask what they planned but the two big men with him suddenly unstrapped the belts securing her body to the bench. They grabbed her before she could struggle, yanked her to her feet, and one of them kicked the bench away. Her body was lifted and slammed hard down on the thick wooden cross. It knocked the air from her lungs as pain shot along her spine and the back of her head where she'd hit the hardest.

The two men jerked both of her arms outright along the beams that made the wood a cross. She recovered and tried to twist away, kicking wildly at them, but it didn't faze them. They secured her from her wrists to her upper arms by wrapping ropes around them, tying her tightly to the cross.

"Don't do this," she pleaded. "This is insane. You can't get away with murder. You'll rot in prison or get the death penalty."

Brother Adam laughed, a sick sound, as he leaned in enough to make sure she could see his face while his two followers began to tie her legs in place.

"We are waging a war against evil and we are willing to die for our cause. We won't have to do that though. I am smarter than them. I've thought of everything."

He believed what he said. It was clear in his crazy stare. Zandy screamed, bucked her hips, but the two men only secured her with rope around her waist. Her gaze locked on Adam.

"The New Species are going to track your worthless ass down and make you pay for this. You better hope the police arrest you on the spot when you drive up to those gates because I know Tiger will tear you apart for doing this to me."

He cocked his head. "Who is Tiger?"

"He's a friend." They might have ended their relationship but she had no doubt that Tiger would avenge her murder by making sure the people responsible were punished. She had faith in that. "He won't let you get away with this."

"I knew you were fornicating with those devils." His gaze narrowed. "They are the ones who will die. Tiger's name will go at the top of our list of who to cleanse next. Thank you."

Her temper snapped. "That devil, as you call him, is going to tear out your heart and make you choke on it."

The son of a bitch just grinned. "I will always prevail over evil. I am the instrument of God." He paused. "Tell the devil I send my regards when you see him."

"You're a loser is what you are. A bat-shit crazy one who gets off on hurting others. What kind of pathetic life have you led that you think this is the right thing to do? You're the one who is going to hell, Adam. Tell him yourself."

Adam's face twisted into an ugly shade of red from anger. "I'm going to enjoy watching you burn. It's going to be music to my ears when the flames start melting your flesh and you start screaming."

They left her tied to the cross while Zandy struggled to break free. She overheard enough to know they had begun breaking camp and what the next step of their plans was. Brother Bruno would drive the motor home to the gates of Reservation and he'd work the winch. Brother Adam would toss the tarp off the roof, address the reporters with the speech he'd written, while pouring gasoline as he spoke. They thought the fire he started would cause enough panic and disarray to escape being arrested.

The ladder creaked in warning that someone was climbing to the roof. Zandy twisted her head to stare at the thin, mousy woman who refused to meet her gaze as she slowly crept forward.

Hope surged that the woman would help her escape but it faded quickly when she reached into her baggy skirt pockets to withdraw a roll of duct tape.

"I'm really sorry to do this to you," the woman whispered as she pulled off a strip of the tape. "They don't want you screaming. Hold still. I don't want to get your nose. You'd suffocate and everyone would be mad at me for killing you too soon."

Zandy twisted her head away to avoid being gagged. "Please don't. I thought Brother Adam wanted to hear me scream while I burn." She tried to use logic, desperate to avoid having her mouth sealed closed.

"Brother Adam will remove the tape before he lights the wood. He doesn't want you screaming before he's ready to reveal your presence. We all have to work together to make sure this goes exactly the way he wants."

Zandy struggled but the woman was able to tape her mouth. Two more layers were added across her lips and down her cheeks to make sure it stayed put. The scream came out muffled when her terror got the best of her. The mousy woman backed away and fled, her job done.

Minutes later two large men climbed over the wood piled on top of the motor home to pull a tarp over the roof. Her terror intensified when the dingy white material they dragged over her body blocked out the sky. It rested on her face and no matter which direction she turned she was unable to get away from it. They had effectively hidden her and the cross.

The motor home engine vibrated slightly when the driver turned it on. Motion assured her that they were on the road as the tires dipped and made the entire vehicle sway under her. Wind whipped at the tarp after the road smoothed to pavement and it picked up speed. She hoped it would fly off but they'd tied the material down tightly.

Zandy closed her eyes and pictured Tiger. He'd be brave and not totally fall apart if he were in her shoes. Of course he could have avoided being taken in the first place. None of Brother Adam's men would have been able to win against Tiger in a fight. Just thinking about him helped calm her rising panic. He'd saved her once in that bar but she knew he couldn't do it a second time. He was in a hospital hours away.

I love you, Tiger. I just wish I could have told you.

Chapter Nineteen

ဆာ

Slade slammed his desk phone into the cradle. "Great. This is just what we need."

Tiger tensed. "What is wrong?"

"Some idiots have called a press conference at the main gate, demanding freedom of speech. The reporters are showing up en masse. Like we need this shit on top of everything else. This group wants us at the front gates too. They said they have something to say to us that we'll want to hear. I doubt that."

Bestial sighed. "I'm sure it will just be insults they wish to hurl at us. These things never go well. It's probably those human-rights people again claiming we're threatening their way of life."

"We have about fifteen minutes before this thing is supposed to start. I'm going down there to see what the hell these idiots are up to. I'm tripling the officers on duty and calling in some sharpshooters. I don't want any unpleasant surprises." Slade ran his fingers through his hair. "I hate these assholes."

Tiger stood. "I will go with you. Security is my job."

Bestial unfolded his body from the chair to stand. "You're still on medical leave, Tiger. We'll all go. It beats sitting here staring at the walls while we wait for word from Tim."

"I've got this," Slade stated. "You're my second, Tiger. We'll deal with this crap together."

The three of them left Slade's office and climbed into a Jeep. Slade used his cell phone to issue orders while Bestial drove. They reached the main gate and took the stairs to the catwalk on the wall where they could see everything. One of the officers passed them bulletproof vests, which they donned. Tiger assessed the twenty sharpshooters on the wall and the thirty officers assembled below on the NSO side of the gate.

Tiger borrowed one of the radios from a male and ordered an additional fifty males to suit up in case of attack. He wanted them prepared to rush to the gates if they were needed. Bestial watched him grimly as their gazes met.

"Best to be paranoid." Tiger shoved the radio in his pocket. "Overkill is a good word when our males are holding the weapons."

"Does everyone have on vests?" Slade yelled to be heard.

Tiger relaxed slightly when they were assured all the high-alert protocols were being followed. He noted the arrival of the local sheriff and four of his deputies. They were there to help with crowd control outside the gates. Sending officers outside wasn't something he wanted to do—it was too dangerous.

Thoughts of Zandy tormented Tiger. He wondered where she was, if she were alive and just wished she were in his arms. Anger gripped him over having to deal with the current situation when all he really wanted to do was make more calls to have more resources focused on locating her. He'd apologize for the things he didn't remember saying and make her forgive him. It didn't matter how long it took but he'd convince her that he was her male.

Bestial growled. "Look at all the news vans pulling up. Who are these people?"

Slade shrugged. "I've never heard of them. They are calling themselves Salvation from Sin." He snorted. "They said they want to tell the world about how evil we are."

Bestial chuckled. "I don't suppose we could just shoot them when they arrive to prove them right?"

Tiger wasn't in a good mood. "Don't tempt me to give that order."

"I want to know how they got so many reporters out here. They are obviously crackpots," Slade said. "They stated they have proof that we are dangerous to humanity and promised the news stations something they'd want to show on the six o'clock news as the top story."

Tiger gripped his radio to address the officers. "They might try to provoke an attack from us. Hold your tempers in check. Do not open fire unless I give the order or you are fired upon first. They are up to something since they wanted so many cameras on scene. Just be prepared for anything. Do we have smoke gas ready?"

"Yes," a male responded. "We are prepared."

Slade sighed. "Great. Just remember to keep your cool, everyone. We are better than these assholes. They want to give some kind of speech and I'm sure it's going to test our restraint. The calmer we appear at their hateful words, the more asinine they seem."

Tiger snorted. "True."

Bestial grinned.

Tiger counted at least fifteen news vans parked along the street but they were far enough from the walls not to be a threat. The protesters had been cleared a good fifty feet away from the gates by the sheriff and his deputies. Sheriff Cooper waved and Tiger acknowledged him with a nod.

"So when is this bullshit supposed to start?" Bestial grew impatient.

Slade glanced at his watch. "Soon. They said they would be here at 5:40."

"There's a motor home coming and a car. Do you think it's them?" One of the officers jerked his head.

Tiger narrowed his gaze, watching the approaching vehicles. "Yes. They have a Salvation from Sin banner on the side of it."

Bestial snorted. "Look how old that thing is. We're being visited by the past."

Slade chuckled. "At least we can rule out them having missile launchers. They couldn't afford them."

Tiger agreed. "Maybe we won't have to worry about them firing on us either. See the rust on that thing? I doubt they can afford bullets."

Tiger tensed when two males climbed out of the cab of the motor home. One walked to the back of it and used a ladder to climb onto the roof where he stood at the back. He bent and lifted a microphone.

"Is this thing on?" The male's voice broadcast from speakers obviously rigged to the vehicle.

"The speakers work," the driver shouted from the front bumper.

"I am Brother Adam from Salvation from Sin. I am the leader of our group. I am here today to tell you that we will not stand for the evil spawn of the devil tainting our women. No God-fearing woman would lay down with a devil. It is wrong and against the word of God to fornicate with an animal. We want the women out there to know that you are condemning your souls to hell by even associating with the spawns of hell that call themselves New Species. Any woman who associates with these demons will burn in hell and I am here to tell you that considering being a bride of the devil will be punished in the fires of hell. Any woman who goes near these vile beings is letting the devil tempt her to be his bride. God has spoken and told me and mine to do this. I am hoping that others pick up the word of God that I preach today and do the same."

"That's a terrible speech," Bestial muttered.

"They spent their money on speakers instead of a publicist," Tiger quipped.

The human holding the microphone pointed up at the top of the wall. "You shall not put your evil hands on our women anymore. Take heed of our warning that God-fearing men will cleanse their souls." He moved over and felt for something under the tarp. He yanked hard at whatever it was.

Slade rolled his eyes. "We came out here for this?"

Bestial chuckled. "I'd enjoy an evil woman in my bed."

One of the New Species males close to them laughed. "Me too. Sinful is best."

"Shit," Tiger muttered, grabbing for his radio. "Alert. The human is unhooking the tarp at the back of the motor home. He might have males hidden under it with guns."

The human male at the front of the motor home bent and the sound of a soft whine started. Slade cursed, putting his radio to his mouth.

"Alert. It could be a weapon."

Tiger rested one hand on the knife strapped to his thigh. He practiced often and had become very accurate at throwing it. His other hand set the radio on the wall and grabbed for the spare gun strapped to the officer on his right, clearing it from the holster as the tarp rose higher. Whatever was under it was at least twenty-five feet tall. The tarp waved in the air and started to drop as it was fully erected.

A scream startled everyone and the sight of a female tied to a cross was revealed as the tarp dropped away. Tiger's knees nearly collapsed under him as he stared at Zandy. The shock of seeing her suspended high in the air on top of the vehicle took seconds to register in his mind. Her hair was messy, a bruise darkened her cheek, and she looked very pale. Thick ropes wound around her arms and legs, securing her there. She screamed again, struggling with the restraints. Her terrified gaze focused on the gates.

"Shoot him," she yelled. "He's going to set me on fire!"

Tiger's gaze jerked away from her to the human closest to Zandy. He was holding a red container and poured the contents out on a bunch of wood chaotically spread across the entire length of the roof of the motor home. Tiger's heightened senses were fully engaged with his heart racing and the stench of gasoline filling his nose.

"Shoot him," Tiger roared, instantly understanding what the human male planned to do to Zandy.

Screams from the humans on the ground filled the air as they realized what was about to take place. Zandy must have heard his voice. Her chin jerked up and her terrified gaze sought him out. Tears slid down her face as gunfire erupted. The human with the gas can jerked as Tiger darted his attention there, watched as three bullets tore through his chest and propelled his body backward to disappear out of sight where it hit the pavement.

"No!" The human at the front of the motor home screamed that one word before he did something with his hands, throwing an object upward. Flames ignited in a whoosh.

Horror jolted Tiger from his frozen stance as the fire spread across the top of the motor home and surrounded the bottom of the cross. Zandy let out another terrified scream that set him in motion before he gave it any thought. He shoved males out of his way, ran on his still-sore leg and grabbed the wall near the guard shack at the gates.

He vaulted over the wall, his body slammed painfully into the angled roof and he slid on his ass to the edge. He hit the grassy area next to the shack with a grunt, ignored the pain and dropped the gun still clutched in his fingers. He needed both hands to shove off, to regain his footing and rush at the burning vehicle.

More gunshots rang out and bullets slammed into the human who'd thrown the lighter that started the fire. Tiger had to dodge the falling body as the male sprawled on his back, dead. He shoved fleeing humans out of the way to reach the motor home where he leaped and gripped the metal edge of it. He hoisted himself up.

Scorching heat from the flames registered but he ignored them, too focused on Zandy to care if he burned. A large body suddenly landed next to him and he twisted his head to stare at Bestial. The male held a fire extinguisher, which he pointed in front of them. He tore out the pin and sprayed the flames. It doused them instantly.

"Get her," his friend snarled, turning the spray to make a path to the wooden cross.

* * * * *

Zandy coughed, choking on smoke from the fire below her as it blinded her. She twisted her head but couldn't find any breathable air until the wind shifted. Tiger had been on the wall above the gates of Reservation. She'd seen him there, heard him order the officers to shoot Brother Adam, but then she'd lost track of him.

"Zandy!" Tiger roared her name and the cross shook enough to make her entire body sway.

She looked down to see if the fire had eaten through the wood enough to make the thick beam collapse. She stared at Tiger below her as he climbed up the cross to reach her. It was his added weight that caused the rough motion. He inched closer until he reached her feet.

Pain lanced through her but she clenched her teeth when he fisted the ropes to pull his body higher. They bit into her skin from the pull of his weight but she refused to scream. He hugged her and the beam when they were face level.

Their gazes locked. His amazing eyes stared deeply into hers and he crushed against her chest. One of his hands released the rope and he suddenly held a knife. He looked away and sawed at the ropes that secured her arms.

"I've got you, little one," he rasped.

"Tiger," she whispered, stunned that he was really there.

"Hang on to me."

One arm was cut free. It hurt to move it but she wrapped it around his neck. He twisted a little to transfer the blade to his other hand and gripped the beam to support their weight.

Sweat beaded his brow and his face was red from exhaustion or perhaps from inhaling too much smoke. She couldn't look away from him. The tug of the ropes assured her that he was trying to free her other arm.

"Hurry," a male snarled from below them. "The canister is near empty."

The wind changed direction and smoke billowed up, making her eyes sting. She tore her gaze from Tiger's face and buried it against the hot skin at his neck. The masculine scent of him and the smoke were strong. The rope gave way and she wrapped her other arm around him, hugging his neck tightly.

The beam swayed roughly again and she wondered if it would collapse with both of them. It didn't. Instead a hand gripped her ankle and the ropes around her legs were pulled away.

"She's free," someone shouted. "I got her legs clear, Tiger. Hurry. The interior is burning now and we are losing the battle with the fire."

"Wrap around me," Tiger demanded harshly.

It took her a second to figure out what he meant but she lifted her legs and hooked them around his waist. He twisted his head to look down. She opened her eyes but regretted it instantly. The sensation of falling made her stomach seem to rise up into her throat before Tiger's feet hit the roof. His body took the worst of the impact and it nearly doubled him over, crushing her between his knees and chest where he crouched.

He snarled—a vicious, horrible sound against her ear. She realized he'd just dropped with her in his arms as he straightened, both arms wrapping around her. She stared at two New Species males who were on the roof of the motor home with them. One of them was kicking burning wood off the sides and using a fire extinguisher to hold back the flames while the other one just jumped off the side.

Tiger followed him to the edge but he limped badly, dragging one leg. Alarm shot through Zandy, knowing he was hurt.

"Throw her to me," Bestial demanded from the ground where he'd just landed. "I'll catch her."

"Let go," Tiger ordered.

She hated to do it but knew there was no time to argue. The thick smoke made breathing almost impossible and it was probably a miracle the roof hadn't given way under them so far. Tiger didn't allow her to stand but instead twisted her in his arms to cradle her there. He lifted her out over the edge and she realized what he intended to do. She said nothing though, the desperation on his features making it clear there wasn't a choice.

She dropped when he released her until strong arms caught her under the back of her knees and around her back. It hurt but she didn't care if it left her bruised. Her head jerked up to stare at Tiger, terrified for his safety.

He jumped down and tried to land on his feet. A roar came from him as he hit. His legs gave out and he sprawled on the pavement. Zandy struggled in the arms that held her but the male refused to let go. He spun with her fast enough to make her dizzy and ran.

The jarring motion was rough but she managed to twist in his arms. She peered over his shoulder and saw the third male escape the roof of the burning motor home. He landed on his feet, bent down and grabbed Tiger.

Glass burst from the motor home windows, fire shot out the sides and Bestial jerked her tighter against his chest. She lost sight of Tiger and the fire as she was rushed through the slightly opened gates of Reservation.

"Tiger!" She yelled out for him, worried for his safety.

"Calm," Bestial demanded, stopping their mad dash. He turned to stare back at the gate.

Zandy saw Tiger then. He leaned heavily against the New Species who'd helped save her. He avoided putting weight on one leg but his gaze was fixed on her as they entered through the gate. The male held Tiger around his waist, being his crutch. He came right at her.

Unshed tears filled her eyes. Tiger had saved her by risking his own life. He and the other male stopped just feet from them. Tiger shoved away from his friend and opened his arms, his gaze leaving hers to stare at the one holding her.

"Give her to me, Bestial."

"Tiger—" the man protested but was cut off when she was yanked out of the black-haired Species' hold.

Tiger staggered with her in his arms. Two Species officers in full uniform were suddenly there, grabbing him to keep them upright. They gently lowered both of them until she ended up sitting on Tiger's lap. He slid his arms out from under her legs and her back and cupped her face.

"I didn't mean the things I said in the hospital. I don't even remember waking." His voice came out softly, pain clear in his tone. "I never meant to send you away."

"Are you okay?"

He growled. "Did you hear what I said? It was the drugs I was given."

"Get a medic," someone shouted. "Both of them are hurt."

Zandy's hands shook as she gripped his shoulders. "It's okay. Don't worry about that right now. Is your leg okay?"

"I broke it again." He licked his lips. "Are you all right?" His gaze lowered to her cheek. "Where else are you hurt?"

None of the bruises mattered. "I'm okay. You broke your leg again?"

"It wasn't completely healed."

284

"You saved me again."

His incredible eyes lifted to hers. "I'll always do whatever it takes to protect you, Zandy. I'm just grateful to be holding you in my arms again."

Her heart pounded.

"You were almost turned into a fire stick and you are worried about me?" Tiger asked.

She nodded. "Yeah." Her brain started to function. "Oh god. I'm on your lap. I must be hurting you." She tried to ease off him but his hold on her face tightened, keeping her there.

"I don't care. I just want you close."

"Tiger?" Slade cleared his throat.

Zandy turned her head to stare up at the man who'd hired her. He stood next to them, his expression grim.

Tiger growled. "Leave us alone," he warned.

"You both need to be taken to Medical right now."

Tiger shook his head. "Later."

"She's hurt, Tiger. We don't know what they did to her. You both need to be seen by our doctors. We'll keep you close together. May I take her from you?"

Tiger stared into Zandy's eyes. "Let him carry you. I can't."

Slade reached down and gently lifted her. Tiger winced and his face twisted in pain, instantly alarming her. She wiggled to be put down.

"I can walk," she stated, glancing at the one holding her.

Slade softly growled. "You two are well matched. Both stubborn and irrational when it comes to each other. Be silent."

He spun, striding away to a waiting Jeep. He gently placed her in the front seat and she tried to look around his big body to find Tiger. Slade leaned in close to draw her gaze.

"Do me a favor, Zandy Gordon. Understand that Tiger has no memory of hurting your feelings and take my word of total honesty that he didn't mean whatever he said. He deserves some trouble for some of the things he's said to males who have chosen human females but I never want to see him sulk again. It was painful to watch when he worried about your safety. Forgive him and maybe he'll return to his rational, mellow ways again."

Slade straightened and jerked his head at someone behind her. "Go to Medical. Hurry so she can be examined before Tiger arrives. I doubt he's in a mood to watch Dr. Harris touch his female."

The Jeep moved and Zandy spotted Tiger finally. Two officers supported his body between them, carrying him to keep his weight off his legs. Worry gripped her over how hurt he really was. The driver made a turn and she lost sight of him.

"Zandy?"

The familiar voice made her twist in her seat. "Smiley."

"I'm glad you're alive." He glanced at her and then back to the road.

"Me too."

"Next time you don't leave Reservation without a full escort."

She relaxed in the seat. "Not a problem."

"Tiger will be fine. We're strong and heal quickly. He shouldn't have been released from the hospital until his bones had knitted firmly but he went a bit insane when he learned of your kidnapping. This set his healing back but it will be fine. Stop worrying."

She hugged her chest and fought the urge to cry. So much had happened that she knew it would take time to recover from it mentally. Her emotions were too close to the surface.

"Don't shed tears. Tiger will heal."

Tiger claimed to have no memory of the episode in the hospital. Her eyes closed as that information settled in. It left her wondering if, in his drugged state, he might have stated what was in his subconscious. Did he think they shouldn't be together? That she really was the enemy?

The Jeep halted and Smiley escorted her inside the building. The medical staff was on alert, all of them waiting inside to handle any emergencies sent their way. Zandy was led to an exam room and a female doctor with a male Species nurse followed her into the room.

"I'm Dr. Allison," the woman introduced herself. "You are?"

"Zandy Gordon."

"She works here at Reservation," the male nurse stated quietly. "She was brought in once before to be treated by the younger Dr. Harris after an incident with the protesters at the gates."

"Thank you for the history." The doctor flashed a smile. "I'm usually at Homeland but the helicopter crash victims needed my attention so I was brought to Reservation. I'm afraid I don't know that many of the employees here but it's nice to meet you. I just wish the circumstances were better." She put on gloves and gently gripped Zandy's jaw, turning her head to study her cheek. "Someone hit you?"

She carefully detailed the attack at her house and consequent kidnapping. The entire story of what she'd endured came pouring out. "So that's all of it. Tiger needs you more than I do. He thinks his leg is broken."

The woman turned her head to glance at the nurse. "Go make sure Harris has it handled, okay? We'd both like an update."

The New Species left the room quickly and the doctor smiled tightly. "Tiger is better off in Harris' care. We had a big argument yesterday. He wanted to leave the hospital but I was adamant he stay there. I'm the last person he'll want working on him. He'd probably snarl at me if I said 'I told you so'."

"He saved my life. He could have burned to death with me if the top of the motor home had collapsed."

"I'm glad to hear it was worth the pain he must be in. Are you hurt anywhere besides your face?" The woman's gloved fingers touched her bruised cheek, frowning. "What are these red marks from along your jaw?"

"They put duct tape over my mouth. I used my tongue to wet it and worked it away from my lips but couldn't do anything about the rest of it. The jerk in charge of that group tore it off right before he tried to kill me. It hurt so bad that I couldn't even breathe for a few seconds. Ouch! Now it just feels tender."

"The skin didn't tear but it's going to hurt for a while."

"My ribs and waist hurt too. They had me secured with belts that dug into me."

"Lie back."

The doctor carefully examined her. "It's just some bruising. I don't feel anything broken. You came out of this ordeal remarkably well. You're lucky. Any trouble breathing from the smoke you inhaled?" The doctor cleaned some cuts she found on Zandy.

"No. It was windy enough to blow most of it away from me."

"You can sit up." The doctor snapped off her gloves. "You were lucky, Zandy Gordon."

"Can I ask you something?"

The doctor arched her eyebrows. "Sure."

"Um…" Zandy hesitated. "Something happened that is bothering me. Tiger said some things to me at the hospital when he woke and he claims not to remember it. Do you think the drugs made him blurt out things that he might feel deep down?"

The woman sighed and glanced at the door, then back at Zandy. "I'm not sure what you were told but you do work for the NSO so I'll assume you can be trusted. Some of the drug cocktails discovered in Mercile's files were experimental. That's what they did. They created drugs to test on New Species. Some of them have reacted quite violently when the drugs were given to them. They were aggressive to the point of being dangerous, while others have had some unique side effects that range from blackouts to severe personality changes while under the influence of some of the drugs. Was whatever he said normal or something you would expect him to say?"

"I don't think so."

"There's your answer. If it's bothering you, ask Tiger. New Species are known for their honesty. I'm positive that he'll want to clear up whatever issue you had with him. Did he threaten you or try to attack? I have spent a lot of time with him and that isn't normal for him. He's actually a sweetheart."

A bit of jealousy rose. "Have you two dated?"

Dr. Allison shook her head. "No. You're not just an employee, are you? I'm guessing you are involved with him?"

"We were before his accident. He...um, kind of ended it with me when he woke up. He said he doesn't remember saying any of it and apologized."

"You have your answer already. Talk to him. The drugs are out of his system but he's going to need to go back on them. They accelerate their healing."

"How?"

Dr. Allison hesitated. "You're with Tiger? I thought those were bite marks when I was examining your shoulder."

"Yes."

"You're in love with him. I see it in your eyes when you talk about him." She smiled. "They were genetically altered. Their DNA was spliced with various animal genes. Mercile was able to manipulate them enough to, well, in layman's terms, make their bodies go into hyperdrive with certain body functions. Their immune systems are amazingly resistant to illness, disease, and they heal very quickly. The drug cocktail we discovered in the records causes rapid healing. He'll need more doses if he did in fact break his leg again. It will heal in days rather than weeks. They hate being down and are terrible patients." A wistful look softened her eyes. "In most cases. I have one patient the drug doesn't seem to work on at all. He's in a coma and we haven't been able to wake him."

"I'm sorry. I hope he recovers. Was he in the helicopter crash with Tiger?"

"No. 880 was rescued and brought to Homeland some weeks ago. I hated to leave him in the care of others but they needed help here. I still have my hospital privileges in this area. Most of the other doctors who have worked longer for the NSO don't since they were brought in from different parts of the country. That's why I was called in." She turned away for a moment then faced her again holding a syringe. "I need to give you this. You have some cuts and this is an antibiotic. I'd feel better giving it to you. I can tell those aren't fresh, probably happened when you were taken, and germs fester in a matter of hours. When did you have your last tetanus shot?"

"Okay. I'm up to date on all my shots. I never miss an annual checkup." Zandy winced and looked away as the needle sank into her arm. She hated shots.

"That was a strong antibiotic and it's going to mess up your birth control."

"I'm not on anything."

The doctor's eyebrows rose. "You aren't?"

"No."

"Okay. I'll spare you the lecture about condoms then since Tiger is already using them. These shots have been known to mess up your cycle. You could skip a period or have two back to back."

"I don't have any diseases. Tiger doesn't have to use condoms."

The other woman turned away to dispose of the syringe and alcohol swab she'd used to clean the injection site. "I wasn't informed you were his mate. They really need to tell us these things."

"I'm not mated to Tiger. I know what the bites usually mean but he just lost control."

The doctor spun, a confused look on her face. "Are you guys trying to get pregnant? I've never heard of one of the New Species trying that before being mated." She shrugged. "I guess they are getting more and more modern in their thinking."

Confusion filled Zandy. "He can't get me pregnant."

Dr. Allison's eyes widened.

"What?" Zandy asked.

"He didn't tell you?"

"Tell me what?"

"Son of a biscuit." The doctor looked angry. "Rules state that he has to use condoms if you aren't mated and he has to inform you that you could get pregnant if he stops using them after you are mated."

Zandy was stunned.

"I'm going to talk to Tiger about this and then I'll have to inform Trisha. She can take this to Justice."

Zandy's arm shot out and grabbed the doctor when the woman tried to leave. "What are you saying?"

Indecision flickered in the other woman's eyes but she sighed. "You work for the NSO so I know you had to sign and read a stack of confidentiality clauses. This is classified information. It's entirely possible that Species males can impregnate us. Humans. Tiger should have used condoms or warned you that it was a possibility. I shouldn't have told you anything but I assumed you knew. Damn. I could get into serious trouble for this but it angers me as a woman that he put you at risk. You have the right to know since you're sleeping with him."

"We had sex while I was ovulating."

"How do you know that?"

"Trust me. I know. Are you saying I could be pregnant?"

"Shit." The doctor jerked away and walked to the cabinet. "I hope not. I doubt the antibiotic I gave you would harm the fetus at this early stage but I wouldn't have given it to you if there was a possibility." She jerked open a cabinet and removed a packaged kit. She turned. "Open your mouth and let me take a swab. We'll find out right now. This is why there are rules and Tiger didn't follow them. I'm a doctor first and I just gave you medication I wouldn't have if I'd known all the facts."

"What?"

"Just let me do this test. I can tell right away if you're pregnant. New Species are different from us and you would test positive for higher hormones within twenty-four hours of getting pregnant. I know you haven't had intercourse with him since his accident."

Zandy was in shock as the doctor jerked open more cabinets after dipping the sample in a clear vial with liquid. The doctor bent, watching the end of the cotton. A good minute passed before the woman straightened.

"It's negative," Dr. Allison informed her, showing her the vial. "It would have turned red if it were positive. It's clear."

"Are you sure?" Zandy's heart was still beating rapidly.

"I'm sure." She sighed. "Either Tiger really trusts his nose to tell him when it's safe to have intercourse with you or he tried to get you pregnant. I strongly suggest you have a talk with him. I'll report this to my supervisor and she'll inform Justice North. Trisha will make sure this doesn't happen again."

"Please don't," Zandy said quickly. She was still floored by what she'd learned. "I don't want him to get into trouble."

"This is serious. Do you know what would happen if anyone found out New Species can have children?"

"I have a pretty good idea. I just spent time with insane fanatics who hate them."

They stared at each other. "Fine. I won't say anything. Invoke doctor-patient confidentiality. That way my butt is covered. You need to talk to him about this though."

"Trust me. I will." She just had no idea what to say though.

Chapter Twenty

☙

The door opened and the male nurse returned. "They just X-rayed Tiger's leg and it's as we thought. He damaged the leg." He stared at Zandy. "Tiger refused to rest until he knows you are fine. He snarled at me to bring you to him."

Dr. Allison shot Zandy a warning look. "That sounds like a man who doesn't want to break it off. You're free to go. Put ice on the bruising if it continues to hurt."

"Thank you, Dr. Allison." Zandy slid off the exam table and shook the woman's hand. "I mean that." She was grateful the woman was going to keep her secret about what Tiger had done and that he hadn't told her what could result from them having sex. "I hope your patient recovers."

"Me too. I've kind of become obsessed with him."

Zandy didn't miss the sadness in the other woman's stare as she followed the New Species nurse out of the room and down the hall. He stopped in front of a closed door.

"He's in there. The break in his leg will be painful until it heals."

"Thank you." She hesitated, taking a deep breath.

Her heart pounded and she wasn't sure she wanted to face Tiger. What if he wanted to stop seeing her? The thought of that prospect made her chest hurt. The only way she was going to find out would be to talk to him. Her hand rose and she knocked.

"Come in," Tiger called out.

The room looked more like a hotel room than a hospital room, much nicer than the exam room she'd just left. Tiger was sprawled out on a queen-sized bed with his leg elevated on pillows. Ice bags had been placed over his lower leg. He'd stripped off his shirt, revealing his muscular, tan chest and flat belly. His hair was down and his exotic gaze met hers.

"Zandy."

The way he softly growled her name made her nipples harden. He had a way of affecting her. "Hi, Tiger. How are you?" She closed the door behind her and stepped farther into the room.

"Come here." He patted the bed next to him.

She didn't hesitate to step to the side of the bed and carefully climb on it. She sat facing him but kept a few feet of space between them. Her gaze left his to glance at his leg before looking.

"How is your leg feeling?"

Broad shoulders shrugged. "It aches and I'm stuck in bed for two days until it heals again. The break wasn't as bad as the original injury." He studied her eyes. "Stay with me here."

Emotions warred inside her. Part of her was happy he wanted to be with her while another part of her worried that he'd toss her out again if he took more of the medication Dr. Allison had told her about. Everyone would know she was sharing a room with him if she stayed too. Their relationship was already acknowledged, no longer a secret.

"Will they allow it? They warned me you could become unstable on the drugs."

"There are officers down the hallway in case I grow aggressive but I won't hurt you. You already stated clearly that you were willing to risk harm to be with me when you refused to leave my bedside at the hospital. This is a more controlled environment."

She wasn't afraid of Tiger. "This is a really nice room."

His blue gaze narrowed and a frown curved his mouth. He watched her. She glanced away again, staring at the blue bedding.

"Zandy? Look at me." His deep voice brooked no argument. It was a demand.

"Are you mad at me?" She held his gaze.

"For what?"

"I had to tell everyone we've been sleeping together to get to see you. Is that why you really wanted me to leave the hospital? You said not to show anyone the bites on me but I was so worried when I heard what happened to you. I—"

His hand rose and he cupped her uninjured cheek. "I don't care who knows about us. You risked your life to reach me. You should have waited for an escort to bring you to me and again when you left the hospital. It's not safe in the out world."

It was cute how he called the world outside the NSO gates that. She knew what he meant. "I kind of freaked out when I heard you'd been in a helicopter crash. I just wanted to make sure you were alive. I had to see you."

"I want you to promise me that you will never leave Reservation without officers to protect you. You were taken because you work for the NSO. They know who you are and where you live."

She didn't want to think about her destroyed house. She'd have to call her insurance company but didn't want to deal with it at that moment. "I have to leave at some point to go home."

A soft growl passed his lips. "No, you don't."

She was unsure what that meant.

He took a deep breath and blew it out, his expression softening. "You can't go home, Zandy. You will stay with me."

A hundred questions sprang into her mind. She tried to decide which one to ask first. Did he mean he wanted her to live with him or that he expected her to stay in the apartment she'd been assigned? Tiger seemed to take her silence as a refusal.

"You're not leaving Reservation." His hold on her face tightened. "I won't allow it."

That stunned her. "What?"

He growled, clearly angry. "Look what happened to you in the out world. It won't happen again. I'm going to keep you safe."

"What does tha—"

He pulled her face closer to cover her lips with his, muting her with a hot kiss. His tongue delved inside her mouth, tasting and exploring. His arm hooked around her waist and she fell against his chest when he yanked her to him. The hand on her face slid to the back of her head where he fisted her hair, making sure she couldn't get away.

Zandy didn't want to. She'd missed Tiger and had thought she'd never see him again. Actions spoke louder than words and the passionate kiss he laid on her spoke volumes that their relationship wasn't over. He pulled her tighter against his chest, almost crushing her to him. The hand at her back fisted her shirt and shoved it up. He released it and gripped her side.

Pain made her gasp against his tongue and he snarled, breaking the kiss. They were both out of breath as their gazes met. His blue eyes narrowed with concern.

"I am being too rough. I'm sorry."

"It's not that. I have some bruises."

Rage tightened his features. "Did they beat you?"

"No. They had me strapped to a bench with belts and they were tight enough to dig into my skin when they were carrying me around. I'm fine."

"Take off your clothes," he demanded. "I want to see all of you."

Her eyebrows rose. "We're in the Medical Center. Anyone can walk in."

"Lock the door."

"I'm fine. Just don't grab me there." She tried to kiss him again but he pulled back.

"Take off all of your clothes and show me."

He looked pretty determined.

"It—"

"Do it."

He was being unusually aggressive and demanding. "Did they already give you that drug to help you heal?"

"Yes. I want to see every inch of you right now."

She just hoped he wouldn't order her to leave and start saying she was his enemy again.

"There is a lock on the door." He released her. "Lock it and strip out of your clothes."

"I'm really fine."

"Do it, or I'll tear them off."

She didn't doubt him with the determined look he gave her as they stared at each other. "Fine."

She rolled away and reached the door. It might be smarter for her to just leave until he was off the drug but she twisted the lock instead and turned to face the man she loved. Her hands trembled a little as she removed her clothes. Tiger watched her with rapt concentration. He didn't look aroused—he looked enraged as he got his first look at the bruises.

"Turn around."

She was naked and cold in the room but did as he asked. A growl came from him that caused her to peer at him over her shoulder. "I told you it's just some bruises."

"Go shower. The bathroom is right there. Hurry and return to me."

She wanted a shower, probably needed one as well, so nodded. Right then didn't seem the time to argue with him about anything. She just headed for the bathroom.

"Zandy?"

She paused and glanced back at him.

"Thank you."

"You know you're being pushy, right?"

"I almost watched you die. I'm behaving extremely well. We are both lucky my leg is broken."

"What does that mean?"

His gaze lowered down her body. "Go shower now. My nose is still messed up from the smoke and gasoline I inhaled. I don't want to scent something on you when it recovers that might bring out my savage instincts. I'm barely holding on to my control. I know I'm being an asshole but do it."

She tried to close the door but he snarled. She paused. He didn't say anything but she got the message loud and clear. Her fingers released the doorknob and she left it open. The shower was a large one that could accommodate a wheelchair if need be. Soap and hair products were inside on a shelf when she turned on the water.

* * * * *

Tiger had to fight the urge to throw away the ice packs on his leg and go to Zandy. He'd crawl if he had to. He took deep breaths, battled his instincts, and ordered his mind to rule his body. He'd nearly lost Zandy and he wasn't over it by a long shot.

The memory of the fire and seeing her suspended by ropes on a wooden cross constructed by those crazy humans would be the source of many nightmares in his future. He'd reached her in time but he could have failed. She could have died and him with her. No way would he have stopped trying to reach her even if he'd known with certainty he had no chance.

She was his mate. His eyes closed as his heart hammered and his fingers curled into fists. He might not have meant to ever take one but he had her. Zandy Gordon had unexpectedly come into his life and blindsided him. He missed her scent. He was hopelessly addicted to it and couldn't wait for his senses to recover just to breathe her in. His lips still tingled from their kiss and he wished he could taste her. A frustrated growl rumbled from him. Dr. Harris had said to give it an hour before the effects of the burning motor home left his system.

The drug he'd been injected with didn't help. His skin felt hot and tight all over his body, his heart rate wouldn't slow to normal and it brought his emotions closer to the surface with the adrenaline pumping through his body. His eyes opened and he glared at his leg. It was stopping him from being with Zandy at that moment. He'd like nothing better than to shower with her and hold her in his arms.

The water in the other room turned off and he watched as she dried her body. The bruises on her waist, legs, and across her rib cage drove him into a frenzy to track down the rest of the humans who'd harmed her. Two were dead but there were more of them. The team that had gone to Zandy's house had scented at least four males. A silent promise was made to himself to track the remaining two humans down and kill them as soon as he was back on his feet.

She stepped back into the room wearing a towel wrapped around her body and she paused there. "I don't have any clean clothes."

"You don't need them. Come here."

He just wanted her at his side, in his arms. He refused to let her out of his sight now that he had her back. *Go slow*, he reminded himself. *Don't frighten her away.* His fingers uncurled and he patted the bed next to him.

"I'll get you wet."

"Come here." He inwardly winced at his rough tone. "Please," he added.

She slowly crept closer, an unsure look on her face.

"I won't hurt you, Zandy. Never."

"I know that. You're just acting really different."

"I'm aware of the drugs in my system and I'm stressed. It's a bad combination but you are safe."

She crawled on the bed and settled down next to him. He reached out and pulled her closer, her wet hair causing water drips to slide down his chest. He didn't care as he hugged her to his side and rested his chin on the top of her head.

"Tiger?"

"Yes?"

She lifted her chin to stare up at him. "I'm okay. Honestly. I'm more worried about you. Are you in pain? Should I get the doctor?"

"I just need to hold you."

"Okay." Her hand flattened on his chest and stroked him gently. "How is your head feeling? They said you had a head injury at the hospital."

"I'm healing fast. I'll be on my feet in two days. We'll stay here until then. They have to keep an eye on me."

"To make sure you're healing okay?"

"To make sure I don't go insane on the drugs and try to harm someone." He forced a smile to assure her when fear dilated her pupils. "You are safe but don't be surprised if I snarl at the doctors. They annoy me."

"That's good to know. About me being safe, that is. I'm glad I don't work here."

He wasn't sure how to respond. The feel of her hand rubbing his chest between his nipples made his dick hard. The purr started in his chest and rose to his throat. Zandy smiled.

"You only make that sound when you're turned-on." Her hand paused before her fingertips traced lower to his belly and her gaze lowered. "And I see that you are."

They'd removed his pants when he'd reached Medical and offered him loose cotton shorts to wear to get access to his leg. The front of them tented from his stiff shaft trapped inside them.

301

"Ignore it. I am trying to. You've been through a trauma and I'm severely stressed from nearly losing you."

Green eyes lifted to gaze into his and her smile widened. "We're both okay and I know a great way to make you relax."

His eyebrows arched.

Zandy wiggled out of his hold. She sat back on her heels and he couldn't stop from growling when her hand rubbed his cock through the very thin material. Desire shot through him so strongly he snarled at her.

Her fingers curled around his shaft and gave him a gentle squeeze. Fear didn't show on her face as she watched him but her smile did fade. He realized his mouth was parted enough to flash his fangs at her. He closed his mouth.

"Easy, baby," she crooned. "And don't move." She glanced at his injured leg. "I missed you." Their gazes met. "Tell me no and I'll stop. Otherwise, just enjoy. I know you're on edge and the drugs are making you prone to violence. You said you wouldn't hurt me and I believe that. I'll ignore the scary sounds."

Her other hand slid into the waist of his shorts and tugged as she bent forward. The feel of her freeing his dick from the cotton nearly made him lunge at her. He wanted to knock her flat, tear off her towel and fuck her. He sniffed to test if she was aroused enough to take him but the stench of burning wood and gasoline still choked his sense of smell.

Hot breath fanned his cock as she bent over him, her wet hair falling as her head turned until he couldn't see her eyes. The feel of her hot little tongue licking at the crown of his dick made him throw back his head and he clawed at the bedding instead of her. Another snarl tore from him, despite trying to hold it back.

She didn't stop at the sound but instead her lips surrounded the tip of his cock and she took inches of it inside her wet mouth. He nearly came when she moved slowly on him, sucking, forcing pure pleasure to take hold of him.

"Zandy," he snarled.

She eased up until her lips nearly left him but she didn't stop. Her fingers gripped the base of his cock and stroked him as she worked it closer to the back of her throat. Every stroke of her mouth drove him insane with ecstasy. Her hand gripping the shorts tugged and he managed to lift his ass off the bed to help her when she pulled the shorts down until they were tangled on his upper thighs and freed his cock completely.

The moans she made sent vibrations right to his balls. He bit his lip hard to hold back the sounds he wanted to make but it made breathing difficult as he panted through his nose. She had barely begun and he was already ready to blow.

"Fuck," he snarled. "I'm coming."

Her mouth eased off him and both hands gripped his cock as she jacked him off, remembering the warning about how strong his semen released from his body. She did something then that really sent him over the edge. Her towel had loosened and she leaned over him more until the crown of his cock rubbed between her breasts, nestled between the soft mounds.

He roared as his body seized, marking her with his semen, making her breasts slick as she rubbed against him to blow what was left of his mind. He shook from how hard he came.

She stopped stroking him and he gasped for breath. His eyes were closed, his head tilted back and the bed moved. The feel of a damp cotton towel made him shiver as Zandy gently cleaned his cock. It wasn't until she curled up against him again and a blanket was pulled up over his lap that he forced his chin to lower. Their gazes met.

Her lips beckoned to him and he reached for her, cupping her cheek. "I'm going to fuck you."

"Your leg—"

"I don't care."

"You just got off."

"I still want you. I always do."

She flattened her hand on his chest and pushed him back a little. "Tiger, honey, I would be lying if I said I didn't want you pretty badly but let's let your leg heal first, okay?"

Someone tried to open the door but the lock prevented them from entering. A fist hammered at it. "Is everything okay in there? Tiger?"

"Go away," he yelled.

"Let me in. I told you not to get out of that bed." The man on the other side of the door paused. "Get me the damn key. He locked the door!"

"Stay out, Harris," Tiger snarled. "Zandy is naked."

Silence. "Oh. I thought you were hurt. Never mind. Is everything okay in there? I heard you and thought you needed help. Is she okay?"

"I'm fine," Zandy called out. She did the last thing Tiger expected. She laughed and lowered her voice. "Maybe next time you should use a pillow and muffle your sounds."

Tiger loved her. The tight feeling in his chest and the way he wanted to pull her onto his lap to hold her assured him of that.

"You shouldn't be engaging in sex. I'm assuming that's what you're doing in there since I heard you and she's in there naked with the door locked. Damn it, Tiger. Didn't you hear me when I said you need to keep that leg still until the bone knits? Miss Gordon? He isn't supposed to be doing that. He needs to lie still."

He wanted to beat on Dr. Harris. Badly. A snarl tore from his mouth and he tried to get up. He'd make sure the doctor left them alone but Zandy pushed on his chest in an attempt to keep him still. He froze. She couldn't stop him if he really wanted up, he was stronger, but his mate stared at him with a pleading look.

"You heard him," she stated softly. "Please do what the doctor said."

He relaxed. "Okay."

A grin softened her features. "I knew a blowjob would mellow you out." She winked. "Now why don't you lie back and we'll take a nap? I'm tired and I bet you probably didn't sleep well last night."

"I'll do what you say on a few conditions." He would use anything he could to get her to agree to his demands.

"What are they?"

"I want you to stay with me. Swear you won't leave Reservation. It's too dangerous. I won't allow you to be put in danger again."

"Okay."

"You're not returning to the apartment. I'm taking you home with me when I'm released from here." He held his breath, afraid she'd refuse.

"I'd love to see your house."

"You'll live with me." He saw surprise on her features and she swallowed.

"Okay but you have to follow the doctor's orders so you get all better."

"I'll do that if you're with me."

She nodded.

He shoved the pillows out from behind him and eased onto his back. His arms opened and Zandy instantly curled against his side, pillowing her head on him. It felt right having her there. The teasing scent of her arousal softly filtered through his nose. It made his dick harden again as his senses returned.

"May I ask you something, Tiger?"

"What do you want to know?"

She hesitated.

305

"Ask me."

"Why do you want me to live with you?"

You're my mate. He didn't say that aloud. She would be resistant to take one after two human males had failed to keep her happy. She'd chosen poorly in the past and he didn't want to spook her. She'd need more time.

"I nearly lost you. I just want you with me." He figured that was safe to say without her wanting to back away from him. "We enjoy sleeping together and you aren't leaving Reservation. We'll be more comfortable at my house."

He heard a catch in her breath. "Okay."

She didn't say anything else and he relaxed again, grateful she wasn't arguing. He'd get her addicted to him. She didn't have a sense of smell to depend on but he wasn't above using sex. A grin curved his lips. It would be a pleasure for both of them when he showed her just how happy he could make her if she agreed to be his mate.

* * * * *

Zandy had a hundred unanswered questions. Tiger was on drugs though and pestering him with them didn't seem like a good idea when he wasn't in his right mind. She'd wait until they left the Medical Center and the drugs cleared his system. Then they'd have a talk. She really wanted to know why he'd had unprotected sex with her, knowing there was a chance of getting her pregnant.

Was he one of those guys who didn't care about consequences as long as he didn't have to use a condom or was there a deeper meaning? She wouldn't ever peg Tiger as being the irresponsible type. She was also afraid if she got too serious that he'd want to cut ties with her. He'd been really clear that he didn't want a lasting relationship. She hoped that if they lived together he might fall for her as hard as she'd fallen for him.

Exhaustion hit her as she lay curled to Tiger's side. They were both safe at Reservation and they were together. She'd take it one day at a time.

Chapter Twenty-One

ॐ

Richard grinned at her. "Being with Tiger agrees with you. Hot sex?"

Zandy stared at him. "Is that the best you can do? I expected you to tease me more."

"Well, I could ask if their dicks are bigger. Creek keeps assuring me that we're smaller. I still refuse to drop my pants for her when she dares me to. So, is it rumor or fact?"

She wiggled her eyebrows at him. "Fact."

"Damn. I'll make sure I never share a urinal area with one of them." He laughed at his own joke. "Are you two going to do the whole mating thing?"

Longing hit her hard. "I don't know. We haven't discussed it."

He frowned. "You've been living at his house for the past, what? Week? He hasn't asked you to be his mate yet?"

"No and stop this line of questioning. I don't want to discuss it."

"I'm your friend."

"I know. It's just that I've been living with him for eight days but I don't know if he asked me to live with him because he knows I can't go home until my house is fixed by my insurance company or if he wants me to live with him. Things are…complicated."

"I'm a man and I know how men think. Tiger is nuts about you. I see him drop you off every morning and the way he kisses you goodbye. He lingers as long as he can because he doesn't want to part from you. Every day he spends lunch with you and he isn't even a minute late at the end of the day to pick you up. That speaks volumes to me. He could have had you stay at the human-housing apartment building after you were kidnapped but instead he had you move into his place. That's something a man does when he's serious. Trust me. We don't give up the bachelor pad easily."

"He's New Species."

Richard waved his hands. "What does that mean?"

"You can't compare him to a normal man."

"Just because his dick is bigger doesn't—"

"Shut up. That's not what I was talking about and you know it. Who knows what it means to him to have me live there. It just might be for sex instead of code for 'I'm serious about you'."

"I don't buy that for a second. He came here yesterday with a surprise picnic and you said he's planning on doing it again today. He was so eager to spend time with you alone that he shoved me out the door before my escort could even get out of his Jeep to take me to lunch. He's nuts about you."

"Maybe. He's got commitment issues though so we don't talk about the mate thing."

Richard sighed. "You guys are just going to play house and leave it all up in the air?"

"That about sums it up."

"What do you want?"

Zandy hesitated. "Tiger."

He smiled. "I'm sure it will work out. You two are happy together. Anyone with eyes can see that." Richard glanced at the front windows. "Ah. My escort for lunch is here a few minutes early." He stood and put his shoes on. "Have a good picnic with Tiger." He winked. "And please don't have sex on my desk."

She laughed. "You're so dirty minded. There are cameras in here and there're no blinds on the windows. Anyone going by can see inside. Do you really think that's what we did yesterday? It was just lunch."

"The security officers who watch the live footage from those cameras would sure appreciate it if you did. It would give them something good to watch for once." Richard laughed as he walked toward the door.

Torrent, a tall, black-haired New Species, opened the office door before Richard reached it. He held a bag in his hand and his gaze fixed on her.

"Zandy?"

She smiled at Richard's escort. "Hello, Torrent. What's up?"

He approached her. "A meeting has been called that Tiger had to attend. He will come as soon as it ends. It shouldn't be long but he didn't want you to go hungry. He ordered your lunch."

Zandy stood and walked closer to him. "Thanks." She held out her hand.

He inhaled and softly growling at her. It shocked her enough to step back. His gaze narrowed as he inhaled again. He growled deeper, his body tensing. Richard and Zandy exchanged glances before Richard moved in front of Zandy.

"What are you doing?" Richard frowned at him. "You're scaring her."

Torrent seemed to shake himself. "I'm sorry." He shoved Zandy's lunch bag at Richard. "I'll wait for you outside. Tiger didn't warn me that she was in heat. I have to leave. The scent drives me nuts. I haven't shared sex with a female in a while and I have to go before I do something Tiger will kill me over." He fled the building.

Richard turned, holding Zandy's lunch, and chuckled. "A laugh a day. You're still ovulating? I thought that was supposed to just last a few days. What are you? A one-woman egg distribution center?"

Zandy felt stunned. "I shouldn't be." Her conversation with Dr. Allison tugged at her memory. "I was given a shot after I was rescued from the creeps who kidnapped me. The doctor said it would mess up my cycle. Maybe I'm ovulating again instead of having double periods. Tiger didn't tell me."

"I wonder why not? Maybe it just started."

"Maybe. I don't know but obviously it's happening. Their sense of smell is amazing."

"Do I want to ask how you know that since you sound as if you're pretty knowledgeable about it?"

"Tiger can tell me what ingredients are in my shampoo just by sniffing at me. I had to change brands because he isn't a fan of avocado. I used it once and he never saw the bottle since he had to go out to do a security check when it was delivered to me. I showered while he was gone and he knew the second he stepped in the bedroom."

"I'm glad my sense of smell isn't that great. I'm going to lunch." He suddenly laughed. "Remember those cameras when Tiger shows up if he reacts the way Torrent just did. The guy looked like he wanted to grab you and take you on the floor."

Zandy carried her lunch to her desk and opened it. She wondered why Tiger hadn't said anything to her about going into what they considered heat. Creek assured her New Species could smell a woman's cycles coming. She suddenly froze in her seat, tensing. That morning Tiger had been particularly frisky.

He woke her up and made love to her until she thought he'd never let her out of bed. He was usually a passionate lover but that morning he'd been more aggressive than usual. It was possible he hadn't noticed or it hadn't started until after he'd escorted her to work. She shrugged it off and ate her roast-beef sandwich, the chips and drank the soda they'd included.

Her phone rang. "Zandy Gordon here."

"Hi, little one. I'm sorry but I won't make lunch. The meeting ran long and I have to wait on a report to come in. I have to call Homeland when it does. I'm stuck in my office."

"Is everything okay?"

"Yes. We're no longer on high alert. The United States government has taken a stronger stance against hate groups after what happened to you. They've been tracking down and arresting the most outspoken hate groups who have made public threats against the NSO. It's rid us of a lot of the more hostile protesters. They're pushing legislation to make it a hate crime to even threaten us."

"That's great news."

He chuckled. "I could almost thank Brother Adam if he wasn't dead. He made sure there were enough cameras and reporters present when he tried to kill you that it made worldwide news. Everyone had to take notice of what we deal with and the public outcry is forcing all the politicians who wish to be reelected to back us."

"You were a hero when you saved me by risking your own life. It showed what great guys New Species are. Plus you're sexy hot." She chuckled. "We're getting fan mail just for you. Most are from women. I hope that doesn't go to your head and you dump me."

"You're the only female I want."

"I'm really glad to hear that because you're all I want too."

Tiger softly purred into the phone and Zandy's body instantly responded. The man made the best noises that turned her on. She bit her lip and closed her eyes and admitted what she was thinking.

"I miss you."

"I'm going to pick you up at four today instead of five."

"What would my boss think?" Zandy teased and knew he'd laugh. "I don't want to be fired."

He chuckled. "Your boss would think I could sexually harass you and you'd enjoy it."

"Promises, promises."

"It is a promise." Tiger paused. "I have to go. The report is in and I have to call Homeland."

"I'll see you at four."

"Yes, you will." He hung up.

She finished her lunch and noticed that Torrent didn't walk Richard to the door when they pulled up to the curb in front of the building. It was unusual since they always did. Richard came in grinning.

"How was lunch with Tiger?"

"He couldn't make it. Something came up but I'm leaving an hour early today. Tiger is picking me up at four to make it up to me."

He chuckled. "See? He's nuts about you. Creek misses you and wanted to know if you'd be having lunch in the cafeteria tomorrow. I said you were in heat and she said she'd see you in a few days."

Zandy turned back to her work and started scanning in letters. They had a lot of mail pouring in. Mostly it had been supportive over the last week. The hate mail was down. It was a nice change.

* * * * *

Tiger watched Bestial swagger into his office and drop his large body into a chair across the desk from him. The male looked amused and Tiger's spine stiffened.

"What?"

"How is your mate? Have you told her yet?"

"No."

Bestial grinned, showing his canines. "You're being foolish. Just tell her she's your mate and be done with it."

"It isn't that simple."

"Sure it is. She doesn't have sharp teeth and she can't fight as well as our females can. I doubt she is as stubborn as they are either. You can handle her if she resists until you change her mind. Don't tell me you're afraid she'll kick your ass. I'd lose all respect for you."

"Shut up. It's complicated."

"Uncomplicate it." He chuckled. "I've fought with you and she doesn't stand a chance."

"This isn't about dominance. She had two humans who were bad mates and destroyed her trust in males."

"You're not being a good mate either if she doesn't even know she has one." He snorted. "Do you want me to tell her?"

"Don't interfere."

"I'm good at it."

"No, you aren't. Brawn still growls at me sometimes if I even glance at Becca when I see them. I took them a gift when their son was born to congratulate them and I thought he was going to attack. You used my name to make him go after his mate when you tormented him by making him think I was interested in stealing her away from him."

"It worked." Bestial laughed. "I've never seen a Species run so fast as when he shot out of our office to reach her. I still think they should have named the baby Sprint."

Tiger grinned. "I dare you to tell them that."

"No way. Kismet was a fine name to choose. You are missing the point. I helped them get together and they are very happy. Let me help you."

"Stay out of it."

"When are you going to tell her?"

"Soon."

"How do you plan to tell her?"

"I don't know. Why are you so curious?"

Broad shoulders shrugged. "I'm bored."

"Learn a new sport or go spend some time in the Wild Zone. Vengeance could use a friend. Go interfere in his life. He's the one who needs help with females. He's mourning the loss of his mate."

"I'd rather help you."

"Go share sex with a female."

Bestial stared at him with narrowed eyes. "I am your friend and you can talk to me. Are you afraid she will reject you?"

Tiger took a deep breath and leaned back in his chair. "Yes." It was a relief to admit it.

"I never thought I'd see the day when a little female would take you down. This is what they call priceless."

Anger stirred. "It's not amusing."

"It really is." Bestial chuckled. "You know we're all enjoying this after all the times you swore you'd never take a mate. Her being human is a bonus."

A snarl tore from Tiger as he shot to his feet. "I can't wait until you meet a female you want to mate. We'll see how amused you are then."

Bestial slowly rose to his feet, all amusement fleeing. "I'll just take her home with me and keep her there if I ever find a female I want to make my mate. I wouldn't allow her to believe we were just sharing a home either once I got her there. I'd claim her. You should try it. You need to do something."

"I am!"

"What are you doing?"

"I have a plan."

"What is that?"

Tiger hesitated. "Zandy has said that the males who didn't make her happy had no idea how to really commit to a female. I'm going to prove to her that I'm nothing similar to them."

"How are you going to do that?"

Tiger held his silence, unwilling to discuss it further.

"Fine. I hope whatever it is works before she leaves. I'd hate to see you moping around and mourning the loss of your mate. Don't expect any sympathy from me if it happens." He stalked out of the office and slammed the door behind him.

Tiger snarled. He was frustrated and worse. Bestial was right. He needed to tell Zandy that he had no intention of ever letting her go. They were mated. He just needed to make her feel secure about him before he did. She might bolt and unlike Bestial, he'd never force her to stay, even though it would tear his heart out of his chest if she left.

* * * * *

Zandy saw Tiger's Jeep pull up in front of the building at four o'clock on the dot. She shoved her feet into her shoes and waved goodbye to Richard. She was out the door before Tiger could reach it. He grinned as his arms wrapped around her in a hug.

"I missed you." He lowered his head and brushed a kiss on her lips.

She laughed. "I would guess so. We're giving Richard and all the cameras a show."

His beautiful blue eyes sparkled. "That wasn't a show. This is one."

Zandy gasped when Tiger lifted her up until her feet left the ground. She automatically wrapped her arms around his neck and he kissed her until she had to fight the urge to straddle his hips with her legs. She wanted to ride him through their clothing just to feel his rigid cock pressed against her clit, instead of where it rested at her lower belly. She desperately needed some relief from the flames of desire burning through her body. He tore his lips from hers.

"Let's go," he growled. His beautiful catlike eyes were passion filled.

316

"Oh yeah. Let's go. Drive fast."

He walked with her in his arms and placed her in the passenger seat. He nuzzled her neck before he let go. "I will." He rushed to get behind the wheel.

She glanced over at him and loved seeing his tense features. That promised really hot sex the moment they reached his house.

* * * * *

Tiger parked in the driveway and climbed out. Zandy didn't wait for him to come around to her side, instead she bolted for the front door. She heard him growl loudly and his heavy footfalls assured her he was in pursuit. She reached the porch steps but didn't make it to the top before hands grabbed her hips. He spun her around and bent, his body bumped her hips. Zandy laughed when she ended up upside down, hanging over his shoulder. He straightened and cupped her ass to keep her in place.

He quickly opened the door and strode through the living room, down the hall and into their bedroom. She gasped when he dumped her flat on her back on the soft mattress. He backed up as she used her elbows to lift her upper body and stare at him.

"Take your clothes off or I'll tear them from your body. I want you right now."

He bent and just ripped off his shoes, throwing them haphazardly behind him. His fingers snagged his shirt, jerking it over his head to reveal his sexy abs and tan chest. Muscular arms rose to yank the hair tie from the ponytail that contained his long hair. He shook his head and the silky strands fell in disarray around his shoulders. His blue eyes narrowed and he growled.

"Now, Zandy. I mean it. I know you like that top. Take it off or it's a cleaning rag."

She sat up all the way and quickly removed the shirt and bra. Tiger opened his pants and just shoved them down and kicked free of them. His cock was thick and hard, pointing right at her. She dropped back down and lifted her hips as she wiggled out of her pants and panties. He was already tugging on the bottom of the legs to get them off. Tiger tossed them behind him to fall somewhere near where his had landed.

Zandy licked her lips when she lay there totally naked, sprawled in the middle of his bed. Tiger's gaze fixed on her mouth and a purr came from him. He put a knee on the bed, dropped forward to bend with his hands braced on the mattress and crawled forward until she was caged under his body.

It was hard to think when she wanted him so badly but she'd had hours to contemplate things before he'd arrived to pick her up from work. They didn't do so well in the talking department on serious issues, each leery of the other, but there was one thing she was determined to get to the bottom of.

"Wait!" She lifted her hands to flatten on his chest before he could drop down over her. "Maybe I should take a shower first. It was kind of hot today and I'm sweaty. I probably smell bad."

He inhaled through his nose and another purr came from him, his chest vibrating against her hands. "No shower. You smell good enough to eat." His gaze lowered down her body and he backed up a few feet until his face hovered over her stomach. "I want to find out if you taste as good as you scent. Spread your thighs wide apart for me."

She really wanted him to go down on her, her clit throbbed in anticipation of that hot, hungry mouth of his and all the wonderful things he could do to her with it. Her nipples hardened and her belly quivered. It was tough but she took a shaky breath and resisted parting her legs to give him access. It was even worse when he dipped his head to place an open-mouthed kiss on the hollow of her hip.

"Tiger," she whispered.

He growled softly and then purred. "You scent so damn good."

He had to know she was in heat. Her mind screamed that at her. "Um, Tiger?"

His lips inched lower, his cheeks nuzzling her thighs, which he wanted open. "Yes, little one?"

"Um, I think you should buy condoms. I'm ovulating again."

His mouth stopped placing kisses on her and he grew very still. It was almost as if he froze as the seconds passed. He finally raised his head and met her watchful gaze, studying her.

"I don't need them with you, Zandy."

Her heart pounded, wondering what he'd say. She was almost afraid of his answer. "Why not?"

He moved suddenly, gripped her inner thighs, and parted them. Instead of answering, his mouth fastened on her clit and sucked on her. The sensations hit her hard and fast as he purred loudly, adding vibrations into the mix. She collapsed flat and her fingers delved into his silky hair, needing something to hold on to as pleasure swamped her.

"Oh god."

Tiger was relentless as he played with her clit with strong tugs of his mouth and licks. He lapped at her rapidly as his purrs grew deeper and stronger. His hands kept her thighs open when it became too intense and she tried to close them. Her back arched and she cried out his name as she came hard and fast.

His hands released her and the bed shifted as he moved. She struggled to recover as she opened her eyes to see what he was doing. He rolled her over onto her stomach suddenly and came down on top of her back. His thighs pushed hers apart and she moaned when the thick tip of his cock brushed against her pussy. He drove into her with one fluid motion that put him balls-deep inside her.

Tiger braced his arms to avoid crushing her upper body under his and he forced her legs wider apart. He held still while her pussy adjusted to the feel of his cock stretching it apart to fit him. His mouth found her neck and sharp teeth nipped her gently. He withdrew almost completely from her before he drove up, fucking her deeply.

Zandy clawed the bedding and turned her head enough to breathe as Tiger rode her fast and furiously. She was totally pinned beneath him. Her climax was still making her twitch and more pleasure rolled through her. Tiger purred and growled, his braced arms shifting enough to tighten his hold on her when he caged her ribs.

"I can't stop," he snarled. "You're so tight and hot. You smell so good." His teeth scored her shoulder, not biting, just grazing her.

"Yes," she encouraged. She wasn't sure if it was for him to keep pounding her as roughly as he did because it felt incredible or if she wanted him to bite her. "Don't stop."

She moaned, trying to shove her ass back to meet him. He moved faster and held her tighter as more of his weight came down until she couldn't move at all. It turned her on more that all she could do was take him as he pounded into her. She screamed as she climaxed a second time, her body not even recovered from the first one. Ecstasy tore through her and she trembled. She went a little limp and knew she was in danger of passing out.

Tiger drove into her deeply one last time, ground his hips against her ass and his roar nearly deafened her. He could have done any lion proud at that moment. He jerked in sharp, tight spasms as she felt him coming inside her.

She panted, trying to catch her breath. Sweat tickled slightly between their bodies. Tiger groaned and collapsed completely over her, going totally limp. He crushed her against the mattress.

"Weight," Zandy gasped.

He seemed to struggle to find the strength to lift his upper body again but he did it until she could breathe again. He lowered his head and licked her shoulder where he'd bitten her in the past. She turned her head enough to see his face.

"Did you bite me again?"

He chuckled. "No, but I wanted to."

Her eyes closed. "Wow."

He nuzzled her neck. "I feel the same."

The ability to think returned as her body recovered. Tiger knew she was in heat and that he could get her pregnant. It was possible that he didn't use condoms because he could be sterile. She frowned, pondering it.

"What's wrong, Zandy?" Tiger nibbled her ear.

"Is there a medical condition that you have that makes you sterile? I know New Species can have babies. The doctor slipped and told me after she saw the bite marks you put on me. She thought we were mated."

His body stiffened against hers. She turned her head and met his gaze. He had paled enough for her to notice and as she studied his eyes, she realized what she was seeing in them. Guilt.

"What is going on?"

He glanced away. "Nothing."

It hurt. "You're lying to me. Look at me and tell me what is going on. I'm in heat but you didn't say a word. Torrent had to tell me. I even had you smell me and you know I'm ovulating. You're even acting different during sex. You're more aggressive. Not that I'm complaining. Why didn't you tell me I'm in heat?"

He met her gaze again. The emotion she saw stunned her. She could almost swear she saw fear. He moved suddenly and his hands encircled her wrists. He jerked them up the bed and kept them there.

"Why are you holding me down?" She wasn't afraid, but *he* was. She was sure that's what she was seeing as they stared at each other.

"I don't want you trying to run from me."

"Why the hell would I run from you and could you at least flip me over if you're going to pin me down? I like to look into your eyes without getting a crick in my neck."

He hesitated but let go of her wrists, flattening his palms on the bed. He pushed up until his body wasn't touching hers. "Roll over."

She did, having to untangle their legs first. The second she was flat on her back he came down on her and grabbed her wrists again. They were jerked above her head and his fingers laced through hers to hold them down on the bed.

His beauty struck her as she studied Tiger. His hair was wild and his amazing eyes were so blue that she felt lost in them. He was her fallen angel, whom she loved. "Why do you think I'd run away from you? Please talk to me. The not knowing is worse than anything I'm thinking right now. Trust me on that. Whatever it is, we can work it out."

He chewed on his bottom lip. It made her attention focus there until he stopped and took a deep breath. He blew it out slowly and her gaze lifted to his. "You've been in heat for two days. It's why I've brought you lunch at work. I knew I couldn't take you to the cafeteria. The males would react and you'd know you were in heat. I had asked Torrent to send a female to deliver your lunch but obviously that didn't happen since you said he told you the truth."

"Why didn't you want me to know? I'm so confused."

"I wanted to get you pregnant."

She gaped at him in bewilderment. It took her reeling brain time to try to let what he'd said sink in. "Why?"

He lowered his face until they were sharing breaths. "I thought you'd be more agreeable to being my mate if you were with child. You would realize I purposely allowed it to happen to show you that I was serious about commitment. You've had males avoid that. I'm not. I hoped you'd also feel more bonded to me if it happened…and that you'd need me."

Her heart nearly stopped. "You want me to be your mate?"

"You already are, damn it." He growled as anger flashed in his eyes. "You're mine, Zandy. You have been since the moment you woke up on the hood of that Jeep and kissed me. I just didn't want to admit it at first but you're my mate and I'm yours."

Zandy could only gape at him. "Let me get this straight. You've been trying to get me pregnant? You didn't think you should ask me first?"

"I'm sorry. I know it was wrong but you've been hurt. I love you. I wanted to do anything to bind you to me as tightly as I am bound to you. You aren't Species and can't become addicted to my scent. You could walk away from me without suffering withdrawal. The thought of losing you drives me insane. I couldn't stand it."

Zandy wiggled. "Let go of my hands."

He hesitated but did it. "You deserve to hit me."

She reached up and cupped his face instead. "All you had to do was ask, Tiger. I would love to be your mate."

She saw his shock. "Really?"

She nodded. "Yes. I love you too. I don't need to own a super nose to feel addicted to you. My heart already is."

His mouth swooped down and covered hers. She moaned into his kiss. Tiger spread her legs with his and nudged her pussy with his cock until he entered her. She tore her mouth from his and moaned. Their gazes sought each other.

He purred. "I'm going to kill myself trying to get you pregnant. I want a baby with you. I want everything."

Zandy blinked back tears. "Then stop talking." She hooked her legs around his waist. "Less talking, more fucking."

He laughed. "I really do love you."

"I love you too, baby. I love how you feel inside me too. Do you really think I can get pregnant this fast?"

"I'm determined," he rasped.

"Lucky me."

She was a little frightened of the idea of having a baby. They were moving so fast. The memory of how close she'd come to losing him though shoved all doubts away. Life was short and she wasn't going to allow fear to stop her from grabbing happiness with both hands.

Epilogue

୭ꝺ

Nine days later Zandy smiled at Smiley. "Thank you for doing this."

He warily regarded her. "Tiger is going to kill me. He said you are to never leave Reservation."

"I know but I really appreciate it."

He nodded. "I have seven highly trained officers in the area. They are far enough away to give you privacy but close enough to know if anyone poses a danger. Tiger will kill me if something happens to you. The others weren't given direct orders where you are concerned."

"You're a good friend."

He laughed. "Not to Tiger. But to you, yes."

Zandy shooed him with her hand. "I know you aren't happy about leaving me here alone but you need to go." She glanced at her watch. "Tiger should be reaching my work about now and Richard will give him the note. I'm betting he will get here really fast. Make sure he doesn't see you on the road."

"No way. I'm hiding until he has you in his arms and knows you're safe."

"You're sure the officers are far enough away?"

He nodded. "You told me what you planned. Tiger will tear them apart if they come this way and see too much of you. It's well known how mates are. Trust me. You have privacy, Zandy. Give me a minute and I'll be so far from here it won't be funny. Tiger is going to scent that I was here with you and be very angry. I'm going to run fast and far to avoid him."

He turned and sprinted into the woods away from the road. Zandy laughed and turned to examine the area by the creek. She smiled and kicked off her shoes, undressing. She eyed the area once more, feeling a little nervous but removed the rest of her clothing to wade into the water.

The sound of Tiger's approach couldn't be missed. Vicious snarls combined with his boots slapping the ground as he ran hell-bent for leather through the woods, crashing through brush, was loud. He sounded really pissed. She smiled, her gaze scanning for sight of him.

He broke out of the trees to her right and came to a halt with a roar that made her start. His hair had come loose from the ponytail and he'd torn his shirt at some point, probably on a low branch. She hoped he wasn't hurt. The wild look in his eyes when his enraged gaze landed on her would have terrified anyone else. She waved instead.

"Hi, baby."

"Zandy. What are you doing out here with Smiley?" He snarled the words. "I'll kill him for taking you off Reservation and putting you in danger."

Zandy was a little shocked at how vicious and deadly the man she loved looked. He was furious and it wasn't pretty.

'Before you do that, why don't you take a look around? Smiley just helped me set everything up. He's my friend who did me a huge favor, Tiger. I needed help because I couldn't carry everything and I didn't know how to use the air pump to fill the bed. I only left Reservation because this is our special place."

Tiger turned and took in his surroundings. She relaxed, knowing he'd cool down. If not, he could join her in the water. The air mattress was neatly made and a picnic lunch was laid out next to it. A camping lantern and a stack of towels held down the blanket spread out on the ground. It looked nice. She glanced back at him to find him watching her intently.

She smiled. "Surprise. There are officers out in the woods who are far enough away to give us privacy but make sure nobody sneaks up on us. I thought it would be romantic if we spend the night out here together. So, do you want to get naked? I'm getting a little cold in here alone."

Tiger slowly smiled. "I'm sorry. I got your note and only read that you were leaving Reservation. I freaked out. Why are you here?" He paused. "It isn't safe for you to leave the NSO. Smiley knows my standing orders where you are concerned."

"That's why Smiley has probably run to another state by now. I bet they heard you roar for miles."

He laughed and kicked off his shoes. "You really did all this for me?"

She grinned. "Yeah and you better do something great to deserve it too." She walked out of the water naked. Tiger's heated gaze roamed down her body.

He softly growled. "I'm going to be doing a lot of wonderful things to you."

Zandy grabbed a towel and dried off as she watched him strip out of his clothes. She walked to the bed and climbed on it and flipped over. She put her head on the pillow and spread her thighs wide. Tiger glanced up and purred.

"Do you see something you like?"

"Oh yeah, Zandy." He was naked as he stalked toward her.

He put his knee on the bed and purred louder. She smiled and opened her arms, reaching out for him. Tiger climbed up the bed and over her. "What do you want?"

"You. Always you. Only you."

"I feel the same way but we need to have a little talk before we do anything."

Tiger frowned. "Before?" He glanced down her body and snarled in protest. "We'll talk later."

She put her hands on his chest. "Tiger, this is serious. We need to discuss something right now."

"Later." He moved down her body and ran his fingers from her knees to the insides of her thighs.

She closed her eyes and took a shaky breath, desperately wanting him to make love to her. *The man has a mouth that...* She shook that thought away.

"Tiger?"

His gaze met hers. "What?" He purred.

"I'll tell you later."

He chuckled. "That's good because I think you'd have a hard time thinking and trying to talk in a second." He lowered his head.

Zandy moaned. All thoughts left her head as Tiger licked her until she climaxed. She screamed out his name as he climbed up her body, gasping as he entered her. She wrapped herself around his body while he rode her. They were both satisfied and out of breath afterward.

Tiger rolled them onto their sides to avoid crushing Zandy. "Ready to eat dinner before I wear you out again? You're going to need your strength."

She grinned, lightly running her fingertips along his jawline. "I do need to eat."

He grinned. "Me too. Only you're dessert."

"This is a special occasion, Tiger."

"Every night with you is special, Zandy."

"I really love you."

He grinned. "I really love you too."

"Hey, Tiger?" She peered at him.

"What, little one?"

"You're going to have to stop calling me that."

A confused expression made him look really cute. "You like that name, don't you?"

She nodded, rubbing her body against his, pushing so close to him that they were skin to skin as much as possible. "I love it but I won't be little for too much longer."

He frowned.

She took his hand and placed it on her stomach. "I'm going to probably get really big but you better still want me." Amusement filled her. "Or I'll never have a second baby."

His eyes widened and his expression stilled. "Zandy?"

She nodded. "I just found out today, Daddy."

She saw tears gather in his eyes. He suddenly rolled her on top of him.

"Why didn't you tell me? I could have crushed the baby!"

She straddled him and straightened. "That's all you have to say?"

He sat up, wrapping his arms around her. "No. I love you. This is the best news ever." His hand cupped her stomach. "A baby? You're sure? Really?"

She nodded. "Trisha confirmed it. I threw up twice yesterday at work and again this morning so I went in to see her. I had my suspicions since my breasts were tender. We're having a baby."

Tiger hugged her on his lap. "Thank you, Zandy."

She hugged him back. "For what? Getting knocked up easily?" She laughed.

He chuckled. "That is a bonus but no. Thank you for coming into my life. I am so happy and you're the reason. You're everything to me. You and our baby."

Zandy kissed him. "You're my life too. You make me so happy, Tiger. You really are my angel."

He grinned. "An angel, huh?" He lifted her and impaled her on his cock. "Does that feel angelic?"

She moaned his name. "Actually, I still think of you as my angel. You take me to heaven all the time."

Tiger thrust up into her. "We'll go there together."

Also by Laurann Dohner

℘

eBooks:

Zorn Warriors 2: Kidnapping Casey
Zorn Warriors 3: Tempting Rever
Zorn Warriors 4: Berrr's Vow

Print Books:

Cyborg Seduction 1: Burning Up Flint
Cyborg Seduction 2: Kissing Steel
Cyborg Seduction 3: Melting Iron
Cyborg Seduction 4: Touching Ice
Cyborg Seduction 5: Stealing Coal
Cyborg Seduction 6: Redeeming Zorus
Cyborg Seduction 7: Taunting Krell
Mating Heat 1: Mate Set
Mating Heat 2: His Purrfect Mate
New Species 1: Fury
New Species 2: Slade
New Species 3: Valiant
New Species 4: Justice
New Species 5: Brawn
Riding the Raines 1: Propositioning Mr. Raine
Riding the Raines 2: Raine on Me
Something Wicked This Way Comes, Volume 1 *(anthology)*
Something Wicked This Way Comes, Volume 2 *(anthology)*
Zorn Warriors 1 & 2: Loving Zorn
Zorn Warriors 3: Tempting Rever
Zorn Warriors 4: Berrr's Vow

About Laurann Dohner

🔊

I'm a full-time "in-house supervisor" (sounds much better than plain ol' housewife), mother and writer. I'm addicted to caramel iced coffee, the occasional candy bar (or two) and trying to get at least five hours of sleep at night.

I love to write all kinds of stories. I think the best part about writing is the fact that real life is always uncertain, always tossing things at us that we have no control over, but when you write, you can make sure there's always a happy ending. I love that about writing. I love to sit down at my computer desk, put on my headphones and listen to loud music to block out the world around me, so I can create worlds in front of me.

🔊

The author welcomes comments from readers. You can find her website and email address on her author bio page at www.ellorascave.com.

Tell Us What You Think

We appreciate hearing reader opinions about our books. You can email us at Service@ellorascave.com (when contacting Customer Service, be sure to state the book title and author).

Why an electronic book?

We live in the Information Age — an exciting time in the history of human civilization, in which technology rules supreme and continues to progress in leaps and bounds every minute of every day. For a multitude of reasons, more and more avid literary fans are opting to purchase e-books instead of paper books. The question from those not yet initiated into the world of electronic reading is simply: *Why?*

1. *Price.* An electronic title at Ellora's Cave Publishing runs anywhere from 40% to 75% less than the cover price of the exact same title in paperback format. Why? Basic mathematics and cost. It is less expensive to publish an e-book (no paper and printing, no warehousing and shipping) than it is to publish a paperback, so the savings are passed along to the consumer.

2. *Space.* Running out of room in your house for your books? That is one worry you will never have with electronic books. For a low one-time cost, you can purchase a handheld device specifically designed for e-reading. Many e-readers have large, convenient screens for viewing. Better yet, hundreds of titles can be stored within your new library — on a single microchip. There are a variety of e-readers from different manufacturers. You can also read e-books on your PC or laptop computer. (Please note that Ellora's Cave does not endorse any specific brands.

You can check our website at www.ellorascave.com for information we make available to new consumers.)

3. *Mobility.* Because your new e-library consists of only a microchip within a small, easily transportable e-reader, your entire cache of books can be taken with you wherever you go.

4. *Personal Viewing Preferences.* Are the words you are currently reading too small? Too large? Too… ANNOYING? Paperback books cannot be modified according to personal preferences, but e-books can.

5. *Instant Gratification.* Is it the middle of the night and all the bookstores near you are closed? Are you tired of waiting days, sometimes weeks, for bookstores to ship the novels you bought? Ellora's Cave Publishing sells instantaneous downloads twenty-four hours a day, seven days a week, every day of the year. Our webstore is never closed. Our e-book delivery system is 100% automated, meaning your order is filled as soon as you pay for it.

Those are a few of the top reasons why electronic books are replacing paperbacks for many avid readers.

As always, Ellora's Cave welcomes your questions and comments. We invite you to email us at Service@ellorascave.com or write to us directly at Ellora's Cave Publishing Inc., 1056 Home Avenue, Akron, OH 44310-3502.

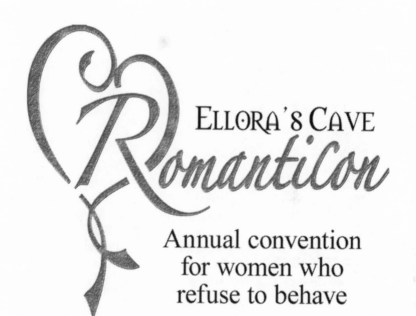

ELLORA'S CAVE
Romanticon

Annual convention
for women who
refuse to behave

www.ECRomanticon.com
For additional info contact: conventions@ellorascave.com

24247448R00198

Made in the USA
Lexington, KY
11 July 2013